T0147730

Zeb Silhouette

Chinyere Grace Okafor

**SUB-SAHARAN
PUBLISHERS**

First published in Ghana 2021 by
Sub-Saharan Publishers
P.O.Box 358
Legon-Accra
Ghana

Email: saharanp@africaonline.com.gh
Website: www.subsaharanpublishers.com

©Chinyere Grace Okafor, 2021

Design and typesetting by Kwabena Agyepong

ISBN 978-9988-550-93-6

DEDICATION

To

Shalom Odokara

My father, Thomas Okafor, a teacher and storyteller, always encouraged us to tell our truths in our ways. My mother, Agnes Illo-Okafor, advocate and business sage, told me to invent and sing in all moods for "it chases away wrinkles and pains." In Indiana, Nawal El Saadawi said, "Never cease to tell stories of women." At Cornell and Syracuse, Micere Mugo counselled me, "keep on the fight with your pen." In Wichita, Carol Konek, champion of women, said everybody should back the cause of women. My poems, plays and short stories have always been about women and other underprivileged persons and groups. I became multiply disadvantaged without family and job in a city where Shalom Odokara, fighter for the oppressed, reminded me of who I was:

"Go to your core and write about it."

These giant shoulders and more gave me strength as I journeyed beyond self to stories of immigrants, which I presented at a writers' conference in 2003, before the metamorphosis that led to *Zeb* in 2011. I am very grateful to all phenomenal people who encouraged me as I wrote *Zeb Silhouette*.

Contents

Foreword

SHADOWS IN A SPECKLED GLOBE: OKAFOR'S *ZEB SILHOUETTE*

The African female writer is, in the main, a historian, a story teller, a social critic, a political activist as well as a strident voice committed to gender parity – a function of socio-cultural regeneration which palpably recognises women and the minority. In the vein of other postcolonial women writers such as Flora Nwapa, Ama Ata Aidoo, Buchi Emecheta, Nawal el Saadawi, Chimamanda Ngozi Adichie and Akachi Adimora Ezeigbo, Chinyere Okafor draws a nexus between female issues and national / global concerns.

Okafor's debut novel, *Zeb Silhouette*, is a convoluted exposé of love, pain and grime which is poignantly, explicitly, and tellingly etched. In the amorous Odyssey, spiked with tinctures of angst and mania, the female protagonist - Zebra Olima - periodically undergoes physical, emotional and psychological battery in the length and breadth of the highly captivating narrative. A victim of child marriage and attendant abuse, Zebra grins and bears an utterly gruelling and loveless marriage underpinned with "bruises, revulsion and vomit". She, nevertheless, later finds love in her affair with Jaja and second marriage with Robert Jefferson in the United States of America. She also achieves her academic aspirations by earning a PhD and teaching in a highly rated Nigerian university.

In her capacity as a writer in the Diaspora, Okafor graphically delineates the immigrant experience lived by the black woman, Zeb, who seeks refuge in the United States, having been exiled by a dictatorial Nigerian Government as a result of her militant human rights activities. Assailed with the realities of her lowly immigrant status as well as the spectres of ethnicity, gender inequity and racism, she valiantly navigates through the clogs of discrimination, oppression and deprivation. She is constrained by the brute force of the vicissitudes of life to fall from grace, in the quest for a new, secure identity procured with the Green Card – immigrant visa.

An array of female figures inhabit the expansive milieu in *Zeb Silhouette*, transcending time and space. Much as glowing tributes are implicitly and succinctly paid to the keen female mind in the opening chapter, the need for a petticoat government in Eden does not really arise. An opportune ambience is, nonetheless, deftly carved out by the author to dismantle varied patriarchal binaries. A daughter is willed to be a great man. Besides antonyms are harmonised to create an effect. White and black [Zebra]; light and darkness[Silhouette], subtly encapsulated in the pithy title of the novel, generate the energies that propel the dynamic female protagonist. Symbols are strategically employed to make political statements. The journey motif that pervades the work, is indicative of the pervasive migrant restlessness occasioned by the trend of a fuzzy globalization. Rape, on its own part, is an index of expropriation, repression as well as predatory governance. A most vulnerable, physically handicapped African servant, Igodoana, is raped by a huge British woman who, incidentally, is his employer's wife. In a reversal and twist of fate, the raped man becomes the rapist in a marriage where Zeb/Chizebe, his child bride - the inalienable victim - is robbed of her "sexual womanhood". An indisposed receptacle to the festering semen of rape sown in her squeamish consciousness, she is continually hounded and later sexually assaulted by a band of armed-robbers. The gang-raped woman, including the raped limping man, emblemises a most vulnerable African nation, grossly exploited by both the Metropolitan powers in the North and the venal postcolonial African leaders, dubbed the vultures.

Okafor's artistic strength lies in her seamless melding of colours, cultures, time, struggles, emotions, alliances, ideologies and spaces. Sorority blends with fraternity to beget an idyllic gender relationship. That the idyllic is pointedly interspersed with the lurid and volatile is a testament of the persuasive author's realistic albeit optimistic vision. Essentially, the politically- conscious author dexterously proffers a kaleidoscopic view of the African woman's traumatic experience in a speckled sphere where women have to ward off encumbering shadows, break the ice of silence - hinged on socio-cultural fetters - to forge ahead.

Chioma Carol Opara Ph.D
Professor of English and Comparative Literature,
Rivers State University,
Port Harcourt - Nigeria.

1

Tribute to Petticoat

It took ten months of rehabilitation and weekly sessions with my Shrink to get me to this happy place in my life. She said that telling the story of my love and travail will boost my healing. I will now take stock of everything that happened in the past that got me to the point of losing it before healing and struggle for my new happy place. The glitch is that I don't know where to begin my story. My good friend, Chioma, suggested that I begin from the most hurtful episode of gang rape. The rape has such negative energy that will surely block my view if I give it a leading place in my struggles. I think that it is better to first write about my old normal, which is not normal to many young women I know. Still it was my normal before the rain began to beat me, before the build-up to the tornadic storm. Then I can rise with my storm breaker!

Ouch! I just stumbled on a stone. Yes, the writing plan sounds great, but... I have just realised that this story is still so painful that I cannot put my emotions in the middle of it. I need to step out and make it a story about someone else. Not an alter ego, but a kind of mirror for looking at the incidents that got me to this point. In this way, I can be on top of everything. I will begin by considering the character that I know very well. I confidently name my fictional character, Zeb.

It is almost six o'clock. Zebra Olima is tired but relieved that she has graded the last of fifty-nine essays. She walks up the stairs to her apartment on the second floor of Friendship Flats. She is drained and slow. Suddenly, she stops. Cold shivers on her arms only. From childhood, she has learnt to trust her sudden shivers. She listens. She feels that somebody or something is looking at her. She retraces her steps and goes through the connecting hallway to the rear steps. She goes another flight of steps in order to take a good look at the surrounding shrubs. She looks through the peepholes. These days of military dictatorship in Nigeria, you have to watch your steps. They pick people up for minor criticism of the government. The Vice Chancellor of the University of Nigeria where she teaches has already cautioned her about referring to the government in her classes. She defended herself by reminding him that relating literature to society was part of the teaching method that made him hire her.

Zeb knows that not all has been well since the students began to agitate for a better government. Many of them have joined the Young African Movement (YAM) that is pushing for the end of the military regime and return to civilian rule. Her eyes move closer to her apartment building, to the shrubs, vegetable gardens, and the long backyard that connects the three apartment buildings usually called The Flats. She observes the bungalow where the domestic workers live and sees only one person in the kitchen area shared by members of the house. All appears normal there, but she strongly feels that something is wrong. She gives out a sigh of relief on seeing a young couple walking leisurely in the yard. Suddenly, she turns round because the feeling of being observed comes from behind her. She sees nothing. She tries to project some bravado by saying in a loud voice, "If you are a ghost or whatever you are, you are a coward." She walks back to the front stairs and down to her apartment on the second floor, still conscious of being watched. She puts her key in the keyhole, waits and twists her mouth in anticipation of danger.

"Zee, I'm the one." The voice is unmistakable. She knows the tone and inflection of the voice. She can recognise the voice of her first love even in her sleep.

"Are you dead?" She says as she swings round.

Jaja emerges from the back of the second floor. He is not wearing his ever-charming smile. Zeb knows that all is not well. They walk through the door and he immediately begins to tell her his mission.

"Zec, I need..."

Zeb interrupts him. "First of all, never sneak up on me again. You could have phoned me."

"Nneoma-m," he uses an endearment to appeal to her, "they will know if they check your phone line. It doesn't require so much intelligence to figure out that I may be with you. Please, I need your help."

"Again?"

"Yes. Again and again."

"What is it this time?"

"They are after me again. They think that arresting me will stop the growing strength of YAM. The growing discontent will soon erupt into something too big for them to control."

"I'm not going to hide you in my house this time." She dumps her bag.

"We narrowly got away with it the other time." She flops on the sofa.

"I know. I can't put you through that risk again. Anyway, I can't stay here because I'm on my way to the YAM convention in the north." He sits opposite her across the table.

"Young African Movement. Is that what they want to prevent?"

"Yes. They want to stop it by arresting the delegates. They know that more students, even high school students, are joining the Movement and they want to frighten them by harassing the leaders."

"So why are you here?"

"You look very tired, my love and you're edgy."

"Tell me why you..."

"I want to see you and I also need you to get my family before they get them. You know that these days, they go after the person's spouse and children if they can't get the person."

"One of these days it might be my turn and without a husband, maybe they'll go after my old mother."

"God forbid."

Zeb knows that they can also go after her son, Dozie, but she does not want to say it because Jaja does not know about him yet.

"Jaa, tell me what happened."

"It happened this afternoon around two. I had a hunch that something might happen because of the proposed meeting. I told the messenger to be on the lookout. I was in my office when Vivian opened the door and came in."

"You mean, Vivian your secretary?"

"Yes. She came in with two men. They identified themselves as State Secret Agents and wanted me to go with them for interrogation. You know what that means."

"Everybody knows what it means when SSA comes for someone. How did you escape?"

"As the two men stood in front of my desk facing me, Vivian left, but she did not close the door behind them. She picked her purse and demonstrated the act of using the toilet. I could see her but the agents facing me could not. She pulled up her skirt a little bit and squatted while waving her bag. It was so funny. Weird is a better word."

"So?"

"I did not understand the meaning of Vivian's antics, so I followed the agents. As we entered the lobby, I said I wanted to go to the bathroom. Just instinct. The men stood in the lobby. I went in there and right there in the cloak room before turning left or right to one of the bathrooms, I saw Vivian's bag hanging on the hook. I have told her not to leave her bag in the cloakroom but you know how she is. 'Yes, sir.' She still does what she wants to do. Anyway, today I was so happy that her bag was there. As soon as I saw the bag, it dawned on me that she wanted me to see something inside it. I opened it and saw her clothes, petticoat, wig and all; very sexy. I wonder where she goes after work with such sexy clothes." Jaja winks at Zeb.

"So what happened?" Zeb suppresses a smile.

"The agents were waiting for a man. I walked out as a very sexy woman but I did not go towards them. I walked out through the back merging with other workers. If anyone recognised me, they did not laugh or show it in any way. I was actually surprised that when I came out of the building through the back door, the messenger..."

"You mean David?"

"Yes, David was there with a taxi. I went home. Told my wife. And ran."

"So your wife saw her loving husband as..." Zeb laughs.

"It's not a laughing matter."

"How does it feel to be a woman?" Zeb is still laughing.

"Safe."

"Wrong and so wrong. A woman feels unsafe every day, every minute and every second because of sexual harassment..."

"Rape and other acts of violence against women. Those are what I deal with as an attorney. But I'm just saying that in my circumstances with the secret agents, I felt safe to look like a woman."

"In that case, let's dress you up like a woman again, because you are still in the circumstance."

"Please, I'm very hungry," he says, moving to a seat near her.

"Look at this man. You left your wife's house to come here and ask me for food. What do you take me for?" The inflection of her voice does not match her words; in fact, her smile shows that she enjoys being Jaja's favourite.

"You look so tired, my love." He rubs her shoulder, "I did not have time to eat in my house, just changed my clothes and gave David the dress before they brought me here. Please, my love." She feels the tingling sensation of his closeness. Jaja smiles knowing the effect of his closeness, but she disrupts it and gets up from the couch.

"Ok. I have some rice and..."

"No-o. Please I need heavy food like *garri* and soup. I don't know when next I'll eat. And I'm leaving soon; just here to gain strength from seeing your pretty face." He gets up to follow her.

Zeb goes to the kitchen. Jaja follows her, but stops to look at the papers beside the computer on the dining table. There is a poem titled, "Vultures." Thinking that it is about Zeb's concern for violence against women, Jaja makes a comment.

"Are you writing a talk for the Women's Forum? I saw the poem about vultures that prey on women." Jaja says as he enters the kitchen.

"Please read it before you comment on it."

"Don't get me wrong. You know I'm against sexual harassment and other forms of violence." He opens the back door so as to make an easy escape in case they come for him through the front door. He goes back to the dining table and reads.

Jaja speaks from the dining area. "Zee. This is very political. It mentions the poet, Saro Wiwa. You know that the government is very sensitive about him."

"Yes. He challenged them. They executed him. I'm a budding poet so it can be my turn next," she says. Jaja is shocked by what she just said. It is true that the government executed the poet but the thought of her being the next target unnerves him, and he is hurt by the casual way she blurts it out.

"Please don't be direct in your writing. The students know about these issues and can make the connections very easily," he says in the living room.

"Please, my dear. Try to play safe," he says, going back to the kitchen.

"Remember what your friend told you," he says.

"Which one?"

"The American woman. She said that you can do more for the Movement through your writing than through joining students in demonstrations and she is right."

"Anise just wants me to leave this country and join her in America," Zeb says.

"Much as I want you with me here, I'll be happy if I know that you are safe in America."

"I'm not leaving this country and all my loved ones," she smiles at him. He does not smile. "Alright, I'll take another look at the poem," she says, "I don't really want my feeling of disgust for the bad situation to overshadow what I write." She smiles at him again.

"Please, I don't want you inside a prison or even near it. You know what they do to women in prisons. You're more effective teaching young people than being inside a prison. You promised me that you'll stay out of trouble." He comes close to her and holds her waist. He knows that his closeness will have an effect on her and it does. She shifts her legs and struggles to maintain her focus on the conversation.

"I know that they do atrocious things to prisoners, especially women. They intimidate, beat, rape and rob them of their dignity. I know all this, but listen. Right now, we have to fix things from the top. You and I know how good things were in this country in the seventies. Many of my students don't have that opportunity to imagine a good life because it has not been part of their experience."

Jaja pulls her closer as she talks. "The country now has thirty percent unemployment because of military control of a government that they cannot manage. Look, we suffered too much during the war and many families have struggled to get back on their feet."

"I know."

"My mother struggled to get the extended family out of poverty after my father's death. Now the government is trying to kill the middle class. I am committed to this struggle-o," she breaks off from his hold.

"Zee, please," he pulls her back.

Holding her by the waist, he says, "We're in this together. I'm just saying that you have to think about your situation as a woman and also that you are more effective with students."

She relaxes. "My poems are about society but they may choose to call them political. I love my kids, my mother, family, you and my fellow citizens of this dear country, so I write poetry with images that anyone can interpret in different ways."

"You think that they are stupid? The secret agents are people like you and me. The only difference is that they have crossed over to the side of the oppressors. They can interpret poetry. They are educated and intelligent..."

"But not intelligent enough to recognise a man in women's petticoat," Zeb laughs and turns round to stir the soup.

"It's not funny." He pushes closer to her.

Jaja rushes through the food like someone is about to snatch it from him.

"Easy, you're safe." Zeb pats him on the head.

"Relax," she rubs his back.

"A person surrounded by lions must be vigilant. I can't relax. I must be on the alert." He has finished eating and goes to the sink with the plates.

"And that in your dictionary translates as eating like a lioness." Zeb follows him to the sink. She places her hand on his shoulder as he washes.

"Will you help my family?" He turns his face to her.

"You know that it is difficult for me to say no to you. That's why you always come to me."

He wipes his hands, turns and quickly pulls her close again.

"It's true in many ways, but..."

"Don't even go there." Zeb steps back.

"I won't. At least, can you give me a kiss? This may be the last time you will see me. Just a friendly kiss."

"If it's just a friendly kiss, you won't be asking for it," she says. She is not sure that she can bear to give him just a friendly kiss. It is better for her not to kiss him at all because she may lose her will power and go the full length. Jaja also knows it. He can read Zeb's body language as no other man can. He looks at her big mouth as it swells up. He knows that her long nipples are now hard. He can see the hard nipples even in spite of the brassiere and blouse covering them. All he needs to claim her is the permission to kiss her. From the kiss every other thing will follow. He knows all this but he will wait for her to be ready to come back to him.

He has never ceased to be ready for her; just the thought or sight of her turns him on. He was in the back staircase of the first floor looking through the back window when he saw her drive in. He began to salivate. By the time she ran up the stairs, he was hard and it was painful. And ridiculous in the circumstances of his situation.

"Just a friendly kiss." Jaja holds her with his eyes. She cannot say yes but cannot say no. She has a very strong Catholic background from her parents, and the nuns that ran the school she attended also enforced the Christian values that restrict her from giving in fully to a married man.

Zeb dated Jaja at the University of Benin when they were undergraduates. He was charming and attentive to her and it was easy to fall in love with him. Right from their first meeting, he told her that he would like to marry her.

"This is unbelievable. You don't even know me."

"I know what I want. I don't expect you to say yes. I just want you to know that I want more than dating and more than friendship from you. I want you always." He had seen her on campus several times. Men usually hung around her. Many of the men had more clout than him. He was a junior and ten years younger than her. The men she hung out with were seniors, older and from rich families. They always had a lot of money to spend, but he was hopeful because Zeb was not dating any of them.

His elder sister, Chika, who was the president of Eden sorority, knew Zeb fairly well as a sorority sister. She confirmed that Zeb had no boyfriend, but told him that she was too old for him. He ignored her opinion and waited for an opportunity to present himself to Zeb in a favourable manner. The opportunity came during an Eden sorority event. He got his sister, Chika, to invite him to speak as a youth organiser. The theme was "sexual harassment on campus." He memorised and practised the speech for weeks. The hard work paid off. His speech was a success. The young women liked it. Zeb came up to him and congratulated him. He did not hesitate to ask her for a date and when she agreed, he told her his intention. That was a mistake. She cancelled the date.

Zeb did not like men to propose to her because it removed the suspense and excitement of a relationship; something that she missed in her life. She had a long plan for herself, and marriage was not part of it. After leaving Igo, all she wanted was education and freedom to be herself as a girl, but she could not be a girl again because she was almost thirty and had three kids with Igo. She wanted education and the experience of being single in her own way, even with her baggage of kids. Although she cancelled the date, she was always gracious to Jaja whenever they met, which was often.

She had a friend, Chioma Okorji, whose boyfriend was Jaja's friend. Chioma was just entering Holy Rosary High School when Zeb left to get married, but fate brought them together in the same university where they became sorority sisters. Chioma's boyfriend, Jo, told Jaja to persist and Chioma encouraged Zeb to reconsider him. Jaja always made himself available to help out with Eden sorority events, but Zeb was the one who presented herself to him at a party. He was the master of ceremonies at his Palm Royal fraternity dance and they had invited Eden women as their sister club. When he announced that a particular dance was for young women to choose men rather than the other way round, he positioned himself near Zeb praying in his heart that she would choose him and she did. That was the beginning of a full blown romance.

Jaja liked what he regarded as Zeb's lack of pretence. She was not reluctant to experiment in bed like many young women of Jaja's generation. During all those years of living with Igo, she kept imagining what it would be like to enjoy sex. She loved to read romance novels and enjoy descriptions of sexual intimacy. She yearned to know all about fore-play and enjoyment. Ecstasy, orgasm and sexual haven did not sound real to her. With Igo she knew bruises, revulsion and vomit. When Chioma told her that she would marry Jo because he could take her to the highest orgasm, Zeb got confused because she had taken what she read in books about sexual ecstasy to be fantasy.

On her own part, Chioma had taken Zeb to be experienced in sexual matters because of her marriage and sexual airs. Zeb could swing her hips, shift her head to attract attention, "pull" her neck and bat her big eyes seductively. Chioma noticed that men always gravitated towards Zeb so she assumed that they detected her sexuality, which she equated to sexual prowess. Through conversations with Chioma about her experience with Jo, Zeb realised that cloud nine experience was real and that she actually totally missed out on it during her so-called marriage with Igo. This made her resent Igo the more for taking away her girlhood and for not knowing about sexual pleasure. She never for a second considered the possibility of having a fault herself until she met Jaja. Experimentation with Jaja never took her to the expected Promised Land of sex but the act of giving him pleasure was joyful to her.

Again, marriage disrupted her link with Jaja. His old father wanted him to marry and give him grandchildren before he passed on. His mother also wanted to be able to boast as other women did about their daughters-in-law and grandchildren. For them, their sons' families were extensions of their own. It made them feel a link with the future.

"My son, make me proud like my fellow women," his mother pleaded. He could never get his mother's plea off his mind.

When Chika told their parents that Zeb was ten years older than Jaja and already had children with another man, they called a family meeting to plan how to deal with Jaja. He resisted family pressure for a while trying to cling to his romance with Zeb and hoping that she would be ready after getting the degree, but she was not. She wanted to have more education so she began to apply for further studies and scholarships. She was successful and won the Commonwealth Scholarship, but she also wanted Jaja. Their convocation ceremony in 1989 was an opportunity to be with Jaja and discuss issues. She was nervous so she took time to prepare how to make Jaja realise that her desire for more education did not imply a rejection of his marriage proposal. She began by telling him about her proposed plan to use her scholarship for further studies in London, but he kept quiet.

"You know my story and yearning for education. I want more education and my people support it. My mother will help me with my kids so all will be well," she smiled. She wanted him to be happy for her, but he did not show happiness. He was thinking about his mother's dream of having grandchildren. He was disappointed that Zeb's dream did not include his mother's dream for grandchildren. He did not communicate his thoughts to Zeb so his silence irritated her and she snapped.

"Alright, you are now thinking about your mother's wish and all I want is for us to discuss the two dreams. I don't want to disrupt your parents' plan and I don't want to begin another fight with in-laws. This is my life," she said. She had thought about this meeting and hoped that it would lead to an assurance from Jaja; that he would wait for her to get her heart's desire first before becoming his wife and that he would protect her from his family's hatred. She did not get this reassurance and Jaja did not want to wait.

When Zeb realised that she got pregnant from that convocation meeting with Jaja, she did not want him to know because she had heard about Jaja's engagement. She was hurting. Fate brought them together again. She returned from England with a PhD in 1995 and took a job as a lecturer in a university located in the same city of Nsukka where Jaja had set up his law practice. At first,

Zeb thought that she could brush him aside. She thought she had moved on just because she was dating other men but in her heart she still had a special place for him and their son was a constant reminder of their love. The first time he visited her in her office, she confirmed that time and experience had not weakened their love.

He often goes to her office to brainstorm on human rights issues, especially issues of women and gender. His law practice focuses on human rights and one of Zeb's close friends, Chioma, is his representative in the big city of Lagos. Jaja and Zeb attend the same church and sometimes, he would meet her with his wife and children after church to say hello. Jaja has a lovely wife whom he respects and two daughters that he adores. His parents are still alive and happy with him for giving them what they want but the hollow in his heart is still there. Now standing with Zeb in her kitchen, he feels like damning the consequences and enveloping her in his arms, but he holds back. He does not want to make a mistake again with Zeb. He feels confident that he will claim her forever at the right time, but he does not know that the future has a lot in store for him and for her.

"You may not see me again." He makes another plea, his arms still holding her. Zeb draws close and hugs him; tight. She places her head on his shoulder in order to avoid mouth-to-mouth contact. He holds her tight and squeezes her. It feels so good that she begins to tear up, yet she manages to push him off.

"You have to go." She wipes her face and opens the back door. He is emotional also as he stands, not pulling her back to his embrace and not moving.

"I'll help your family."

"I trust you. Goodbye, my love."

Zeb gets a feeling of emptiness. She usually feels this way after meeting with Jaja. It is a complex feeling of hurt and joy. It has a tingling edge that excites her. It is intense this evening. She feels like weeping but at the same time, she hugs herself in pleasure like she is still holding Jaja. The warm feeling begins from her heart as if it is swelling and fills her whole body with joy. Yet she feels lonely because she never freely allows her feeling for Jaja to overrun her self-control. She knows that it is a struggle and wonders how long her self-control will last. The only other guy she has ever felt something for was not available.

She met Aracebor in London and felt immediate attraction to him. He was handsome, cultivated and was interested in African culture but she soon realized that he was not ready for her. Zeb does not want to dwell on her tough luck with love. She wants to run Jaja's errand. For her, the task is not just for Jaja but also for Jaja's kids who are her son's half-sisters and for her people because Jaja is "fighting" for their rights. She picks her car keys and looks at her watch. It is almost eight o'clock at night. She is still tired but feels obligated to run Jaja's errand.

2

Under the Blackout

Zeb looks out through the balcony of her apartment into Ikejiani Street. Many huge trees need trimming. Their leafy branches block light from the few street lamps that have not burnt out. The shadiness of the street suits her purpose. People often look out through their windows and can tell whose car is passing and who is inside it. Jaja's visits to her office have generated a lot of gossip. Seeing her and Jaja's wife together in her car will certainly create a bomb of a gossip when it happens. She walks out through the back and makes her way to the garage. She puts on the parking light as she eases the car out of the garage. It is a 1990 Ford Mustang, which makes roaring sound when you rev it. Zeb makes sure she does not rev the car as she roles it into Ikejiani and drives west to Elias Avenue, not eastwards to the main gate but to the side gate on the north side beside the Vice Chancellor's lodge. It opens into a dirt road that runs through a semi-traditional village with many mud houses lit by traditional candles made from palm fruit fibre. Few of them have electricity, illegally tapped from loose wires that hang near the university fence, but they do not have outside light so the surrounding is dark and suits Zeb's secret purpose.

She does not mind the darkness and does not encounter any other car as she drives through the hilly and winding dirt road. Driving becomes easy when she enters the tarred Market Road. Since the market is closed at night, she does not encounter the usual hold-up in the market area. She smoothly turns left onto Enugu Road and makes her way to the gated community of Ugwuja Estate. Driving to Jaja's compound, Zeb wonders how to tell his wife, Anene, to come with her. She is not friends with her and always gets a funny feeling whenever they meet. She never says much but the way she looks at Zeb gives cold shivers to her arms. Aney, as Anene is called, sees Zeb's car lights shine on the gate. She knows Zeb's car and promptly tells the gate-man to open the gate.

Zeb drives into the compound and to the front of the main house. She bangs her car door and walks straight to the front door with her head held high; trying to banish the guilty feeling for loving the woman's husband. Aney meets her at the door.

"Good evening Ma." Aney bends her knee to show deference to an older person. She's more than a few years younger than Zeb but Zeb's education and status intimidate her.

"How are you, dear?" Zeb sounds condescending.

"Is my husband with you?" There is ice in Aney's voice and Zeb feels it.

"Can I sit down in your house?" This is a way of putting Aney down, and showing that she is not hospitable to a visitor and older person. She is testing the young woman's pride in being a proper wife. It works.

"Sorry Ma. Please sit down." Aney is formal and still cold.

Zeb perches on the couch. Aney pulls a side table and sits opposite her. She looks at Zeb directly expecting some news.

"Mr. Okorafor told me to take you and the children to my house." Zeb does not want to say "your husband" or even "Jaja." She wants to keep it formal and non-personal.

"Where is my husband?" Aney puts a lot of strength on the word, husband.

"Get the kids ready. Bring the money in the second drawer of his computer desk. Get your packed bags. We have to leave now before anybody can see us." Zeb rolls her eyes thinking, "No need to feel guilty, after all it was another woman that took Igho from me. And Ja was mine before this woman rushed him to the altar even without his heart." She juts out her mouth as she wonders how a woman can willingly get into marriage when the man does not love her. She too lived and had children for a man she did not love. She feels bitter that he forced her to live with him and have his kids. She pouts as she remembers that chapter of her life.

Aney is surprised at how calm she sits on the passenger seat of the woman she hates most in the world. She sometimes longs for an opportunity to beat Zeb up. The woman has everything she needs. She has education, independence, and above all, she has Jaja's heart in her pocket. Aney suspects that Jaja does not want them to have another child because he still hopes to marry Zeb and have another child with her. The gossip is that Zeb knows how to have sons. Maybe he hopes that Zeb will have one for him. Aney has conflicting emotions towards Jaja because of Zeb. She hates him for loving Zeb, but she is so hopelessly in love with him that she feels powerless to confront him about Zeb. Her marriage to him was arranged.

Some people had visited their home to talk with her parents. It was later that her mother told her they wanted to find out whether Aney was ready for marriage and whether the family would like their son Jaja to court her. Their son was a lawyer with a lucrative practice somewhere in the East.

"Is he an Igbo man from the East, Mama?"

"Yes, he is from a very distant part of eastern Igbo called Aro but his father is the postmaster here in Ibusa."

"Mama, what does he look like?" Just five feet two inches tall, Aney liked tall men.

Her mother showed her a photo. Aney beamed when she saw the image of a tall good-looking man. She traced the facial features with her hands; big nose, big eyes and big mouth. Just opposite of her small features. She suddenly covered her face in embarrassment because she saw her mother observing her reactions and smiling.

"Don't fall for a photo my daughter. Wait till you see him."

"When?"

"On Sunday when we go to church."

Aney took an unusually long time to prepare for church that Sunday. She chose a mini skirt so that people would see her beautiful legs. She chose a blouse that covered her breasts so that she would look like a good girl. She got her friend, Jane, to braid her hair with shiny thread in the latest style called "king's cap." Her father even teased her when he saw the hairstyle.

"Is this the one they call 'boys-follow-me?"

"Papa, this is called *okpu-eze*, king's hat. How do you even know about such things?" She giggled. Her father was pleased that she liked the idea of marrying Jaja Okorafor.

Aney's father spoke a little about his prospective son-in-law. "Jaja's mother's family is part of Umueze village in the notable Otu-Odogwu clan of Ibusa. His father is not from these parts but I am happy that he is from the famous people of Aro in the eastern side of the big river. He was the postmaster here in Ibusa for many years before he retired but still lives in Ibusa. He is a good man who has trained all his children in universities." He hoped that his son would be a good husband like his father, but he did not verbalise this thought.

When Aney eventually saw Jaja, she was speechless. The photo did not do him justice. He was the most handsome man she had ever seen in her whole life of seventeen years. He was educated. He was a big lawyer. He had a very beautiful car. She had never seen a Mercedes Benz 350SLC in her village of Ogbe-Owelle. Very few people had cars in the village and they were mostly old cars. Only the headmaster had a new car; a Volkswagen Beetle. On her way to school, Aney liked to look at cars on the Benin-Onitsha highway and she had not seen Jaja's type of car. That made him special. She met him in the company of their parents after church. After curtsying to greet, she did not say anything; just stood there and wriggled her toes. From that first meeting, she became the happiest person on earth. But this was brief.

Soon after marriage, Aney discovered that Jaja was not complete as a person. She would catch him stare at nothing and sigh. He would call out a word in his sleep. Zee. In their most intimate moments, he called Zee. When she asked, he said that she should not worry about it. When he named their first daughter Zebra, everybody was against it. It was not a family name. It was not even the name of a person. He ignored the traditional way of naming children. Of course, they got names from grandparents, but Jaja insisted on Zebra as the first name of their daughter. It was years later, when Aney saw Zebra Olima that she connected some things that puzzled her about her husband. Now sitting in the passenger seat with Zebra driving her, she feels like choking the woman. She looks at Zebra intently from head down to her feet even though she cannot see her feet on the gas pedal. Zeb is aware of the gaze. She smiles. It is not the first time that a woman has stared at her with disgust. Some cannot stand the fact that she is not married and miserable as many of them are, she thinks and smiles at her selected misconception of the gaze. In truth, she is not sure why some women choose to gaze at her. She understands that of men. Her smile widens. Aney is aware that Zeb is smiling but misconstrues the smile. Maybe Zeb is relishing her time with her husband. By the time they enter Zeb's house, Aney is so full of anger that she can throw up.

Aney assesses Zeb's living room. It is not as big as hers is. There are too many plants and not enough space for children to play. She makes a face at the dining table with a computer and books and papers. It indicates that Zeb does not have an office in the apartment as her husband does. She does not even live in a single house, but a rented apartment. Aney concludes that she is of higher class than Zeb. In spite of this superiority feeling, she is still jealous of the woman.

"Where is my husband?" Her voice is harsh.

"Let's take care of the kids first."

"Auntie, is my Daddy here?" Zebra Junior says. Aney touches the five-year-old on her mouth indicating that she should keep quiet. She does not want her child to refer to Zeb as Auntie, but does not want to correct the child in front of Zeb.

"No darling, your Daddy is not here," Zeb says.

The children have gone to bed when Aney repeats her question.

"Where is my husband?"

Zeb goes to the kitchen and turns on the stove to warm the food.

"I can smell him here." Aney speaks from the living room.

"He left. And don't shout. Do you want to eat?" Zeb says.

"I'm not hungry." Aney enters the kitchen.

"I'm taking you out of here later tonight. You may not find food later when you are hungry. So you better eat now," Zeb says.

"Get a plate from the rack there and serve yourself," Zeb dishes rice and beans for herself.

"Which plate did my husband eat with?"

"He dumped them there after washing them. Just touch them and see which ones are still wet," Zeb makes a face. She does not see why Aney wants the plate used by Jaja.

"In my house, he doesn't go into the kitchen. I can't believe that he washes plates for you." There is so much anger in her voice. Zeb shoots a look directly at her, feels like kicking her out of the place, but remembers her promise to Jaja. She turns and goes to the dining table with her food.

Zeb has barely slept a few hours before she springs out of bed. She presses the light button but lights do not come on. She gropes in the dark, finds her flashlight and checks her watch. It is four o'clock in the morning. She goes to wake Aney up. The children are co-operative. No crying. No noise. They whisper as they see Zeb and their mother do.

"I want the light," Ebere says.

"Sh-sh-sh. NEPA has taken the light," Zebra Junior says to her sister. Her voice is low. The Nigerian Electric Power Authority (NEPA) is notorious for not being able to control power outages.

"I want my Daddy."

"Sh-sh-sh. We'll pray for him. That's what Mummy says," Zebra Junior says.

In the car, Zeb puts on the parking light only and drives very slowly. Aney is not in the passenger seat. She is in the back with the children so that if they are stopped anywhere, Zeb will say that the children are ill and she is taking them and their mother to the hospital. They made the children lean on their mother in the back as Zeb drove. At the university gate, the Security Officer flashes the light at the back of the car. As soon as he sees a woman with children, he lets the car out. Zeb speeds up with the car's full beam.

"If anybody kills my Daddy, I'll take a gun and shoot that person and he will die death." Little three years old, Ebere, is half-asleep.

"Where will you get the gun dear?" Zeb says.

"From the soldiers."

"Where will you see the soldiers?" Zeb says.

"TV."

Zebra Junior laughs.

"Nothing will happen to your Daddy," Zeb smiles.

"And children should not talk about shooting. Alright?" Zeb says.

"Yes, Auntie."

Aney juts out her mouth in disgust. Her little girl still refers to her enemy as Auntie.

"Daddy is a hero. He will not die," Zebra Junior says to her sister.

There are glimpses of light in the few houses beside the road leading out of Nsukka town. It becomes brighter by Queen's Secondary School with light in the school's fields illuminating part of the road, but soon after that, the road becomes dark. Zeb begins to rely more on the full beam of her car that skirts the outlines of the road lined by shrubs and forests on both sides. In normal times, Zeb would have remembered many folk tales about ghosts and spirits that roam the forests at night, but tonight her thoughts are focused on getting to her destination without suspicion. The scenery appears dreamy as the car winds up and down the rolling hills of Nsukka landscape, and the light picks clusters of forests scattered in the grassy hills, but Zeb does not notice them. Even Aney holding her children does not seem to notice anything, as she keeps quiet like a refugee avoiding enemy lines. The children are asleep and Aney's eyes follow the movement of the light even though she is aware of only the road and not the surrounding scenery. She, however, knows when they exit Enugu Road and enter the Highway towards Ninth Mile. She is aware of branching off the Highway into a dirt road.

"Where are we going to?"

"The seminary in Egede," Zeb says.

Their journey is without interruption and in about one hour, Zeb drives into the mission compound of the Marian Fathers in Egede South. No one stops them at the gate. She drives through the winding bumpy road lined by mango and *dogon-yaro* trees. The darkness is dotted by lights coming from lanterns carried by seminarians who are already up getting ready for Mass. She drives slowly to the house of the chaplain behind the big hall. Father Egbujie has come out with a lantern to see who is paying them a visit at this time of the morning. He remembers how security agents visited them earlier and searched the compound, so he stands at the entrance waiting and anticipating another incident with security agents.

Aney and the children remain inside the car as Zeb discusses with the priest.

"Soldiers came here and searched the whole place last week. I cannot keep them here."

"Did they find anybody?"

"Nothing and nobody. They apologised. Said it was a wrong tip-off. Donated money to the orphanage and left. We're still looking into the matter in order to find out who their informant was."

"Let's talk with the woman," Egbujie says and they walk to the car. Aney says that she can go to her parents' house in Ogbe-Owelle village of Ibusa.

"That's the first place they will look for you if they don't find you in your house."

"We will not stay in my parents' house. We have remote farms and settlements where they can never find us."

"It is settled then," Egbujie says.

"The kids can easily fit in with the orphans going to your site in Onitsha and she can fit in as a worker or dress like a Reverend Sister or something," Zeb says, showing her knowledge of the seminary operation.

"Leave the details to me. I'll take care of everything. Keep up the good work and God bless you in the name of the Father and of the Son and of the Holy Spirit," Father Egbujie makes the sign of the cross on Zeb's forehead.

Zeb's drive home is uneventful. She enters her apartment and throws her pocket book on the couch. What she wants most is to lie down and catch a breath before getting ready for classes, but the telephone rings.

"Good morning."

"Sorry to wake you up. This is Anise."

"Of course I recognise your voice. You didn't wake me up. I've been up since four."

"Writing?"

"Not really. NEPA failed. There is total blackout." Zeb says.

"Then why were you up?"

"Some political situation that I can't discuss on the phone."

"I have told you to leave that country."

"I just came back to the country barely two years ago, so I just can't turn round and run."

"I'm not telling you to run away but to come out to a better place where you will be more useful to your country. This is your chance because your United States visa is still valid, not so?"

"Yes."

Anise continues. "The US is tightening up on Africans coming to this country. You may not get another visa when the one you have expires. So use it now and come out-."

"Because."

"I'm afraid that if you continue to stay in Nigeria, something may happen to you."

"Nothing will happen to me," Zeb says.

"Ye-ar right. Are you better than all those who have been thrown into prison for nothing? We heard in the news yesterday that soldiers raided the University of Jos campus and arrested some students and as usual raped female students."

"We did not hear it."

"They will hide it from you guys. But they can't prevent our American network from getting information."

"Is that why you stayed up? It must be around..."

"After twelve midnight here in Maryland. I'm begging you my friend, leave that sick country of ours. You can be a better citizen of that country from over here. Trust me. You can write in the papers here and get the world to help. Over there, they just muzzle everybody and your views cannot get out of the country."

"Coming out will be difficult for me," Zeb says.

"Because of your boyfriend? Leave him alone. He's married!"

"First of all, Jaja is not my boyfriend. And you're right; he's married."

"Good. So what's tying you down there?"

Zeb does not reply immediately. Such a question from someone who has known her for a long time surprises her. Her friendship with Anise goes back to their early middle school days when they met at School's Debate in Enugu.

Anise was in Queen's School team and Zeb was in the opposing team of Holy Rosary High School. Although her team lost to the Queens, Zeb was highly admired because of her wit and delivery. She and Anise became pen pals. The Nigeria-Biafra war disrupted their communication, but Zeb did not give up. She wrote many letters to Anise after the war. When Anise finally got one of them, she replied immediately narrating how she attended the only secondary school in Biafra, where her mother was a teacher, and was ready for university education by the time the war ended. In Anise's subsequent letters, Zeb followed the story of her meeting with a handsome man called Alex and leaving the country with him.

On her own part, Zeb narrated the story of her false marriage and the joy of watching her kids grow. It was in 1994, almost thirty years since their first and only meeting, that they met again. Zeb took out time from her study at Columbia University in New York to visit her in Washington DC. They had caught up on a lot of things that happened in their lives especially their love for their children, so Zeb is surprised that Anise would ask what is keeping her in Nigeria where her children live.

"You know that I have my kids and old mother here," Zeb's voice does not show her surprise. She is just tired.

"Then discuss it with her. Tell her that you have a friend who has a big house and who has promised to house you free of charge till you get settled."

"Are you sure?" Zeb is elated.

"I made this offer to you before. Did you think I wasn't serious?"

"Why do you want to do it?"

"We're friends. I just don't want you to waste away there. I always remember how smart you were and how everybody praised you way back at schools debate."

"After all these years, you still remember."

"Yep. Everybody said that you deserved to be in Queens rather than in that school where Reverend Sisters made you tie scarves to cover your hair as they do."

"You don't miss an opportunity to put my school down," Zeb chuckles.

"I tell you girl, take your chance now," Anise says.

"It will be difficult for me to leave. I've got the education that I wanted and finally come home to settle with my sons."

"Think about it. Discuss it with your loved ones."

"Anyway, how are you and lovely little Wendy?"

"We are all fine. She's now a big girl. Eight. She likes to point you out in her birthday photo album and say 'Auntie.'"

"How is Alex, your boyfriend cum lover cum husband?"

"Asleep. Everything is great."

3

Going Underground

eb is teaching "Global Literature" class in the arena of Paul Robeson Building and quite unaware that the Chair of her Department, Professor Ode, has quietly left his office on the second floor of the Arts Building complex and is making his way to her class. He knows that there are secret agents everywhere and that students are against the government. He does not want to agitate the students or the secret agents so he tries to minimise interaction with people in order to hide his feeling about the issues. He answers greetings from the secretary and messenger in the general office ignoring their sad faces. Stepping out of the building, he does not use the front yard that connects with the right side-walk to Robeson, but takes the back short cut used by hackers making easy escape with their wares when they see security agents. Leafy izorah hedges in dire need of trimming line the short route. Dust has coated the leaves giving them a brownish hue, so he makes sure that no leaf touches his impeccable white shirt as he eases his heavy body through the opening.

The students are absorbed in a heated class discussion of vultures, scavengers, cesspits, and madness in Zeb's new poem, when Zeb sees Dr. Ode through the window. She hurries out of the class to meet him in the hallway.

"The Vice Chancellor phoned me now. He said that he wants to see you in his office." The look on Dr. Ode's face indicates that not all is well.

Zeb looks at her watch. It is ten minutes to four.

"My class will end in ten minutes."

"He said right away, so you have to go now?"

"Is anything wrong?"

"He did not tell me what it is, but I sensed that all is not well. I'll be waiting for you in my office."

"Let me tell the class."

"I'll let them know." The Chair enters the class with Zeb following him.

"I've been summoned by the VC. The Chair will explain everything to you." Zeb does not smile. She picks her handbag and just leaves the class. She sniffs back some tears. She is tired and emotionally drained. In less than twenty-four hours, she has dealt with Jaja and Aney, driven to Marian seminary in the dark, had no rest, and now she's going to face the Chief Executive of the university. She lets the tears flow down her cheeks and onto her blouse.

The Administration Building is a four-storied complex with a long yard whose frontage borders Robeson building, so it is quite convenient for Zeb to walk, but she does not. She enters her car and heads south to Club Road that joins Zik's Drive that leads to the university's Exit. She, however, does not proceed to the exit but turns left on Zik's Drive towards the Admin Building. She parks in the large parking lot and walks almost the same distance that she would have walked if she hadn't used her car. The long drive and walk give her ample time to control her emotions and collect her thoughts.

The VC's Peugeot 505 SR is parked at the entrance in front of the Security Office. The officers reply to her greeting, but do not ask her any questions as she passes the Foyer. She walks the two flights of steps and enters the long hallway to the spacious waiting room. Many people are seated on comfortable seats waiting for their turn to see the VC, but the door attendant promptly opens the door for Zeb.

As she enters the office, the Vice Chancellor picks a piece of paper on his table.

"What does this mean?" He hands it to her.

"Good evening Professor Ikoku," Zeb says taking it and staring at a copy of her poem in astonishment.

"Sit down and tell me what it means," he says. Zeb takes her time to sit down opposite the VC while thinking of what to say.

"This is my new poem. We just used it in class today." She tries to make her voice normal.

"Secret agents came to my office to report that you are still inciting students. They gave me the poem as proof."

She stares at her poem, "Vultures."

VULTURES

Poet killer and forager of the dead.
Public cesspit should be your place,
For you stink; of murder and idiocy.
Your endless brutality gives no peace,
Corruption unlimited is your choice.
Hell is yours for abuses uncensored.
Bros, there's turmoil in our paradise,
When madness carries our village gong,
And commotion wears the elders' cap.
Sis, there's turmoil in our paradise,
When our mouths are locked with padlock,
And safety lives in the custody of scavengers.

"This poem?" Zeb says looking at it and thinking of her defence. Should she beg Ikoku to help her? No; that will be an admission of guilt and she has not done anything wrong. In any case, Ikoku cannot do anything if the government has already decided to take her away. She has done nothing wrong; she emphasises this in her mind.

"It is just a poem about vultures." Zeb's voice is not even. Deep down, she knows that the poem is a political indictment of the rulers, yet she argues that it is not.

Ikoku shakes his head from side to side and laughs. He laughs because she is right and wrong at the same time. On the surface level, the poem is about vultures, but its deeper meaning is political.

"Why did you choose to write about vultures?"

"It is a significant image in our oral tradition and students use it to learn how to connect with society." Her voice is even. Ikoku's laughter has eased her tension.

"You are a very smart woman, but there is a limit to how I can protect you. They also said that you are hiding Mr. Okorafor in your house and they wanted..."

"This is so ridiculous!" Zeb interrupts and thrusts her right hand in the air to demonstrate disgust. Her handbag falls on the floor.

"And so insulting," she says.

"Do the agents think that the best I can do for myself is to keep a man in my closet; a married man for that matter? For what?"

"Look at me." Zeb stands up.

"Am I so ugly that I can't get my own man and must hide someone's husband under my bed?"

"Sit down," the VC says. "I'm sorry that you are upset but I don't want you to be hurt. I just want you to be careful."

The door flings open. "Students are demonstrating outside, Sir," the secretary says from the door.

Ikoku gets up from his chair and goes to the window. He slides it open. The words of the demonstrators filter into the room. "All we are sa-aying ..."

"What are they saying?" Zeb says.

"They want you. They think that you have been arrested." Ikoku closes the window. "I'll go out and talk to them. Then I'll call you to tell them that you are alright."

The Deputy Vice Chancellor comes in with the Chief Security Officer.

"It started from the Paul Robeson Building and the Arts Building," The Security Chief says.

"Another group is marching from the Freedom Square," the DVC says.

"We gathered that some arrived by bus. I'm not sure that they are all our students," the chief says.

"I'm going to meet them," Ikoku says.

"No, this might be a set-up. Wait."

"For what?"

"We have to gather all the intelligence," the chief says.

As they talk about it, Zeb picks her pocket book from the floor and leaves the office. They do not notice.

From the hallway, she can hear two voices address the crowd. She goes to the balcony and looks out. More than a thousand students are out there. Two of them are on top of the Vice Chancellor's Peugeot 505 car. One is a man and one is a woman. Zeb walks down the stairs. There are security officers at the entrance preventing people from coming in. She walks past them and goes towards the parking lot as she listens to the voices of the speakers.

"They are not interested in us or our education. They come in here and pick our lecturers whenever they want. We do nothing." The voice is a strong bass.

A strong soprano voice takes over, "This time, we say 'enough is enough.' They have touched a woman. How many women lecturers do we have in this university?"

"Not many. They shout about women's education. How can women feel free to come to the university if you abduct the few women who teach here?"

"They won't come."

"We must say NO to oppression." The two voices shout and the loudspeakers boom. The crowd begins to chant. Zeb can make out some of the words of their chant.

"All we are sa-aying...

Army must go.

All we are sa-aying ...

No more prison."

Some of the students see her. They are not her students and do not react to her presence, so she believes that they do not recognise that she is the subject of their rally. They do not prevent her from entering her car and driving out. In fact some of them clear the way for her and she waves at them. She drives off but does not stop at the Arts Building where the Chair is waiting for her or turn right at Club Road to go back to her class. At the campus gate, she stops for a check. The police officer looks into the trunk of her car. She heaves a big sigh as she heads straight out of the campus. All she wants is peace and she heads to where she believes she will get it.

She wants to hurry out of town before they come after her. She changes the gear from two to three and four as she speeds on the University Road. She is still angry about the idea of hiding Jaja in her house, but she smiles; it means, "they don't know where he is." She wonders whether her replies to the accusations were believable. But how did they get a copy of the poem? Could they have gone to her apartment? Could there have been an informant in her class? Her reverie is interrupted at the junction of University and Enugu Roads as she slows down because of a "go-slow."

She looks at the car's clock. It is ten minutes after five. Most offices have closed, so people are going home and too many cars clog the main street of the small city of Nsukka. She changes the gear to one and drives very slowly. An unscrupulous driver of a *kia-kia* bus tries to cut corners by driving on the shoulder of the road. Zeb watches in disgust as he negotiates the untarred shoulder thereby raising a lot of dust. Zeb's car is air-conditioned so the dust just settles on the body of the car, but this is not her concern as she constantly watches the rear-view mirror to see whether anyone is following her. The lawless driver soon encounters a huge pothole on the shoulder and tries to veer into the main road in front of a stubborn taxi-driver who won't let him in. Their vehicles bump each other. It is slight but it causes more obstruction.

Zeb heaves a sigh of disappointment and turns off the air conditioner, but she is also relieved that any government agent looking for her would also be halted by this holdup. She winds down the car windows. Music filters into her car from studios located on the left of the road. She tries to calm herself by concentrating on Celestine Ukwu's musical lyrics about how some people are enjoying while others are crying. She glances to her right. Children with empty buckets and cans line up to fetch water from a tap beside the gate of Bishop Shanahan Hospital. Most of the children are in washed-out clothes and tattered shirts. Zeb feels that the clothes were probably bought from leftover in *okirika* piles. She is familiar with grades of used clothes because her mother used to buy used clothes, which she repaired and sold in village markets. Zeb guesses that the kids are probably from villages that have been "swallowed" by the city's expansion and whose traditional ways of life have been impacted by modernity. They have polluted their streams by industrial waste and they have no alternative water source except the occasional Good Samaritan who allows them to fetch water from their tap. Zeb shakes her head from side to side, as she recalls the Main Streets of London and New York with paved sidewalks used for walking and not for children to line up for water. They would classify the plight of these Nsukka children as child abuse in England, but here it is just necessity, family survival and joggling of old ways with hectic city life.

Zeb's thoughts are interrupted as the drama of the reckless mini-bus driver takes a new turn. People have gathered. Some rebuke the reckless driver whose bus is stuck on the shoulder of the road. Others beg the taxi-driver to let him in. A woman comes out of the car behind Zeb to join the crowd. Zeb adjusts her mirror and sees that the woman has two children in her car, probably going to an after-school lesson programme. These are privileged children, Zeb thinks. She looks at the children struggling to get water from the taps. She imagines that their mothers are probably lining up to buy kerosene for lighting their cooking stoves, since they lost their firewood forests to the city's development. The fathers are probably selling their labour at construction sites. She recalls the new immigrants who flock into London to sell their labour cheaply just as the parents of these children. A major difference is that these Nsukka villagers are not immigrants but indigenes, a bit similar to the situation of many Native American communities that were forced out of their land by immigrants from Europe. Thinking about these things adds to Zeb's bad day as the drama in front of her takes another turn.

The woman bangs the door of the taxi. She pleads with the taxi-driver. "Driver! Please allow the stupid man to enter," she yells. "The kids in my car are dying of heat. Please!"

"If not for dis fine woman and her children, I for show the idiot pepper!" The taxi driver obliges.

The *kia-kia* bus driver tries to save face by attacking the woman. "Madam, who you de call stupid man? Go get driver and enjoy ya life like big man, instead of roasting your children in the heat," he laughs.

"Foolish man," the woman retorts, going back to her car.

The cars move a bit faster. Zeb sighs again, but it is that of relief. She winds up her car windows as she drives up to the market area. She puts on the air conditioner, grateful to see two *Yellow-Fevers* in the traffic booth managing the traffic at the market junction. True to their nicknames, they wear the characteristic reddish-yellow shirts; a colour that the famous musician, Fela, associates with yellow fever disease in his satire of the government. Zeb smiles at Fela's use of a disease to describe a government that creates a bad situation and then appoints wardens to make it right knowing that the poor wardens are not capable of repairing the roads or the country for that matter.

Zeb drives up the hill relieved that no car is following her. She speeds up. Approaching the famous Opi Junction, she sees a long line of cars and slows down. It is a checkpoint. When it gets to her turn to be checked, she comes out and opens the trunk of her car. The police officer also wants to check her handbag.

"What for?"

"None of your business," he says.

"It is unusual for men to poke their noses into women's bags," Zeb says; it is a kind of grumble.

"This is an unusual time." The officer's voice is brisk.

"You're right," Zeb unzips her bag. She takes her class folder.

"Do you want to search my lecture notes too?" She opens the folder.

"No Madam. You are a doctor. I saw your name."

"Yes."

"Madam. Your Mama born you well-o. So beautiful and educated too. God bless you. I'll tell my daughter about you. I want her to be like you, but her mother always tells her to cook and clean so as to learn how to be a wife."

"How old is she?"

"Sixteen; just a baby in school," he says.

"Bring her to the university sometimes so that she will see many others like her and learn how to be whatever she wants to be."

"What department Ma?"

"Languages."

"Thank you, Dr. Olima. God bless you." He bows.

"God bless you, too."

Zeb feels good about the incident with the Police Officer. She thinks that things are not altogether bad. There are glimpses of hope even in the chaos. A bully of the oppressive regime admires education and wants to support his daughter to be educated.

Things were not too bad when she left the country in 1989 but on coming back six years later, she found the country in shock as the government executed some people including the poet, Saro Wiwa, on allegations of treason. It was not the first time they executed a poet. They executed Mamman Vatsa when Zeb was an undergraduate in Benin. She remembers that a delegation of Nigerian writers including the renowned Chinua Achebe and Wole Soyinka had gone to plead with the military leader but they disregarded their plea. When they announced the execution, students went on demonstration. Zeb and Jaja participated in the demonstration. It never crossed their minds that nine years later, a similar scene would play out in the killing of Wiwa and his group. Zeb shudders as she remembers these events that show how ruthlessly the government can deal with those regarded as opponents. Jaja is right to tell her to be careful, but she wonders how careful she can be in a situation that threatens her mere existence as a poet whose writing must conform to... She does not know what they expect of her. They could have tried Wiwa in a civilian court not a military tribunal like Vatsa who was a soldier, but none deserved to be executed. Zeb shakes her head from side to side in disgust at a government that kills its own. She veers right into Enugu highway.

Driving to Enugu is always a delight. The prospect of seeing her son and her mother brings a smile to her lips. She surveys the vast countryside of grassland with a range of hills and valleys. She smiles. In spite of human attempt to create ugliness, nature always comforts you with a beautiful scenery. She slows down and goes to the right lane. The mild amber of the sun gives the scenery a golden tinge. She turns off the air conditioner and winds down the glasses of the windows. She turns off the music. The only noise is the sound of the car. The triplet hills are on the right of the highway as she drives through the valleys of Ukehe. She knows that very soon, the hills will be on the left as the car winds to another direction. She slows down. There is another checkpoint with two police officers, each with a rifle. She feels cold shivers. She massages her arms and waits for her turn to be searched. Her mind seeks comfort in days of her childhood.

In the sixties, they did not have checkpoints where they routinely stop and check people. That was because civilian rulers managed the country then. They confined soldiers to the barracks. Then the Nigeria-Biafra war started in 1967. The easterners had seceded from Nigeria because the country did not prevent the pogrom that they endured in parts of northern Nigeria. They called their new country Biafra, so the rest of the country loyal to Nigeria fought them. It was a reckless three years of warfare. Millions of people died. Biafrans gave up the fight and became Nigerians again in 1970, but a major harm had been done to governance. The military that fought the war remained in political control of Nigeria and continued to rule since then, except for a brief civilian government from 1979 to 1983.

Checkpoints have become a feature of Nigerian roads. Zeb recalls Jaja's view that checkpoints are used to intimidate people. Zeb nods her head in agreement. They use it to promote military culture of command and obedience under the pretext of protecting people. After looking into the trunk of her car, the police officer asks Zeb for the engine number of the car. Zeb is surprised.

"You have to show me the engine number before I let you go." His voice is loud.

"What do you want engine number for?" Zeb does not even know about engine numbers.

"You want to query me?"

"Just want to know," Zeb says.

"Ok stand there." The police officer attends to the next car in line. He completely ignores her.

She does not know where the engine number is written in the car's engine. She notes that he did not ask anybody else for the engine number. She follows him.

"Please come and finish..."

"Shut up woman! When *deez ol* men buy cars for *deez small gals*, they *tink* they can talk to people anyhow," he waves at other drivers to pass. Referring to a woman of about forty as a small girl shows how young Zeb looks, but it is not complementary to her and is not meant to be. She pretends not to have heard him. The anger that was building up when she left the campus begins to resurface.

The other police officer goes up to her.

"Just bring a little something. I'll beg him to let you go," he says.

"What in the world do you mean by that?" Zeb says to the second officer. She knows that he wants money from her and it makes her angrier.

"Hei. Don't blow too much grammar on me-o! He thinks you have a rich boyfriend who has bought you a car. All he wants is for you to share your loot."

"What?" Zeb's mouth opens in shock, and then she says, "I'll ignore that insult."

"You call me an insult?" The officer yells at her. He is really close to her so she steps back.

"Is your name insult?" Her voice is loud. More cars stop for check.

"*Ashawo.*" The officer spits and walks away.

Zeb's mouth flies opens again in shock. "You call me a prostitute?" The pout on her face shows how angry she is about this unwarranted abuse.

"You are the fattest prostitute in the world. Look at you!" She is very loud.

An elderly woman jumps out of her car and says, "Prostitute what?"

"He called me *ashawo*." Zeb points at the officer.

"Did you call this gal *ashawo*?" The woman yells at the police officer.

"Women." The officer sucks his tongue making a loud hissing noise.

"Don't insult women-o. I get respect for my Mama-o." A man shouts through the window of a bus that has stopped. People in the bus begin to rain insults on the officer.

"Frustrated man!"

"Instead of finding a good job, you stay on the road to harass people."

"Suffer-head!"

"Your Mama na *ashawo*! See ya fat belly."

"*Afo awufu.* Bribery belly."

The two officers move towards the bus from where all the insults are coming.

"You better leave now that the people are dealing with them." The elderly woman says to Zeb. Zeb smiles at the people. "It is the second time today that I have walked away from a bad situation because people intervened." She waves as she drives off.

4

Light The Candle

 eb is aware of being awake but unsure of where she is. She sneezes. At least, she is alive. Her eyes open and she sees that there is light in the hallway next to her room. It is really her room in her mother's house. She remembers her mother saying, "You look very, very tired. Go and shower. By the time you come out, your food will be ready." But she can't remember showering or eating. She feels her body. She is tying a single wrapper across her breasts. A knock on the door. Her mother enters the room and puts on the light.

She looks at Zeb and knows that it is time to talk. "My child, what happened?"

Zeb tells her everything except the part involving Jaja coming to her house.

"Which one are you not telling me? Tell me my child. There is nothing new under the sun. Are you still following that boy Jaja?"

"Mama, I'm not following him. We are just friends."

"M-hm." Angel grunts as she folds her hands across her chest.

"There is a cloud in your forehead. Did anybody hurt you, you know, touch your heart?"

"Mama, the police officer called me *ashawo*?" Zeb brings this up to divert her mother's attention from Jaja.

"Are you a prostitute? You are not a prostitute. From head to foot, you are proper, very intelligent and beautiful, the top. Your father saw this when you were born and you have never stopped being the best. Don't forget who you are and worry about what people say. Remember your name. It is special. Do not allow anybody to take away your pride and joy. Let me go and tell them to bring pepper soup for you. Dozie is asleep but I'll wake him up to see you."

"No don't wake him up. I'll go and sleep in his room and see him when he wakes up. And Mama, I'm not eating any food again."

"Pepper soup is not food." Angel is already at the door.

Zeb's eyes rest on the large framed photo hanging on the wall. She was three months old in the photo. She remembers what her father said when she was a child as they looked at the photo together. "My man, as you go up, remember where you started even before crawling." She smiles at the memory. Her father told her that she was cut out to be a "man" among men and women. At the time of her birth in 1955, her father, Ibuchi Olima, was a teacher in the village of Ama-Enugu in Eke town where they believed that each child came to earth with its own blessing from the Almighty Chi-ukwu. Gifted people were able to read and predict the child's destiny. Ibuchi did not need to consult a psychic to know that his daughter was special.

The local midwife had said that he should take his pregnant wife, Angel, to the hospital because the child would come out with her legs. At the point of her birth, the baby quickly turned round and came out normally with her head first. Her mother called her Chizebe, which meant that God warded off the misfortune of wrong positioning of the child and would continue to ward off evil on her path. People were the ones that shortened Chizebe to Zeb. Her father, Ibuchi, tried to read the child but she closed her eyes, so he gazed at her forehead for a long time.

"I saw the star on your forehead when you were born and knew that God had washed you from inside to outside. I called you Ugo-Nwa, the eagle child," Ibuchi said.

"Eagle is a beautiful swift bird. It is swift and strong like a Gazelle but prettier. God and nature favour it. Trees vie to have it perch on their branches. Animals are blessed when they see it. You will be great like your grandmothers. My mother was the greatest singer and dancer in our community. Everybody loved her. Your mother's mother was a successful long distance trader, but she never broke a slate or touched a chalk for writing. She was a stark illiterate who could not say "come" in English. I knew that you would be educated like no other man in our family or your mother's family. The names Ugo-Nwa and Chizebe fit you. God clears misfortune from the path of a swift and intelligent man; a gazelle that scales the forest unscathed. That's just you, my child."

Zeb smiles again at the irony of her father's reference to her as a man. It was considered a compliment for a girl to be told that she would be a "great man" rather than a great woman. Many stories portrayed women as wives of great men so one hardly thought of women as great in their own right. Zeb treasured her father's explanation in her heart and tried to learn how to become "a successful man" by imitating her father. Zeb's father was highly respected in the community as a teacher so Zeb took her studies seriously and memorised the catechism with the aim of becoming a teacher like her father. At school, she got another name from other children because of her athletic prowess. They called her Zebra.

Zeb has finished eating the pepper soup when Angel tells her that there was a big demonstration in her university. They heard it on the evening news when she was sleeping. They said that some lecturers and prominent Nigerians incited the students. They mentioned many names. Zeb and Jaja are in the list.

Her mother tells her that she should not go back to the university but wait and watch how events unfold.

"I'm not going to run away."

"No, but you cannot rush to a fight head-on. It always pays to watch, calculate and plan a strategy that will work. This is the wisdom of the hen. That's how she deals with the menace of hunter birds, conniving cocks, and thieves," Angel says. Zeb laughs just thinking of what a chicken can go through.

"I'm going back to campus very early in the morning. I have a class by nine," she says.

"You are leaving this house now."

"Now?"

"Yes now, but you are not going to the campus and you are not staying here. They'll probably have looked for you in your flat at the campus. The next place will be here and that may be this night or early in the morning."

"You're right. Ma-ama di Ma-ama! Your brain is always sharp."

"I've been dealing with emergencies all my life."

"Yes, I remember that your premonitions of danger saved you people during the Biafra-Nigeria war."

"The only time that it failed me was when I could not save your father from being enlisted in the German war. We prayed and luckily, he survived, but the harm was already done. Now he is in heaven."

"Mama, please let us not talk about him now."

"You are right, my child. Now, we are facing another kind of war that is not called war. The wise old woman of our people's proverb said that if the hill learns to break her waist she will learn how to rest a little, catch her breath, and continue climbing the hill. That is how she will succeed. So my child, get ready to move. You'll spend the night somewhere else. When things cool down, we'll plan how you'll go back to Britain and join your sister. That way, they'll never catch you."

"Mama, I can't go back there. I'm done with living without my children and you." Zeb gets up.

"Time will come. The country is not done with you or maybe you are not ready to conform and live in this country. You have to go where it is safe for you and don't keep me worrying about you."

"Mama, so you don't mind my going away again?"

"What I want most in the world is to have all my children living in this country where I can see them as often as I want to. But I'll rather have them safe somewhere than have them live in danger here. My grandchild Dozie keeps me active. But I need peace of mind to raise him until you're ready for him."

"Mama that will be very soon."

The telephone rings. Angel goes to the living room where the phone is located. By the time she gets there, her goddaughter, Eunice, is already talking on the phone.

"Who is it?" Angel says.

"Mr Okorafor." Eunice gives Angel the receiver. Angel cannot believe that Jaja is phoning her house to look for Zeb. She suspects that he is the reason why she has been rejecting suitors. In her opinion, Zeb's recent suitors are better than Jaja. David is more educated and established than him. William is the son of their family friend. He has a PhD and a good job. Angel feels anger towards Jaja.

"Good evening Ma. This is Jaja."

"E-hen? So you are still following my daughter. Leave my daughter alone-o!"

The reply that comes to Jaja's mind is that his bond with Zeb has not been broken by marriage and that he will never stop loving her. He knows Angel's strong religious beliefs about marriage, so he just gives a simple reply to her question. "Mama, I'm not following her. I just care for her and this is why I'm phoning because I heard her name on the television. We are sending someone with a letter that you will keep for her. It is about whom she will contact. We want her name to be out of the list of the wanted persons. We can't send the message to her place because they will be monitoring it by now. Please Mama."

"When is the person coming?" Angel does not tell him that Zeb is in the house. She does not know who else is listening or tapping the conversation.

"As soon as possible." Feeling that Angel has cooled down, he wants to play on her sympathy.

"Mama, my wife and children are underground as I am. I don't even know where they are."

"So things have come to this?" Angel says.

"It's a war, Mama. But we will not talk much because it is telephone."

"God bless you my child and protect your family."

Angel lives on the second floor of a block of six apartments owned by her. She is a market-woman who deals in gold and women's clothes. She began her business by trading in used-clothes called *okrika*. She used to travel to the city of Aba in order to meet her supplier at Ariara market. The man used to buy up the rejects that sellers could not sell. He would ring a bell and chant about the durability of the clothes without mentioning that they were not normal-used but castaway *okrika*.

"Come and see wonder clothes! Wash them a thousand times, they remain strong." His voice was usually strong and loud. People would gravitate towards him to watch his demonstration.

"See this shirt," he would say raising a khaki wear and ringing the bell.

"I call it *akwa-a akwuru*, Push-and-it stands firm. Come touch dis ..."

The first time Angel witnessed the man's performance, she closely examined the clothes and realised that some of them would sell in the villages because of their durability. That was the beginning of her trade in clothes. She would buy them, wash, repair, iron them with coal iron, and resell them in village markets. Later, she began to travel to the neighbouring country of Togo to buy them in bales that she sold wholesale in Enugu. That was how she managed to support Okpara, Dokki and Kordi in school. She now has a store that deals in clothes and gold.

Positioned in the centre of Agbani Close and with a large yard, Angel's house is easy to locate. Friends and neighbours who have heard that Zeb is in danger visit Angel early in the morning to show their concern. Angel is surprised to see Zeb's cousins, Okpara and Udokamma called Dokki. Angel brought them up as her children and they relate to Zeb as brothers.

"Good morning, Mama!"

"I thought you were overseas," Angel says to Okpara.

"I returned last night and heard the news. I tried to phone Dokki but did not get through so I went to his place very early before he left for work."

"NEPA took our light so I didn't watch the television and my phone lost contact," Dokki says.

"I gave him the bad news. We decided to check on you first before going to Nsukka for Zeb."

"I hoped that NEPA also took your light so that you wouldn't have heard about it," Dokki says to Angel.

"Well, we know about it. That is why all these people are here."

The brothers greet and shake hands with a few people in the living room.

"Why are people gathering in the front yard?"

"To pray for your sister, Zeb."

Agbani Close has three classes of people. It began from the home of Aga who lives where the close branches off from Airport Road in Enugu. Aga's father was one of the elders who were present when the government negotiated to take vast lands to build industries and an airport. The people were happy that they would "get development." The establishment of a Mercedes Benz factory and an asbestos industry enabled local people to get low-income jobs that helped them pay for their children's elementary education. Income from such jobs as janitors, messengers, servants and house cleaners was not enough to sponsor children for higher institutional learning.

Most of them usually end up in the low-income earning jobs like their parents. Some of them augment their income by selling some of their family land to enterprising property owners who build for renting to industrial workers of the fast growing city. Angel is highly respected because she lives with the tenants in the same house and interacts with the low and high. Upper middle class people also built mansions on the street, so it is common to see new expensive cars alongside old second-hand cars and motorcycles. The houses face each other on the street so it is easy to see what goes on in the balconies, yards and the road. They know who drives what car and who uses *legedis-benz*, which refers to walking.

When someone drives into Agbani Close in a blue Golf and parks beside Angel's house, people know that it does not belong there. When two agents come out of the car and begin to ask questions, people are suspicious of them. The woman agent asks a boy for the house number.

"Good morning Ma. I don't know-o. We don't use numbers here. We just know the houses."

The agent approaches the praying group in the front yard of Angel's house and speaks to one of them. Dozie runs upstairs to alert his grandmother.

"Mama, don't worry. We'll handle them," Okpara says and pats Dozie on the head.

"We will all talk to them," Dokki says.

"Thank you everybody. You are the reason why we pray to have people. Money cannot buy you or your support. Please follow us. Let us meet the agents outside."

The agents are coming up the stairs when they see people walking down. They step aside until the last person has gone. Eunice locks the door as instructed and is about to go downstairs when one of the agents speaks.

"We are looking for your mother."

"Good morning. Sir. Good morning, Ma. Everybody is outside praying." Eunice walks down. The agents follow her to the yard.

"Who is looking for me?" Angel shouts from the front yard.

"We are Special State Agents. We were sent to ask you some questions." They raise their badges.

"You are interrupting our prayers to God," one man shouts. He is an indigene of the village who is fanatical about his traditional ways even as modernity overwhelms his surroundings.

"Did your mothers not train you in good manners?" The man adds.

"Please, let us hear them out. They said that they were sent, so they are acting on somebody's authority," Okpara says.

"Sorry-o, my brother," he says to Okpara and fixes his gaze at the agents as he continues, "but I don't care about that kind of authority. In this our land, we have respect for elders. We have gathered in the house of an elder to pray for our community this early morning. We want to pray to our God."

"Nothing is more important than God and prayer for our community," another person cuts in.

"Say what you have to say in front of everybody," a woman has joined the small crowd. She is carrying a basket of oranges to Airport Road, which is the main street where she will board a bus to Ogbete main market. Another woman helps her to put her load down. More passers-by stop to listen and make comments. The woman agent looks at the man. She does not like the idea of harassing an elderly widow. In fact, she does not like this kind of assignment. They convinced her to accompany the male agent because Angel would be more co-operative with a woman. The male agent did not expect to deal with a crowd.

"Madam, we have to come back another time," the agent says. They go back to their car and drive off. Mama thanks the people and tells them to come back in the evening after work for entertainment.

Zeb leaves her car at the Marian seminary. Father Egbujie's driver takes her to Nsukka Motor Park where she boards an *okadah* like ordinary people. She does not go through the main entrances of the campus. She directs the motorcycle driver to a path behind her apartment block where she gets off. She walks through the narrow path boarded by shrubs and small farms. Some children are playing soccer in the yard behind the block. She looks at her watch. It is eight o'clock in the morning.

"Good morning, Ma."

"Why aren't you at school?"

"They closed our school because of students' demonstrations. When is Dozie coming back to play with us?"

"Soon."

Zeb has heard from the *okadah* man that they closed the university but she did not know that the primary school is closed too. She goes up the stairs through the back entrance and makes it to the back of her apartment. She has that sense of foreboding. She rubs her arms to erase the cold shivers as she retraces her steps. She goes to her neighbours' apartment on the ground floor. Their children are playing in the hall and the door is open. Zeb puts a finger across her mouth to prevent them from talking or greeting her. The parents of the children tell her the latest news on the matter. The Nigerian Bar Association has made a public statement condemning the government for naming scapegoats who they will persecute without trial. The president of the Board said the government should release all political prisoners.

"They talked about you specially but did not mention your name," Odunze smiles.

"They said what kind of soldier is afraid of a girl with a poem?" his wife laughs.

"Sister, keep on writing. The pen is part of our hope," Odunze says. They decide to go out together.

"From afar, you will be seen as one of our teenage daughters."

The Chair is in his office when Zeb enters.

"They came looking for you here and I could not account for you. You made me look like a fool and an incompetent Chair."

"I'm sorry." Zeb feels that he has crossed over to the other side. She feels unsafe in his presence and decides that she must leave immediately.

"Where were you?"

"I went home."

"No one could get you in your place. I phoned you."

"I was exhausted from everything and I was sound asleep."

"How could you have been asleep when the campus was on fire that you caused?"

"I did not cause anything." Zeb turns and walks out.

"Hold on Dr. Olima. I don't want you to put this department or our students in jeopardy. It will do us all a lot of good if you can either remove yourself from your trouble-making cohorts or leave us in peace."

"Yes sir." She bangs the door. Her mind goes to her mother's wish that she should leave the country. She remembers her telephone conversations with her friend, Anise, who has offered her accommodation in America.

Zeb goes back to her neighbours' apartment. She has lunch with them. The children scout the whole apartment area looking for strangers or agents. The couple eventually goes to Zeb's apartment to search the rooms for any intruders. Zeb is already in her apartment when her cousins arrive. They support her plan to leave the country. Okpara gives her advertisements for American jobs that he cut from the Chronicle newspaper during his recent trip.

"Bro, were you planning for me to leave the country?"

"I thought it might be useful to you or your colleagues."

"Thank you. I will look at it and see whether I can begin to apply for jobs immediately."

Her cousins help her to pack her property while she concentrates on packing two suitcases for her trip to America. They throw in advice here and there.

"We are lucky that your visa to the United States has not expired. They are now pretty tough on Africans."

"Make sure you take the names and contact information of your friends in America."

"Cousins and other family members."

"Phone our sister in England. Don't isolate yourself. I would have told you to go to her house but they will get you more easily in the colonial centre of London than in America."

"And extradite her as they did some politicians."

"Things will be hard initially in America but just have patience and things will work out, Okpara says.

"Adopt the wisdom of the chameleon."

"Hei Bro Dokki. What does the chameleon do?"

"It moves gently and puts on the colours of the environment. It always succeeds in the new environment and still retains its chameleon self."

"Even the chicken has its own wisdom," Okpara says.

"I know it. It stands on one leg to survey a new place."

"Exactly; be gentle and observe before you leap," Okpara says.

"We will take care of your things, sell those we can, and send you the money."

"Don't worry about Mama. We'll take care of her."

They load their two cars and leave with Zeb before daybreak. They are going to Enugu so that Zeb can say goodbye to Dozie and Angel before leaving the country.

5

Welcome To Sunlight

Zeb Oli jerks her foot backwards as if she has kicked off some muck; then she steps into the Immigration Hall of Dulles Airport with a smile on her face. She feels that she is ready to face the world. She stands for a minute, surveys the vast entry point, and opens her mouth to "drink" the American air thinking that all of her problems have ended and she is ready to go. She feels some reassuring warmth inside her body even though the weather is cold for her. The warmth is from a feeling of excitement. She likes the feeling. She smiles. She remembers the first time she experienced such a feeling. It was back, when she was five years old. Her parents were taking her to the doctor in the city of Enugu. Although she was shivering with fever, she had a very warm feeling when she saw all the cars and the pattern of houses that were different from what she had seen in their town of Eke where they lived in compounds. She now smiles as she remembers her father's prediction when he saw the sparkle in her eyes.

"This child will go places," he said.

"Let her survive first," Angel said.

"See how her eyes sparkle at the sight of the city."

Zeb remembers wanting to jump down from her mother's arms, but her mother would not let her.

"Leave her," her father, Ibuchi, said.

"She's still having fever," Angel said.

"Let her feet touch the ground. The ground is pulling her," Ibuchi said.

"Tufia! May Earth not pull my child," Angel said jerking one hand in the air.

Even at a young age, Zeb showed that she must find her way just as her father predicted. She jumped down. The lace of her right shoe had come loose. Her left foot marched on it as she tried to run. She tripped and fell immediately. Ibuchi picked his daughter up. Angel just shook her head at father and daughter.

"You spoil that girl," she said.

The hall of Dulles Airport is huge. So many people! She looks at everything like she's studying it for an exam. A few people catch her eyes. There is a woman in purple gown. She classifies the gown as *a boubou* and identifies the style as *Baule* because of the way it exposes the woman's shoulders just like the gowns of West African women traders she saw at the airport in Lagos. There is a man in red wrapper and long white shirt. He wears a white turban also. She believes that he is from an Indian sect. People are in diverse attire. Three-piece suit, mini skirt, jeans and all are free and in motion. Exciting! The world in different shades! God's own country! She takes out her journal and pen to describe the scene. Her hand shakes. The pen falls. She frowns. It gives her a bad feeling. She does not write. She resumes her survey of the scene.

US Citizens. Non-citizens of the US. Diplomatic. She reads the signs and joins the one for non-citizens. The line stretches from the Immigration booth, and snakes from left to right and back, forming three rows. She stands on the third row, but soon it fills out to a fourth row. The line does not move.

She surveys her surrounding again. The Immigration Officers are seated inside booths. She watches the people on the line of "US Citizens." A large man in very tight blue jeans is on a similar spot to where she stands. He wears an orange safari shirt. Beautiful! She likes the colours. She brings out her paper and pen. Again, her hand shakes. Her papers fall. The man moves. He moves again. Zeb does not move.

Having nothing to do, she looks at her feet. They are Hausa leather shoes. They are brown but have black lines that snake from the back to the tip of the shoes. She notes that the black lines are similar to the line of non-US citizens. Her shoes are made of snake leather, but her line is made of live human beings. That is the main difference, she thinks. The lines of the shoe can afford to look like that permanently, but human beings cannot be on one spot forever. People must move. She has never really looked at her shoes closely since she bought them from Tejuosho market in Lagos, Nigeria. The Immigration Hall now reminds her of Tejuosho market. They are both crowded. The human beings in the market move. In this hall, there is no movement in the non-US line.

Zeb is bored. She shifts her weight to the left leg and supports it with her right hand. She looks around. She shuffles her right foot. The woman in purple *boubou* and the turbaned man go through the "Diplomatic Line." Their line is fast. She twists her mouth indicating that she is irritated by standing on one spot while other lines keep moving. She stretches her hands and yawns. Her line moves. One-step. US citizens keep moving. She searches for the man in blue jeans, but can't find him. He has moved on, probably in some bar having a cold beer. She smiles wryly. A woman occupies his former position. She has a child in her arms and drags a buggy. She steps aside to manage her baby. The people in front of her are fast. Her baby cries. Zeb envies the child's freedom to cry. He can cry and not look strange. "If I cry, they'll look at me like I'm strange; maybe hurl me to some mental hospital." An attendant comes to the aid of the woman with a child. He takes the pushchair. She moves. The people behind her move on. Their line runs. Zeb's legs ache.

Zeb's line moves again. There is hope. Zeb brings out many papers from her bag. She has anticipated many questions from the Immigration Officers, and has papers ready to support her answers. She reviews the questions that she believes they will ask her. "Where will you stay in America?" She has the letter of invitation from Anise and her husband, Dr. Alex Esomonu. She has the photograph that she took with them at their daughter's birthday party in 1994 when she visited them from Columbia University during her study abroad from London. She also has a bank balance that shows she is capable of supporting herself. The line moves again. She smiles and thinks of something pleasant as she waits.

A week ago while staying in Lagos, she gave her friend, Chioma, an application to fax to the University of Florida. She was surprised that they soon got back by email inviting her to an interview. She feels that she will get the job and begin to send money immediately to support the Movement. Jaja will be proud of her. It is a job to teach World Literature. She researched on World Literature when she was a PhD student at the School of African and Asian Studies in London. She has published a paper on it. "I'll get the job," she whispers to herself even though she also thinks, "you can never be sure of interviews." Maybe they will prefer a beginner whom they can train to suit their needs. Who knows? Her legs ache. The good thing is that her line moves.

There are many people in the Waiting Area, some carrying posters with names of their visitors. Zeb sees Anise and Alex before they see her. They are in the crowd on the side of the exit. Anise hugs and whirls her round.

"You are so tiny. Don't they feed you in that country of ours?" She speaks in their Igbo language.

"I'm just slim," Zeb says in English. She notes that Anise has added a lot of weight. She feels awkward as Alex looks at her figure approvingly. She tries to change the topic.

"I left a message on your house phone that we were delayed, but I didn't phone your office because you said your boss doesn't like people to phone you there."

"That's okay. We haven't been here long. Girl! You're petite," Anise says.

"That's the trend, girl." Alex smiles nodding at Zeb and taking the cart from her.

Anise rolls her eyes at Alex. She weighs about sixty pounds more than Zeb's one hundred and twenty-five pounds. There is a pillar with a glass panel. Anise looks at herself in the glass, and tries to fix her hair.

"You're still popular," she looks at Zeb.

"Why?" Zeb says.

Anise glances at Alex, frowns, and says to Zeb, "You have two phone messages."

"Already?" Zeb says.

"From a woman called Gloria," Alex says pushing the cart.

"You listened to her message?" Anise says.

"Didn't you?"

Zeb doesn't want to be caught in-between the couple, so she turns to their daughter, Wendy.

"You are quite a big girl now."

She smiles and stretches her hands for a hug.

6

Grab a man

Gloria and Zeb go back a long way from their high school days at Holy Rosary High School in Enugu. Reverend Sisters from Ireland managed her school and regimented their daily life, with the help of Nigerian teachers. They were there in the morning for prayers. They were there after night prayers to see that the girls were in their beds and all the lights were out before the security guard turned off the generator that supplied the light. The nuns were there to punish you if a teacher or prefect reported you for misbehaviour. They once punished Zeb for speaking her mother tongue, Igbo, in class. Her friend, Gloria, was the one that made her speak the language in class. She had raised the cover of her desk as if she wanted to bring out a pencil, but turned to Zeb sitting behind the desk on her left and whispered.

"See. The woman *na atabi anya* like she is out to catch someone for whipping today-o," Gloria said.

The way Gloria described the Sister's blinking of eyes in a mixture of English with Igbo sounded funny and Zeb did not want her to continue in case she said more funny things. She reprimanded Gloria.

"Shut your mouth, *Mechie onu*," Zeb said. She put her hand across her mouth and pretended to be scratching her face, but Sister Claudia knew the trick.

During recess when others were in the field playing, the Sister told her to weed the grass near the classroom area as punishment for speaking Igbo. Gloria joined her.

"You caused it Gloria."

"You are lucky that Sister didn't flog you. I would not have helped you with that."

Zeb did not like to be flogged. They all knew that the best thing was not to get into trouble. Most of their teachers were women who made sure to bring the girls up in the Christian way, loving Jesus and honouring the Blessed Virgin Mary by imitating her ways. In spite of the occasional punishment, Zeb was very happy in the school but her education was cut short by the death of her father and her early marriage. She and Gloria reunited many years later at the wedding of one of their schoolmates.

The Esomonus have left for work when the phone rings. Gloria is anxious to get to the point.

"Are you still free?" Gloria says.

"What?"

"Still single?"

"Why?"

"Things are easy, if you're single."

"Why?"

"You can get a guy; he'll give you a Green Card, so you can get a job."

"What!"

"Listen. I remember that you used to be arrogant and all that."

"Me arrogant?"

"Come on, cut that humility stuff. It's outdated."

"Gloria?"

"Yeah. Same good old Glow. Listen! Just listen."

Zeb is surprised by Gloria's new way of speaking. She does not engage in pleasantries and just asks her questions. This irritates Zeb and she wants to drop the phone on her, but her friendship with Gloria compels her to listen.

"Are you there?"

"Yes." Zeb swallows, and breathes heavily. "I'm here," she says.

"I have great news for you, but let me explain something first. I don't mean arrogance in a bad way. You were beautiful, intelligent, sports star, songster, dance star and I heard how you joined the women's club at the University of Benin and later-."

"Don't flatter me or narrate my life history," Zeb cuts her off. She does not want Gloria to keep going on because it may end up with asking her about Jaja or her son. She cannot deal with the emotions that they will trigger. There is a lot going on in her life with her narrow escape from Nigeria and not knowing anything about Jaja.

"I don't sweet-talk anybody. Just telling it as it is," Gloria says.

Zeb knows that Gloria is telling the truth but they were brought up to be humble. Their parents, the teachers and the Reverend Sisters told them the same thing about their talents. "God gave them to you. They were not of your own making, so you should not feel superior."

Zeb is confused by Gloria's boldness and believes that it must be Gloria's way of being American.

As if Gloria read her mind, she says, "This is America. Humility and stuff don't work here! Don't be shy about your good points. Advertise them. And when people praise you, accept the praise dramatically. Do you still walk arrogantly?" She laughs.

"You call me arrogant!"

"Honey, you still don't get it," Gloria laughs. "I've said that I don't mean arrogance in a bad way. You used to walk straight, talk gentle with your head upright. It was graceful. It was arrogant. I wanted to be like you, so I became your friend," Gloria says.

"Really?"

"Not kidding," Gloria says, "And I'm serious about what I want to say. I know that you'll be offended, but I'm going ahead to talk as your friend."

Zeb's heart begins to beat fast.

Zeb says, "Remember that we've known each other from way back."

"And that's why I want to tell you that you have to use all that you have to get what you want. This is America. If you don't, you'll be the loser. Nobody will feel bad for you."

"What do you mean?" Zeb says.

"You know what I mean. Use your beauty to hook a man who will give you a Green Card. You're lucky to be single so it will be easy to catch a guy." The way Gloria said 'catch' jars at Zeb's ears and she winces as she remembers that the term is used for hooking fish.

Gloria continues with her speech. "I don't want you to suffer as many foreigners do when they come here. Be street smart and get a man that will apply for a.Green Card for you."

Zeb is still thinking about the use of the word, "catch" and visualising Gloria and her at the fishing line.

"Zeb?"

"Zeb, are you there?"

The phone begins to make beeping noise. Gloria has hung up. Zeb lies down on the bed and covers herself with a blanket. She snuggles under the blanket and wraps her hands around her shoulders. She wants to hold her baby. She misses him and he must be missing her too. She remembers how he hugged her so tight the night her mother told her to leave the house and go to the neighbour who would accompany her to the seminary. Angel had given her pepper soup but she ate just a little and took it to Angel's room to meet her son. He was fast asleep on Angel's bed. Zeb sat there admiring his face. He looked so much like her father. She stretched her hand to trace the features of his face. He woke up and wrapped his hands around her neck. Thinking about Dozie, Zeb bites her lips and rubs her eyes. She tries to control her emotions and focus on the present, but her mind goes to Jaja. She jumps up from the bed and shakes her head.

The phone in her hand brings her to the present. She sits on the bed thinking that it is nice of Gloria to have phoned her, but a pity that Gloria has developed some bad ideas. Hook a man! Crude expression with crude intention! Go out to the streets and get a man who might be a killer or some kind of sadist. Every hour, the television warns people about the criminal killing women in parts of Maryland and Virginia.

"Oh God! I don't know whether I locked the front door after Anise and Alex left for work." She runs out of the room.

She remembers that she locked it, but-. She stops abruptly.

"What about when Wendy took the school bus? Did I lock it?"

She rushes out of her room, down to the front door. She is the only one in the big house.

She locks the front door. If the killer has entered and is inside the house, she will be in the house with him or her. The telephone rings. It is Gloria.

"Did you hang the phone on me?" Gloria says.

"Please help me. I left the front door open and I don't know whether the killer is already inside with me."

"Don't panic. Where are you?"

"I'm on the first floor."

"Is there a basement?"

"No."

"Okay. I'll be on the phone. Check every room. If you run into trouble, I'll call 911."

"What?"

"I'll call the police. 911 is the number you dial in an emergency," Gloria says.

Zeb runs across the family room and bangs the computer room door.

"What's that noise?" Gloria says.

"It's the door of the computer room. I opened it."

"Ok."

The computer and all the papers are just as Zeb left them when she used the Internet last night.

"Do they have a garage?"

"Yes."

"Check the garage. Be careful. I'll stay on the line in case of anything."

Zeb holds her breath. She tries the garage door. It is locked.

"Thank God."

"What?" Gloria says.

"It is locked."

"Go on. I'm here."

She opens the bathroom door. Empty. Her feet make thudding sound on the floor as she runs up to the second floor.

"Are you okay?" Gloria says.

"Yes."

"Talk to me as you check the house."

"The living room is okay, bathroom is okay." She opens the door of the bathroom.

"Check the closet," Gloria says.

"Here is the closet." She shakes two coats on the hanger, as if the killer can hide inside a coat.

"Here is the kitchen."

"I can draw the house from your description." Gloria laughs.

"Wait. I still have to check the bedrooms upstairs."

"There is a third floor. Go ahead," Gloria says.

"These people have a swimming pool in their bathroom!"

"What kind of swimming pool is that?" Gloria says.

"It is the size of five big bathtubs. It has inbuilt seats, different levels. What are you laughing at?"

"It is not a swimming pool. It is a Jacuzzi." Gloria laughs.

"It looks like a small swimming pool," Zeb says and checks the walk-in closet of the master bedroom.

"It is a small swimming pool. You can call it what you like!"

"What's that noise?" Gloria says.

"The dust bin just fell." Zeb says.

"Call it 'trash can' as an American and not 'dust bin' as a British or Nigerian," Gloria says.

Zeb closes the door of the master bedroom and walks back to her room.

Gloria continues, "In America, you have to call things by their proper names. If you want biscuits, say cookies because that is what we call it here. Learn to say candy instead of sweet. Jacuzzi is not a giant-bath. Anyway, you'll learn from experience. First things first."

"First, Thanks for checking the house with me," Zeb says.

"You're welcome."

"Why?"

"You're welcome' means that it's my pleasure to do it," Gloria says.

"So why not say 'my pleasure?" Zeb says.

"We don't say that here. Better learn American expressions from me before you go out and embarrass yourself. What did you speak when you were in Columbia on study abroad programme?"

"Proper English."

"Anyway, anytime you want someone to talk to or explain things to you, just call me. I'll call you back."

"Why?" Zeb says.

"I know what it means not to have a job in this country, so calling you back is the least that I can do. The most important thing is to help you get a Green Card so that you can be on your feet."

"I want to go to the bathroom."

"Take the phone with you so that we can talk."

"I have to go."

Zeb goes to the bathroom. It feels good to get off the telephone and Gloria's idea of getting a Green Card. She relaxes on the toilet seat. It looks like a good space to think without Gloria telling her what to do. She fumes. Look at all the trouble it took to make sure that there is no intruder in the house. Yet, Gloria wants her to open herself to intruders and just get a man. She believes that any of her previous suitors would have been better than a stranger. She remembers Jaja. She was not ready for marriage when he proposed and she blamed him for not waiting for her to be ready. Her experience with other suitors helped her to discover something about herself that made her to stop blaming Jaja. She found out that she was afraid of the marriage contract, afraid of what it would bring, afraid of another failure, afraid of disrupting her education and good life. Because of her bad experience with Igo, she lacks courage and tends to see conflict and the bad side of marriage. She now tells herself, "I'll remain with what I know - single and happy with my books. Coward."

She retracts. She should not be too harsh on herself. After the frustration of losing Jaja and additional heartache at Aracebor's inaccessibility, she decided that marriage for love was not her luck. She wanted to settle down with Oji but he began to act funny. He even believed that evil spirits possessed him. Zeb thinks that he was just scared of marriage. Knowing the fear of marriage herself, Zeb understood his plight and moved on with her life when he began to see visions. Having gone through all that and escaped all that, Zeb does not see why she should venture into the business of marriage now because of a Green Card. She prefers to be in control of her life instead of mortgaging it to a card that is not even as important as the marriage contract.

7

Miss Has-been

The telephone rings.

"Are you done?" Gloria's voice is harsh.

"Done what?"

"I knew you weren't going to the bathroom," Gloria says.

"That's not true."

"Anyway...?" Gloria clears her throat.

"I'm listening Gloria. Go ahead." Zeb gets ready for a confrontation.

"Then listen good! Nneka came here two years ago. She is already married to an American."

"Nneka? Who is Nneka?

"Nneka Jebata who is now Mrs. Nneka Fortney," she says.

"Nneka, our classmate?"

"Yes."

Zeb leafs through her address book to check the list of her classmates in the U.S. Ada Enendu, American

University, DC. Ada was her sorority sister at the University of Benin, but she withdrew in their second year.

"Do you know Ada Enendu?"

"No," Gloria says.

"I knew her in Benin. My friend, Chioma, gave me her address. She's at the American University, DC." Zeb reads out the address and zip code.

"That's in your area. Check her out," Gloria says.

"I'll check out her number in the phone book and give her a call first," Gloria says.

"You want to call her?" Zeb says as she leafs through her address book again.

"I'm saying that you should call her. I'll also give you Nneka Fortney's number."

"Fortney?"

"I told you that Nneka Jebata is now married to Fortney," Gloria says.

Nneka's name and Surname have not changed in Zeb's address book. She needs some clarification here.

"Glow. Are you talking about Nneka, the one we called the 'Holy *Wedge*' of our Reverend Mother Principal?"

"Yes," Gloria says.

"Nneka Jebata is the wife of Obi Jebata in Lagos and they have two children. As far as I know, they are still married. I saw Obi about two years ago at a wedding and he was there with one of their children. He did not say that he was divorced." Zeb closes her address book.

"As far as you know is not current," Gloria laughs.

"What are you laughing at?"

"The way you talk reminds me of home. I like to talk like that. I never try to change it."

"Why should you change it?" Zeb says.

"It changes on its own, but Nneka forced the change. She went to a school in New York to change it. She now speaks like an American."

"She does not want to be a Nigerian again?" Zeb says.

"She married an American. She is now Nneka Fortney, and she has a Green Card. She works and sends money to her family. Period. She is useful to herself and her family, because she did the right thing."

Zeb is silent.

"Nneka is now the holiest wedge of two families." Gloria laughs.

"Gloria. Are you making this up?"

"I am not kidding."

Zeb tries to think about Nneka's situation.

"Does it mean that she loves and lives with the one in the United States while paying the one in Nigeria to take care of her children? Is that the idea or does she love the Nigerian while she uses this one in the United States for what? What's the arrangement?"

"I don't know what the deal is," Gloria says. "I guess she loves both of them, and loves her children that now go to the best private schools in Nigeria."

"This is ridiculous! What about love for herself?" Zeb says.

"She loves herself also; she wears the best attire. You need to see her at parties."

"Attire doesn't appeal to me that much because I have worn the best when I was married to Igo but I still wasn't happy. What about her heart; is she happy?" Zeb says.

"Her heart is with her all the time. It is taken care of in America and in Nigeria. Big deal."

"Did you marry a guy to get your Green Card?" Zeb says.

"I'm an RN. Registered Nurse. I work for an agency in the city. It applied for my Green Card."

"I can be lucky too; after all I have a job interview soon," Zeb says.

"They don't do it these days. Marriage is what works for Green Card now. Do you want Nneka's number?"

"No thanks. I don't like her stupid … crazy style!"

Gloria's voice becomes harsh again. "When the months roll around and the payment of bills hit you, you'll know that it is not stupid to do what you can to get a job. When your folks back home tell you things that need to be done, but can't be done because there's no money, you'll know that Nneka is not crazy. When they tell you that your loved one is very sick, and money is needed for hospital bills, you'll know that Nneka is smart. When they tell you that one more colleague of yours has been thrown into prison, you'll do anything to raise money and help the opposition."

Everything that Gloria said is true. Zeb knows this, but that of her colleagues being thrown into prison is the one that hurts her most. Her family is fairly alright at this time, but if Nigerian leaders continue to mismanage resources and the economy continues to go downhill, her family will be in serious trouble like many Nigerian families. Gloria's reference to colleagues in prison takes her mind to Jaja. She does not know where he is or what is happening to him. Her anxiety for Jaja overwhelms her.

She feels very hot. She cannot stay on the bed anymore. She throws off the blanket and moves to the chair, but cannot sit. Her heart is beating so fast. She rubs her chest. She can still hear Gloria's heavy breathing at the other end of the line. Both of them are aware of how things have changed in their country and how the changes have affected all of them, and made people to do things that they never did before. Some have moved to other countries. Zeb has also changed her life plans; left her loved-ones, and come to America alone. She feels bad for Nneka too.

"Are you there?" Gloria's breathing is still heavy. Zeb can hear its sound and it disturbs her as it seems to parody her own breathing.

"God, do something about this heavy breathing," she whispers.

"I'm here." She says to Gloria. The room is hot. There seems to be no air. Zeb wants to feel the world outside. She moves to the window. She opens it to look out, but Gloria's voice follows her.

"When you realise that you can save those you love and preserve their innocence, the type of innocence that you still have, you will do what you can to save them. It is a kind of sacrifice. It is holy."

"I know these things." Zeb leaves the window but does not close it. She begins to pace the room.

"I also sacrificed my comfort at home to come here and start a new life. I really do understand." Zeb pants.

"Do not allow your sacrifice to be in vain." Gloria breathes in-between her words like someone who is jogging.

"Do what you can to help our country in any way you can. If you operate underground, it is good. If you are on the ground or above it, it is great. Just get a job and begin to play your part as a member of a country in need. Many families at home are still alive because of the sacrifices of family members who have come to work here. You've done the right thing by giving up all your comfort to come here. But you cannot get a job without a Green Card. You can get a Green Card through a man. So get out there and get a man!"

Zeb presses the off-button on the phone.

Zeb cannot bear the heat. She tries to run from the heat by leaving the room. She walks towards the front door. But the heat follows her for it is coming from within her soul. She walks very slowly, because she is very angry but trying to control it. She is angry at her friend for the truth that she has told her. She is angry at the leaders of her country for messing things up, and making them to leave the country. She is angry at America for the harsh option that is the lot of emigrants. She is angry at herself for leaving her country. She is angry at herself for coming to America. She is just like a bundle of anger. It is the kind of anger that leads people to punch things or hit people. She needs to stop the anger. She needs a lot of air. She opens the door and runs.

She is at the end of the road. The wood is thick with trees and branches that cuddle so tight. She can't tell which leaves belong to which trees. They entangle as if in a wrestle. All of them form a thick green maze with yellowish mesh. Green is life.

"Green wood, show me a light!"

She believes that her stomach cramps. It is actually her heart. She hugs herself tight and looks up.

"Please!" The sun dazzles her eyes. Nightmare. She believes that she has really reached the end of the road. She closes her eyes and looks into her soul. She perceives only a weakened spirit. She wraps her hands round her shoulders. And waits.

"What's wrong with you?"

Zeb jumps out of the edge.

"The man has killed five women? Do you want to be his next victim? Don't do that in my house!" Anise says.

Zeb stares at her.

"Are you okay?" Anise reaches out and touches Zeb's cheeks. Zeb is so glad to see her. She enters Anise's car.

"I was angry, very angry." Her voice quivers. Anise holds Zeb's face in her hands and looks at her eyes to see if she is alright. She doesn't ask why Zeb was angry. She just drives down the block.

"You should have hit the wall or something, instead of coming outside at this time that a serial killer is around!" Anise parks the car outside. The recklessness of Zeb's action upsets her. Not only did she expose herself to danger, but she also made the house vulnerable to the intruder. Zeb raises her hand to hit the wall. She can't bear the violence of it. She tries to slap herself but instead her two hands rub her cheeks. Anise observes her actions and knows that Zeb is having an emotional turmoil. She holds Zeb's hand and leads her into the house. Zeb walks up to the living room. Anise locks the door.

Zeb's head aches. Gloria's words still echo in her mind. Getting a man would be like bastardising herself and throwing away her values. What about all the things that go with marriage? What about love? What of touching? What of companionship? What about dating and the various steps involved in marriage. This new kind of marriage that Gloria talks about pulls up the fear of marriage that was buried deep inside her. At the same time, the need to get what it takes to live in America is urgent because she has to play her part in the Nigerian struggle.

8

Spicey Interview

A knock on the door. Anise enters.

"Just checking the house to see that no one is hiding somewhere."

"Oh my God." Zeb opens her eyes.

"We have checked everywhere except your room." Anise opens the closet.

"All is well. Come for dinner." Anise pulls at her blanket.

"I am not hungry."

"Come and keep us company. Alex and Wendy want to say hi."

"I'm coming," Zeb says. Her window is still open, so she closes it and goes downstairs for late dinner.

"I hear you almost lost it today," Alex says.

"I'm sorry."

"Nothing to apologise for, adaptation can stress you out. You've got to take it easy," Alex says.

Zeb is silent.

"If you don't want to talk about it, that's okay," Alex says.

"It's not okay. She needs to tell us what is going on," Anise says.

"I'm really sorry that I left the house unlocked. Please forgive me."

"That's okay. We understand." Alex says.

"It's not okay!" Anise pauses and glares at Alex, then she turns to Zeb.

"It's not just the house. It is you also. If anything happens to you, the state will ask my husband and me a lot of questions. This is America!" Anise says.

Zeb looks down at her plate, thinking, "As if I don't know that it is America. As if I don't know that Alex is her husband," Zeb does not say it loud.

Alex says, "If there is any problem in the house, you can phone my office."

"You can also phone my office, but don't ever leave my house just like that," Anise says.

"You said that your boss doesn't allow private calls so why do you want me to call your office?" This question immediately comes to Zeb's mind, but she does not say this out loud. It's as if she is too tired to talk, but she has also sensed the anger in Anise's tone and decides to keep quiet. She just raises her head from the plate and looks at Anise across the table.

"You're alone in the house. You never know who is watching," Alex says.

"They have had their say and I will not apologise again," Zeb does not say this aloud. She is silent and just pushes her plate.

They eat. Nobody talks. The only noise is the sound of their cutlery. Wendy is in the living room watching the television. Zeb looks at Alex across the table. He looks at his food. Zeb looks at Anise. She looks back.

"It is harsh out here in America especially for those of us without support from family," Anise says.

"You need someone with whom to share your problems," Anise does not remove her eyes from Zeb's face.

"I have you and Alex and I have..."

Anise cuts in: "I mean your own special person." She drags the words for emphasis.

"You forget that I was married before." Zeb still looks at Anise.

"Will you call what you had with Igo a marriage? It was more or less a forced kind of arrangement." Anise's voice is harsh.

"Anise, that's rude," Alex says.

"Well, no matter how you describe my relationship with Igo, it was a kind of marriage that produced lovely children."

"Whatever!" Anise rolls her eyes.

"What were you mad at?" Alex looks directly at Zeb.

"I had a call from a friend, well, a former classmate of mine phoned me." Zeb does not want to use the word "friend" to describe her current relationship with Gloria. She is no longer sure that a woman with Gloria's ideas of love and marriage can still be her friend. She considers Gloria's ideas weird.

"Was it bad news?" Alex says.

"She told me to get out there and get married." Zeb makes faces. The tone of her voice shows disgust.

"So?" Anise says.

"She told me to grab a man!"

"So?"

"You don't see anything wrong in that?" Zeb is surprised at Anise's attitude and antagonism. Anise does not say anything.

"When I arrived in Amsterdam from Lagos, I spent six hours waiting for the flight to Dulles Airport. I'm still jet-lagging and sleepy." Zeb is trying to be polite to her hostess but tears begin to crowd her eyes, begging to be released, but she controls them. She feels that she had a very bad day from Gloria and now from Anise, not to mention the scare of the Maryland intruder and the loneliness she feels. She stretches and yawns to indicate that she is no longer interested in the conversation, but Anise ignores it.

"That classmate of yours is a good friend. She gave you good advice." Anise digs the fork into her food, but Zeb does not want her to have the last word. She opens her mouth and quickly closes it to prevent herself from verbalising her thought. "Why would this woman who knows that I suffered abuse from my former husband want me to gamble with a man, just for a card? You have something else bogging you woman." Zeb looks very hard at her friend, but does not verbalise her thoughts.

"Thank you," Zeb says. Her voice does not match the fire in her eyes.

"You haven't touched your plate," Alex says.

"I'm not hungry," she gets up.

Inside her room, the tears that she had managed to control begin to flow. She lets them flow because there is no one to see them or feel that she is behaving like a child. She feels alone and lonely even though Anise, Wendy, and Alex, are in the house. Something seems to be wrong in her friendship with Anise and she cannot figure out what it is exactly. She just can't connect with her. She needs someone to be on her side and there is nobody. In Nigeria she had her brothers and mother. She had her neighbours. She had Jaja as a friend to count on. She kneels down, raises her hands and cries out to the Ultimate Spirit to save her from the danger that looms:

ARE YOU STILL THERE?

Go-o-d, are you still there?

Are you still there for me?

Please help this soul, this spirit before you.

Help me, please; there is a pit before me.

I do not want to fall into it.

Why am I tackled by marriage talk?

A talk that should be soothing,
Is turned to intrigue and plot.
I ask you who created marriage,
Is it worth this assault?
You potted me as I am.
Will you let them shake me,
Like a plant without roots?

She goes to the window, opens it to look at the sky, to feel the Supreme Spirit. Cool air massages her face. "I am not a plant without roots." The trees are there. She cannot see the moon, but all appears normal, and quiet. "You are there, you are here, and you are everywhere. Help me. Please," she says. She thinks that a tree sways. She goes to the bed. She pushes off the address book from the bed where she left it after talking with Gloria in the morning. She goes into a troubled sleep, but still wakes up early in the morning to prepare for a telephone interview.

Zeb's heart misses a beat when she opens her door and sees Anise coming up the stairs.

"Why are you dressed up this early in the morning? Where are you off to?" She says to Zeb without exchanging pleasantries.

"Good morning to you my friend." Zeb stresses the word, 'friend.'

"How are you?" Anise says.

"I'm ready for my interview," Zeb says.

"But it's going to be a telephone conference. They won't see you."

"It doesn't matter. I see myself."

Anise begins to laugh. Alex sticks his head out of their bedroom.

"What's so funny this early in the morning?"

"She's dressed up for phone conferencing."

"That's cool." Alex laughs also. Wendy runs up the stairs from downstairs to join in the fun.

"Auntie is dressed-up for a job interview." Anise tells her. Wendy turns and goes back downstairs.

Zeb looks at herself in the mirror. She rubs brown rouge on her dark chocolate cheeks. She smiles and lines her eyes with mascara. She looks like chocolate in a green wrap. Her green suit has a single gold leaf embroidered on the left lapel. The gold matches her gold neck-lace and earrings. She knows that Angel will be proud to see her look so good. She smiles at the thought of her mother who would sometimes tell her to turn round for inspection. Zeb would dramatise her movement as beauty queens did on the television. Her mother would laugh. Zeb now laughs at the thought of her dressing up as if her mother would inspect her outfit. She feels some relief as she thinks about her mother.

Growing up, Zeb felt that her mother gave her conflicting messages. On one hand, she always told Zeb not to focus on physical beauty because it would fade, but on her own part, Zeb observed that her mother wore the best wrappers and fashionable blouses. When she mentioned it to her mother, she was told that physical beauty was one thing and body adornment was another. Zeb grew up looking different from her mother, shorter with a different kind of elegance. She liked beads and costume jewelry, but her mother liked gold and had a special goldsmith that always personalised her jewelry. Zeb smiles as she notes how she is becoming like her mother. She wishes that her mother could see her wearing gold like her.

Zeb looks at her watch. Eight o'clock in Maryland should be two in the afternoon in Nigeria. She phones her mother. She is lucky. Her mother is at home.

"Good afternoon Ma."

"Is it Kordi?"

"No Ma. Zeb."

"Oh! Zee Zee. How are you?"

"Very well Ma. How are you?"

"I am well. Dozie is fine. We thank God. How are your friend and her husband and child?"

"They are fine. Ma, I won't be long on the phone because I have an interview for a job. I just want you to wish me good luck."

"You know that the sign in your hand is special, and God will always give you all that are yours. You will get the job if it is the will of God. If it is not, don't even waste a frown on it. A frown will give you a wrinkle."

"Mamma, you and your funny bits," Zeb laughs.

"I am telling you the truth. Listen to me. The water that you will drink will not pass you as it flows. It will allow you to drink it. It will not flow away from you. Remember that. May God continue to carry you, amen."

"Mama, what of Dozie?"

"He went to catechism class."

Zeb sits on the couch. She knows that she will try her best.

"If this job is mine, I'll have it. I feel good about myself," Zeb affirms. If fact, she feels so good that she has to knock her head. Her hand hurts, but her head doesn't. She goes to the bathroom mirror. She checks her hair to see that she did not scatter it with the knock. The phone rings.

"Hello. Dr. Alex Esomonu's residence." She says this in her best voice.

"Have you found a man yet?" Gloria laughs.

"Gloria! Be serious." Zeb laughs also.

"Practise that voice a lot more. It will get you a man in no time."

"Glow. I can't talk with you now. I'm waiting for a telephone interview."

"What time?"

"Nine."

"Make sure you ask them whether they'll apply for Green Card."

"You mean work permit?"

"Any," she says.

"I will."

"Good luck. I'll call later."

Zeb feels that her success at the interview will put an end to the whole talk about getting married in order to get Green Card. It is not that she hates the idea of marriage per se. The use of marriage as motive for getting a Green Card annoys her. As her thoughts drift to the Green Card issue, she checks herself. This is not the time to think about men and marriage and Green Card. She gets up. The wall clock strikes. She counts. Nine times. It is six in Florida. She is not sure why they have to call her so early, but she is ready. She sits down, and crosses her legs. She waits for the call. She uncrosses her legs. She looks at her watch. "What are they waiting for?" The phone rings. She breathes in and out. Her breath is heavy. Again she inhales and exhales to calm herself down. She picks the phone at the third ring. They are three at the other end.

They take turns to ask her questions. The wall clock strikes once. Zeb knows that they have spent thirty minutes and that the interview will end soon. It does.

"Thank you Dr Olima. Do you have any questions for us?"

"How soon will you make your decision?"

"Well, the fall semester will start in two and half weeks, so we shall make our decision and let you know as soon as possible."

"Will the university apply for a Green Card for me?"

"We have a lot of foreign students and faculty here, and an office that handles their matters. I'll fax the information, so you can contact them."

"I have no other questions."

"How was the interview?" Anise says.

"I think that they were impressed." Zeb makes the sign of the cross. She hopes to get the job and move out of Anise's house. She cannot understand what is going on, but she knows that she is definitely uncomfortable with her friend as her host. She treasures the friendship and does not want to jeopardise it with living in the house.

"Congratulations!" Anise says.

"Well interviews can be unpredictable but I'm hopeful," Zeb says.

"So we have our fingers crossed."

"I feel good about it," Zeb says.

"We still have to worry about the Green Card, because you can't take a job in America without it."

"They will fax me the information about whom to contact in the university."

"They said that?"

"Yes."

"Then you've got the job. But the Green Card will still be a problem."

"They said that I'll contact someone in the university."

"Let's wait till you get that fax and contact the officer. I'm telling you, colleges no longer help with that. I have a friend-."

"On whose side are you? I don't want to hear any more stories of failure!"

"On our side," Anise says.

"I trust that the professors who interviewed me know what they are talking about."

"They may not know."

Battered Stranger Syndrome

eb does not want to go along with what Anise said about colleges not helping employees to get Green Card. She believes that Anise may not know a lot about the academic profession since her experience is based on her work as an Assistant Manager at Marriot Hotel. Zeb believes that the specialists at the University of Florida will help her with Green Card. Meanwhile, she does not want to "put all her eggs in one basket." She wants to keep busy and spend less time thinking about loved ones back home. Every time she remembers home, she wonders what is happening to different people. Jaja does not know where she is and she does not know what is happening to him. Instead of sitting in the house worrying, she plans to visit colleges in the area to see whether they have job openings. This will also give her the opportunity to know Maryland before she leaves for Florida. What she does not count on is failure at getting the Florida job. She goes down to the computer room. The Internet has a list of colleges and universities in Maryland. She hopes that one of them may need her services. She decides on the University of Maryland in Baltimore. She plans to go there tomorrow.

She gets off the bus at the University Plaza, looks to the left and the right and marvels at the vastness of the university. She thanks her God that she is wearing flat shoes. The fall weather is cool and dry, so she walks leisurely through the streets of the university that is so vast that one can call it a small city. She finally makes it to Davidge Hall on Lombard Street and to the Personnel department. The long walk energises her.

"Excuse me, Madam?"

"Can I help you?" The officer says.

"Do you have openings for teaching jobs?"

"Credentials?"

"I have degrees in Language."

"Go to the Language department."

Zeb gets directions from her, and begins to navigate the streets again in order to locate the department.

"My name is Zeb Oli." She likes to shorten Olima to Oli so that people can say it with ease.

"Yes."

"I want to see the Head," Zeb says.

"What can I do for you?" The secretary says.

"I'll like to see the Head of the department."

"What?"

Zeb remembers the American term, Chair, so she repeats the sentence but replaces 'Head' with 'Chair.'

"Do you have an appointment with the Chair?"

"No, but I was directed to see him."

"Who directed you?"

"I don't remember the person's name in the personnel..."

She cuts off Zeb's last word as she says "Do you want a job?"

"Yes."

"The Chair does not deal with jobs. You have to go back to the person that sent you." She turns to the computer.

"I still want to see the Chair."

"He is at a meeting right now. If you choose to wait, that's okay."

"May I sit down, please?"

"Sure." The secretary does not raise her head from the computer.

Zeb sits, but a bit uneasy about the secretary. She is not sure that the secretary is being helpful.

"Where're you from?"

"Nigeria."

"Where's that?"

"West Africa."

"Oh. Africa. You have a strong accent." She still looks at the computer.

"Thank you," Zeb says.

She notes that the secretary does not say "You're welcome" as Americans do.

After about thirty minutes, the secretary informs her that the Chair would not return from the meeting till after lunch.

"He may not see you because he will go to another meeting."

Zeb is silent. She glares at the secretary for wasting her time.

"Do you wish to make an appointment to see him some other time?"

Anise listens to the story of Zeb's visit.

"Your problem is that you're not aggressive," Anise says.

"Should I have attacked her? She said that the man was at a meeting and that was that! Would aggressiveness have brought him out?"

"Zeb, don't yell at me."

"I'm not angry or anything. I just want to know what aggression could have achieved." Zeb does not lower her voice.

"You didn't handle it well. You told her that you were sent. That's putting you down." Anise's voice is soft.

"But I was directed by the officer in the personnel department. That was the truth."

"Nobody asked for that truth. You have to know how people like that secretary think about things. Is she white or black?"

"I'm not sure. This colour thing is sometimes confusing," Zeb says.

"You talk as if this is your first time in this country."

"I've never got used to knowing people by colour. If the features do not fit the typical description or media portrayal, I'm lost. Anyway, the secretary has blond hair but her colour was..."

"She could have dyed her hair blonde."

"Did you tell her that you're a professor?"

"No. Why should I?"

"You caused the problem. That secretary has issues. Maybe she thought you were after her job."

"Really?"

"Yes. This is America. No beating about the bush. Just show that you're somebody."

"All of you tell me that this is America, and yet you don't speak American."

"What do you mean by all of you?"

"You and Gloria."

"Do you want me to lose my identity?" Anise looks directly at Zeb.

"No, but you criticise my Nigerian ways."

"Only the ones that draw you back in America," she says.

"Like not introducing myself as doctor or professor? I can't do that."

"Did you steal your degrees?"

"What do you mean?"

"Why can't you say what you are? If you had said you had a PhD, that secretary would not have said you had a strong accent."

"Strong accent is not bad," Zeb says.

Anise laughs. "Next time you go there, give her your résumé to pass on to the Chair. If you don't blow your trumpet, nobody will blow it for you. Don't let your trumpet die in silence. Blow it!"

Zeb takes Anise's advice as a ctiticism of her ways so she defends the culture that she spent a long time cultivating.

"I was polite and cultured."

"Like what?" Anise asks.

"I asked her whether I could sit, said 'please' and 'thank you', appropriately like a civilised person. I have good breeding; it shows my sophistication."

Anise laughs again and shakes her head.

"What's so funny?" Zeb says.

"You got a lot of learning to do, baby girl. But, learn one at a time. Number one, always blow your trumpet. It is called packaging."

Zeb wants to tell her that what she regards as her "trumpet" does not belong to her but was freely given to her by God to use with humility.

"Don't argue with me. I have been there, so learn from big sister! Period."

Zeb is now on her bed. She stares through the window. She sees nothing. She thinks about Anise. She is a different person from what she used to be when Zeb visited her from New York three years ago. She was considerate and respectful. Anise admired her for the way she went after her dream and shared her regret for not having a college education because of family.

"Anyways, my children are well-educated like Alex. My sacrifice for them paid off," Anise said then. From the time they met during their high school days, Zeb knew that Anise always has strong views about issues. Zeb is also like that, but she struggles to understand why Anise now tries to force her views. This makes her uncomfortable in Anise's presence and she is disturbed by it. She will make efforts to accept Anise's criticism. At the same time, she knows that she can't accept all that Anise says.

"Blow my trumpet." Zeb laughs. She can imagine her mother throwing up her hands in exasperation if she hears that Zeb blows her trumpet. Zeb still remembers her mother's reaction the day she called another girl, "ugly."

"Let me never hear you again call another person 'ugly.' You're not the one that made your beauty. Our God gave it to you, so let it never get to your head. Do you hear me?"

"Yes Ma," Zeb always said.

10

Mama's Bird List

Ojiugo was the original name of Zeb's mother. Marriage to a man who worked for the Christian Mission led to her having additional names. In the fifties when she got married, the priests would not accept African names for baptism, so Ojiugo had to get a name that befitted the baptismal water. Since she did not know many English names, she relied on her husband, Ibuchi, to give her a name. Ibuchi had a long list of names, but Ojiugo did not like any of them because he could not say what they meant.

"Even trees and stones have names that say something to you. Why will I, tall grass of a girl, have a name that says nothing?" She rejected Elizabeth, Virginia, Eucharia and many other names. She chose the name Angel when Ibuchi brought it up because it was similar to the Igbo personal spirit concept of Chi, which Ojiugo was familiar with. Her mother raised another objection by saying that the name Ojiugo should not be rejected because it was her grandmother's name. That problem was solved through a translation of Ojiugo to Gold Kolanut, but she still was not very satisfied with the names. She resolved to educate her children so that they would never rely on anybody to translate English for them.

She nurtured her children to aspire to get into her bird list. At a time and place that kids did not have expensive toys or designer clothes, their biggest aspiration was to get into their mother's bird list. Angel used to cook a fowl for any of her children who took the first position at school or won a prize. She would buy a live chicken, wild goose, or any other bird for celebration. Although everybody would eat it, knowing that it was cooked in your name was a thing of pride.

Zeb was in Grade Three when she won the Catechism contest. They were living in their town of Eke now in Enugu State, Nigeria. Zeb treasures how her father hugged her and threw her up. "Up in the air! He threw me up again and caught me. I was so happy!" Zeb always smiles at this recollection. She also remembers her mother's mock objection to the special treatment.

"Don't spoil her. She's a big girl." Her mother hugged her and wouldn't let go.

"Don't spoil her with that big hug." Her father also drew attention to how her mother appreciated her. He read out the details of the report card for all to hear.

"I'll cook a fowl for you," Angel said.

"For me too. I helped her to learn it," Dokki, her cousin said.

"Everybody will eat the fowl," Angel said what they all knew, but they still liked to dramatise and joke.

"I'll eat the heart of the fowl because Zeb won't eat it."

"Not you, little man." Her father picked Aik and threw him up.

"I'll eat the heart because I filled the forms for her."

"I'll eat the heart because I'll cook it," Angel said.

"I told her to enter for the competition," her father said.

"I helped her to learn it." Okpara, another cousin came into the living room to share in the excitement.

"Okay." Their father put Aik down.

"I'll settle this matter. Zeb will eat the heart." He looked at Angel. Both of them laughed in anticipation of Zeb's reaction.

"I hate it!" Zeb said.

"It is delicious."

"I hate it."

"I'll eat it!" Anyi, her little cousin ran in from outside.

"I hate it!"

"I'll eat it!" Anyi did not know what was going on; just excited by the attention.

"Stop the noise." Their father and uncle went to the veranda.

Zeb stood on the stage with teachers as the head teacher praised her. The school cheered. Her class teacher,

Miss Antonia, gave her a diamond cross. She was a star. When the teacher saw that she was ahead of her class, she promoted her to the next grade. For Zeb, it meant that she was better than other kids in her former class. She was promoted again. She went up two times in one year! Yet, Angel counselled that she should be humble. That confused her because she understood her mother as saying she should pretend that she was not the best.

When she won the prize, Violet told her to teach her Catechism. Violet was older than Zeb but Zeb was two grades ahead. Violet wanted to win the next competition. Zeb had no problem with that. She gave up part of their playtime in order to teach her. They sat under the pear tree beside the main house and Zeb tried to make Violet learn by repetition. Violet was not a fast learner, so Zeb was frustrated. She called Violet 'dunce.' She did not know that her mother heard her from the house. She was quite surprised to hear her mother's voice.

"Zeb! Stand still where you are and don't move an inch."

Zeb obeyed. Violet also stood.

"Stupid!" Zeb rolled her eyes at Violet.

"You put me in trouble." She rolled her eyes again.

Angel came out, and told her to sit on the floor. Violet was about to sit when Angel told her to bring a chair. Zeb sat on the floor while Violet sat on a chair.

"You see that she is now higher than you?" Angel said.

"Yes Ma."

"You are down there on the floor and she is up there on a chair. Why is that?" Angel said.

"I climb a tree better and faster than she does, and I can be higher than her if I want to, but you put her there and put me on the floor." Zeb began to sniff, but Angel continued with her questions.

"Is anybody higher than me?"

"Papa is higher than you!" Zeb wiped a tear with her hand and rolled her eyes, but her mother ignored it and asked her another question.

"Is anybody higher than your Papa?"

Zeb looked up, thought for a while and answered, "God."

"If I can put Violet on the chair, and put you on the floor, because I do not like your calling her bad names, God can take her higher because God is higher than me. What did I tell you the other day and the other day and the other day?"

"Whatever I have was given to me by God, and I should not be proud."

"Good girl. God made Violet as she is, and made you as you are, so be happy to be the one that teaches her. When it is her turn, she will teach you something."

"She cannot teach me anything. I am good at everything."

"What did I tell you the other day and the other day and the other day?

"Whatever I have was given to me by God and I should not be proud."

"Always remember that." This was how Angel inculcated values in Zeb. Angel was repetitive and persistent because Zeb was strong-willed.

During the Easter celebration, Violet's mother organised a dance session for girls in Ama-Enugwu village. On the day of performance, Zeb told everybody to line up behind her. Her friend, Violet, wanted to know why Zeb was at the forefront.

"Because I am very beautiful," Zeb said and the kids laughed, but they still lined up behind her. It's like people enjoyed to humour her aggressive stance. It was not usual for girls to be so pugnacious because of their nurturing, but it was different with Zeb because of her father's support. Her father read to her, played soccer with her and the boys and always told her that she was very intelligent and would be very important in the society.

"It is true. I'm the best!" Zeb put her hands on her hips and looked directly at Violet.

"Look at you!"

"Yes! Look at me, and tell me what is not good in me?" Zeb began to sway her bony hips from side to side daring Violet or anybody to challenge her.

Another playmate of hers called Vicky was peeved by Zeb's pride even though she admired her boldness.

"Look at you." Vicky said and smiled.

Violet's mother stepped in. She was the leader in charge of the children's dance group and the one who taught them the dance movements.

"Zeb, you must never use your own mouth to say that you are beautiful. Let other people say it and when they say it, you must pretend that it is not true."

"I know why. It is because the spirits might become jealous of her and harm her." Violet was happy to draw some attention to herself.

"Yes," Violet's mother said. She explained to the children the motive for the pretence.

"Don't you see some people, one day you'll see big rashes all over their bodies. A jealous spirit has put the rashes there. You see a child who passes examinations. One day the intelligent child falls down to failure, *kpum!*" She cupped her left hand and hit it with the right hand to produce a big sound, *kpum!*

"Maybe the child had boasted and annoyed a dangerous spirit," Violet repeated what she had heard many times from her mother.

"Maybe the child didn't read her books," Zeb said.

"You are a stubborn girl," Mamma Violet said.

"I'll report you to Angel," Mamma Violet said.

When Zeb's mother got the report from Mamma Violet, she said, "God, you are my witness. I, Angel, Gold Kolanut, daughter of Nnanna Enyi and wife of Ibuchi Olima, will not live to see my daughter boast about the good things that you gave to her. Help me teach her how to be gentle and humble. Zeb, what did I tell you the other day and the other day and the other day?"

"Whatever I have, was given to me by God and I should not be proud. I was not proud, Ma. I was just telling the truth."

"Wait here, let me get my bible."

Before Zeb went to bed that night, Angel made her memorise psalm 131 so that she would never forget it. Zeb narrated this incident to her father whom she regarded as her biggest ally.

"Papa, was I wrong? You told me that I am the best. Am I not the best?"

"You are the best, never forget that."

"But Mama said-."

Her father did not want her to dwell on any misconception of the notion of humility so he steered the conversation in another direction.

He said, "Don't worry about it. Just work hard and continue to be the best, but don't boast about it-o. I agree with your mother that you should not be arrogant. Pride is good. It means that you believe in yourself and what you can do. Saying it to show other people that they are not talented is not a good thing."

"I did not say it to make them feel bad."

"Good," Ibuchi said. "Now, come let me show you how you can make your mother's anger turn to a smile." He took Zeb out of the house and they took the path to the stream where he usually told her the names of the flowers and trees. On this occasion, they did not study nature, but music and song. Her father used the tune of a church song to teach her the psalm.

"You will see that this will please your mother."

When Angel told her to recite the psalm that she memorised, Zeb sang it like a song. Angel shook her head from side to side and tried to suppress a smile.

"You like the song. Why not tell her that you like the song," Ibuchi said.

"Okay." Angel smiled and patted her on the cheeks and hugged her. Angel's body language showed Zeb that she liked the song, but did not want to praise her because it was a punishment. Zeb liked it too and sometimes she would chant it when she had problems.

MY HEART IS NOT PROUD
Lord, my heart is not proud,
Nor are my eyes haughty.
I do not busy myself with great matters,
With things too sublime for me.
Rather, I have stilled my soul,
Hushed it like a weaned child.

Zeb chanted this psalm several times as a child, but did not know the meaning of all the words. She only understood that God said she should not be proud. She internalised the message as she kept repeating the song and as she taught her friends how to sing it. Angel was happy with the outcome of the punishment. The song helped to socialise Zeb to despise arrogance. This incident took place in 1963 when she was eight years old.

Thirty-four years later in her room at the Esomonu residence in Germantown, Maryland, Zeb affirms her lack of arrogance. But she asserts it with mixed feelings. She is no longer sure that the quality suits her goal in America, but she is sure that Anise despises her inability to show off.

"I am still not proud," Zeb says. Her voice is lame. She tries to resolve her situation through prayer. She reaches out to the Ultimate Spirit for help in unlearning the values that took her mother a long time to cultivate in her. She stretches out on the bed almost immobile like a statue, under the blanket. She closes her eyes and listens. She seems to hear her spirit pleading. It is her heart pounding as she tries to make sense of how to change her personality and become more assertive. Her mouth is shut. The house is quiet. Without thinking of the Maryland killer, she shoves off the blanket and goes downstairs to the computer room. She wants to make sense of her confusion by writing it down. She titles it "Trumpet of God."

TRUMPET OF GOD
You made this humble statue.
You made humility a virtue.
How can I flaunt arrogance?
Teach me the vain habit,
So that I too can delete
Gentleness and humility.
And learn to blow the trumpet of God.

11

This Mountain Will Fall

The Chair of the Department of Languages and Literature phones to give Zeb the good news. Zeb got the job.

"If you need some time to make up your mind-."

"I don't need any time," Zeb cuts in.

"I'll take the job," Zeb says without asking for how much she'll be paid. Zeb is not familiar with the American system of employees negotiating their individual salaries with the employer. It is different from what she is used to in Nigeria where payment is uniformly based on qualifications and experience of employees.

"Ok. Great. I'll go ahead and notify the Registrar's Office. They'll send you the appointment letter. Meanwhile, I'll send you a copy of the book we use for the course."

"What about Green Card?"

"Here's the number of Foreign Scholar's Office.

They understand how such things go. The search committee has done its part. Congratulations."

"I feel great! I have to phone Mama and give her the good news. Very soon she'll have to send Dozie to me. I can't wait to settle down properly again." Zeb is loud even though she is the only one in the house.

"It's too late to phone Mama." She dials Gloria's number.

"Congratulations!"

"Thank you." Zeb is overjoyed.

"What about Green Card?"

"They gave me the phone number of Foreign Scholar's Office."

"Have you phoned?"

"I just got this good news and want to share it with you. You see, there are other ways of getting Green Card, not just through marriage," Zeb laughs.

"Call that office and let me know."

"Maam. It's the law?" The shrill voice of the officer in the Foreign Scholar's Office is harsh in Zeb's ears.

"Maam. You have to present your Social so that we verify the Permit before the university sends you a letter of appointment," the officer says.

"My understanding was that the university would get me the permit."

"Who gave you that understanding?" The officer says. Zeb thinks that her voice is ruthless. It does not occur to Zeb that the officer is merely stating facts.

"The university professors who interviewed me."

"This University does not get work permit for applicants. I have to attend to other matters. Have a nice day Maam." She hangs up.

Zeb holds the telephone receiver. She seems to hear the sound of her heart, *kpum, kpum. kpum*. She does not feel the wetness on her face until the tears begin to soak her blouse.

"If you want to make a call, hang up and try again." The recorded message on the receiver warns her that she has held the receiver for too long. She throws the receiver and her body on the couch. She hits her leg on the couch. It hurts. She hits it again and again. She runs to the bathroom. She does not wash her face or use the toilet. She just sits on the toilet seat. Her chests heave up and down. She thinks about her job in Nigeria; a job that did not require a Green Card. Her mind goes back to how she got blacklisted by the Nigerian government.

It all started in Benin when she went to her sorority reunion at the University of Benin. The activities were over but she decided to spend one more day at the guesthouse. She wanted to relax and buy some things that she had missed in Benin including Bini masks and special dried fish called *ehuru*. There was gas scarcity and the alternative-market price was too high for her, so she decided to use public transport. She would conserve the gas in her car for the journey back to Nsukka the following day. On her way to take a bus to the local Uselu market, she wondered why there should be gas scarcity in an oil-rich country like Nigeria. Since she returned to the country, she had noticed that the situation had got worse than it used to be. The Nigerian currency had fallen in value yet things had become very expensive. Many people had lost their jobs and many were dying because they could not cope with the economic depression. The situation was different for some people especially those in the military or connected with the military government. They had a lavish lifestyle with mansions and beautiful cars.

As she thought about these things, a car pulled up beside her. Jack introduced himself and offered her a ride since she was going in his direction.

"What a beautiful car!"

"Thank you very much," Jack said.

"What make?"

"Toyota Camry XLE," he laughed.

"Five speed automatic," he laughed. He was loud. He smiled and turned off the air conditioner.

"Maybe you'll like some fresh air." It was a statement rather than a question for he did not give her the chance to reply before he pressed a button and the glass roof slid open. He pressed another button to turn on the stereo. The music soothed her senses as the cool evening breeze caressed her body. The setting sun spread an orange hue on the environment.

"The world can be beautiful for some people and

they don't care about what is going on in this country," she thought.

"Fasten your seat belt, Miss, and enjoy the fresh air," he said. He smiled at her and his eyes lingered on her legs. She wore a pair of shorts. She relaxed on the comfortable seat but soon realised that the wind disturbed her hair. She complained. Jack immediately turned off the sunroof and put on the air conditioner, which was soothing.

She wondered how Jack was able to have such a brandnew car in the university when the average lecturer found it difficult to feed well. She became curious.

"What department do you work in?"

"I don't wotk in the university. I'm Special Assistant in charge of special duties at the-."

Zeb interrupted him in order to clarify her understanding of the man.

"So you work for the government?"

"Yes, for the army."

"Did you say enemy?"

"No no no. I said army."

They were silent. As they approached the market, Jack slowed down because of a crowd beside the road.

"Thanks for the ride. I'll get off here."

"I'll come along and help you with your shopping," Jack said.

Long lines of vendors spread their commodities in a large field before the stalls. Zeb approached a vendor.

"Sister, how much be the fish. No be you dey sell?" Zeb addressed the fish-seller in Pigeon-English, but the seller was busy demonstrating and pointing towards the crowd to the amusement of other vendors that constituted her cheering spectators.

"Wetin dey happen there?" Zeb addressed a seller-attendant.

"Na *winch*," the attendant said and ran off at top speed to join the crowd. Jack became anxious.

"It looks like one cannot do any buying in this market today. Let us be off. It is getting dark," he said.

"Off to where?"

"I'll take you to dinner. You don't have to cook dinner tonight," Jack smiled.

"Thanks, but no." She licked her lips at the thought of relaxing at dinner, but shook her head at the thought of going out with someone she did not know.

"Before going into the market, I want to know what is going on in that crowd," she said as she walked towards the crowd.

"Look here Miss, a mob can be dangerous." Jack pulled her hand.

"What can they do to me? I'll just be one of them." Zeb removed her hand from Jack.

"What of my brand new car? Look here, I cannot risk my car for this kind of people."

Zeb pushed through the crowd to see what the attendant had called a *winch*. The crowd had blocked the road thereby causing a big traffic jam. A military van was also being delayed in the jam. Zeb pressed her body in-between people and managed to get to a position where she could see the figure of what looked like a man. She counted seven prominent and protruding lines on the thoracic region of the man's body. A worn-out brown pair of shorts was the only attire 'gracing' his exhausted frame. His legs looked like hockey sticks, but they quivered. It looked like the quivering was due to the figure's eagerness to escape from the scene, but it probably was due to hunger. Zeb wondered whether he was a real human being. The sunken eyes and the muttering mouth suggested the former existence of a face. There was no hair on the head and no flesh decorated the skeleton, but a generous pot of flesh 'sat' on his pelvis.

From childhood, Zeb had learnt to detect the signs of malnutrition. Her part of the country in the east was a battlefront during the Nigeria-Biafra war. There was famine that caused an epidemic of kwashiorkor in Biafra and people still talked about it. Zeb knew a lot about it from her mother's tales and pictures she saw in an exhibition in Enugu, so she was familiar with the signs of kwashiorkor. She felt that the man was suffering from lack of good food. For the crowd of Uselu market, however, "Di man na *winch*." They believed that his protruded belly was pregnancy, which was induced by his witchcraft.

An officer came down from the military van and got busy. He cleared a space so that his van could pass through. If he noticed the man, he did not show it. He even pretended not to have noticed the stones and sticks carried by some individuals in the crowd. Zeb was making her way out of the crowd when she heard the relevant question that even the officer with authority did not have the courage to ask the menacing crowd.

"How una sure say na pregnancy be dat or something else?" A woman shouted.

"Yes, how can anybody be sure that the man is pregnant? It could be something else." Zeb echoed the woman's words as she remembered the exhibition images of the children that starved in Biafra.

Zeb wondered why the officer was not dispersing the crowd and protecting the victim.

"Why can't he carry the man away in the van? Why can't somebody rescue him before they kill him?" Suddenly, Zeb knew how to solve the problem. Jack was the solution that came to her mind. The man who was kind enough to offer her a ride would surely do the same for a more helpless person.

"To the hospital, to the hospital, Jack, Jack, Ja-." Jack's car was no longer there. It hit her like the harmattan cold, sudden and harsh. Jack was gone.

It was getting dark. The crowd had started moving with their victim. The cars too were already moving oblivious of the crowd.

"Na ignorance go kill us for dis country," someone said. Zeb peered in the darkness to see the owner of this voice of wisdom. The same woman questioned the authenticity of the man's pregnancy. Again, Zeb agreed with her and decided to do her shopping.

"Hei, hei. My purse. Chineke-e. Who took my bag-o-o? My bag!" It was only then that she realised that someone cut off her bag and she was holding on to the strap of the bag. She ran. It was getting dark but she ran all the way to the Teaching Hospital. From there, she walked through the campus to the guesthouse.

Zeb did not eat dinner and went to bed very sad as she thought about the incident. She woke up in the middle of the night and switched on the button, but there was no light. She groped in the dark and found a box of matches to light a candle. The kwashiorkor man was still on her mind. She sat on the chair and rested her jaws on her hands. She decided to write about the man, but instead wrote a poem titled, Vultures. When she went home to her apartment in Nsukka, she polished it and took it to her class. She told the students that the culture was changing and people were mirroring the insensitivity of the military. She referred to the way the military disregarded public opinion and executed people on charges of treason without clarifying what they meant by treason. Do acts of treason include opposition to government policies? The students discussed the meaning of treason and some narrated other gruesome events that they had witnessed. She was enjoying a very exciting class without knowing that spies had already taken her poem to the authority.

Still seated on the toilet seat at Esomonu's residence, Zeb thinks about her present circumstances.

"That kwashiorkor man! Why didn't I just mind my own business like Jack and leave the downtrodden to their plight?" she says.

"Tufia!" She says and flings her hands to contradict the thought. She inhales and exhales through her mouth, but the thought of her former life in Nsukka will not go away. The image of her four-bedroom apartment comes up on her mind.

"I had my own place. Now I am squatting in Anise's house."

"Tufia!" She says and flings her hands again.

"God forbid. I'm not squatting and I'm grateful to Anise and her husband." This does not divert her mind from the thought of her country and all the poitical prisoners. She wonders about Jaja. What she wants most in the world is for the military to leave the governance of Nigeria and for things to become normal so that she won't have any reason to be in another country looking for Green Card and be constantly criticised by Anise. "There is fire in my soul." Zeb is still sitting on the toilet seat.

"They said that birds cannot sing under fire, but my heart is so hot that I can sing volcanoes." She does not just think this, but says it loud as a poem begins to form in her brain.

THE PROMISE IN MY HEART
We sang our way to prison.
We sang our way to exile.
We made plans underground.
Sang utopia and subversion.
Promised Land was far away,
But promise was in our hearts,
We dug at the mountain,
With iron hearts of hope.
I need my old iron heart
In this freedom card fight.

Zeb gets up from the toilet seat. She no longer thinks about the bad news given to her by the University of Florida officer. Her Green Card problem is not at the fore of her mind. She wonders whether it was right to leave the country. Maybe she should have stayed and faced the problem like Jaja. Is it not cowardly to run away from her country and her children? She goes downstairs to the computer room, sits down in front of the computer and writes to herself:

"How can I escape from Ani that keeps my umbilical cord in its bowels? Ani keeps my father and all my forebears in its bowels. The land will also receive all my loved ones and me when it is our time. We cannot run away from Ani, our land. My father used to say, 'If available is not desirable, make desirable available.' The economic depression made politics undesirable and life unbearable, so I followed my father's counsel. I joined in digging the mountain of undesirable oppressors in order to establish desirable governance. I am not running away. I am on a journey. So help me God. The volcano building up in my country will surely explode. I am here to give myself a new opportunity to support the movement. This new place! Open for me. Let my job not slip away from me because of Green Card."

Zeb gets up from the computer desk to phone Anise. She knows that Anise's boss does not like people to call her unless there is an emergency. She believes that her situation is an emergency.

"Don't lose hope. Call the Chair of the department. They want you, so they have to help you," Anise says.

"But she already made it clear that she does not handle this kind of thing."

"Just call her. Have faith."

"Thank you."

"We are in this together. Don't worry."

Zeb phones Florida and speaks with the Chair about her situation.

"I've sent you the book. Try to get the work permit. We still have two weeks before classes begin," the Chair says.

"How do I get it?"

"I don't really know about it. Maybe an attorney or somebody would know," the Chair says.

"Thanks."

"As I said, we still have two weeks, but I need time to find an Adjunct to replace you if you don't get the permit. I'll hold the job for a week, so let me know as soon as you get the permit." The chair says.

"Are you there?" the Chair says.

"Yes." Zeb's voice is thin and low.

"Replace me, you said?" Zeb drops the phone.

12
Between the Mountain and the Canyon

eb picks up the phone book beside the television to look for attorneys. She flips through the yellow pages. She smiles when she sees the section on attorneys. It has subdivisions. Accident. Bankruptcy. Divorce. Medical Malpractice. Her heart misses a beat. She does not see any subsection on Work Permit Attorneys. She flips through the phone book again.

Social Security. This is it. She smiles and dials the phone number on the page. It goes into a machine with a list of options. None of them is "work permit." Zeb's heart beats fast. She feels hot. She pulls off her jersey and takes the phone book to the dining table. She begins to flip through it again. Most Legal Problems. This is it. She heaves a sigh of relief. And calls the number.

"We don't deal with immigration problems."

"I don't have immigration problem. I want permission to work."

"That is immigration problem. Call Immigration."

"Thanks."

Zeb goes back to the living room and sits on the couch. She picks up the yellow pages again. One listing only. Immigration and Naturalization Consultants. This is finally it! She dials the number.

"Catholic Charities. Can I help you?"

"Sorry, wrong number." She checks the number again. It is correct. Oh! She notices that Catholic Charities is listed as the consultant. She dials again.

"Catholic Charities, can I help you?"

"Yes. I need work permit."

"What's your name?"

"Zeb Olima." She smiles. At last, she seems to be making a headway.

"Hold on a minute while I look for your name. Are you registered with us?"

"No."

"You have to register."

"How do I register?" Zeb says.

"Which country are you a refugee from?"

"I am from Nigeria."

"Nigeria is not listed as refugee."

"I didn't say I am a refugee."

"Sorry. We deal with refugees."

Zeb's head flops. Her eyes face the red carpet of the living room, but she appears not to see the carpet. She thinks of what to do. She thinks of Anise but decides not to phone her again. She will call Alex. He is his own boss, so there is nobody to frown at her call.

Surprise. A woman answers the phone. "Rocco Pharmaceuticals. Can I help you?'

"Sorry, wrong number."

"Do you want to talk to the CEO?"

"No."

"Are you sure that you don't want to speak with Dr. Esomonu? The Caller ID indicates that you are calling from his house."

"Sure, I want to talk to him. I thought I had the wrong number," Zeb says.

"Hold on."

"Zeb, Anything wrong?"

"I need an Immigration Attorney."

Alex says that he does not know an immigration attorney, but that he will find out from the pastor of their church. Many immigrants attend the church and may have useful ideas.

"I can't wait till you go to church on Sunday. I need to get a work permit within one week."

"I'll see him on my way from work."

"Okay thanks."

Alex returns with Wendy and gives Zeb two names and numbers that he got from his pastor.

"They've all gone for the day. I'll call in the morning," Alex says.

"I'll call now, just to make sure that the numbers are correct," Zeb says.

The first number announces that they are closed, but that the caller should leave a name and number. Zeb leaves a message.

"You are happy?" Alex says.

"Not quite." Zeb phones the second number.

Surprise! "Yes can I help you?" It is a deep male voice.

"Yes. My name is Zeb. Zeb Oli. I need a work permit."

"The office is closed to the public. You'll have to phone tomorrow and make an appointment with my secretary."

"Are you the attorney?"

"Yes."

"Thank you." Zeb begins to dance. Wendy laughs.

Zeb wakes up very early in order to make it to the attorney's office. She gets off the bus at Annapolis Road. It is easy for her to see the huge building called Victoria Place even though it is far from the bus stop. She goes through the automatic sliding door that faces the Information booth.

"I'm going to Mr. Colin's office," she says to the officer in the information booth.

"Fifth floor, but no one is there yet," the information officer says.

"I'll wait."

In a few minutes, another young woman walks in. She is about Zeb's height, wears a black three-piece suit, and carries a matching black briefcase. Zeb hears the information officer talk to the woman.

"That's your client, Ms. Barnes."

"Good morning," Zeb says to the woman.

"You want to see me?" Ms. Barnes smiles.

"Yes please."

"Come along then."

"Yes, what can I do for you?" Barnes swings her chair from the computer to face Zeb.

"I need to see Mr. Colin. It is very urgent."

"I've heard that line many times. Tell me what it is."

Zeb sees opportunity in the face-to-face contact with Barnes. She believes that Barnes can't dismiss her easily as she would have done on the phone. She looks at her straight in the eyes with eyes that are desperate. She thinks of how to begin her appeal, but the other woman cuts her short.

"What is it?" Barnes blinks.

"I have been offered a job as a professor in a university-"

"That's great! Congratulations."

"But I need a work permit within a week or I lose the position."

"Let's see your contract."

"What's that?" Zeb says.

"Their communication of the job offer and its conditionality. That is the contract."

"They have not given me the letter of appointment yet. They gave me the job on the phone."

"We can't work with a phone promise. We need documentation," Barnes says.

"They want to see my work permit before they send the letter." Zeb leans towards Barnes.

"We can't convince the Immigration Department that you have a job without evidence of the job offer. We need a commitment in writing."

"Let me see the Attorney," Zeb believes that the attorney must know how to solve the problem.

"There is a non-refundable consultation fee of $50. He'll say the same thing that I've said, and it will be a waste of your money. Try to get the letter. Then call me and make an appointment. You don't need to come all this way for that."

"I still want to see the Attorney."

"He is fully booked till..." She checks on the computer for appointments.

"I need to see him today."

"He is fully booked today."

"Can I wait? There might be a little time between clients. Please."

"That will be a long wait. He will come in today by one and he has appointments till five."

"I don't mind." Zeb is prepared. She brings a novel from her bag to keep herself busy. When she eventually meets with the attorney, he tells her to go back and bring all the letters that the university has written to her.

Zeb opens the door. Anise comes in with lots of material.

"What's all these for?" Zeb says. Anise dumps the material on the couch, and slumps beside them.

"Do you know how to sew?"

"Why?" Zeb does not answer her question.

"Sew as in stitch clothes!" Anise does not answer Zeb's question.

Zeb thinks that Anise is in one of her moods. She knows what would help her shake off the mood. Zeb goes to the kitchen.

"We are going to make Halloween costume for Wendy." Anise is loud so that Zeb can hear her from the kitchen.

"You allow her to get involved in that?" Zeb shouts back. She opens the fridge and brings an orange.

"Halloween is a nice American custom." Anise's voice is loud from the living room.

"Isn't it a kind of devil worship with costumes? Zeb takes a knife from the drawer.

"It is a kind of fun for kids!" Anise's voice is louder.

"Don't they wear costumes that depict devils and ghosts?" Zeb shouts back slicing the oranges. She puts them in the juicer.

"Catholics started it. You are a Catholic, so you tell me!" Anise's voice is louder still.

"Impossible!" Zeb is loud. The juicer is making noise.

"Don't yell at me." Anise shouts.

"Who is telling who not to yell?" The noise of the blender drowns Zeb's voice. She does not want to get into an argument about something she knows little about.

"They started it from the Catholic celebration of All Souls." Anise is still too loud.

"Didn't you hear me? It is the celebration of a Catholic feast," Anise shouts.

Zeb keeps quiet for a moment. Then she decides to say something even if it annoys Anise.

"All Souls day is when you pray for people who died, and they are not witches. Halloween is dominated by witches and devils."

"Whatever!" Anise drags the word. Zeb notes that Anise has not asked her about her visit to the Attorney.

She gives Anise a glass of orange juice. Anise drinks.

"Just what I needed." Anise puts down the empty glass. Zeb gives her the other glass. Anise sips and gives it back.

"Did you think that I would drink all?" Anise speaks in an even tone.

"You were in a nasty mood," Zeb says.

"It's the heat. This fall is too hot for me."

"Imagine a Nigerian complaining about heat," Zeb laughs.

"It's never this hot in Nigeria," Anise says.

"I'm teasing. Don't you want to know what the Attorney said?" Zeb says.

"I was coming to that," Anise says.

"He saw me after closing time."

"Will he help?"

"He told me to bring my passport and all the letters that the University of Florida wrote to me."

"That's good news. You charmed him."

"God heard my prayer. The Reverend Sisters of Rosary High School will be proud of how I always seek God's guidance."

"I went to the best school." Anise sneers at Zeb.

"Queen's School is the best school in the east," Anise adds.

"Just because you went to Queens doesn't make it the best. You guys had no religious teaching."

"Our parents did that at home," Anise says.

"You thought that you were better than girls from other schools but you were not better. No moral teaching. That was why you guys used to follow boys." Zeb says.

"You guys used to dream of boys." Anise laughs.

"Your school was just good at showing off wealth because you were from rich homes."

"Hey! Not all of us. I was not from a rich home," Anise says.

"Like hell."

"Just don't jealous the princesses of Queen's School," Anise says.

"You mean show-offs of Queen's School?"

"If I squeeze your mouth now," Anise says.

"I'll turn the other cheek like a good girl from a Christian school," Zeb laughs.

Anise laughs. Her laughter is very loud. Both of them laugh because of what Zeb said about Christians turning the other cheek. They know that according to the bible, Christians are supposed to turn the other cheek if you hit them, but they also know that Muslims criticised Nigerian Christians for not turning the other cheek when Muslims hit them. There was once a conflict between the representative of the Muslim community and the spokesperson of the Christian community in Nigeria. Actors later played out the conflict in a national television drama that became very popular in the country. Anise stands, puts both hands on her hips and re-enacts the drama.

"You Christians of Nigeria are not good Christians." Anise kicks the bathroom door. Zeb gets it. She pretends to be angry. She throws two punches in the air. Anise runs. Zeb goes after her to the kitchen, round the table and back to the living room. They both enact an aspect of the National drama as opponents.

Anise: "I said that you Christians fight and kill. You are not good Christians."

Zeb: The bible says, 'Judge no one and you won't be judged."

Anise: "*Walahi*, mine is a statement of fact. You do not imitate Jesus."

Zeb: "In the name of God, I challenge you to prove it."

Anise: "*Walahi Talahi!*"

Zeb: "I say, prove it or I curse you in the name of Jesus."

Anise: "In your Bible, Jesus said that you must turn the other cheek when your brother hits you. But you Christians of Nigeria are not brotherly. You strike us Muslims when we hit you."

Their laughter is so loud that they do not hear Alex open the front door and walk up the stairs to the living room.

"What's going on here?" Alex says, but they do not hear him for they are absorbed in the drama.

"This infidel!"

"This unbeliever!"

Alex stares at them. He does not take off his coat.

"Infidel!" Anise throws a pillow at Zeb and laughs when she sees Alex.

"Unbeliever!" Zeb catches the pillow and throws it at Alex.

"What's wrong?" Alex says.

"Declare your stand!" Anise says to Alex.

"Are you an infidel or an unbeliever?" Zeb holds her stomach and tries to stop the laughter.

"I'm nothing of the sort." Alex holds the pillow.

"You are an infidel from Nigeria." Zeb throws another pillow at him.

"You are an unbeliever from America!" Anise throws another pillow at him.

"Infidel from Nigeria!" He throws the pillow at Zeb.

"Infidel from America!" He throws the other one at Anise. Anise throws at Zeb. They laugh. They throw pillows. They call each other "infidel" and "unbeliever."

"You are home early honey," Anise says.

"I knew that I was missing something," he says.

"You just had to come and be thrashed by two women," Zeb says.

"I defended myself very well. Once a soldier always a soldier."

"He was an officer in the Biafran army," Anise says.

"I need to retrieve a document from my home computer. I'll go back to work immediately," Alex says.

"Oh no," Anise says. Anise winks at Zeb, because she knows that she also doesn't want Alex to interrupt their story.

"Honey, do you want some coffee or something?" Anise says to Alex.

"Let's go to the bedroom," Alex says.

"What for?"

"Ask me that question in the bedroom," Alex says.

Anise laughs and winks at Zeb. Zeb winks back. They go to the kitchen to make coffee, but Alex comes down and declines the coffee. He has to go back to his office before picking Wendy from school.

Alex and Wendy return home. Wendy runs up and dumps her backpack on the couch.

"Hi sweetheart. I'll make Halloween costume for you. I'll make a Kenyan giraffe. You remember that one you liked at the zoo?" Anise hugs her daughter. Wendy shakes her head indicating her dislike for something.

"You don't want to trick or treat?" Anise says.

More shaking of head.

"What do you want dear?"

Wendy goes to the magazine rack, picks up a Teen Magazine and opens a page. She shows her mother the picture of a vampire with its front teeth sticking out.

"You want to be a vampire." Zeb looks at the magazine.

Wendy nods. Zeb shakes her head. She cannot understand why a nine-year-old girl wants to dress up like a vampire.

"Your daughter wants to be a vampire at Halloween," Anise says to Alex who is coming up the steps.

"You want that dear?" Alex says.

Wendy nods.

"And what do you say, wife?"

"I know you're up to something whenever you call me 'wife.' What do you want now?"

"Do you want her to be a vampire?" Alex says.

"Why not be an angel?" Zeb says to Wendy.

"No!"

"Okay honey. We'll buy you the costume. I don't even have time to sit down and make a complicated costume that will look like a giraffe," Anise says.

"What about all the material that you bought?" Zeb says.

"I'll return them to the store."

"How was your day with the Attorney, Zeb?" Alex says.

"I had a..." Anise interrupts her as she talks to Alex.

"You didn't ask about my day," Anise throws a pillow at Alex.

"I phoned you at work, came home and found you enjoying live drama." He catches the pillow and throws it at Zeb. Zeb catches it.

"Me me me!" Wendy is excited. Zeb throws it at her. She falls with it on the couch.

13

The Killer In My Neighborhood?

"You are almost fifty minutes before time Ms. Oli." Barnes looks at her watch.

"Only one bus was very late, the others were on time."

"How many buses do you take to come here?"

"Four."

"Four?"

"One from Germantown to Shady Grove. From Shady Grove to Silver Spring. From Silver Spring to Prince George's Plaza. From PG to here." Zeb talks fast. She is happy that Barnes is friendly but nervous about the prospect of meeting with the attorney. She wants to keep talking.

"Wow!" Barnes says.

"I add extra one or two hours to my travel time, because of the buses that come late. Today was one of my lucky days. I lost only forty minutes. I hope I'm lucky with Mr. Colin." She talks fast.

"Why don't you take the metro? It's faster," Ms.Barnes says.

"My friend said that metro is expensive for me. With buses I pay eight dollars."

"That's expensive."

"One dollar for each bus ride."

"You don't have to pay for each bus ride," Ms. Barnes says.

"Who will pay?"

"One ticket lasts for two hours. Who told you to pay one dollar every time you enter a bus?"

"Nobody. I just slot the money in the machine as I see others do." Zeb explains.

"Find out about bus passes," Ms.Barnes says.

As Mr. Colin examines the documents, Zeb watches his face for signs of approval. His face does not give away any emotion. Zeb remains anxious.

"This letter acknowledges receipt of your application." Colin goes through the letters again.

"Yes," Zeb says even though she does not see the particular letter. She is seated on the opposite side of the table from Colin.

"This one states that you made it to the finalist list."

"It says congratulations, you-." Zeb does not see the letter but she knows the contents by heart.

"Congratulation is not a commitment," Colin cuts in. "But it shows that I am a possible candidate." Zeb's heart beat fast.

"This is a letter of invitation to an Interview," he says.

"And the interview was successful," Zeb says.

"There is no evidence of that."

Zeb is shocked. She thinks that Colin doubts her. "It is the truth. I am not lying. You can phone and ask them. I have their phone number."

"I can intervene on your behalf, but institutions try to avoid litigation. They don't like to deal with Attorneys," Colin says.

"What can I do now?"

"There must be individuals in that institution who can influence decisions. Talk to the Chair. If they want you, they should meet the Dean or the President. Time is a key factor in this case. You need people in authority to act fast."

"Please talk to them on my behalf? You know how to go about it. I am new in this country. " Zeb remembers how Anise criticises her Nigerian ways.

"I have not yet learnt enough of American approach to things. Please do it for me."

"That will cost you money, and there is no guarantee that it will work. They might become defensive when they know that an attorney is involved."

"I am desperate. My father always said that a desperate situation requires concerted action."

"Is your father a cop?"

"A teacher."

"Give me a call when you decide on what to do?" Colin says.

"How much is your fee for talking with them?"

"Representation will be one thousand dollars. It might be a lot of money for you, but that's the standard fee. I'll knock off ten percent for you."

"I want you to represent me," Zeb says.

"Call my secretary to confirm. She'll prepare a contract."

Zeb arrives home late. Alex hears her try to unlock the front door. He goes to open it for her. She enters. He raises his left hand to look at his watch. Zeb knows that it is a deliberate act. She also looks at hers. It is fifteen minutes after eight. She begins to explain that she missed the bus and had to wait for one hour for the next bus.

"You have to call home and let us know. The State is not safe now because of the sniper," Alex says.

Zeb wants her host to understand that she was aware of the lateness and that she tried to do what she could.

"The public phone near the bus stop was not working. When I got to Shady Grove station I took a taxi because it was late," Zeb says.

"You should have called me."

"I didn't want to disturb."

"Don't be silly."

Zeb walks up the steps to the living room. She is slow. Alex believes that it is because she is tired. But Zeb walks slowly because she wants to delay her meeting with Anise whom she believes is waiting for her in the living room. She expects Anise to tell her off and she dreads what will come out of Anise's mouth. She is relieved that Anise is not in the living room. Anise has gone to bed early, because she is coming down with flu. Alex gives Zeb a large envelope. It is from Florida. She smiles. She does not sit down before she opens it while telling Alex about her visit with the Attorney. He is eager to know the details. He listens to everything without interrupting her. She brings out a book from the envelope and reads the title: *The Empire Writes Back.*

"I've read this book by Ashcroft, Griffiths, and Helen Tiffin," she shows it to Alex.

"Do you really want to pay him nine hundred dollars?" Alex gets up and goes to the fridge.

"Yes." Zeb flips through the pages of the book. She is now sitting on the couch.

"Don't you want dinner?" Alex says.

"I'm not hungry."

"You need to eat. You need to take care of yourself. The last thing you want is to be sick or something. You don't have health insurance." Alex says from the kitchen area.

"You don't think that Colin should represent me?" Zeb says.

"I don't know how much money you have, but to pay nine hundred for something that the Attorney is not sure will work blows my mind!" he shakes his head, closes the fridge and goes back with a small bottle of orange juice. He places it in front of Zeb.

"Thanks," Zeb drinks it down and keeps the empty bottle on the table.

"Why not sleep over it."

Zeb is in her nightgown. She is just about to get under the blanket when she hears a knock. Anise enters her room. Zeb does not sit. She braces up for Anise's criticism of her coming back late.

"What's this I hear? That you're going to throw away nine hundred dollars, just like that?"

"What do you want me to do?" Zeb says.

"Your sister called from London. She said that your mother wants to know how you are doing," Anise says.

"I phoned her last week."

"She wants you to phone again. She probably feels that her baby needs her," Anise says.

Zeb sits on the bed. Anise sits beside her. She throws her left arm round Zeb's shoulders.

"Don't throw away your money. You need to be careful about how you spend your money, because nothing is coming in," Anise says.

"I know. But I need to spend money on work permit to do the job."

"I know what you need and I'll work on it." Anise sneezes.

"I have to go before I pass the flu to you." Anise gets up from the bed.

"Good night my friend." Zeb is happy that Anise is not mad at her.

"Remember to call Mamma."

Zeb has to keep awake till twelve o'clock midnight when it will be six o'clock in the morning in Nigeria. She puts on her jersey and goes down to the computer room. The book she got from Florida has given her some hope. She believes that it is a sign that she will do the job. She wants to work on the syllabus. She does not want to be unprepared when she gets the work permit and goes to Florida. She wants to have the syllabus and the first week's lectures ready. As she enters the computer room, she feels a chill all over her body. She is surprised by this because the room is warm and she has her jersey on. She remembers the killer. She panics. She runs upstairs to the living room and puts on the television. Instead of watching it, she begins to read the book from Florida. She doses off. She opens her eyes when she hears a sound on the floor beside her. She jumps. The large book has fallen from her hand. She yawns and stretches. She glances at the television. Breaking news.

"The Maryland sniper has been spotted in Silver Spring area of Maryland. Montgomery County is on the alert! People should report any suspicious character or movement to the police."

Zeb runs upstairs. She knocks on their bedroom door. Alex comes out and she tells him the news and narrates how she suddenly got frightened on the first floor. He says that he has already heard the news. That was why he was worried when she did not return in time.

"Go to bed."

"I want to call my mom."

"Take the phone to your room."

Zeb's mother, Angel, has heard about the Maryland killer.

"The police are looking for him," Zeb says.

"And I don't go out that much," Zeb says.

"Use your eyes very well."

"Yes, I'll be careful," Zeb says.

"What is killing your heart?" Angel says. Zeb cannot tell her mother that she worries about Jaja because she will not like it. She can't even ask her mother whether she knows anything about Jaja.

"I'm okay," Zeb says.

"Didn't you get that job?"

"I got it but I haven't got the permission to do it," Zeb says.

"It is good that you got the job. You are still our bright girl. Your father's heart will be sweet in his restful place. And your heart should smile also. You are quick to show America that your brain is very hot. Well done, my child."

"But Mama. I can't do the job without permission."

"Is there a problem on your way?"

"It is a little problem. A lawyer wants to try and get the permit for me, but he is charging a lot of money just to begin."

"How much?"

"Nine hundred."

"How much in Nigerian money?"

"Like ninety thousand naira," Zeb says.

"We use money to make money. If that is what it costs, pay it and get the problem out of your way."

"We are not sure that the lawyer will succeed," Zeb says.

"And he wants to eat your money even if he does not deliver the prize?"

"Yes," Zeb says.

"That's not a good lawyer."

Zeb is silent. There is a wavy sound on the line.

"What do your friend and her husband say?" Angel's voice is muffled by the wavy sound.

"They are not in support," Zeb shouts because the line is faint.

"Follow the advice of people who know the land. If you don't get it now, don't worry. I don't even like that Florida," Angel says. Zeb knows that her mother twists her mouth because of the sound of the words. She smiles.

"Why? What do you know about America?" Zeb laughs.

"I asked your brother about America," Angel says.

"Okpara?"

"No. Dokki knows a lot about Florida," Angel says.

"Dokki may know about England but he has not lived here in America," Zeb says.

"You know that he reads a lot. And he has friends. Anyway, Dokki said that there are too many mosquitoes in Florida."

"Is that all he said?" Zeb says.

"That it is beautiful," Angel adds.

"Okay, he said that it is too far from where your relations live. We want you to get a job near them so that when your father's brother goes to America, he won't have to go all the way to see you. As for me, I don't want you to go to a mosquito land and get malaria there. You know that children easily get mosquitoe bites so the place will not be good for Dozie"

"Mamma, their mosquitoes don't carry malaria disease."

"I don't trust any kind of mosquitoes. If they don't carry malaria, they'll carry something else. My child, please hear my words, I don't like the place."

"Mama, call Dozie for me."

"He's already waiting. As soon as he heard the phone ring, he woke up. 'That's my mummy.' "

"He said that?"

"Yes, here he is."

"Mommy, good morning." He says the three words like they are one.

"My baby, kiss kiss." She makes the sound of kissing. He makes the sound also and laughs.

"Mummy, uncle bought me a beautiful book. It has red cover. He said I should write on it everyday."

"What will you write?"

"About you and Queen Grand Angel."

"Is she a queen?"

"Yes mommy. She tells everybody what to do. She owns the house and gives people where to live and gives out food."

"Do you know any other queen?"

"Yes, Queen Elizabeth rules England and people also obey her. Queen Amina ruled Zaria in the north of Nigeria and people obeyed her, but she fought wars and killed people. I don't like that," he says.

"What else will you write in your journal?"

"Uncle Okpara and Uncle Dokki. I'll also write about my friends at school. Mommy, Queen Granma says that we should not be long on the phone because it is costing you a lot of money. I love you Mummy."

"Kiss kiss."

"Kiss kiss."

Angel has come to the phone. Zeb feels like asking her about the riots, but her mother will know that she wants to hear about Jaja,

"Mama. Are you well?"

"I am well, my child. Do you eat well?"

"Yes Ma."

"Look after yourself very well. If you don't have money let me know and I'll tell my sons Okpara and Dokki to send money to you."

"They have their own problems," Zeb says.

"It's not their money. I still get a lot of money from my business. The women who manage my store are good. They pay money into my bank account," Angel says.

"Mama, I got money from my property auctioned by Okpara and Dokki," Zeb says but does not disclose that her money is going fast. Her mother is the one that brings it up.

"Money runs like harmattan fire when nothing is coming in. I don't want you to worry about money. Just let me know."

"Yes Ma."

"Good. Remove your mind from the mosquito place."

Zeb laughs. Angel laughs also.

"Di Ma-aama!"

"That's me!"

"Always Di Ma-aama!"

"Yes! God is carrying you, and your Papa is in heaven. You are blessed. Always remember that."

14

Women's Room

Zeb opens her eyes at the sound of the telephone ringing. It is her friend, Chioma, callimg from Lagos, Nigeria. Zeb has not been in touch by phone because they tapped Chioma's phone. She works in Jaja's Lagos Office and is in the team of lawyers representing Jaja and other YAM members.

"Is it safe for you to phone me?" Zeb says.

"Don't worry. This is not my phone. I just talked with your mother. She told me about the job thing. Tell me about it," Chioma says.

"You think that as an attorney in Nigeria, you can do something?"

"Of course not. I just want to know the steps that you are taking."

Zeb explains everything to her. They agree that Zeb has to look for other jobs, visit libraries and schools in the area.

"There might be a school in Maryland that needs someone with your capabilities. Don't just focus on Florida," she says.

Zeb is silent. She is sad. She feels that what she has in her hand is slipping off. Not the telephone.

Chioma continues to talk. "Talk to people. Most of our sorority sisters are in Britain or here in Nigeria, but just talk to other immigrants. They have gone through similar problems and will give you useful advice."

"Gloria thinks that I should marry a man who has Green Card," Zeb's voice is low. She expects Chioma to be shocked or annoyed. Chioma is calm. Her profession has made her familiar with the way immigrants try to cut corners.

"Does she know any man who can do that for you?" Chioma says.

"No."

"Look in your old address books. There might be other people who you know in America."

"There is someone."

"Who?"

"Another classmate, but Gloria said that she is a student."

"It doesn't matter. Get in touch with her. Just go out and keep meeting people. Something will work out. You'll see."

"I hope so," Zeb's voice is still weak.

"Are you crying?"

"Just about."

Chioma has known Zeb as a strong woman, so to hear her crying is confusing. She has made the call to tell Zeb about Jaja and his family, but she decides to cheer her up by saying that Jaja is well. Telling her the whole story may be too much for Zeb in her situation. After Zeb left the country, the demonstration against the military government took a new turn that had been building up for years. The government had borrowed a lot of money from foreign banks and put the country in heavy debt. Some leaders embezzled money and banked them in their personal accounts in Europe and America. At the same time, they withdrew government support of public hospitals, transportation, education and even jobs. Majority of the people were frustrated as they dwindled in poverty while seeing the lavish lifestyle of the military class. They wanted the soldiers to end their rule so that they could vote civilians to power. The civil unrest started from the university campuses. Students left the campuses and filled the streets chanting:

NO MORE

Army must go!

Back to barracks.

Army must go!

No more guns.

Army must go!

The country was on fire! The fire of military dictatorship! The fire of the gun! Fire of economic depression! The government became desperate and more brutal. They began to advertise the names of people in their "wanted persons' list" and promise huge amounts of money to anybody with information about them. Chioma wanted to tell Zeb how they captured Jaja's family, but knowing that Zeb is already distressed, she continues talking about Zeb's situation.

"Don't be sad about the work permit thing. Just connect with your inner self and remember that you are special. You'll get a better job, if this one doesn't work out. But get in touch with that classmate soon."

"Tell me more about the struggle?" Zeb says.

"I know that you want to hear more about Jaja."

"Is he well?"

"Sure. The riots are over. They have arrested more people and thrown them into prison. We're very lucky that you were able to leave the country at the time you did. The prisons are full. Prison guards are overworked. Many of them are kind to our people. Even some members of the police force are kind to us. Don't worry about the struggle. Just focus on getting settled. We need you to work."

Zeb is so upset that she phones her cousin, Kordi, who relates with her as sister. She just wants to tell someone about her anxieties for Jaja, job and Anise's unfriendly attitude. They talk at length and it performs the trick that she hopes for.

"Will you go to our cousin's party in New Jersey?" Kordi says.

"I'm thinking about it, but they haven't sent me a card. His wife, Ijeoma, told me about it on the phone, but she hasn't sent a card," Zeb says.

"It'll be nice to travel out of your State for a change."

"I guess."

"Don't be sad. After all, Mom doesn't want you to feel bad about not going to Florida, so she made up that story about mosquitoes," Kordi laughs.

"Is that the deal?" Zeb laughs.

"I just love Mama. She's wonderful," Kordi says.

"I'll go to Trenton, New Jersey. She'll like that."

"You'll like it too. You like parties. And who knows?"

"Knows what?"

"Just relax and leave yourself open to possibilities."

Zeb snuggles under the blanket and as is usual with her these days, her mind goes to her situation. Coming to America has exposed her to unprecedented criticism about her ways and the way she thinks. She has come to see her personality as having two aspects. The part that she calls her spirit is always strong even when she cries. She feels an inner strength in "my mind and my soul," she thinks. Sometimes, when she is hurt and feels physical pain, her spirit remains strong. This seems to be the case now. She is hurt about not having the permit to do the job that is hers. But her spirit is strong. It became very strong after talking with her mother, friend and sister, yet she still feels sad. She wants to make new plans, but her body feels weak.

Zeb can be assertive in the sense of setting goals and moving towards them without allowing things to distract her. Her life as a girl was put on hold during the war when she got married at twelve. She was in her late twenties when she left her husband. She did a lot of catching up on growing up as a girl by interacting with younger people in the university. She was girlish in many ways but there was still a tough streak developed through her type of marriage. She will not allow you to denigrate her but she often chooses to ignore things that she thinks waste her time. Her habit of ignoring things is what Anise criticises as a sign of weakness. It is not easy for Zeb to be forceful even though she tries to show Anise that she can be. It took years to cultivate her character. Her parents, peers, schools, and teachers contributed to the formation of her personality. It is not easy to unlearn what took her decades to learn.

As a child, Zeb expressed great individuality and vanity, but her mother made it a special task to curb these traits, which she regarded as uncharitable. By the time she entered middle school at ten her character had developed to her mother's liking. Zeb was concerned when she saw girls who had not curbed their vanity, but she also admired them. Under the blanket, her mind goes back to her years at college in Benin. She was almost thirty when she entered the university, but she still tried to cling to some of the values she got from her mother as a girl. She remembers one young woman called Ngozi and the way other young women criticised her in the shower room. The shower rooms were open on top and under the doors. If you cared, you could tell who was bathing in which room by looking at the feet. The lights hanging from the ceiling brightened all the rooms.

All the shower rooms were occupied, so the students stood outside waiting for those inside to come out. Ngozi's roommate stood outside the shower room where Ngozi was bathing. It was easy for anyone to hear the conversation that was going on. Zeb listened from one of the bathrooms.

"I'm beautiful, so men like me," Ngozi said to her roommate, Biddy, who was waiting for someone to vacate a shower room.

"You don't have to say it, if it is true," Biddy said.

"Men always say that I am very beautiful," Ngozi said again.

"Men can lie. They can tell you anything when they want something from you. My boyfriend said that he loved me more than any woman on earth," Biddy said.

"That's a lie. What about his mother?" Ngozi said.

"Of course I knew it was a lie. He also said that I was the prettiest girl on campus."

"Another lie. I am the prettiest. Everybody says so," Ngozi said.

"I've never heard any girl say that you are beautiful," a voice shouted from one of the shower rooms.

"Because they are jealous," Ngozi said.

"Those who are beautiful don't need to say it, because we see it with our own eyes. Those who say it are hiding something!" A girl said this from another shower room.

"What am I hiding?" Ngozi shouts.

"You have spindle legs!" This voice came from the end of the shower area.

"Hockey sticks!" Another shouted. Laughter from different shower rooms. Zeb did not join them in castigating Ngozi, but she laughed also. She pitied Ngozi and blamed her mother then for not teaching Ngozi humility as Angel did for her. At that time, Zeb believed that Ngozi's family were not Christians and did not read the bible, and so were not able to inculcate good values in their daughter.

Zeb's mind goes to her graduate school days in England. She remembers Kate, the American girl, in her class. There were only three girls in a class of eight. The young men in the class didn't like Kate. Even Meg, the other girl in the class, didn't care for her. As far as Zeb was concerned, Kate did not insult or hurt anybody, so she liked her. She also wanted to know why others did not like Kate. She began to watch and analyse Kate's actions. One day, she got a hint as they were discussing their project in one of the study-rooms.

"Got to eat something." Kate walked out. Dan and Sam stopped chatting to look at her. Zeb watched their faces. Mean looks. The door hadn't closed behind Kate when the boys showed their resentment.

"Bloody American!" Dan said.

"What did she do?" Zeb asked.

"Too arrogant!"

Zeb didn't understand.

Kate usually wore jeans while Zeb and Meg wore dresses or formal long pants. Zeb liked the way Kate walked. Kate's chest pushed forward as she walked with her head high, as if she was challenging you. She always said her mind without permission. She did not say 'please' or hesitate when she talked as the other young women did. She just said what she had to say. She could get into a conversation without saying "excuse me." This was considered rude. The one that surprised Zeb most was the incident with Sam. Sam was beside the door of the Green Room when Kate pushed the door open. It hit Sam.

"Ouch!"

"Excuse me!" Kate said. Everyone expected her to say "sorry," but she just sat down. People exchanged glances. Some shook their heads in exasperation.

Zeb also thought that it was rude. But arrogance? She never found any arrogance in Kate. Life in America has made Zeb to remember Kate and have a better understanding of her ways. She has realised that Kate was not rude. She had an aggressive personality. Anise admires that kind of personality, but Zeb lacks it. Zeb yawns. She knows that she will soon drift to sleep. Her mind comes back to her own character and its interaction with American culture. Neither her mother nor the wisdom of the women's shower rooms allowed her personality to develop its full assertive potential. She now feels that she liked Kate because Kate had a personality that she would have had if her mother had not suppressed it.

"Now! It's time for me to develop my suppressed personality. I'll try out my aggressiveness at my next visit to Baltimore." Zeb pulls the blanket over her head.

Ada Enendu is on her mind when she wakes up in the morning. She looks though the phone directory. Surprise. Enendu is listed. She dials the number to leave a message. Someone answers the phone. Zeb apologises for calling her early in the morning and begins to remind her of who she is.

"Zeb Olima. Of course, I remember you. Who won't remember you? Where are you at?"

"Germantown."

"What are you doing there?"

"Nothing. I want to see you," Zeb says.

"Of course. I'm at school till five. So I can come and pick you after that so that we can hang out."

"That will be nice, but I'm going to Baltimore today. Can we meet tomorrow?" Zeb says.

"I'm off to a conference tomorrow. We'll arrange something when I'm back. I see your number on my caller ID," Ada says.

"Ms. Zeb Oli." The Chair is at the door of his office. Oh God! Zeb forgot to send in her résumé to enable him appreciate her credentials as Anise had instructed. He pronounces Zeb very well but found Oli difficult. He says it two times in different ways. Zeb says it. The Chair says it right the third time. Zeb smiles. She feels that his trying to be correct is a sign of friendliness.

Zeb holds her head high like Kate and follows him. She has planned to sit down without being asked, but now she just can't do it. She stands, but does not say, "May I sit down please."

"I'm Eric Fenton." He sits as he motions Zeb to the seat. Zeb sits also.

"What can I do for you, Ms Oli?"

"Well, I am new in Maryland. I live in Germantown, and I am looking for a job. I want to find out whether you have an opening in your department." Zeb looks at him directly trying to read his reaction.

"What kind of job would you be interested in?"

"I am interested in teaching." Zeb notices that his brows twitch. She thinks that it may be a sign of amusement or surprise or maybe a mixture of both. Oh dear! Zeb made a mistake. She should have told him her background as a professor and mentioned her degrees before telling him about her need for a job.

"What kind of teaching?" He says. Zeb is sure that he is amused.

"Teaching in this department," Zeb keeps her eyes on his.

"Do you have a college degree?"

"Yes." Zeb seizes the opportunity of the question to give him a copy of her résumé.

He bends his head to read it. Zeb watches him and pretends that she is not. She puts on her large-framed dark bifocal, and pretends to read from the folder in her hand. She sees one of his brows go up. He glances at her and continues reading. She looks up and sees that both his brows are up. She continues "reading."

"You are a distinguished woman," he says.

"Thank you."

"So you were at Columbia University as an exchange student from Britain."

"Yes," Zeb wonders whether he doubts the information in her résumé. She thinks that she needs to portray confidence and prove her Columbian connection. She talks about how she enjoyed her stay at Columbia and how nice the people were. She mentions that one of them is now an assistant Dean in the institution.

Fenton explains the hiring situation. "We have already planned the schedule for the semester, so we may not be able to fit you in now. But the department is planning to review the programme. Some of the courses that you have taught sound interesting and new," he says.

"Which ones?"

"Global literature. African Diaspora literature." He flips through the pages of her résumé.

"Some of our students might want to try them. So, I'll have this in mind when we review the programme." He places his hand on the résumé.

"When will that be?"

"In a couple of weeks. I'll be in touch with you." He walks her to the door. Zeb smiles. She hopes that she'll be in Florida before then, and may not need their job.

"It was nice meeting you Dr. Oli. I'll be in touch." He shakes her hand.

"Thank you." As Zeb leaves, she wonders how Anise would rate her assertiveness.

"How was your visit to Baltimore?" Alex asks.

"I think that it was fine, but I don't know what Anise would say." She looks at Anise.

"Did you meet with the guy?" Alex asks.

"Yes, and we had a good conversation." She tells them about the meeting. She mentions that the man was impressed and called her a distinguished woman.

"Great! Any promises?" Alex asks.

"He'll call me."

"Like hell he will!" Anise says.

"You never know," Alex says.

"You don't think that he'll call me?" Zeb says.

"He may," Alex says. Anise shakes her head.

"Why?" Alex says.

"I don't know. Just don't trust smooth-talking whites," she says, looking directly at Alex, as if daring him to disagree.

"You always find an ugly side of things," Zeb says.

"I live in the real world," Anise says.

"I don't want you to be disappointed. That's all. You're too trusting," Anise adds.

15

Germantown Unlimited

Zeb has settled into the routine of going out in the morning like everyone else in the house. The only difference is that she returns before everyone else. She has to get back to the house before two o'clock in order to be there when the bus drops off Wendy. Zeb spends the evening in the reading room where she searches for jobs on the internet. The absence of news from Nigeria disappoints her. This is 1997, yet most Nigerian newspapers and media agencies are not on the internet. The military government does not know the value of the Internet. What a shame.

This morning, Zeb missed her bus. She asks the driver of another bus whether his bus can get her near Whiting Station where she would board another bus to her destination. He says that he will let her off where she will catch bus 46. She asks him where she can get a bus transfer, because Ms. Barnes at the Attorney's office said something about it. He gives her one and explains how it is used.

"Show it to the driver of the next bus you enter. It shows that you've paid to get to your destination."

"Thank you."

"You're welcome."

Zeb recalls the first time she wanted to take a bus in Germantown, she asked Anise about the cost. Anise told her it was ninety-nine cents. She is a bit concerned that Anise did not tell her about transfers. The information would have saved her a lot of money. She makes a quick calculation and realises that she will now save five or six dollars from her usual transport budget for one day if she uses transfers. This means that she can now afford to take the metro. She takes the metro on her way back from Whiting library. She reclines her head to rest, relieved that the metro is very fast. It does not experience delays as the buses. It has its own track and does not wait for pedestrians to cross as buses do. Very soon, the officer announces that the next station will be Shady Grove. Zeb gets up and waits for the door to open.

As she comes out of the station, bus 51 drives off. She is lucky that the driver looks at the mirror and sees her running and waving her hand at the bus. He stops. As usual, Zeb brings out one dollar to slot into the machine.

"Didn't you come out of the metro just now?"

"I did."

"You should've got a transfer from the metro."

"You mean that I should have bought a ticket from the metro?"

"No. There is a machine with a red or blue button. When you come out of the train, just press the button, and the machine will give you a bus transfer. Your train ticket should get you to your destination. And when it doesn't, you take a transfer from the metro machine. You have to slot in a token of twenty-five cents before you enter the bus though."

"Thank you." This is yet another way of saving money, Zeb smiles.

"You're welcome."

She tells Anise her experience of wasting money on buses.

"Oh really? I don't know about such things. We always use our cars to and from the metro."

"So you never used the bus in this country? You have always had cars?" Zeb says.

"They change rules every time," Anise says.

Zeb is silent.

"What?" Anise says.

"You think I knew about all these transfers and stuff and didn't tell you? Well, you should have asked other people instead of blaming me!" Anise says.

Zeb is silent.

"In America, you have to talk to people and learn how to survive. Nobody baby-sits anybody," Anise says.

"You think that you pamper me if you tell me about bus transfers, but you want to force me to marry any man on the street!" Zeb says.

"Wow! Easy."

"If you think that I want you to pamper me-."

"Peace. Don't take it that way."

There is a message from Zeb's sister, Kordi. "Hello Zeb. This is your sister, Kor. Just checking on you. I talked with Mama yesterday. She's fine. She said that you should call her when you have the time. Love you."

Zeb has a lot of time now, but she has no phone card. She puts on her coat.

"Where to?" Anise says.

"To buy a phone card."

"For?"

"I want to call Mama."

"Is it urgent?

"My sister said to call Mama."

"It is a bit too late to go out. You can use my phone. Tell her that you'll call her again soon."

"Thanks." Zeb smiles.

"Peace?" Anise says.

"Peace." Zeb smiles.

"Kor?" Angel says.

"Mamma, you never know the voices of your children."

"I like it when you say that. I like to think that you all sound like me. After all her late mother sounded like me also. You remember her Zee."

"So you recognize my voice now?" Zeb does not want to talk about her other mother who died during the Biafran war. It might bring up sad memories of her loved ones who have died.

"Of course, I know your voice even in my sleep," Angel says.

"How are you?"

"My body is good. And you?"

"Fine also. Kordi said that you want me to call you."

"Are you still worried about Florida?"

"I still want the job."

"Listen, my daughter. The one that God gives you is the best."

"God made me to pass the interview."

"I said, listen," Angel says.

"Okay."

"Tell me about America."

"Mama, what do you want?"

"My son, Okpara, said that you live in a place called Germantown. Are there many Germans there?"

"No, just a name."

"Is it near where your brother Okpara used to live?"

"No Ma. That's Michigan."

"It is not near Germany where my brother studied?"

"No Ma. You know that America is not near Germany. You have something to tell me. What is it?"

Angel laughs. She knows that Zeb is used to her style of talking. Zeb laughs also. She has shown her mother that she knows her ways very well.

"Be patient. You will eat the most delicious food if you have the patience to let it cook very well. Have patience. Do you hear me?"

"Yes Ma."

"Don't put your whole mind on the job in Florida. You like to make songs and poems. Write about America. Write about that place where you live. Germantown without Germans." Angel laughs. Zeb laughs. Her mother passes the phone to the love of her life, Dozie.

Zeb is in the library. She reads The Chronicle of Higher Education. She is disappointed when she opens the section on job advertisement. There is no vacancy in her area of specialisation. She drops the newspaper and begins to recap her conversation with her mother. She plays with what Angel said about Germantown.

GERMANTOWN WITHOUT GERMANS
This name from the land of Germans,
Germantown sits in a maze of charm,
That decks the place with colours,
And faces that would shock a Hitler
In this town that speaks not German.
The wood lures me to its hall,
Greenness that calms my heart.

The leaves touch lips, they sway,
They waltz with the air and sun,
In this land that means not German.
Birds have fun and ride the sky,
Hike the woods and tango the sun.
Sing songs and weave their tale,
That wraps this town of Germantown.
These birds, take my tale with you.
Spread my dream on Earth and sky,
So that I too can dance and play,
And waltz this land of Germantown.

16

Gold Digger

Zeb's meeting with Ada Enendu is an inspiration to her. She comes out of Rockville library as Ada drives in, and her first thought is, "What a flashy vehicle for a student."

Ada stops the car, comes out and gives Zeb a very warm hug.

"You've not changed," Ada says, and wraps her arms around Zeb.

"Still looking young and beautiful," Ada looks at her.

"Thanks. And you've changed; looking better than before." Zeb looks at Ada from head to toe. Ada wears a loose gown that is popular in Nigeria with matching shoes and elaborate braids packed above her head. She looks relaxed and comfortable.

"Nice car," Zeb says.

"Thank you."

"What's the make?"

"BMW, latest model," Ada says with a lot of pride.

They enter the car and Ada drives off.

"You still like Nigerian music," Zeb says as highlife music comes from the CD player.

"Of course, I'm a Nigerian who lives in America. I brought that CD last month when I went home to Nigeria," Ada says. To Zeb, this information communicates the confidence of someone who does not seem to have Green Card problem; someone who is free to travel in and out of the country.

"What was the political situation when you were there?"

"No change. The place was buzzing with the news of the arrest of a civil rights lawyer and his whole family?"

"Jaja Okorafor?" Zeb says.

"Yes. Do you know him?"

"Oh my God. So they have finally got Ja." Zeb cries.

"I'm sorry to give you sad news."

"Did you say his whole family?" Zeb sniffs.

"Yes, first his wife and children, then he came out of hiding and gave himself up. Then they let his family go."

"I'm sorry." Ada stretches one hand and touches Zeb on the cheek, "Didn't think you know them."

"He was my boyfriend at the university. Don't you know him? He used to attend our sorority events."

"You forget that I left in my second year. I didn't complete the second year in Benin. I remember you because you were everywhere: sports, music and sorority; just everywhere."

"Well, he was my boyfriend and we're still very good friends even though we are no longer lovers."

"I understand; an emotional bond is still there."

"Yes. It's not that strong anymore but..."

"Don't bother to explain. It's taking you some time."

"Exactly. We're both in YAM organisation and I was also in the list of those wanted by the government."

"You're in YAM? I contribute to the organisation. You people are the only hope for that country."

"Thank you. Supporters are our strength."

Zeb is not surprised to hear that Jaja is in jail but she is sad. She feels happy seeing someone who supports the organisation. She wipes her tears and looks at Ada who shows the kind of confidence Zeb used to have when she had a job in Nigeria. Her jobless situation and especially the lack of Green Card and its promise have eroded a lot of her self-assurance. During their long drive to the university, they both keep quiet as if they are focusing on the highlife music, but Zeb's mind has gone back to their sorority days. Ada was not outstanding, was not even missed when she withdrew, yet she has made it big in America. "And I have not yet started," Zeb thinks. She hopes to find out how Ada has managed to become successful in America. On her own part, Ada empathises with Zeb. She has been in a similar situation and can imagine what a new immigrant goes through. She decides to be there for Zeb in any way she can.

"Ada Enendu, Ph.D" is written on the door of Ada's office in Calder Hall of American University. Zeb is shocked, but she does not show it. She did not know that Ada is a professor and not a student. She stands by the door. Ada sits in front of her desk and phones her Chair. Zeb listens as Ada tells him that she will bring a professor friend to meet him. When she drops the phone, she explains that she will be going on sabbatical at the end of the semester and wants the Chair to meet Zeb.

"We are still looking for a professor to teach my courses while I'm away," Ada says. Zeb's hope rises, but she remembers that she has no Green Card.

"I don't have Green Card," Zeb says.

"Don't worry about it yet. I want the guy to meet you first. He has to meet you informally and form his impressions. Then when I later bring up the issue of you replacing me, he will know who I'm talking about."

"This is Dr. Zeb Olima. Her area is global literature and she is a specialist in fictional semantics."

"Nice to meet you Zeb." Jim Noel is a tall thin balding man. The blond hairs at the back of his head are tied together in a ponytail.

"How did you two meet?" He removes some books on a chair and motions Zeb to sit.

"We were at school together," Zeb says.

"She is more accomplished than me though," Ada sits on the other chair.

"Not really," Zeb says.

"She has degrees from England and Nigeria."

"Impressive." Jim sits facing the women.

They have coffee as they discuss world literature.

Back in Ada's office, Ada tells Zeb to sit down. She looks at Zeb intently. She switches her mouth to the right and to the left, closes her eyes a bit. The facial gestures signify her trying to decide on whether to tell Zeb something or not. Finally, she decides to talk. She says that Zeb looks anxious, but she does not ask Zeb what the trouble is. She already knows.

"Are they telling you to marry someone for Green Card?" Ada says.

"How do you know?" Zeb says.

"I went through a lot. By the time I got this job, I had put restraining order on a man."

"Tell me."

"I'll tell you stories that will give you courage. Just be patient and keep looking for a job that will help with your Green Card. Don't let anybody push you to use marriage. Some of our men here are gold diggers," Ada says.

Zeb laughs because people usually generalise that women are gold diggers. Zeb has always known that in real life, gold diggers are men and women who care to dig other people's gold. It is so agreeable to hear a woman turn it round on men for a change.

"Did he want to marry you by force and give you Green Card?" Zeb says.

"Something like that. I had no job at the time I met him, but he knew that I would get a good one."

"What was he?" Zeb says.

"Nothing."

"Nothing?" Zeb says. How can a person be nothing?

"Well, no degrees, no skills, no job." Ada explains.

"He must have been making a living somehow," Zeb says.

"He came here to study as he said, but ran out of money and married an American nurse who applied for Green Card for him. They are divorced and she pays him alimony."

"What?"

"I've heard about it but never known any real life example of a woman paying a man," Zeb says.

"That's American law. Alimony is both ways. If a man has no income, the woman pays him alimony."

"And he takes it?"

"Why not? It's his right. That's why you should be careful about marrying anybody for Green Card. They know that you'll get a good job. And if the man is lazy and shrewd like Adaka, my ex-boyfriend, he can hang on you forever."

"God forbid."

"Well, you have to forbid it yourself and make sure that it doesn't happen," Ada says.

"But there must be sincere men out there."

"I'm not saying that all our men are bad. Just be careful. Don't let anyone use you. It's good that you keep your intellect busy as you do in the library instead of thinking about your situation and developing psychological problems from worrying. Just hang in there. Something will work out."

"I can't believe that our men can be that vicious," Zeb says.

"All men can be vicious. All women can be vicious. That's why people are very careful. Some American men were good to me. Jim for example recognised my talent when I presented a paper at a conference. He invited me to apply for this job. Since then, we have remained very good friends. He and his wife, Barbara, invited me to Thanksgiving and after I settled down, I also began to invite them for parties in my house. That's how life goes. Some are good, some are not. We owe it to ourselves to ally with the good people."

"You're right."

"But I had a horrible experience from another person."

"Adaka."

"Adaka was a small fish. No, from a big one. Let's go to lunch. I know a nice Indian restaurant two blocks from here. I don't have any more classes today, so we have all the time to catch up on the past."

As they wait for the elevator, two women join them.

"Hi," Zeb smiles at them. Nobody says anything. Zeb's smile hangs on her lips like a permanent feature of her face; like a mask. She finds it odd that Ada does not greet them. As soon as they come out of the elevator, Zeb asks Ada why the women did not answer her greetings.

"Is it because they don't know me? Even then, it's simple courtesy to reply to my greeting," Zeb says.

"They know me. I know them," Ada says.

"Why didn't you greet them?" Zeb says.

"We greet when we meet alone."

"What do you mean?" Zeb asks.

"I noticed that when they see me alone, they greet me, but when they are with someone, they don't."

"Why?"

"Another professor told me that it is not politically correct to be seen to be on familiar terms with an African especially one that is very dark and who speaks with an African accent as I do."

"That's so ridiculous." Zeb says.

"Well. It's my reality. Maybe they see me as ugly or dirty or wrong or all of the above." Ada laughs.

"But you're very beautiful," Zeb says.

"In your eyes. Some people don't see beauty in a woman who is not white and thin and all American."

"You're kidding."

"Watch the media and tell me the kind of women that they project as beautiful."

"This is crazy," Zeb says.

"Lots of things are crazy in this world."

The weather is mild and bright, so they walk leisurely. Zeb feels so happy about meeting Ada and seeing her office. She holds Ada's hands and swings it as they walk to Rasheka restaurant. A group of African American students sit under the oak tree beside Barnes and Noble bookstore. One of the students greets Ada.

"Hi Professor Enendu," he says.

"How're you doing, Rashard."

As they walk down the steps by the Theater building, Ada points at the concrete form in front of the theatre as the spot for white students. About eight white students are there with their lunches.

"Asians also have their own spot," Ada laughs.

"So American University is not racially integrated?" Zeb says.

"You can see that I mix very freely with my Chair who is a white blond. That's integration." Ada laughs.

17

Dating Dispute

Ada takes Zeb back to Rockville library and invites her to visit on Saturday.

"Why not tomorrow?" Zeb says.

"Tomorrow is a busy day for me. I have two classes and office hours. Saturday is only three day's away," Ada says.

"What time on Saturday?"

"I'll phone you. Remember to get your résumé ready, so that I can give it to Jim," Ada says.

"I'll bring it with me to the library on Saturday. You can come at any time. I'll be in the library."

"Right," Ada replies.

Zeb goes back to the booth where she sat earlier. She wants to continue reading. No sooner has she opened the page than Ada's experience comes to her mind. She is inspired by Ada's perseverance. Ada did not derail from her principle in spite of the pressure but stubbornly held on to it. She conquered the temptation to cut corners and take the supposed easy way to achieving her dream. Zeb nods her head and promises herself that she will not allow Anise and Gloria to make her abandon her principles. She will persist and go after the Green Card legally. Zeb's mind is so full of her meeting with Ada that she just cannot read the book in front of her. She decides to leave the library. She checks the bus schedule. She needs to be at the station in fifteen minutes in order to catch Bus 51 on time. As soon as the shuttle bus from the library stops her at the station, she runs all the way to the bus. She sits behind the driver panting for breath. She smiles at other people running to the bus.

The driver waits. He turns and looks at Zeb. Zeb also looks at him. He winks.

"What?"

"I didn't say nothing." He turns to the steering. After some time, he looks at her again.

"I'm sorry if I embarrassed you," he says.

"You did not embarrass me. Just funny."

"Where're you from?" he says.

"Nigeria."

"Don't Nigerian men look at pretty women?"

"They do, but not like that."

"Tell me how they look at women. I'll leave in a minute, so give me your number. I'll call you, so you'll tell me how to look at you." He drives off.

As the bus leaves the station, Zeb sits back on her chair. She looks out through the window but she does not focus on the scenery. Her mind has gone back to Ada. Zeb is barely aware of the bus driver adjusting his rear view mirror to look at her. He follows the direction of her eyes, but does not see any unusual sight or happening that she is gazing at. A few people are on the sidewalk. The traffic is smooth. Zeb's eyes seem to focus on the scenery, but she is thinking about Ada and her own experience. She believes that she too has not had it easy with settling down. She is always watching out for Anise's feelings and her moods that are not predictable. Anise is kind and generous. She often treats Zeb like a sister and sometimes even like a mother yet Anise is not much older than she is. Zeb feels that it will be unappreciative to complain about her at this point.

She becomes aware of the bus driver when he reminds her to give him her phone number. They are near Shady Grove station.

"My husband will not like it," Zeb says.

"You have a husband?"

"Yeah."

"He didn't give you a ring?" He looks at her finger.

"We don't use rings to marry in my culture," Zeb says.

"I have a lot to learn from you. Take my number and give me a call."

Zeb automatically takes the piece of paper yet she is not interested in contacting him. She frowns at her action and immediately reasons that she took it because she wants to be polite.

"Thank you." She leaves the bus.

"I have no intention of being rude to a man just because he looked at me," she thinks.

The driver does not drive off immediately. Other passengers get off and more passengers enter the bus. As Zeb is about to enter the station building, he presses the horn. Zeb looks back. He waves at her. She waves back and at the next trashcan, she drops the piece of paper with the phone number.

Zeb has got off her last bus. She is walking down the street when Anise drives in and they enter the house together. Zeb relates the incident with the bus driver. She does not say that he asked for her phone number, or that he gave her his own.

"You should have asked for his phone number," Anise says walking up to the living room.

"Why?" Zeb follows her.

Anise turns on the step to face Zeb.

"He likes you," she says. She looks at Zeb in the eyes.

"So I should collect the numbers of everybody who pays me a little compliment?" Zeb looks back.

"Why not? You need to check out as many men as you can and get one of them to marry you." Anise turns and continues to the living room.

"I should check out even bus drivers?" Zeb follows her.

"This is America. The man's status is not important. What is important is what he can bring to the table.

When they see you two together, nobody will know whether he is a bus driver or not." Anise throws her pocket book on the couch.

"But his background will clash with mine, and we won't have the same understanding."

"Let me tell you something. In this place, many cab drivers have degrees and even PhDs. Driving is the only job they can get, so they take it. How will you feel if someone looks down on you because you have no job?" Anise says.

"At least, they have jobs," Anise walks to the kitchen. She turns again to face Zeb.

"Listen to me my friend. You need a job. You need to be on your own. Think of the best way to get going." Anise turns and walks into the kitchen.

Zeb stands on the same spot. She takes Anise's advice as an indirect way of saying that she sponges on her. Zeb decides not to take it in a bad way so she tries to make a joke of it.

"You want me to go man hunting not job hunting?" Zeb follows her to the kitchen.

"Man hunting will get you a husband and a husband-."

Zeb completes the sentence for her, "will get me a Green Card that will get me a job."

"I like you," Anise says.

"You learn very fast. If you are lucky as I think you are, you'll get a good man who will love you and you can settle with him for good," Anise says.

Zeb's mind goes to Ada's story, "And if he is a bad man who can be up to some mischief and who can use me as a sex toy and threaten to report me to the police if I don't comply..."

"You have to think positive my friend!" Anise gets some water from the fridge. She bangs the door of the fridge.

Zeb tells her how Ada got a restraining order against a man who wanted to marry her, help her apply for Green Card, and use her.

"Did you ask her whether the man is still available? But knowing you, you'll think that you have to reject him just because your friend did." Anise drinks, drops the cup, and goes back to the living room. Zeb feels agitated. She feels that she cannot have a good conversation with her friend without her turning it to Green Card issue. She finds it very unhealthy, but feels helpless in the situation. She senses that the best thing for her is to leave Anise's house. She shakes her head. Maybe Anise does not mean any harm. She follows Anise to the living room.

"Anise, you didn't listen. Adaka wanted her to get green card so that she could get a job and support him."

"What's wrong with that?"

"I don't understand you Anise."

"Is your friend married now?" Anise laughs.

"I didn't ask her."

"How did she get her Green Card?"

"I didn't ask her the details but she kind of implied it was through her work because-."

Anise interrupts her "So you spent all this time with her without asking her the important question." Anise picks her pocket book and walks upstairs.

Zeb flops on the couch. She opens her mouth, inhales and exhales deeply. This is one of the times that Anise's attitude drives her crazy. She tries to analyse Anise. She is caring, but sometimes she just acts like she doesn't care at all. She can be rude also. Just imagine the way she walked away from Zeb. Zeb gets up from the couch to go to her room. She cannot get Anise out of her mind. She makes to knock on Anise's door to tell her that she was rude to her. She might have had a bad day at the office so this may not be a good time. She goes to her room still thinking about Anise. "Why does Anise get on me? And why did I follow her to the kitchen? Why do I have to tell her everything just because I live in their house? And see how she treats me like I don't know what I want."

18

Giving Back

Zeb is happy about the possibility of getting a visiting professor position in Ada's department. But the Green Card issue-. She shakes her head. She does not want to think about it and get depressed. She wants to be positive. Again, she feels lucky that she is not in the kind of trouble that Ada found herself in. She will be very careful with men who use Green Card to get vulnerable women. She will take Ada's advice and be patient. Being patient may mean waiting for a long time and this requires a lot of money. Her bank balance is not that good. She stretches out her hand and picks her balance from the table. She looks at the balance. A lot of debit and no credit. If she does not get a job soon, she will be in serious trouble. She wonders how she spent all the money. She does not indulge herself; does not buy clothes or spend money on any kind of luxury whatsoever. She does not spend money on rent. Zeb spends a lot on transportation, photocopying and mailing of applications. Everybody reminds her that she must maintain a healthy lifestyle because she has no health insurance. She exercises her body and brain. She also spends money on organic food but she is not a big eater. In her country, organic food was cheaper than the inorganic ones that were imported. She finds that it is the opposite in America. Organic food is expensive. Maybe it's time for her to change her diet totally to inexpensive pizza and fries because she needs to save money.

Anise has just finished her coffee and is about to put moisturiser in her hair when Zeb comes down. Zeb needs to know how Anise feels about her living in the house all this while. She takes the moisturiser from Anise.

"Let me help you." She sprays Anise's hair and begins to rub in the moisturiser.

"Anise," Zeb says. Anise turns round. The comb falls from Zeb's hand.

"Why do you jerk your head?" Zeb says.

"I want to see your face. Why do you call my name like that?"

"I want to ask you something."

"Then say it. Don't call me as if you don't know that I'm here," Anise says.

Zeb picks up the comb.

"When you invited me, you said that I could stay here for as long as it took to get a job."

"E-hen. Has anything changed that?" Anise says.

"It's just that I never expected that I would stay this long; three months already and no job." Zeb parts her hair with the tooth of the comb.

"What's your problem?"

"I don't know how you feel about it," Zeb says.

"Feel about what?"

"Staying in your house indefinitely. That's what it looks like to me," Zeb says.

"You won't stay indefinitely," Anise says.

Zeb has parted the hair from the front to the back and begins to massage the scalp.

"This feels good," Anise says.

"Maybe I should open a hairdressing salon," Zeb jokes.

"Do you know how to braid hair?" Anise says.

"Not professional braids, just simple stuff."

As she massages Anise's scalp, she thinks about the telephone conversation that they had when she was about to come to America. She told Zeb that her children had moved out of the house and that Zeb should stay with her instead of staying with her cousin. Zeb said that she hoped to get a job as soon as possible and have her own place. Zeb remembers Anise's reply. "Just get here first and we'll worry about other things later." Zeb had thanked her and asked her whether there were things that she wanted her to bring to her from their country. Anise wanted some Bini masks, the type that Zeb brought when she visited for Wendy's birthday. She wanted one more. Zeb brought it and a world cup wooden sculpture.

"What are you thinking about?" Anise breaks Zeb's contemplation.

"I'm thinking about my continued stay in your house. Am I a burden to you?"

"I have no problem with you staying here. My husband likes you. Wendy likes you. Even my kids that don't live here like you. So no problem."

In spite of her assurance, Zeb still worries about her situation. Since high school, she has never stayed in anybody's house for more than one week, except in her parents' house of course.

"Think positive. Don't worry too much," Anise says.

"I'll think and act positive." Zeb thinks.

Zeb is happy about Anise's assurance that she is not a burden to her. She, however, wants to make herself more useful in the house. She begins to play with and teach Wendy. She teaches her how to say a new word everyday. Wendy likes to dance, so Zeb begins to dance with her, and teach her singsong phrases.

"Hei Papa," Zeb sings.

"Say it to your daddy when he comes back. Hei Papa." Zeb swings her shoulder to the left and right. Wendy laughs.

"When you feel good about your daddy, you say 'Hei Papa." Zeb swings her shoulders. Wendy laughs.

"Hei Papa," Wendy says and imitates Zeb's movement.

"You say to your mom, 'Hei Mama."

Gradually Wendy begins to say, "Hei Auntie," to Zeb, and sing the name of her brother when he visits. Zeb is happy to be able to reach Wendy in a special way.

Anise and Alex are pleased to hear Wendy's new words. On her own part, Wendy begins to dote on Zeb. She likes to stay with Zeb as she works in the computer room. Zeb shows her the photo of her son Dozie.

"My child." She touches her heart and touches the photo. Wendy looks at the photo. She also touches her heart and touches the photo.

"You like him?" Zeb says.

"Yes."

Zeb brings out the photo of her sons living with her ex-husband. She kisses the photo and puts it back in her wallet. She sends her résumé as an attachment to Ada and prints a hard copy that she will send by post. The print thrills Wendy. She runs her fingers through the pages. She is excited. She fingers the words on the paper, and says the words that she recognises. Seeing that printed words excite the girl, Zeb prints simple words and sentences and teaches her how to say them. She likes it. Zeb prints more words that will appeal to her:

WENDY WENDY WENDY

Wendy is a good girl.

Wendy is a great girl.

Mummy loves Wendy.

Daddy loves Wendy.

Brother loves Wendy.

Wendy. Wendy. Wendy.

Wendy is pretty.

Wendy is smart, bright, and gifted.

Fingering the sentences and saying the words become Wendy's favourite pastime. Sometimes, Zeb chants them with her; they swing their shoulders and have a good time. Sometimes Zeb tests Wendy's mood by singing, Wendy Wendy Wendy. If she is in a good mood, she will reply, "Hei Auntie!" Zeb is pleased with herself for being able to connect with a specially gifted girl. It is the first time in her life that she got close to a girl like Wendy with special ways of expressing herself and getting you to appreciate difference.

It is arranged that Anise will pick Wendy from school and take her to buy a costume for Halloween, and that Alex should bring Zeb to the school. Alex and Zeb arrive at the school as Anise is parking her car. They walk to the field to watch the parade.

"You have two cameras," Zeb says to Alex.

"You can help me with this." He gives Zeb the Canon camera, and begins to film the place. Zeb passes the camera to Anise.

"She doesn't bother with cameras," Alex says.

"Why should I, when I have Alex?" Anise says.

"Alex the cameraman," Alex says.

"Hi there." A man waves at them.

"He is the father of that boy. His wife ran away with another man," Anise says.

"Why not introduce him to Zeb." Anise nudges Alex.

"How's the big boy?" Alex walks up to the man.

"He's playing Indian tonight." He shakes Alex's hand. "This is Zeb."

"I'm Kevin."

"Nice meeting you," Zeb says.

"You have an accent," Kevin says.

"So do you," Zeb says.

"I don't mean it in a bad way."

"I don't either." Zeb feels Anise's pinch, so she adds, "I like your accent though."

"I have an accent?" Kevin sounds surprised.

"Will you like to come to my Thanksgiving dinner? I'll have a small party. Maybe your son can play with Wendy." Anise talks to Kevin and winks at Zeb.

Kevin is tall and good-looking, but Zeb is put off by his attitude.

"Thank you, but we have planned to be with my parents in Aspen Hill."

"Maybe another time," Anise says.

"Sure."

"Are you out of your mind?" Zeb says as soon as Kevin leaves.

"He is a single father," Anise says.

"Let me leave you girls to your talk." Alex walks away.

"He thinks he's all that," Zeb says.

"So?"

"He thinks that I have to speak like him."

"This is America! People must comment on your accent. Some people will even wonder at your black colour; whether it will dirty them, but it doesn't matter. Just ignore such comments. You're so used to seeing black men in Nigeria. In America, men come in all colours. You get?"

"Why didn't you marry a white man yourself?" Zeb says.

"Colour was not an issue when I married Alex. You know that. But here in America where it is important, Alex can pass for white if he likes. In Nigeria, they call him *oyimbo* pepper. That's the fairest of fair complexion."

"Didn't it embarrass you that people referred to him as white in his own country?" Zeb says.

"The only thing that I did not like was when a friend asked me personal questions about our private life, you know, his private parts with him being a black that looks white." She looks at Zeb directly.

Zeb has never asked her whether Alex snores in his sleep, how good he is in bed, or the size of his secret parts, so Zeb looks back at her without any guilt. Zeb does not see why Anise should be angry about such questions. Women usually share such secrets with close friends and usually keep them secret. Why is she touchy about their private life?

"You are very quiet," Anise says.

"You were talking about Alex's colour," Zeb says.

"Some people have asked us if Alex has a white parent. Wendy took his colour and the little fairness in me, so people say she doesn't look like she has any black blood in her."

"That's America," Anise says.

"I didn't know that blood can be black. I thought all blood is red." Zeb laughs at Anise.

"Thinking biology, yes. Thinking society's way, there's black blood. Skin colour is used to differentiate blood even though we all know that it is red."

"That's a lot of headache," Zeb says.

The parade ground is an arena arrangement. Part of the classroom block forms one side of the arena while the second side is part of the Assembly Hall from where the children file out. Parents and visitors stand along the two other sides. The children parade in pairs. The crowd cheers. Leading the parade is a thin long figure in white. It has no arms and legs. It just glides forward with open mouth and hollow eyes. Zeb shudders. She finds it strange that the kids are not afraid of it. Beside the ghoulish figure is a black figure. Zeb guesses that the figure is Wendy. She feels that the vampire mouth of the costume is recognisable. She focuses the camera and takes a picture of the figure.

"That's Wendy." She points at the vampire.

"No. Wendy's costume is velvet. This one is leather," Anise says.

"So where is Wendy?" Zeb looks through the line. So many vampires file out. Alex moves to another side to have a better focus.

"That's Wendy!"

Wendy holds hands with her partner, who is dressed like a bat with very large red wings.

"I thought that she would pair up with Kevin's son," Anise nudges Zeb.

"You want to marry her off so soon?" Zeb says. She takes another picture.

"Don't be silly, I want us to talk about Kevin. The way he looked at you." Anise giggles.

"I didn't notice," Zeb says.

"He looked interested, even though you tried to mess things up when you said he had an accent."

"You mean when he said that *I* had an accent?" Zeb says.

"Whatever!"

Zeb looks at Anise and shakes her head. A verse runs through her mind, "woman for sale."

WOMAN FOR SALE
This affable home of mine,
You treat me like crayfish,
Spread in the marketplace,
For men to poke and puke.

19

Routes To Victory

Zeb has three mails. She looks at the senders. Two are letters from two universities. Her hands tremble. She opens the first one. It is disappointing. She drops it in the trash, and reads the other one. She retrieves the one in the trash and compares the two. Their contents are similar.

They received "numerous applications from candidates with excellent credentials, but unfortunately yours was not selected for interview."

She folds the letters and puts them in the book that was sent from Florida. She glares at the book. Even though she has lost the Florida job, she has left the book on the table. She looks at the book with hostility and thinks that it adds to her stress because it indirectly reminds her of her missed opportunity. She throws the book into the trash. She opens the third envelope. It contains an invitation to the naming ceremony of her cousin in New Jersey. She does not like the idea of going to New Jersey without a job. It will cut into her savings. In addition, relations will be there. They'll feel pity for her. "I don't need anybody's pity at this time. I won't go." She opens her journal folder on the computer and writes:

How can I go merrymaking?
With a load of many worries,
That hangs in my dear heart?
How can I conquer this country?
And carry my head with victory?

She scrolls back and gives the verse a title, "Conquer this country." The idea of victory is important in Zeb's life. She and her cousins remember it as one of their father's favorite words. Their father believed there are many routes to a person's goal in life but that each person has to discover his or her own best path. When Zeb was angry at not being chosen to be in the women's netball team at the university, her brother reminded her of their father's idea.

"Why must you join the team?" Dokki said.

"You know brother; I am much older than other students in the university and need a lot of exercise to keep fit."

"Easy. Find another way. You don't have to do it like other people. Papa taught us that-."

"All roads lead to victory, just choose one and focus on it," Zeb completes his sentence for him.

"So you remember. Of course, why not, you were Papa's baby."

"Bro, I still miss him after all these years."

"That's why he came back to you. Just think of your second son whenever you miss Papa. You know, sometimes when I visit Abeokuta, I just delight in looking at him. He even has the black bump on Papa's left wrist."

"I know, but he's still my child not my Papa."

Back at the university, Zeb continued to go to the games to help the team. They appointed her warden of the netball team and she accompanied the team to tournaments. At the National University Games event, she and Jaja noticed that students from the University of Nigeria were not adequately kitted like students of other institutions. Some of them did not even have spiked running shoes that were basic for athletes. They asked questions and discovered that they did not fund the university adequately. Located in war-torn town of Nsukka, the institution focused on infrastructure and academics and had little left for sports. The university was a battlefront during the Nigeria-Biafra war and had lost a lot of time and assets in the war. It was in a hurry to gain back its premier position among other universities. Many professors did not give athletes any credit for representing the university in sports. Some in fact penalised those who were absent from classes when they were involved in sports activities. This was contrary to the situation in Zeb's institution in Benin. Jaja saw this as a human rights issue. "They have to support everybody; academic and non-academic. They are all equal as students and they all contribute to the university."

Zeb knew that they discriminated against her at the selection of the netball team because of her age. During the mid-term break, Zeb went home to Eke to see her mother. Her cousin, Okpara, was also visiting. She brought up the matter just wanting to hear him condemn her University for discriminating against her because of her age.

"After all I look like those twenty-year-olds and as energetic as they are." She had Jaja as proof. He was close to the age of those twenty-year-old girls, yet he found her more attractive than they were. She hoped that an experienced teacher like her cousin would understand her take on the matter. His reaction confused her at first.

"There are many roads to victory," he said just like their father.

"What do you mean?"

"Take another road to progress. Read more and write more. Run with your friends for fun. Come. Run with me," he laughed as he entered his car to leave.

"You mean I should run while you drive the car?"

As he drove off, she ran after his car until it disappeared. He brought out his hand through the window and waved. She stopped running. She turned back and took the alley that she used to know when she was younger. As a child, she used to explore outdoors with her cousins Dokki and Aik as well as her friends, Vicky and Violet. They would trace their way to the cashew forest and eventually make it to the savanna of wild fruits where they collected fruits like *utu*, *icheku* and *ube-oji*. As Zeb walked through the alley back to her house, she was grateful to her brother for reminding her of what their father said about diverse routes to progress. Back at college, she began to walk instead of taking taxis to places. One of her favourite places was the Agricultural farm where she and her friends collected fruits. The first time she suggested that they should walk instead of using a taxi, they refused. Eventually some of them walked and enjoyed it. Walking to and from the farm turned out to be a lot of fun. Zeb no longer missed the sports field as much as she did earlier and she continued to work behind the field as a warden.

Running has always been a good antidote for situations that upset Zeb. The Maryland sniper is no longer a threat, so she can run in the trails. Maybe it will help her to overcome her situation of helplessness and lead her to the path of victory. She settles in front of the computer and reads her last poem. She repeats the last line. "How can I conquer this country, and carry my head with victory?" She goes to the Chronicle of Higher Education website. There is a new edition with many advertisements. She scrolls down. Language. Literature. Translation. There is nothing for her in these sections. She scrolls down some more. Fellowships. Something excites her from Harvard. She reads the description of the Fellowship and method of application. The application involves a lot of material. They want two samples of short stories about poverty, résumé, evidence of award, and ISBN pages of a published book. They also need six copies of each item. Zeb thinks about the expenses involved in producing all the material. They will be expensive to produce. She finally decides that she will do whatever it takes to get the Fellowship. She types another poem:

I shall walk over spikes and climb steep hills.
Whatever loves this job is mine with speed.
A touch of care and skill, garnished with diligence,
Is medication swallowed with hope and vigilance.
I shall wash my face in the waters of harmattan,
Flush dullness from brain and gird my heartland.

She titles it, "whatever it takes." It gives her some hope. She prints it. Now in a better mood, she picks the Florida book from the trash. She has good news that she can share with her relations when she goes to New Jersey.

"Reject will turn to Victory!" She puts the poem beside the reject letters in the book. She begins to go though her published stories and research papers. She wants to select the best for the Fellowship application.

Anise opens the door.

"Hi," Anise says.

"You are back early."

"Yeah. I have some hours off from a previous overtime." She sees Zeb's application letter on the computer screen.

"You saw a new job opening?" Anise says.

"Yes."

"Did you phone Florida?" Anise glances at the Florida book.

"What for?"

"Just to feel them."

"No need to get myself worked up again," Zeb says.

"Do you want to take a walk?" Anise says.

"Are you not tired from work?"

"I am, but I need to relax and release the tension. Working in this country is very stressful when you don't belong here, when you're not what they regard as all-American," Anise says.

"Let me get a job first, I won't bother about belonging."

"You will. I know you," Anise says.

"What's the problem?"

"You won't understand how it feels to be more qualified than the person that is your boss and who doesn't know the stuff. This thin blond girl is just out of high school, younger than all my children except Wendy. I have diplomas and training for the job. I've done it for many years. Great evaluations and all that. But this one comes straight from school to boss me. I plan the work, supervise, and do the job. I'm also required to teach her because she has no experience. I do all that, yet she likes to humiliate me. Can you imagine that?"

"Did she do anything to you today?" Zeb says.

"Last Friday, I filled the form for time-off and gave it to her. Today I reminded her that I would take some time off. Can you imagine what she said?"

"What?"

"'Do not expect anyone to baby-sit you. You have to do your work till it's time to go.' That's what she said. Imagine that!"

"Did you explain to her?"

"I had to! Then she looked for the form."

"Did she find it?"

"Yes."

"Did she apologise?"

"Not on your life! I did a lot of overtime to save her butt when she had issues with her boyfriend and made lots of mistakes at work. You teach her something and she says that she understands, but she still does the wrong thing. When they find out, she claims that it was because of one reason or the other. And they accept it."

"Don't worry about it. She is young and inexperienced. She may not get away with it for too long," Zeb says.

"But she is placed there above me! But I do most of the work."

"Let's go for the walk," Zeb says.

"Shopping Center."

"How far?" Zeb says.

"Like two miles."

"No big deal."

They walk in silence. The air is cool. Zeb hopes that it will cool Anise's mood. They get to what appears to be the end of the road. Zeb wonders whether Anise knows where she is going to. Anise diverts to a narrow path that leads from the road.

"Is this a new path? I didn't see it when I came here," Zeb says.

"You were so mad that you didn't see it."

"I've never seen anybody use it," Zeb says.

"People were afraid of the sniper. That's why they did not use it. I'm happy that the danger is over." Anise says.

"I hope so."

"Why?"

"They haven't confirmed the identity of the man they caught. I saw this on the Internet," Zeb says.

"Oops!"

"Do you want us to go back?" Zeb says.

"No."

They walk through the wood. They are alert and silent. They look around for any sign of an intruder.

"What's on your mind?" Zeb glances at Anise.

"Are you happy?" Anise looks at Zeb.

"What do you mean?"

"Are you happy in my house?"

Zeb does not reply. She is not sure why Anise always calls it "my house" rather than "our house" as if it does not belong to her and Alex.

"Why do you always say 'my house?"

"It's my house."

"What about Alex?" Zeb asks.

"You're looking out for Alex?"

"Well."

"Don't worry. I know you like Alex. Women like him."

"No! Not in that way," Zeb says.

"Of course, I know that. You are my friend."

"Then why do you say that women like him?"

"Because they do."

Zeb's mind goes to Jaja. If only Anise knows Jaja and the type of men she dates, she will understand that Alex is not her type. For Zeb, a man who cannot look you in the face and have a hearty disagreement is not for her. Jaja is able to stand on his feet and confront the military oppressor of their country. On top of it, he has no gun while they have all the guns. That's her kind of man. Alex is always the nice guy. Zeb smiles because she remembers what such men are called back in her country. They are regarded as *k'ewe sikwa*. This refers to someone who wants everybody to see him as the good guy. Such people cannot stand firm. They are afraid of being on the wrong side of the bully or oppressor. Zeb does not find Alex physically attractive. He is tall but too thin for her liking. He is bald also. Zeb relents a bit.

What she thought about Alex not standing firm is not true. He has sometimes defended her against Anise. He does not bother with fixing the world. He just likes his good life, yes. Zeb softens the more as she remembers that he loves her friend dearly. He has a good job and spoils Anise with presents. He's considerate and kind. He's not moody like Anise. Alex is a good man, but "he's not my type."

"Women may tell you what you like to hear and not tell you everything." Zeb looks at Anise.

"Is there something about Alex that you are hiding from me?" Anise says.

"You started it."

"Are you hiding something?" Anise says.

"Let's leave Alex out of this. Why did you invite me to walk with you? What do you want to tell me?"

They come out of the wood and cross Woodcutter Road to the sidewalk. Anise takes Zeb's hand and holds it as they walk. Zeb knows that this is a friendly gesture, so whatever Anise has to say can't be bad. Anise swings her hand. Zeb smiles.

"I don't want you to take this in a bad way. It is about Alex and me," Anise says. Zeb drops her hand and moves away from Anise. Anise holds her by the waist. Zeb pushes her. She laughs.

"What is it?" Zeb says.

"I'm worried about you." Anise holds her hand again and swings it.

"Is it about Green Card?"

"No. It is more than Green Card." Anise holds her by the waist again. Zeb is sceptical about all the friendly gestures. Maybe Anise wants to say something that is harsh, and wants to assure Zeb of her friendship. Zeb thinks that this may be the reason for all the holding.

"What?" Zeb wants to hear it and get over with it. The light is red, so they wait for the light to change.

Zeb and Anise are crossing the road when a man shouts at them from a car. "She doesn't want you. I saw it. Leave her alone!" The woman on the passenger seat laughs.

"Why is he screaming?" Zeb says.

"They don't like women to hold each other here. That's why he's yelling at us."

"Why?"

"It is not their culture," Anise says.

"It's not his business."

They are at the parking lot of the Shopping Center. Cars pass. They move in-between cars.

"You haven't told me anything," Zeb says.

"It's noisy. I'll tell you later."

"I can hear you very well. Say it now."

"Too many people." Anise pulls out her cell phone.

"Honey. Great. We'll be done in thirty minutes," Anise says on the phone.

"Well, since you won't tell me what you have in mind, I'll tell you mine," Zeb says. A car drives between them in the lot but they manage to shout and hear each other.

"What?" Anise shouts.

"I'm going to New Jersey for a party."

"Good for you!"

"What!" Zeb does not hear her.

Inside the store, Zeb pushes the cart. Anise loads many items.

"So much food," Zeb says.

"It's for Thanksgiving."

"You celebrate Thanksgiving too?"

"Why not?" Anise says.

"I forgot, Alex has naturalised and is an American citizen."

"I'm American too," Anise says.

"What are you thanking Columbus for?"

"Not Columbus. I thank God for bringing me to America. It is great for me." Anise dumps a large turkey on the cart.

"It will be great for you also." She dumps another one.

"How many birds will you send to hell fire for Thanksgiving?" Zeb asks her.

"You and your use of words." Anise laughs so much. Zeb doesn't find it funny.

"Seriously, how many?" Zeb says.

"I'll invite friends. You know our people. They'll take things home," Anise says.

"You do that here in America?" Zeb says.

"Sure. I have plastic plates for packing food for guests."

"Who do you expect?"

"One American couple, one Nigerian couple, another couple from Canada and our pastor. He is single." Anise winks. Zeb frowns.

Zeb is on the line with the cart. She leans on the cart. A hand touches hers.

"Hi Alex." She looks up.

"Where is my wife?"

"She forgot to get some stuffing," Zeb says.

"She usually makes Nigerian stuffing."

"She bought two birds," Zeb says.

"Different stuffing for them," Alex says.

"You got it."

"I know where to find her." He goes.

20

Asoebi Wedding

After dinner, Alex dumps the plates in the sink. Zeb begins to wash them.

"That's okay. I'll load the washer." Alex cleans the plates and puts them in the washing machine. Anise puts the vegetables on trays. She's silent, but makes a lot of noise in the way she places the trays on the table. What's on her mind? "What did she want to tell me at the Shopping Center?" Zeb thinks.

"Zeb, are you done with the computer? I want to use the Internet," Alex says.

"Go ahead. I want to help with the Thanksgiving stuff," Zeb says.

"Coming Wendy?" Alex says.

"No!" Wendy watches Buffy on the television.

"Okay buddy. No hassle." Alex is on his way downstairs.

"Anise."

"What?"

"What're you mad at?" Zeb says.

"Come. Sit down."

"I don't want to sit."

"Hey, come and cut the green peppers." Anise pushes the plate of peppers opposite her.

"So?" Zeb sits opposite her.

"You see how Alex helps me out all the time," Anise says.

"Is there a problem with that?" Zeb says.

"You know that it is not like that back home."

"Yes."

"Back home, I won't rely on my husband for helping out in the kitchen."

"Yes. Just get to the point!" Zeb says.

"Okay. It's harsh out here in America especially for those of us without support from family." Anise clears her throat.

"What's your point?" Zeb says.

"Don't be mad. Our pastor..."

"You want to match me with your pastor! You don't have to take me all the way to the shops in order to say that. After my appeal that you should respect my emotions."

"For a married man! I'm sorry; I cannot respect it. I'm a married woman myself and will hate any woman who has an affair with my husband."

"I'm not having an affair; I'm just..."

"Don't talk to me about it. You also need to respect my emotions as a married woman with a loving husband."

"I shared something with you as a friend for you to understand and not for you to shove it on my face," Zeb says.

"Calm down. Don't fight me. Believe me, I'm doing this because I care for you as my own sister," Anise says.

"Please don't ever bring up the issue of me marrying your pastor. Alright, I get it. You want me to marry and leave your house?"

"No! Don't even think like that."

"So what is it? Just go straight to the point."

"I want us to have a woman to woman talk," Anise says.

"Yes?"

"You know how wives sit together and gossip about their husbands," Anise laughs.

"I'm not a wife so I don't remember how they bitch people! Get to the point." Zeb is mad that Anise should bring up the issue of her pastor and have the nerve to condemn her feeling for Jaja. The marriage thing is going overboard, but she feels that she has to take it easy. Maybe Anise does not mean any harm as she says.

"You're in a bad mood. I know what you need, but I won't say it. You'll hit the roof," Anise laughs.

"Another secret?"

"You need TLC - tender loving care," Anise laughs.

"That wasn't what you had in mind," Zeb says.

"I'm sure you know what it is, but I can't say it, because Wendy is around." Anise winks.

"Let's be serious. You need someone with whom to share the problems. That's the only way to survive the stress of life here with your people so far away. You think that the only trouble is not having a job. Wait until you get the job. Then you'll get into other difficulties and guess what?"

"What?"

"You'll have to live with them."

"I don't want you to think that I hate marriage because of my past experience. I like chasing and dating. I don't like match-making." Zeb cuts a green pepper with the sharp edge of the knife. Anise shakes her head in disapproval, and goes to the kitchen.

"There is no chasing here. America is direct. If you want somebody, you say it. If that person wants you; good. If not, you go your way. If you don't, that will be sexual harassment. You can go to prison," Anise says.

"There is no fun in that." Zeb cuts the same pepper again.

"I know." Anise comes back with another chopping board.

"Don't slice green pepper like that. I want them in small cubes that will contrast with strips of red pepper," Anise says.

"Why not use the grinder," Zeb says.

"It won't have the same effect that I want," Anise says.

"Fussy."

"Zeb, I know that you hate cooking and domestic work."

"I do domestic work in this house," Zeb says.

"But you wish that we have servants as you had back home."

"You wish it too," Zeb says.

"I'm the housegirl and Alex is the houseboy." Anise laughs.

"As you like it," Zeb says.

"It works for us."

"Why not pay someone to help out sometimes, like two or three times a week? Alex is rich. If you two do everything, how will you have the time to do fun things?"

"Fun is a luxury here," Anise says.

"But Americans always have fun."

"We say we're having fun, but it's not all that fun. You can't have fun when you're not relaxed, your mind is on this bill and that bill, shooting here and shooting there, who watches you because of your skin colour and who is favoured because of race or something else. Even when we go to the movies or the theatre, our minds are on many stressful things. The good thing is that we do it together as couples, so we share the stress."

"Isn't it boring being with one person all the time without fun?" Zeb says.

"We had a good courtship at home and even when I joined him here, it was great. I still remember everything, full of fun."

"You are too young to live on memory," Zeb says.

"Courtship is a lot of fun here, because nobody cares what you two do. You can go anywhere together. You can kiss on the street. You can have sex. You can live together."

"Why do you get married, if you can do all that?" Zeb picks another pepper.

"If you don't get married, you miss out on the ceremonies. The engagement ring, wedding gown, honeymoon and all that. You know what I mean, pretty much the same as we have back home," Anise says.

"You have been here for too long. You have forgotten that Nigerian marriage typically has three wedding ceremonies. And everybody prepares and dresses as if it is his or her own wedding." Zeb stops chopping the pepper to look at Anise.

"Why not blend the onions instead of that. You'll cut your fingers," Zeb says.

"If I blend them, we'll be done in a minute. We won't have the joy of talking while we share the work."

"You want to punish me? You know that I don't like to do this?" Zeb makes a face.

Anise laughs. "I miss home. You and the way you talk are my closest to home."

"How did you cope before I came here?" Zeb says.

"I clung to the only home I had."

"Alex."

"Yep!"

"Sweetheart, you're sleeping," Anise says as she goes to check on Wendy.

"No!" Wendy shouts.

"Go on Zeb."

"Yes. We all celebrate our own lives with the bride and groom. I like *asoebi.*"

"Tell me about *asoebi.*" Anise speaks from the living room.

"Don't they wear *asoebi* here at Nigerian weddings?"

"They do, but I want to know how it is done at home now," Anise says.

"It is a word from the Yoruba language."

"But what does it mean?" Anise says.

"The closest translation would be a kind of uniform worn by a group. A husband and a wife can wear a suit and a gown respectively, but their attire is similar because they are of the same material. That's *asoebi.* The bride's family, bridegroom's family, bride's friends, mother's friends, each can have *asoebi.* At a wedding, you know groups by their attire."

"That's pretty similar to what they do at Nigerian weddings here." Anise does not sit, but stands engrossed in Zeb's description of Nigerian wedding.

"Some people have more than one uniform depending on how many groups they belong to. When my cousin got married, I wore *asoebi* with our association and also wore another one with our family."

"How did you wear two attires at one wedding?" Anise says.

"I wore three, one as her maid-of-honour in the church, and one when she was dancing with our age grade association at the reception. I changed into our family's golden wrapper and white top when we went to their home to present the dowry."

"This sounds exciting." Anise stands across the table with a sparkle in her eyes.

"What did your family give her as dowry?" Anise says.

"A car-."

"Automobile?"

"Yes. It was not brand new, but it added to the prestige of our presentation," Zeb says.

"What else?" Anise sits down.

"Television, radio, cushion seats, just anything you can imagine in a living room. We also gave her kitchen things like electric cooker, fridge, freezer, and so on. Even bedroom items. The only thing that was missing was a house, but it was assumed that her husband and his people would give them one."

"That is a modern version of what they did in my village long ago."

"Tell me what you remember. You are home-sick," Zeb says.

Anise shifts on her seat. She smiles. "Okay. This is a test to see whether I still remember the Igbo culture of my village in Aruzo town. I got married thirty-four years ago but I still remember the wedding ceremonies." Her face lights up.

"Okay, tell me about the marriage," Zeb says.

"In my village, there are four basic events. The first one is when representatives from the man's family go with wine to show interest. In my case, a man from my village in Umuaro who worked with my father-in-law in the railways was the go-between. He brought a few people from my husband's family to ask whether their son was allowed to court me."

"It is called *iju ajuju*," Zeb says.

"I know that, and I know that it translates as 'asking questions.' They asked one question and that was the point of the whole ceremony."

"Sorry, go on." Zeb says.

"When they left, my father asked my mother and my mother asked me whether I knew the man and if I wanted him."

"Don't tell me that you pretended not to have been sneaking behind your parents to meet hm."

Anise laughs, "You know me. I did not pretend. I said yes, so they sent a message to them to come for the next stage."

"It is called *iku aka*."

"I know that. I also know that it translates as 'to knock on the door.' If you tell me what the stages are called one more time, I'll shut up," Anise says.

"Do you want me to go on?" Anise asks.

"Please."

"I'm enjoying it, but do not interrupt me again," Anise says.

"It is like a trip home." Zeb did not go through these stages with her ex-husband. She keeps the knife on the table.

"Okay, let us enjoy the trip. The third stage is the pricing." Anise coughs.

"I wanted to see whether you will interrupt me," Anise laughs.

"I know, because the cough sounded fake."

"I think that my child is asleep. Let me check on her again." Anise gets up.

"Go on!"

"At this stage, there was a lot of goings-on between Alex and me." She sinks her neck on her shoulders and twists her body. Zeb laughs at her demonstration of clandestine movements and her narration of it.

"Alex came back from America with degrees and everything. Every girl in my village knew him and wanted to be the one."

"So you got him through clandestine..."

"Shut up. My daughter is in the living room, so let me go on with the next stage. I can't really say *Igba-ngo* in

English. There is dance and prize in the word. Of course there is a lot of music and dance around the prize, me," Anise touches her heart, "and there is discussion about money to be brought by his family and that is pricing. Yeah! Dancing to win the prize with a price!" Anise dances to the music from the television.

"I have heard people call it 'bride-price' but that's not a good translation," Anise goes to the living room.

"My baby!" Anise says.

"Mom," Wendy says sleepily.

"Go, put on your nightie."

"You know," Anise returns from the living room.

"When I knelt down and drank palm wine from a cup and gave the remaining to Alex to drink from the same cup, I felt like the whole world was at my feet. People clapped. Alext drank from the cup, and then he raised me from my kneeling position and put me on the chair beside him. That was my paradise and position as his wife."

"Why did you kneel down?"

"That was the tradition. I had to kneel down as a woman and acknowledge the earth mother that is special to women."

"But Alex did not kneel."

"He's a man. I'm the one that is close to Ani, the earth goddess. His mother and sister can kneel to drink of the wine prepared by Ani but not him. Don't you know that palm wine is ready-made on the tree that comes from deep down the bowels of the earth?"

"I know, still men don't kneel."

"Do you want to hear another special thing?"

"Sure."

"This one happened at the engagement party. When Alex knelt down on one knee and put a twenty-two hundred dollar ring on my finger." She pauses. She sits opposite Zeb. Zeb thinks that there are tears in her eyes.

"I felt great like I was the queen. He called me his queen."

"And still treats you like one."

"Tell me about the traditional wedding day, if you can still remember."

"Yeah. *Igba nkwu*," Anise says.

"We now call it wine-carrying," Zeb says.

"That is not a good translation of it. *Igba-nkwu* is more than carrying wine. The traditional attires, different groups, kola nut ceremony, dowry presentation, music, dance, feast, and so many things that make *igba nkwu* interesting are not reflected in your translation of it as wine-carrying," Anise says. Zeb's eyes water; she never had the advantage of a proper marriage.

"Which item of *igba-nkwu* d'you like most?"

"Definitely the dowry. Oh God, my eyes hurt." Anise hurries to the bathroom.

"It's from the onions."

"Come on. I want to wash my face." Anise says. Zeb follows her.

"I also like bride-wealth so that all my relations who contributed money used in purchasing items of my dowry can share in the wealth that I bring." Anise splashes water on her face.

"But the item that I like most is the dowry itself." Anise takes the towel, wipes her face and continues to talk. "My family gave me different kinds of cooking utensils. They gave me mortar and pestle, three sizes of tripod stove, sets of plates and clay pots. They also gave me brooms, pillows, chairs and stools. What I liked most were the colourful mats. I gave away many items of my dowry because I was coming here." Anise takes some tissue papers as she leaves the bathroom.

"Why do you like mats?" Zeb follows her out of the bathroom.

"I also like beds and couches. In America, I like to trade them in and get better newer ones," Anise says.

"You know what they say about women who like beds?" Zeb says.

"I don't care." Anise sways her hips.

"They also say something about those that like kitchen utensils," Zeb adds.

"Whatever."

"Is it true, what they say about you people who love beds?" Zeb says.

Anise taps her right leg and her hips shake. They both begin to laugh.

"Do you remember something?" Zeb says.

"I know that you know that I am sexy. And I have a man who appreciates it." Anise flops on the couch.

Anise is back to good mood. She stretches on the couch and props her head with one hand.

"What?" Anise says.

"You're very beautiful." Zeb cups her mouth with her hand and adds, "When you are not in a bad mood."

Anise picks the pillow. Zeb takes cover on the floor. The pillow hits Zeb's back. Zeb springs up. Anise runs upstairs. Zeb also runs. Anise is opening their bedroom door when the pillow hits her. Zeb laughs; loud laughter.

"Wife. I've been waiting for you to come to bed." Alex's sleepy voice is loud enough for Zeb to hear by her bedroom door. Zeb laughs out loud, and opens the door of her room. The pillow hits Zeb's back. She turns to get the pillow.

"Go answer your wifely call!" Zeb hugs the pillow.

"Good night!" Zeb hears Anise's voice. Their door shuts.

Zeb enters her room. She feels cold chills all over her body. She looks around for what is wrong. The window is open. She is alarmed. The police had put an advertisement on the television warning people not to leave their doors and windows open because of the killer. Everybody forgot about the advertisement when they thought that the killer had been caught, but it later turned out that they got the wrong person. The killer is still at large. Zeb hopes that the intruder has not entered the house through the open window. She runs out of the room. She knocks on the master bedroom. Alex comes out.

"I left my window open. I don't know whether the killer has entered from the window. I had chills all over my body when I entered the room."

"That's not likely. Your room is on the third floor."

Seeing that Zeb is still not convinced, he offers to check her room. As he follows her, Anise comes out and follows them. Anise stands by Zeb's door as Alex checks the closet. Zeb kneels down to look under the bed.

"This is not a Nigerian bed that is high. Nobody can hide under your bed." Anise laughs. Alex locks the window.

"Your room is safe. Lock your door if that will make you feel better," he says and leaves.

"Thank you."

"You're welcome," he says.

"Lie down, baby sister," Anise follows him.

She sits alone and thinks about marriage. Marriage was thrust upon her as a girl but she has never thought this much about it in her life. What is it about Anise's house that fills her mind with thoughts of marriage? She believes that it is a combination of things; Anise, Gloria and Green Card. It does not occur to her that she could be lonely because she had not given any time to fun since her mind is preoccupied with situating herself in America. She believes that she has internalised Anise's words about needing a special person in her life. It does not surprise her that she is not thinking about a job or Green Card, but about the need to let Jaja go. She thinks that she can only let go by opening herself to other men. She gets up from the bed and takes her address book. She flips through the book. One name sticks out. Rob Aracebor. But he is married. She assures herself that he is just a friend. She has not written to Rob for some time now. She did not even tell him that she is now in America. She wants to send him a message immediately because she may not have the time for it before she leaves for New Jersey in the morning. She goes down to the computer room.

21

They Stick Together

Zeb drags her suitcase out of the metro and joins the people moving to the elevators. They go in different directions as they come up the elevator. Zeb does not know which way to take. She stands for a moment. She sees an imposing entrance with a metal banner. She reads the name on the banner, Union Station, Washington DC. She makes her way through the entrance. Barnes and Noble bookstore is on the left as she enters the station. Zeb cannot resist the array of books she sees though the open doors. She enters and begins a tour of the fiction section. Many people stand around. Some are reading and waiting for their train.

From where she is, Zeb can see more people come up the elevator and go to different directions not leading to the trains. She wants to explore the station and know where all the people go to. She leaves the bookstore and follows the people going in the direction opposite the bookstore. There is an art gallery with paintings of American presidents. She joins the tour. People eat and drink while they look at the arts. Zeb is thirsty. She has to buy some soda. There are many shops. There is a food court as well as cafés. She soon discovers that Union Station is like a shopping mall. She thinks that it is more interesting than a mall because of the art gallery, bookstore and transportation. It has metro and train terminals. On her way to buy soda, she cautions herself that she needs to buy her train ticket before she is carried away by the interesting station.

She buys an Amtrak ticket to Trenton, New Jersey. The train will leave by twelve. She looks at her watch. She does not have much time. She decides to go to the gate and wait. She stretches her legs. It's a good thing that she is wearing flat sandals. It makes all the walking easy. A train stops by seven minutes to twelve noon. She's about to enter when an Inspector shouts at her.

"This is not your train. This is metro line," he says.

Zeb retraces her steps and goes to him.

"Isn't this the train to New Jersey?" she says.

"Your ticket is for Amtrak!" He blows the whistle. The train leaves. Zeb looks at her ticket. It says Gate 12. She looks at the gate sign. It is Gate 12. She looks at her watch. She is confused.

"Do you want Amtrak?" A man sits on the bench.

"I guess."

"It will be here in a short while."

"Are you going to New Jersey?"

"New York."

"I want the train to New Jersey."

"It's the same train. Where are you going to in New Jersey?"

"Trenton."

"You'll get off at Trenton station, and then I'll continue with this train to its final stop in New York.

"I see."

"Where are you from?"

"Germantown."

"I mean originally," he says.

"You mean my nationality?"

"Yeah."

"I'm a Nigerian. What about you?"

"I'm a New Yorker."

Zeb goes to an empty seat by a window. The New Yorker walks to the seat at the other end across the isle. The train takes off. Zeb heaves a sigh of relief. She is finally on her way to New Jersey. She smiles, sits back; this is her first travel by train in the US so she is open to see what it is like. She looks out of the window. She sees so many tracks as the train leaves the station. It is hard for her to imagine the number of trains that use all the tracks, maybe leading to different mega stations. The houses near the station look worn-out and ugly. She looks away. She needs to find something to keep her busy. She takes a novel from her bag and flips through the pages. She does not really feel like reading. She looks out again. Great. They are now passing through the countryside. Lots of trees and shrubs. It reminds her of the birds in the park across the road from her bedroom window in Germantown.

"Baltimore Washington International Airport station!"

The announcement is loud and clear. Zeb looks out. She cannot see the airport. There are shuttle buses. They will probably take people to the airport.

A couple that enters the coach diverts her attention. The two hold tight and their four legs get in the way. Zeb shakes her head and suppresses a smile. She thinks that the couple surely demonstrates Anise's idea of a man and woman sticking together as one. She continues to watch them with her mind still on the birds that she often sees through her bedroom window. They habitually perch and skip on the huge tree. They face the harsh elements together and have the freedom to roam the horizon. She wishes that she can have the freedom of the birds that do not bother about Green Card.

The bird imagery brings up the idea of how to get a man. Maybe she should roam around like the birds and look for a partner. Searching for men may be fun. It is different from her usual practice of picking from those who present themselves to her. Zeb is beginning to realise that her style limits her choices. She has no status, no car, no house, no job, and no affiliation to any club. Where in the world will she find the right men? This question jars her mind as she thinks of her experience with the bus driver. She promises herself that she will take control of the situation and search and "hunt men." She smiles. It's fun to think of herself as the hunter of men. In a hunting mood, she closes the novel in front of her and puts it back in her bag. She brings out her address book to check the men with US addresses. She looks at the men listed under A. She searches from one letter to another. None of them seems good enough to hunt. Zeb does not give up. She says to herself, "How can I know the flavour of a dish, if I don't taste it?" The one that she is interested in is married or maybe married when they met.

Rob Aracebor. Zeb still remembers how she met him even though it happened several years ago. It was in the summer of 1994, when she was doing her PhD at the School of Oriental and African Studies in London. Rob and Cara Aracebor were spending their vacation in London and exploring different areas of the city. She met them at Sunday outdoor market in Liverpool Street where they were shopping for African items. Rob went up to Zeb and introduced himself. Zeb noted that he did not introduce Cara whom she assumed was his wife. Zeb helped him with his shopping and Cara did not seem to mind as they went through the stalls looking at the items.

"Those are beautiful fabrics."

"They are wrappers."

"I want to purchase one."

"What will you do with it?"

"Souvernir."

"We wear them," Zeb says.

"How?"

"Just wrap it round the waist. It looks like a long skirt but then we wrap a second one that gives the attire a characteristic sexy look."

"Sounds cute. Do you wear it yourself?"

"I'm going to wear it tonight. The Africa Students' Association will have a party to welcome new students and I intend to wear a traditional attire."

"Can I get a ticket?"

"You don't need a ticket. It's free. You and your wife are welcome. You will even add some excitement to the party. People love to meet Americans."

"Thank you. I'll be there. Just give me the address."

Zeb still remembers him at the party. He admired her attire and paid her compliments and a lot of attention. There were many Africans from different countries. He admired their gorgeous clothing and the ease with which they moved in the huge gowns. Zeb went round meeting people. She knew that Rob was doing the same, but somehow, they kept bumping into each other, as she thought. But they were not accidental bumps at all. Rob deliberately arranged them. He cautiously kept an eye on her and made sure that he appeared near her when she was alone. He did not want to ask her about her marital status because he did not want to talk about his situation with Cara and reveal the secret of his marriage. He was sometimes detached because he was not sure whether she had a man with her who was also keeping an eye on her.

The first time they bumped into each other was when she was going to get a drink. He did not see a man with her so he also went to the bar for a drink. She smiled when she saw him. He looked regal in his darkish blue kaftan that she helped him pick at the open market in Liverpool Street.

"The kaftan looks very good on you," she said.

"Thanks to you. Do I look like an African?" Rob says.

"Not just an African. I can place you in Nigeria with the Fulani people."

"Why?"

"Your colour-."

"Colour? You have that problem in your country."

"It's not a problem. Many people from my Igbo ethnic group are light-skinned like you but your height places you more with Fulanis."

"Your men are not tall?"

"Ok. Some are tall but not usually as lean as you."

"I didn't know that you differentiate by colour in Africa."

"It's not like white and black in this country. There are many other things."

"Such as?"

"The language, culture, attire, name and and other things that instantly identify someone's ethnicity."

"Ok. It's more of culture."

"Yes. You just look like a FulanI but it's easy to know that you are not Fulani as soon as you speak."

A small girl carried on the shoulder by her mother had stretched one hand and pulled Zeb's head-wrap. Rob was there to help the mother remove the child's hand without doing much damage to Zeb's head wrap. Zeb remembers how surprised Rob was when she removed the head-wrap and showed it to the girl who touched and kissed it.

"You remove it like a hat?"

"And put it back like one," Zeb said putting it on. Rob was in awe as she quickly retied the ends that were dislodged by the girl. He liked the way she carried her small figure like she was so tall. He couldn't wait to record it in his journal.

They did not meet again but spoke a few times on the phone. Zeb remembers her phone conversations with him. He seemed to know a lot about Nigerian soccer players. He had a better knowledge of their names and clubs than she did. She thought it weird that he never mentioned his wife in his conversations with her. At a seminar, she had heard an anthropologist talk about open marriages and she then wondered whether his marriage was one such arrangement. She wanted to ask him about it, but changed her mind because it might give him the wromg signals. She was still hurting from Jaja's marriage and trying to get on with her life. After the party, they e-mailed back and forth even after he went back to the United States. But Zeb could not keep up with his messages when she went back to Nigeria. It was burdensome going to the computer department of the university to check her email. They had only two public computers and used to grant each person just twenty minutes to use the computer. That never used to be enough for Zeb and she could not keep up with email messages. That was how she lost contact with Rob Aracebor. A couple of days ago, while leafing through her old address book, she saw his information and sent him a line, "Are you still there?"

After reminiscing about Aracebor, Zeb keeps the address book. She rests her head on the window and stretches out her legs smiling at memories of Aracebor. The smile is still on her lips. The thought of planning how to get a man intrigues her. Hunter! She laughs but she does not pick up the address book. It looks like she has already given up on her decision to hunt men as she continues to think about one man. The first thing will be to find out if he is married.

22

New Jersey Connections

Trenton, New Jersey is a lot of fun for Zeb. The get-together is not an ordinary party for a new baby. It is also a celebration of the baby's parents, Tom and Ijeoma. It feels like a family reunion, because, relations came from different parts of the United States. It is also more than family reunion because friends, in-laws and neighbours are also there. The party does not begin as scheduled, but the music is good and the bar is open and free. People drink and talk.

"Hei!" Zeb runs into her uncle Sylva Okolo. She is surprised to see him. No one told her that he is in the country.

"Nze," She addresses him with his title and bends down in greeting but he pulls her up and hugs her.

"Uncle, I didn't know that you were here."

"Come." He holds her hand and takes her to the outer room, but there are so many people there.

"Let's go outside," Zeb says.

"It's cold."

"Uncle, it is not yet cold-o."

"My blood is not young like yours. Let's go downstairs."

Zeb's heart misses a bit. She knows that there must be a serious issue. She frowns. She glances at him and hopes that nobody is seriously ill or dead.

"I am here for treatment," he says.

"Are you ill?"

"Not serious. Prostate problem."

"Is Tom treating you?" Zeb says. Tom is his nephew and Zeb's cousin.

"No, Eddy's friend is my doctor." Eddy is also his nephew and Zeb's cousin. He and his girlfriend have a daughter named Kim.

"What did his friend say?"

"He said that it is not cancerous."

"Did he send you for blood test or something?"

"Yes. Many tests. I feel much better than when I arrived," he says.

"You are very precious to me." Zeb hugs him and holds his hand.

"Your son is very intelligent."

"You saw Dozie?"

"Of course. I visited your mother to tell her I was coming here. Your son is carbon copy of my brother. It brought tears to my eyes looking at him, just like your father when as children we used to roam the bushes looking for wild fruits. Your mother is doing a fine job raising him. He heard us talking about my trip so he asked me whether he could come with me to see you."

"He said that?" Zeb places her hands on her chest.

"You mother told him that he had to wait till you got a job. 'Can we go together Grand Angel,' he has such a lovely name for your mother."

Zeb wants to know something about Jaja, but her uncle is not the right person to ask. With her hands still on her chest, she asks about the political situation in Nigeria hoping to hear about Jaja.

"Uncle, why didn't anybody tell me that you have come to America?"

"I came here just a week ago," he says.

"That is not an excuse. Eddy or Tom or Tom's wife should have phoned me," she says. She feels slighted and thinks about her situation. Maybe they do not reckon with her because she has no job, and is no longer relevant, she frowns. Okolo notices the frown and knows that she is really hurt about the exclusion. He tries to convince her that it was not a deliberate act of omission.

"You know how busy they are. One is at work during the day, the other one works at night," he says.

"Don't make excuses for them."

"Don't be angry. How are you?" he asks.

"I'm okay," she says.

"You look well. What about work?"

"I am still looking." She shrugs her shoulders.

"Papa!" Eddy shouts from upstairs.

"Let's go. Maybe they want to begin."

Okolo clears his throat. Everybody keeps quiet.

"Put off the music completely," he says.

"I am Nze Okolo. I thank all of you for being here. I want to make it short because we need enough time to eat all the food that my son and his wife have provided. We all know why we are here. We are here to welcome our new child into our community. As the oldest here," he pauses to see whether anyone will challenge him. People look around. It is as if no one is older than he is.

"As the oldest here, I can say that..."

One woman coughs loudly. Everybody looks at her. She is sitting beside Tom's wife, Ijeoma, who is carrying her baby. There is a brief silence. Everybody looks at the woman. She is small, about five feet. She ties a very big *gele* that sits on her head like a water pot. She carries her head straight; no slouching of the shoulder. She looks around. Everybody looks at her. She looks at Okolo.

"I was a full maiden when the war of Hitler began," she says.

"If my memory still serves me well, history said that the war started in 1939."

"Correct!"

"Very well. In that case, I doff my hat for you, Madam. It is because of people like you that we are alive and kicking. Thank you for coming here," Okolo says.

Okolo clears his throat again.

"This boy here." He points at Eddy.

"This boy is my son. The father that begot him sucked our mother's breasts before me."

"The father of this one sucked after me." He points at Zeb.

"This one here," He points at Tom.

"Tom is the second child of the last child of our mother." He says still pointing at Tom.

"You can see that all of them come from children of those that sucked from the same breast that I sucked, so I am their big mother's child; what you call uncle in English," he says.

"This is our new wife and our new child from God." He points at Tom's wife, Ijeoma, and the baby.

"Madam, we are happy to have you here." He says to the elderly woman who has come up to him.

"Thank you, my brother," She says to him before she turns to the gathering.

"As for me, I am Lolo Nwanyi-bude," she says.

"Her grand-daughter is my good friend," Ijeoma says.

"That's me!" A voice is heard from the back. The speaker comes out. She does not look like her grandmother. She is tall and big, with a sizeable behind. She deliberately sways her hips. She unties her second wrapper, sways her hips stylishly and ties her second wrapper again. She knots it at the side, pushes down the knot and leaves her hand there. She looks round and smiles at everybody, probably wanting their approval.

"You are the great child of my child." The Lolo approves of her action.

"My brother, you can continue," Lolo says to Okolo.

"This is a very good gathering. We want one person from every age group to come over here, so that this baby can see how rich she is," Okolo says.

People file out and stand beside him. Ijeoma remains seated with her baby. A ten-year-old girl kneels beside Ije and begins to kiss the baby. A woman sits her baby on the floor so that he would represent the baby's age group. He crawls towards Okolo with his eyes on the microphone. She brings him back and gives him a toy.

"Sit there. Let me take a photo of you and the baby."

"He may be her future husband!" Someone shouts from the back. People laugh.

"You never know!"

"I said that I will make this short," Okolo says and continues.

"Action speaks louder than any words. You can see that this baby is blessed on her left and her right, behind and in front of her. As you all know, her naming ceremony was performed in Nigeria. This party is for us to tell you her names and celebrate with her. Before we announce her names, we have to perform a very important ceremony. Breaking of kola nuts."

Tom brings a plate of kola nuts.

"These kola nuts were sent from Nigeria for this occasion, and they have been blessed." Tom gives the plate to his Uncle.

"I brought them with me from Nigeria. I was at the burying of the baby's umbilical cord in our village. My brother's son, Okpara, came all the way from Uwani to pick me from Amuvi in Aro where I was visiting my mother's brother. We made the long journey together, all the way back to Enugu. For those of you here who don't know, we are from Eke town in Enugu State in Nigeria."

"Where is Amuvi, sir?" The voice came from the back. Everybody turns towards the back.

"Amuvi is one of the nineteen villages in Aro. I hope that you know where Aro is. In case you don't know, it is near the Cross River at the Igbo side of it. It is a great town. In those days, the people fought with British people three times and defeated them in the first war and the second war. They lost the third one in 1902. The British were helped by soldiers from other parts of Nigeria and West Africa that they had already conquered."

"They were traitors." The same voice shouted from the back.

"No. My brother's son, Okpara, wrote a book about that war. He did not call them traitors. They had become part of the British Empire and were forced to serve the Empire by British law. When Aro was defeated, the

British took over and Aro people lost everything. They also joined the British Commonwealth army and fought the First World War and the Second World War with other Africans. My brothers, Eddy's father and Zeb's father were soldiers in the war. They used to entertain us with stories of London, Burma and other places where they were stationed."

"We are learning history here." It is the same voice from the back.

"Yes. And don't forget it." This is Tom's voice.

"And who is this voice from the back?" Lolo says.

"Brian. My name is Brian Ogafele. Yes Ma. I'm Tom's friend." The man goes forward for people to see him. Zeb notes that he has an imposing personality. She smiles at him. His eyes are on Eddy who is speaking.

"The kola nuts for this party were blessed by the elders. Our cousin Okpara wrapped them in fresh plantain leaves so that they would remain fresh. Then he put them in a cellophane bag," Eddy says.

"It was his wife, Ifenyi, that wrapped them," Uncle Okolo says.

"I bought that plate holding the kola nuts from the market in China Town. It looks like the *okwa* that we use for kola nuts at home," Ijeoma does not want to be left out of the kola nut issue.

"The story of kola nuts never gets to the end," Lolo says.

"I will leave the story of the kola nuts and make this ceremony short," Uncle Okolo says.

"As the oldest member of my family here, I present these kola nuts to you all from my *ikwu* and *ibe* at home and in the United States."

"What is *Iku* and *ibe?*" The ten-year-old girl looks up from where she is cuddling the baby.

"Sh-sh!" her mother says.

"Don't hush her," Lolo says.

"It is a good question." "*Ikwu* are relations from our mother's family. *Ibe* are relations from our father's side. We always make the connections to remind us of the two sides of our identity."

"Kelly, say 'thank you' ," the mother whispers to the girl.

"Thank you Sir."

"Thank you, my daughter. As I said, these kola nuts are from our *ikwu* and *ibe*. We shall break them, call on our forebears, and share the kola. The baby will eat also."

"That is child abuse!" Kelly shouts.

Everybody laughs. The baby begins to whine.

"The baby has no teeth and can't chew." Kelly really thinks that they will make the baby eat a kola nut. People laugh.

"It is true that the baby can't chew the nut, but we shall touch a kola nut on her lips. She will taste the bitterness and the sweetness that follows. That will be her first communion with us who are living and the forebears that blessed the kola from their place in the other world."

Lolo whispers to the girl, "From a young age, we begin to show children that bitterness is followed by sweetness and teach them to work hard which is bitter, so that they can enjoy which is the sweet part of it."

"Who will help me with the prayer?" Uncle asks Eddy. Eddy turns to Tom. They did not remember to put it in the programme. Lolo volunteers to pray.

Okolo breaks the kola nut.

"Igwe, Ani, take kola." He holds one piece up, then points to the floor before he drops it on the floor.

"You were there when we prayed over these kola nuts in our village of Ama-Enugwu in Eke. Sky and Earth, you are still here, but many here were not in Eke with us. We thank you that they are here for this occasion to thank God."

Lolo begins her prayer. "Our big spirit that we call Chi-ukwu. You gave us life. All of us take our spirit from you. We thank you for putting life into us. We thank you for bringing us to America. We thank you for those who are at home in Nigeria. We do the same thing. We make our land to grow at home and abroad. We thank you for bringing all of us here for this special event of *omumu*. We thank you for *omumu*, the special thing that you gave to women." She looks at Ije. Ije smiles at her. Every woman feels something whenever the power of child--bearing and nurturing is mentioned. Women feel connected to child-nurturing and the reverence for that special gift that connects all women. Men also feel the bond with their mothers.

Lolo continues. "It is because of *omumu* that we are here today. You have given us another life that will join women to enjoy and endure everything about *omumu*." She pauses.

"We thank you for fathers and all men that complete the circle when we celebrate *omumu*." She pauses again. She looks around at the men, then at Eddy and uncle Okolo. Finally she begins to point at the baby as she speaks.

"This new baby. Your *omumu* will be rich. May all the gifts in the lines of your palm bring prosperity. May we all be blessed and protected by God. Our God, good spirits of our land, America, and all the earth, you hear our voices."

"Ise."

"Amen."

"In Jesus' name!" Lolo's granddaughter adds, looking around like Lolo and daring anybody to contradict her. Traditional Ikoro drum music follows immediately from the player. The kola nuts are cut and shared.

23

Sweet Tango

kolo takes the stage again. "Our daughter and sister has six names. Her grandparents in Nigeria sent four. Two are from her parents here. The names from her grandparents are Chinonso, Chika, Ada, Eberechukwu." Okolo looks at Tom.

"Trinita. My parents, Ije's parents, Ije and I, make up three parts that are joined in this baby, so I call her Trinita." Tom says. People clap.

"Cool name!" Kelly says. She is still kneeling beside Ije and the baby.

"Here is my own!" Ije says.

"Once God has marked something, written it, or said it, it must happen. God has said everything that happened between Tom, me, and the coming of this baby, so I name her Odera. Chukwudera," Ije says.

"U-u-u-u-u-u..." Lolo ululates. Ije ululates. Zeb joins. The room comes alive with ululations in different voices. People clap. Trinita begins to cry.

"That's her way of cheering," Lolo says. Ije takes the baby to the room. Kelly runs after them. People begin to eat and chat.

The disc jockey plays a mixture of music from different African nations. Although a few people dance in pairs, majority are not paired. Zeb dances alone until Eddy's daughter, Kim, takes her hand. Zeb begins to dance with her. Kim tries to make every move that Zeb makes. Zeb gets it. Kim wants to learn Zeb's dance steps, so she makes simple movements that are easy for the girl to follow. Kelly also joins them. A boy joins them. Soon, Zeb has five partners; all children. They dance High-life, Juju, and Kongo. The dance steps are different from what the children are used to from the television. Initially they fumble with the steps, but soon demonstrate that they learn fast. The music changes to American pop music. Some older people leave the floor. Zeb's young dance partners are in tune with pop and dance without her help. They rock fast. Zeb pauses. It is her turn to learn from them. She watches their movements to make sure that she is not too old -fashioned.

"Do I dance well?" She says to them.

"Yeah."

The little boy takes her hand. They dance as partners and follow the rhythm in simple movements. Soon he begins to make complicated movements with his neck and shoulders. Zeb is not able to keep up. Kids, teenagers, and the young-at-heart now dominate the dance floor. The music changes to Hip-hop. Zeb decides to leave the dancing floor. She goes to get something to eat.

"You dance pretty well," someone says beside Zeb. He is the same young man who spoke from the back during the kola nut ceremony. Zeb remembers that he made an impression on her.

"Thank you," Zeb says. He is a head taller than she is. Zeb assesses his height. She is five feet and two inches, so the guy must be about five feet eight or nine inches. She feels that he is not that tall for her kind of man. But he's big framed. Surprisingly, she does not compare him to Jaja.

"I'm Brian." His eyes focus on hers.

"I'm Zeb," she smiles.

"Lovely name."

"Thanks." She smiles up at him.

"You want something to drink?" He touches her hand; a slight touch.

"Yes." She likes the touch. Good feeling, her heart wells up.

"What do you want to drink?" He smiles at her. Zeb looks at his set of teeth. Very good set.

"Juice or something."

"Come on. Do better than that." He has a charming smile too!

"Okay, let's see what they have," she says.

They both go to the bar section.

"Red wine, white wine, palm wine," he says.

"They have palm wine here?'

"Sure."

"Let me see." Zeb reads the label on the bottle of palm wine. Nigerian Oil Palm Research Company in Nifor made it.

"I know the place. It's near Benin-city. I'll drink palm wine from my city," Zeb says.

"You're from Benin?"

"I used to live there during my undergraduate years. Great historical city," Zeb says remembering that he commented on history during the kola nut ceremony.

"Are we going to learn another history lesson from you?"

"Not on your life. I need some food," Zeb is in a light mood.

"Good."

They leave their drinks on a table and go for food. Zeb has not seen such an array of Nigerian dishes since she came to the United States. Goat meat pepper soup. Fresh fish pepper soup, *edi ka-ikon, moyin-moyin, ugba, akara, fufu, egusi, ogbolo*. All of them look delicious. Because of her love for vegetables, she goes first for the *edi-ka-ikon*.

"Here is pounded yam for your vegetable soup or do you want to eat it with *garri*?" Brian says.

"I don't need any *fufu*, only the vegetables." She takes more *edi-ka-ikon*.

"Just what I like to eat; mixture of various green vegetables with fish and ingredients," she says.

"You don't have to watch your figure tonight. You look great as you are and we're celebrating," Brian says.

"Thanks. I'm not watching anything; I just like vegetables." Zeb smiles at him. He is charming to her.

"There is no heavy stuff on your plate, not even meat," he says.

"I'll take some *moyin-moyin*," she says.

"Bean pudding. It's good for you," Brian says.

"You sound like my mother."

"Do you like your mom?"

"I love her."

"That's good," he says. "Comparing me with your mother shows that you'll like me." He prefers to take her comment in a good way.

They go back to their table. The music changes to waltz.

"I really like this music. Will you do me the favour?" he says.

"My food will get cold."

"I'll warm it up for you. There is a microwave over there," he points.

"The music is damn slow!" she says.

"It will become faster soon." He holds her hand. His grip is firm. He places his hand on her hips. They dance.

She can feel his hand move. It soon wraps round her waist. She feels his body and thinks that her hundred and thirty pounds frame must look small in his hands. She rests her head on his shoulder. He pulls her closer. He moves smoothly on the dance floor for someone who is that big.

"You smell so good," he says. She feels his breath on her ears.

"You sound so good," she says.

"Thank you." His breath brushes her ears. She feels good. He is a gentle dancer, and a good one.

"Nne-oma." He pulls her tighter. Zeb is happy to hear that familiar endearment that men in her cultural area often use to express their admiration. The music ends. Someone is talking. Brian's hand lingers on her waist as they go back to their table.

"Why did you call me Nne-oma?" Zeb says.

"Because you are a beautiful woman. You're ebony, petit, and dazzling," he says.

"Thank you." She is quiet. Her heart is racing, but her brain tries to call it to order. She wants to be in control of herself. She ponders on what he said about the name that he called her and doubts that he has an accurate translation.

"Nne-oma translates as 'good mother.'" Zeb does not mean to correct him, but she has done so many translations in her life that the practice comes naturally to her and in this case it comes unexpectedly. Brian maintains his stand. He takes her hand and explains that it refers to a beautiful woman.

"You are as dark as the prettiest ebony and your skin is fresh like palm tendril. You're charming," he says.

"Thanks. I'm sorry; my profession gets in the way sometimes."

"Mine too," he says.

"You like women."

"I like you." He looks at her directly. She casts down her eyes, but sees him with the corner of her eyes.

"Don't be shy with me." He squeezes her hands. She feels that he may like shy women. It dawns on Zeb that she has not practised the art of playing shy in a long time. She enjoys playing it now. She glances at him fully and quickly casts down her eyes again to hide her amusement.

"When did you come to the United States?" She looks up still smiling.

"Six months ago."

"I'm also new." She casts down her eyes.

"Where do you live?"

"Germantown, Maryland." Her face is still down.

"All the way?" He touches her jaws and pushes it up towards him.

"Yes. You live here?" She looks at him.

"Yes."

"You work in the same hospital as Tom?" She says.

"No. I am yet to take the American Board exam."

"You trained at home?"

"Yes, and did my specialist course in England," he says.

"What did you specialise in?"

"Obstetrics."

"And you don't have a job yet?"

"I'm lucky. I work at a gas station," he says.

"As a doctor?"

"As an attendant," he says. He puts his plate down.

He is silent. He does not look at her. He sips his beer.

She is silent. She does not look at him. She thinks of her situation with the Florida job.

"It is tough."

"We'll survive," he says.

"Yes."

"I'll like to keep in touch with you."

"Yes."

"Do you have a phone number?"

"Yes."

24

Forget Me Not

Zeb wakes up with a smile on her lips. She stretches and makes to continue with her sleep when she remembers that they have to take Trinita to church. She needs to shake off the sleep. She stretches and yawns. She has not felt this good in a long while. She gets up and puts on her jogging gear. She opens her door into the living room.

"Hei husband, you are up early." Ijeoma greets Zeb with the traditional respect that wives give to their husband's relations especially the ones that they like. She is busy in the kitchen.

"My wife, is that you?" Zeb reciprocates Ije's respectful greeting.

"Yes, my good husband," Ije comes out of the kitchen with a canister for watering the plants.

"Did you sleep well?"

"Very well. And you?" Ije waters the plants. She takes the pot of forget-me-nots and puts it beside the sliding door.

"What of my little cousin?" Zeb says.

"Odera is very well. The only problem is that she eats too much." She goes to the kitchen to wash her hands.

"And what's the problem with that?" Zeb says.

"She's expensive." Her laughter shows that she is happy about the baby's large appetite. She puts more water into the canister. Zeb takes it from her.

"We are all expensive in this family, in many ways." Zeb waters the plants.

"I'm beginning to see that." Ije goes back to the kitchen and washes her hand. She takes the feeding bottle and begins to mix baby food.

Zeb waters all the plants and pays particular attention to the forget-me-nots.

"These are beautiful colours," Zeb says and fingers the purple flowers.

"Tom gave them to me on my birthday, and I replanted them after the fragrance of birthday died." Zeb looks into her eyes to feel her soul. There is joy. Ije is happy. Her cheeks bubble as if they are ready to smile anytime. Zeb smiles at her.

"You want to go out, my husband?" She smiles and gestures at Zeb's jogging suit, as if she sees it for the first time.

"Just to take a little walk and drink Trenton air." Zeb opens the front door. Cold air slaps her face.

"It is a safe neighbourhood. But don't be long. You know that we are going to ten o'clock Mass."

"Ten?" Zeb winces at the cold air.

"Yes, ten. So that people from out of state can attend the church service and still have enough time to get back to their states."

"In that case, I can't jog now."

"Sorry."

"No problem. I'll do it in the evening."

Ije goes into their bedroom with the feeding bottle. Zeb is happy about the way Ije tries to show courtesy to her as Tom's kin by addressing her traditionally as her "husband." Ije has been in America for two years and is still close to her Igbo-Nigerian ways. Zeb gives her credit for trying to be traditional. Some of her friends in Nigeria do not bother with traditional ways. Many of them attended schools where they were taught that their culture was not good enough to be proud of. The schools prevented them from speaking their mother tongue languages. Since Zeb's education was cut short by early marriage, she retained her tradition and grew to like the way it helped her maintain her sense of self. She teaches her students to promote the good aspects of tradition and not to make the mistake the older generation made by diminishing Africa as they embraced English culture. She goes into her room thinking that Tom is lucky to have a wife like Ije. She takes care to select a huge *boubou* with a matching *gele*. She spreads the *boubou* on the bed and places the *gele* beside it. She selects the jewelry that goes with the attire and brings out matching shoes from her suitcase. In the shower, she feels like the water is massaging her body. It will be nicer, though, to have a gentle hand do it for her. Brian has such large fingers, but they are gentle, she smiles.

Okolo and Eddy are in the living room when Zeb opens her bedroom door to enter the living room. At the same time, Tom comes out carrying baby Trinita.

"Hei, Cousin. This your attire kills!" Tom says. Eddy and Okolo laugh. Zeb takes the baby from him.

"See the way the *gele* sits on your head like a crown," Eddy says. He and Okolo stack the chairs in a corner.

"She's a monarch! She will turn somebody's head today – o," Tom says.

"Brian will not be in church," Zeb says.

"I did not call anybody's name – o," Tom says. Everybody laughs again.

"I did not hear anything," Okolo says.

"I don't know what you people are talking about." Ijeoma comes out laughing to indicate that she knows that they are teasing Zeb.

"Like hell you don't," Tom says. They laugh and make their way to the garage.

Okolo calls everybody in the house for a brief meeting before he goes back to New York.

"Bring the baby," he says. Zeb picks up Trinita from the buggy.

"Tom. I thank you and your wife, Ijeoma, for organising this reunion. I know that it is a celebration of our *Ada*, but it is also a family reunion. I don't know the last time that all of you came together."

"Long time. I saw Tom last when we went to Nigeria for Ije's wine carrying," Eddy says.

"That's over two years ago," Tom says.

"And you live in the same country," Okolo says.

"Too many demands and no family support," Eddy says.

"You got it," Tom says.

"That's why you should buckle up and do what I've done." Tom holds Ije by the waist and winks at Eddy.

"I hear you," Eddy says.

"Hear him very well," Okolo says.

"I'm working on it, Uncle. At least, I have Kim when she's not with her mother."

"Come home, and we'll help you find a good woman to marry," Okolo says.

"No thanks," Eddy says.

"He's working on it," Zeb says.

"I've never seen as many of Tom's relations in the US as I saw at yesterday's party," Ije says.

"The same with me. I had the opportunity of seeing some of your people I have never seen even though they live in this city," Tom says.

"You see why it is good to have this kind of coming together. You all must continue to do it. You don't have to do it in a way that will break your hand. Do it in a small way, just as much as your hand can carry. Our people said that slowly and gently is the way to lick soup that is very hot. You cannot bring everybody together at once. Just do what you can, as long as you keep bringing people together, even in small numbers." Okolo looks from Tom to Eddy.

"Yeah. We can also do it the American way and ask people to bring food and drinks," Tom says. No sooner has he said it than his wife claps her hands and jerks her shoulders in rejection of his idea.

"Tufia! God forbid!" Ije says. Eddy smiles. Okolo maintains a straight face. Zeb watches for Tom's reaction to this outburst.

"What's wrong with that? After all, at home people give money and even food items to help if you're doing something like this," Tom says to all of them looking from one to the other.

"Yes, people can bring things if they want," Ije says to Eddy and turns to Okolo.

"But we are not the ones to tell them to bring things," Ije adds.

Tom tries to maintain his stand. "It is an American custom that works. Once in Rome, act as the Romans do."

"I'm not going to tell people to sponsor my party. That's all." Ije stamps one foot for emphasis.

"Our wife wants to do all the buying and cooking. My son, that is a woman's province so let her decide on how it will be done."

"I give up then." Tom laughs. They all begin to laugh.

"The important thing is that we maintain family connections here," Eddy says.

Okolo clears his throat. They all know that it indicates that he still has another important message. "And never forget those who are at home in Nigeria. Their sacrifices made all of you what you are today. Many of us, your fathers and mothers, went to school because families contributed money, and in some cases sold their land in order to raise money for school fees. It is a good tradition to help others and support them in any way we can." Uncle Okolo nods his head in affirmation of his advice.

"That is for the Welfare Department in America," Ije says.

"Our families and communities are our own welfare, so I pray that you younger ones will continue with our tradition of support, and pass it on to younger ones. May God give all of you the good head that is wise, so that you'll be able to be what you are, and have the strong heart to become the most that you can be. Never forget who you are. And may goodness remain in you always."

"Ise." Ije and Zeb say.

"So be it," Eddy says.

"Amen," Tom says.

"What do you say, Ada?" Okolo touches Trinita's cheeks. She smiles.

"Say something." Ije tickles her cheeks.

She makes a sound.

"Cousin, I hear you had a job offer but could not do it because you have no work permit," Eddy says.

"Yes."

"Have you discussed with the Immigration Officers about the best way to get a Green Card or work permit?"

"No. Should I do that?"

"Yes of course. You are here legally so you have nothing to hide. A friend of mine got his permit in that way. He just went to the Immigration Department and explained his circumstances. They gave him forms to fill and that was it."

"Are you talking about Andy?" Tom says.

"Yes."

"He has many books and other publications," Tom says.

"I have publications too," Zeb says.

"Then go for it. Make a trip to the Immigration Department and have a chat with them," Tom says.

"Where is the Immigration Department," Zeb says.

"We'll look it up from the Internet," Tom says.

"You can also phone Information," Eddy says.

Eddy and his uncle have phoned to say that they are back in New York. Zeb and Tom relax in the living room. Zeb decides that this is a good time to tell Tom about her concern for his attitude.

"You know Tom; I wanted to tell our uncle that our family in the US should also help those of us who are in need in the US. It is not only those at home in Nigeria who are in need." Zeb goes to the fridge to get some juice.

"I agree with you. People here suffer a lot, but some go home and give wrong impressions about America. They do all kinds of menial jobs here and save as much as they can. Then they go to Nigeria and pretend that all is well with them here. People in Nigeria don't know how we suffer here."

"Because we don't say it," Zeb says.

"You got it," Tom says.

"But it has to stop. The pretence has to stop," Zeb says. She gives Tom a glass of cranberry juice.

"Thanks." He takes a sip and keeps the glass on the side table.

"I like the fact that people take some of their money to Nigeria to help people who are suffering the outcome of military oppression, but some of us suffer here too because of the same military oppression that made us to leave our country."

"I agree with you Zeb that we have to talk about the harsh reality that we face in this country everyday," Tom says.

Zeb sits on the cushion seat near Tom, "I know that it is good to support people at home. That is why many of us are here." She turns to face Tom as she speaks.

"But Tom, people don't talk about those in need of support here in America. I have no job and nobody has asked me how I manage or given me even one dollar to help with my transportation." She looks at him directly because she expects him to give her some money. She feels that even if he has spent a lot of money for the party, he can refund her transport money, at least one way.

"Things are very hard for people here. There are bills to be paid. By the time you finish paying all the bills, there is nothing left," he says.

"It is worse if you have bills to pay and no job and no hope," Zeb says.

He is silent.

The telephone rings. Tom stretches his hand and picks it.

"It's for you." He gives her the telephone and goes to the bedroom.

"Nne-oma."

"Hey Brian?"

"Is it okay to talk with you now?"

"Sure." "*Nne*, you've been on my mind. I'll like to see you."

"Where are you?" Zeb likes the way he says *Nne*.

"I'm on my way to work."

"Work?" Zeb looks at her watch. It is almost eight in the evening.

"I work at night. I get off in the morning."

"They must pay you a lot of money."

"Three dollars an hour."

"That's below the minimum wage of five dollars and fifteen cents."

"It's a great favour. I don't have work papers," he says.

"May I come and see you tomorrow? I can't get you off my mind. I need to see you," he says.

"Since you work at night, don't you sleep during the day?"

"I sleep in the morning. My afternoons and evenings are free."

"I'm here. Whenever you like," Zeb says.

"Is one o'clock okay?"

"Sure."

25

Sentimental Journey

he train pulls off. Brian still stands waving at the
train. Zeb still stands by the door of the train.
She no longer sees Brian but she still waves. She
continues to look through the window even though she
no longer sees him. The smile is still on her lips when
the ticket collector comes to her seat.

"Great guy."

"You saw him?"

"Yeah, he sure digs you." He winks at her and takes
her ticket. He gives her the stub and puts the slip on the
raft. Zeb inclines her head and closes her eyes, but she
does not sleep. She thinks. It was nice of Brian to have
visited her yesterday and again today. She is concerned
that he came straight from work today without any
sleep. She hopes that he will go home and sleep rather
than to the library. Her head slides to the corner of the
headrest. It feels comfortable between the headrest and
the window. She pictures Brian walking home, smiling

and thinking about her. She is sleepy. Still smiling, she dozes off.

"Newark Station! Newark Station!"

Zeb opens her eyes. She looks at her watch. She cannot believe that she slept that long. She picks her suitcase and bag and hurries so as not to miss the southbound Amtrak to Washington DC. Her shoes hurt. She should have worn flat shoes for travel, but because of Brian, she wore high-heeled shoes that are sexy fit for her skirt and blouse. Brian liked her attire very much; could not stop complementing her. The train is about to leave when the inspector sees her running with her suitcase. He steps down from the train and picks her suitcase.

"Thank you." She jumps into the Amtrak.

"You're welcome."

With that problem over, her mind immediately goes back to its happy place. She knows that Brian has touched her in a special way and she wonders what it is about him that excites her so much. He is not that good-looking. But, he is just a great guy. He is attentive, caring, hardworking, intelligent and focused. He is his own man. Even though he has friends who own houses, he does not "squat" in their houses as Zeb does in Anise's house. He lives in his own place no matter how dingy it is and maintains himself with his meagre pay. Zeb thinks about all these and drifts to sleep again.

Her head jerks forward and back against the headrest. The train slows down, and then moves fast again. She looks out through the window. The forest is thick and still green. She remembers her Trenton experience and all the people she met; her uncle, Ijeoma's relations, her cousins and their friends. She nods. She is happy that she made it to Trenton. It was really a good get-together. All the prayers and food made the party like Thanksgiving. She is amused at the idea that they have done their own Thanksgiving prayer. No need to gorge themselves with more food at Thnksgiving.

"Baltimore Washington International Airport!"

She looks at her watch. She cannot believe that she slept for over two hours. She looks at the shuttle buses waiting to take people to the Airport. Then it occurs to her that she should get off too and go to the Immigration Department in Baltimore before going back to Germantown. That will save her some money. She hurries out of the train. Once inside a taxi, she gives the taxi driver the paper that Tom gave her with the address: Fallon Federal Building, 31 Hopkins Plaza, First Floor. Baltimore.

"You're going to the Immigration Department. I know the place," the driver says.

The Immigration Department is on the first floor of the Plaza. There are many men and women of different races and classes. There are kids, and babies in buggies. Many are casually dressed in jeans, but some are formally dressed in suits. The lines are long, but there are many officers in different booths so the lines move fast. One section operates with numbers. You take a number and sit down until your number is called. Zeb has no idea where she fits in so she goes to the Information Officer.

"Do you have an appointment?"

"No"

"What are you here for?"

"I want advice on how to get a Green Card."

"Go over there." He points.

"How can I help you?" The officer is a young woman in her twenties.

"I'm here on a visitor's visa but I want a work permit to be able to work here."

"What kind of visitor's visa?"

"I don't understand," she looks at her brown eyes.

"What is the category of your visitor's visa? B1 or B2 or what?"

"I believe it is a B2," she says still looking at the brown eyes with blue tinge. Her eyes look kind, she thinks.

"Do you have a PhD?"

"Yes." Zeb smiles, happy that someone could expect her to be college educated.

"Do you have books or international awards?"

"I have books and awards," Zeb smiles.

"Then you can apply for yourself as an alien of extraordinary ability."

"How do I do that?" Zeb's eyes still focus on her face.

"I'll give you the forms," she says. She brings out a folder.

"You have to read the instructions carefully." She gives her the forms.

"They'll ask you for evidence of your awards or books. Anyway, you will see how you fit in and what you need to submit with your forms. After filling the form, you can send it to the address at the bottom. I wish you good luck."

"Thank you very much." Zeb gives her best smile to the brown-eyed officer whom she thinks has the kindest face.

"You're welcome." The officer smiles at her.

Zeb places the forms on her chest and closes her eyes; just for a second. She is so happy. A woman sitting on one of the benches is touched by Zeb's demonstration of joy. As Zeb drags her suitcase near the bench, she greets her.

"Good luck," she says.

Zeb stops and turns to the speaker. The woman smiles and gets up from the bench.

"I'm Esi."

"I'm Zeb."

"I saw you touching the form on your chest. What is it for?"

"Green Card."

"I can relate to that. Let me help you." Esi drags Zeb's suitcase as they talk. Esi is from Ghana but has a lot of experience on immigrant matters. Zeb wants to maintain contact with her.

"Can you visit me sometime or maybe..."

"I work two jobs but I'll make out time." Esi gives Zeb her business card. China Palace Restaurant.

"I'll phone you," Zeb says as she enters a taxi.

Back at the train station, Zeb waits for the next train. She is in a very happy mood. She thinks that this is a wonderful opportunity. She wonders why nobody has told her about it, even Anise that seems to know everything; "many things" she corrects herself smiling. She feels happy that she will be the one to apply for Green Card for herself. She will always treasure her New Jersey trip. As soon as she enters the train, she asks the officer how long it will take to get to Union Station.

"About twenty-five minutes," the officer says.

She looks at her watch. The train might get there before six. She settles on a window seat and looks out of the window at the houses and shrubs that seem to rush past. As the train gets nearer Washington, Zeb's mind diverts to Germantown. She decides that she would shop at the station and buy a present for Wendy. She wonders how Wendy will react when she sees her.

Anise, Alex, and Wendy are at Shady Grove station when Zeb arrives. Anise gives her a bear hug. Wendy throws her hands around both of them. Zeb feels so welcome and great.

"How was the trip?" Alex is driving out of the parking lot.

"She enjoyed herself so much that she forgot to call." Anise looks back from the front passenger seat of the car.

"I called and left a message," Zeb says.

"That was all. No more," Anise says.

"We were busy," Zeb is all smiles.

"Busy having fun."

"Hei Auntie!" Wendy nudges Zeb.

"Hei Wendy! I have a present for you."

As soon as they get back to the house, Zeb goes to the computer room. She brings out the Immigration forms. It has twenty-five pages and requires many original documents. She puts them back in the envelope. She will go to Kinko's and photocopy them so that she can use the copy as a working-copy. When she's done, she will transfer the content of the copy to the original one. First, she will phone her brother to get documents from her schools. She checks her phone messages. Zeb smiles as she listens to Ada's message that she received Zeb's résumé, "Very impressive résumé." Gloria phoned. Zeb phones Gloria to tell her about the forms, but the answering machine comes on so she leaves a message. "This is Zeb. Just to let you know that I'm back from Trenton, New Jersey. Met a great guy. Had a wonderful time. Call me." She checks her email messages. Aracebor has replied her message. "Hi Beautiful, I've been away in Europe and did not have easy access to the Internet, so I didn't read your mail until I came back. I've missed you all this while." He gives her his phone number and asks for hers and the best time to call her. Zeb phones him immediately, wondering how he would sound. She is thrilled and thinks it funny that she should be excited about him in spite of her feelings for Brian.

As soon as they exchange pleasantries, Zeb goes to the question on her mind.

"How is your Cara?"

"I suppose that she is okay. We are divorced."

"Oh, I'm sorry," Zeb says.

"Not your fault."

"It was just my way of expressing concern," she says.

"No hassle. Let's talk about you. How long are you here for?"

When he learns that Zeb is looking for a job, he whistles.

"What's that for?" Zeb says.

"It is tough, but if you do the right things, you'll get there soon," he says.

"What are the right things?"

"We'll talk about them when we meet." Rob wants them to meet because he needs to explain a lot of things to her.

"Is there any chance of your coming down here sometime?" he says.

"Where are you?" Zeb says.

"Chicago"

"I have no plans."

"Will you come if I invite you? It is a beautiful Midwestern city. Some of your people are here. You'll like the place. You have to see as much of America as possible now that you have the chance. And there are lots of opportunities for highly qualified people like you, so, don't say no."

"Well, even if I want to come to Chicago, I would not be able to afford it now because I have no job."

"That should not be a problem. Greyhound and Amtrack-"

"I travel by air." Zeb cuts him short. The fact that she has no job does not mean that if she has to visit a guy, she'll travel cheap.

"I'm sorry. Forgive my thoughtlessness. I thought that you may want to travel by a means that will enable you see the countryside; I remember you like that kind of thing," Aracebor says.

"I like nature, but I always decide what I want." Zeb laughs a little to diffuse the harsh delivery of the sentence. She likes Aracebor, but she wants to know how far he can go in his desire to see her.

"Of course, I often seek advice from those who are knowledgeable," Zeb adds.

"My apologies please," he says.

A call is coming through.

"Please hold. I have another call," she says.

"You can take the call. I'll be in touch with you soon. Just think about my offer," he says.

"Okay," Zeb smiles. It crosses her mind that he may not phone her because he might be offended by the way she rejected his greyhound offer. She shrugs her shoulder as if she does not care, but she cares a lot in spite of Brian.

Alex and Anise are in the kitchen when Zeb joins them. She is still excited about her trip and the Green Card application.

"I stopped over in Baltimore."

"What for?"

"I got some forms from the Immigration. They said that I can apply for Green Card as an alien of extraordinary ability."

Anise rolls her eyes.

"Don't discourage her," Alex says.

Zeb opens her mouth. She wants to take her information back. She closes her mouth. She hates Anise's negative spin on things. Maybe she should begin to keep things to herself.

Alex goes to bed after listening to stories of Zeb's trip. Anise and Zeb stay back on the dining table.

"You really had a great time."

"Yes, the kola nut ceremony was something else," Zeb says.

"I love those ceremonies. Naming. Kola nut. Wedding. All ceremonies. They remind me of good old days and they are a lot of fun." Anise smiles and looks up.

They hear Wendy's footsteps. She goes to her mother, kisses her and leaves. Then she runs back and kisses Zeb.

"Hei Wendy!"

"Hei Auntie!" Wendy runs upstairs.

"You like my child."

"I adore her. She reminds me of my baby; they're almost the same age."

"But she's a girl. You have no girl. Don't you want to have another child, maybe a girl," Anise smiles at Zeb. She is not sure of what Anise is up to with the question.

"I'll like to." Zeb looks at her directly before adding, "That's not my priority though. I need to be able to take care of the ones that God has given me."

"You can do both; take care of them and have another one. Time doesn't wait for women. Let me be frank with you as my friend. You may look very young but your biological clock knows that the time for having babies will end sooner than later."

"I understand but if I'll have another child, it must be planned."

"What's the difference? A baby is a baby no matter how the baby comes."

"I really don't want to discuss this further," Zeb says.

"I'm not yet done. Let's be realistic. Jaja didn't marry you because you were too old for him."

"No, because I wasn't ready to marry him."

Anise smiles. She knows how to pinch Zeb's vulnerability and she goes on with her purpose. "Ok. I guess what I'm trying to say is that an eligible bachelor will not want to marry a woman who is over forty. He'll want *someone* who can have children unless he's old and already has children from another woman. In that case, he won't want children."

"Are you done?"

"Yes," Anise smiles.

"This phase of my life is about what I want. So this matter is closed," Zeb does not smile.

"The problem with you is that you're stubborn," Anise says.

"Thanks. That's my business."

"Our pastor is very nice." Anise is amused by Zeb's reaction. She hides her smile by looking down.

"Pastors always look nice," Zeb says and continues to explain what she means. "After all they are the centre of the stage and the one that the congregation looks up to."

"Just give this one a chance." Anise looks at Zeb and waits for her reply.

"Please respect my emotions as a friend." Zeb glares at Anise and keeps silent. It sounds so crude asking her to marry someone that she does not know, just because he is a pastor. She thinks it is disrespectful and annoying, but does not want to let Anise spoil her happy mood. She tries to divert her mind to the idea of filling the immigration forms and applying for a Green Card on her own merit. She smiles.

"What's on your mind? What are you smiling at?" Anise is confused by Zeb's change of mood.

"Nothing."

"I like to see you happy and I want you to continue to be happy. Let's talk about marriage. I'm not telling you to marry anybody. I just want you to know reality not romance; romance is in novels only." Anise says.

Zeb laughs. She is loud. She finds it funny that Anise thinks that she doesn't know the reality of married life.

"Ok my friend, go on," she stops laughing.

"When you get a job, taxes will be very high because you're single. Marriage is very important because you will get tax break as a married couple. Marriage will give you legal rights. Marriage will bind the two of you. You'll do everything together. Pay your bills, file taxes, and do insurance and other things together. The church is all about family. If you are single, you can feel like a misfit in a church," Anise opens the fridge.

"Then I will stop going to church," Zeb says.

"Where else can you go to as a foreigner?" Anise opens a can of Budweiser.

"Join clubs," Zeb says.

"Who will recommend you? Church is the only place that you can walk in—."

"And be accepted," Zeb adds.

"No. Not all churches. Some do not allow foreigners. A friend of mine in North Carolina. Her name is Ann. Her husband got a job there so they moved. They went to this church on Sunday. Nobody sat near them. They felt so odd because people would not sit near them or even shake hands with them when it was time to exchange greetings."

"Sometimes people just complain about other people without making the effort. Why didn't they go and sit near the Americans or shake their hands? Why did they have to wait?" Zeb says.

"Let me tell you something," Anise goes back to the table and continues talking from there.

"In my church, it can't happen. Once you are a visitor or you are new, there are people who will welcome you. At a point in the service, our good pastor will ask all new people and visitors to stand and introduce themselves. We'll get to know them and chat with them after service," Anise says.

"Well, all churches are not like yours." Zeb does not want to talk about Anise's church and hear about her pastor. She suspects that it is Anise's way of bringing up an issue that irritates her. She talks about Anise's friend in North Carolina.

"I still think that your friend should have made the first move," Zeb says.

Anise insists, "She did. After service, the priest stood by the door and shook hands with everybody. She and her husband went for his handshake."

"Don't tell me that the priest refused to shake their hands because I won't believe you."

"He shook their hands, but he told them not to come to his church again because the parishioners would not like it. He referred them to another Catholic Church in the city."

"This happened in a Catholic church?" Zeb says.

"The Catholic Church in this country is different from the one back home in Nigeria," Anise says.

"You won't see many African Americans in Catholic churches here," Anise adds.

Zeb is silent. She thinks about the churches that she has been to in America and believes that Anise is exaggerating.

"Things are changing though, especially with the growth of the Hispanic population. They have many Catholics," Anise says.

26

The Way Love Goes

Zeb is no longer interested in chatting with Anise. She is eager to go to the computer room to fill the forms. She pushes her chair to get up. Anise pushes hers too.

"Yeah, let's go to the living room and watch the TV," Anise gets up.

It is obvious to Zeb that Anise still wants to talk. Anise might have missed their conversations when Zeb was in New Jersey and probably had space to rethink her attitude towards Zeb. Zeb feels it is better to stay and chat with her friend and deal with the forms later. Once in the living room, Anise stretches out on the sofa. The television is on Disney channel where Wendy left it. Anise does not change the channel but continues her argument about the issue of churches and marriage.

"Anyway, whatever church you go to, it is better for you to go there with your husband just as you do other things with him," Anise says. Zeb sits on the couch adjacent to the sofa. She has lost interest in the issue, but feels compelled to keep the conversation going.

"What about the freedom to choose not to go to church together or file taxes together for that matter?"

Anise laughs. She is loud.

After laughing, Anise gets up from the sofa. She turns towards Zeb, "In this country, a lot of things tie you two together even if you don't want it. You don't hang out a lot with other women as they do back home, no plaiting hair sessions, no festivals, no market outings, no social meetings, no dance sessions, no moonlight gossip, and no story sessions. Here, the older women may play bingo but for most of us, you stick with your husband all the way. He is your life. So it is difficult for him to leave you."

"But they still leave," Zeb says. Anise looks up in the direction of the bedrooms. She gets up and walks to the staircase that leads upstairs.

"Alex." She walks to the steps and calls again. Alex does not answer. She smiles and climbs down the stairs.

Satisfied that the door to their bedroom is closed and her husband cannot hear her, Anise says, "Yeah, if he leaves, he'll lose the house, custody of Wendy and many other things. It's different at home where a woman leaves the man and also leaves the house because it is the man's house. She only takes her dowry and she'll be lucky if items of the dowry are still in good condition."

"Don't generalise. Remember Adaka, Ada's ex-boyfriend? He was receiving alimony from his ex-wife," Zeb says.

"That's probably because his ex-wife earned a lot more than him. In majority of the cases, the husband earns a lot more than the wife does. Some of the wives do not even earn money but they get the house and the children. I tell you my sister; this place is good for women. The man loses all. You take all."

"So if I marry the bus driver or one of the other men that you push me to, I'll pay them alimony when we divorce?"

Anise is silent. She stands by the television. She is not comfortable with Zeb's question. She picks the remote control and changes the channel, but Zeb is not letting her distract her attention.

"And you never told me," Zeb says without looking at the television. Anise changes from one channel to the other and finally settles on Bill Crosby show.

"Anise I'm asking you a question."

"You may not make more money than a bus driver," Anise is still beside the television.

"You have to think positive, my friend. We'll always be there to help you out." Anise does not go back to the sofa. She leans on the wall by the television. Zeb thinks that Anise is condescending by saying that she will look after her if she marries a bus driver. She is irritated but does not blame Anise for the attitude. She blames herself. She has put herself in the situation by living in their house all these months. It is time to move out and be her own woman in her own place where nobody will try to organise her personal life.

Anise feels that she is losing Zeb's attention. She begins to emphasise how Nigerian women get a bad deal at divorce.

"America is good. In Nigeria, the woman leaves the house and takes only her dowry, the items that are still in good shape." Anise says again.

"That's because the women here don't have dowry to take?" Zeb says. Her voice is harsh.

"What's the matter?" Anise says.

"How can it be right to kick a man out of his ancestral home?" Zeb looks directly at Anise who does not answer the question.

"Wow! Here, we don't live in men's ancestral homes. A man loses the property not his ancestors. The woman gets all!" There is a glint in Anise's eyes.

"I get it. In Nigeria, the woman won't get all. So, it is better in America where the woman takes all? That's not fair. Nobody should take all." Zeb shakes her head.

"And that's probably why women stick with their marriages at home even when the marriage is no longer happy. Because they can't take all," Anise says.

"It isn't. It's because of their children, not the house, not the man. Just children," Zeb says.

"I see. You might be right. They stay for as long as it takes them to plan to leave with their children, just as you did."

"I didn't leave with my kids."

The telephone rings. Anise picks it, hands it to Zeb and goes to the bathroom.

Gloria says, "I have flu and I'm drowsy and my throat hurts. I want to hear all about your visit when I am better. But who is this guy that you met?"

"Brian."

"American?"

"No. Nigerian," Zeb says.

"Does he have Green Card?"

"No."

"Dump him before your emotions get in the way. Do you hear me?" Gloria's voice is hoarse.

"Dump him. Period."

Zeb notes that Gloria and Anise say 'period' when they think that they know it all. Just because they have been in America for a long time, they think that they know more than everybody and want to dictate her life. She wonders what they mean by period. It is something like *quad erat demonstratum*, which they used to say in high school when they used a mathematical theory to prove a point. But her situation is not exact science. It is life with flesh, blood, and emotion. These are not like simple mathematical equations. Gloria has no right to tell her to dump Brian. She feels that her jobless situation has made her vulnerable. It has put her in a situation where they tell her who to love and who not to love. She cannot believe that Gloria will tell her to dump a man who she does not know anything about. She is upset when Anise comes out of the bathroom.

"Who called?"

"Gloria. She has flu so we didn't talk"

"You look angry. What did she tell you?"

"Nothing. She has flu and her voice is bad."

"Whatever," Anise says.

"Okay. I told her about this guy that I met."

"Oh yeah? You didn't tell me."

Zeb tells Anise about Brian, how they met, danced, chatted, visited and how he met her at the train station.

"So you really like this doctor whose background you don't know?"

"Yes, I like him. His name is Brian."

"Don't put your hope on him," Anise says.

"Even if he cares a lot for you," Anise adds.

"Well, don't judge him; you don't know him," Zeb suspects that Anise has another reason for not wanting her to be excited about Brian. It's true that she knows very little about Brian but her cousins know about him. All the men that Anise wants her to date are complete strangers. Bus driver, pastor, and a man suffering from his wife's rejection of him are all unknown to her, yet Anise wants her to believe that she is worried about

Brian's background and not that of complete strangers. It just doesn't add up.

"Are you thinking about the doctor?" Anise asks.

"Yes."

"Thinking of wedding bells and ceremonies?" Anise smiles.

"I'm not hooked on ceremonies like you," Zeb says. Her voice is harsh.

"Ceremonies are great. After all you enjoyed the kola nut ceremony in New Jersey. Just have an open mind. Don't shut off other men because of the doctor."

"His name is Brian!" Anise's refusal to call his name annoys Zeb..

"Whatever."

27

Moving On

It is Saturday morning. Zeb goes downstairs and sees that the Esomonus have left. She goes to the garage and brings the vacuum cleaner. She cleans the computer room and the hallway. Then she cleans the living room and kitchen. She tries to focus on the cleaning even though her mind occasionally drifts to Brian. She writes a letter to her cousin in Nigera telling him to send her some documents that will support the new immigration forms. She also writes a letter to Columbia University for her transcript. She is having breakfast when the phone rings.

It is Aracebor. Zeb tells him about the forms she got from Baltimore. He likes the idea and says that he has another proposal. Zeb asks him whether it is a marriage proposal.

"How did you know?"

"That's what everybody tells me these days."

Aracebor explains. "It's the easy way. I know how it works. You can pay somebody to do it for you or get a friend to do it as a favour. Which one do you like?"

"What are involved in each arrangement?" Zeb says.

"You discuss it with the person in question and agree on something."

"How will I make sure that he will keep his side of the bargain?"

"There is some kind of gamble there, but like every business it has its own risk factor," he says.

"I don't want to gamble with my life. I can gamble with money or business, but certainly not my life," Zeb says.

"Don't take it too badly. It works for some people."

"Did it work for your marriage?" Zeb asks recalling that she did not see a lot of demonstration of love between him and Cara when they met in London. Rob is silent.

He is trying to decide whether this is a good time to come clean with Zeb. He has a lot to tell her and he does not know where to begin and what her reaction will be. He does not want to scare her or lose contact with her again.

"I'll tell you about it when you come to Chicago," he says finally. Zeb nods. She suspects that he might have married Cara because of a Green Card. Small world.

"When do you want to come?" he says.

"I haven't made up my mind."

"It takes you pretty long to make up your mind."

"Worse than that, I may not make up my mind at all," Zeb laughs. She finds it easy to talk with him.

"You're really complex."

"Thank you," Zeb says guessing that it's not a compliment. She's just happy about her decisions.

"Listen up. Make up your mind and let me know. I want to see you."

Zeb laughs; she feels that the man has a crush on her and she feels good.

Rob does not have a crush on her. He feels deeply for her and finds it strange because he barely knows her. The feeling started the first time he saw her in London. He was in London for a short vacation with Cara. The vacation was Cara's gift to Rob for helping her at a time she was vulnerable and facing the threat of deportation from the United States. She knew that her case was complicated and this affected her usual ebullient personality that endeared her to colleagues at HealthMaster. She was a Care Co-ordinator in a small business that relied on immigrant workers. One of the traits that endeared her to Rob was that she treated everybody equally, so when he heard about her imminent deportation, he went to sympathise with her. It was during the discussion that he learnt about Green Card marriage. While Immigration officers were deciding on whether to send Cara to Britain from where she immigrated to the US or to Albania whose passport she carried alhough she kept insisting that she was Italian, she got married to Rob. The terms of the marriage were clear. Rob agreed to an open marriage. He was the one that offered to help free, but gladly accepted the huge sum of money when Cara insisted that it would make her more comfortable in the arrangement.

Grandmother-Emma raised Rob and his brother, Cedric, to work hard and achieve economic success. He started work at an early age and learnt how to invest his money. He was lucky that his brother, Cedric, was an investment banker and always gave him good ideas about the market. He continued to hold jobs as waiter and janitor while he was in college in Baltimore and invest almost all his earning because he had merit scholarships. In spite of the wealth he had amassed over the years, he maintained a simple lifestyle. He had almost completed his PhD programme except for the required work experience in a health facility. The Chair of his committee helped him get a job at HealthMaster in Chicago where he met Cara. As soon as she got the Green Card, he resigned from the job and took another one at Amoco Company while waiting for re-admission to finish his studies.

Rob was eager to get back to his life as a bachelor. He never imagined that getting into that kind of marriage contract would disrupt his life the way it did. Although he was free to date women, it was not the same because the girls always regarded him as a married man when in fact he was practically and emotionally single. He could not freely explain his marriage situation to people. Another complication was the name Aracebor that he and Cara took up in their restricted marital social circles. They figured that the fake marriage required a fake name that would be discarded when the marriage ended. They made up Aracebor by combining letters in their names.

He remembers his first meeting with Zeb as if it happened yesterday. He recorded it in his journal and delights in reading it especially when Zeb was in Nigeria and he thought he had lost her forever. He is lucky to have found her again and happy that he is no longer married and it looks like she is not married either. One thing he wants to straighten out is the issue of name. He needs to explain his marriage and divorce and tell her his real name. Zeb's mention of Green Card marriage was an opening but he feels that the explanation will be better when she visits him in Chicago. He smiles at the idea of seeing her again and hopes to take her to the popular Amaco parties. What he does not know is that the company will soon lay off up to thirty percent of workers and that he will be one of them.

Zeb is expecting Esi, the Ghanaian woman she met at the immigration office. She hopes to finish cleaning before her arrival. She has not received the long-awaited phone call from Brian. The door bell rings. Zeb opens the door. Esi gives her a hug. One of the things that helped Esi during her years of quest for the Green Card was the way some people related to her as a person. Warm hugs meant a lot to her. They made her feel at home.

"Wow! This is a big hall," Esi says. Zeb is about to take her upstairs to the living room, but Esi goes straight to the family room on the ground level.

"What room is that?" Esi gestures towards the room beside the computer room.

"It's an extra room for visitors."

Zeb invites her to the living room upstairs. Esi does not sit down immediately. She walks around the spacious living room, looking at the pictures.

"This house is really big. How many rooms?" Esi says.

"Three bedrooms upstairs."

"You have a room to yourself?" Esi turns her gaze from the mask on the wall to Zeb sitting opposite the television.

"I have a room and a bathroom. I use the computer room downstairs as my office."

"You're comfortable, so why do you want to move? Is it too expensive?" Esi says.

"I don't pay money."

"Are they your relations?"

"No, but the woman is my very good friend."

Esi looks at the mask again and says, "A married woman living with her husband and a single woman sounds like fun but it can lead to jealousy and trouble."

"Are you talking from experience?"

"Yes, but all are not personal. Before I came here I was the leader of a women's association and through that got to know a lot about what happened in marriages outside mine," Esi says looking at Zeb. She notes that Zeb frowns. Zeb does not know whether she can confide in Esi and tell her the problems she had with Anise. Esi knows that having no job and green card creates a feeling of helplessness and being under someone adds to the feeling.

"Are you really comfortable?"

Zeb nods her head. Esi notes that Zeb noded too quickly and is now looking down, which does not communicate confidence in her nod. She looks at Zeb for a while. Something in Zeb connects with her. She sits beside Zeb.

"My husband left me and the children six years ago," Esi says.

"I'm sorry. Does he pay alimony?" Zeb says.

"No. I don't mean that we're divorced. It was physical separation at that time. He travelled to our country for his father's burial, but they refused to renew his visa, so he could not return to join us here." Esi sees that the frown on Zebs face deepens. Zeb can relate to the situation of Esi's husband.

"Is your father living?" Esi asks.

"No, and I can relate to someone who wants to attend his father's funeral," Zeb says.

"I understand the need to bury the dead, but in his case, our Green Card interview was pending and all of us in the family were in his application. He had people at home who would have given his father a befitting burial. I told him not to travel, but he still left. He said he would be back within a week, but they did not give him visa to return to the United States. That was how I got stuck here with my children. I had to abandon my education at Montgomery Community College in order to fend for my kids." Esi is surprised at how she easily shares her story with someone she barely knows. She trusts her instinct that Zeb is reliable.

"It must have been hard."

"It was terrible. I began to look for a job. Our two kids dropped out of high school and began to look for jobs." Esi frowns. It is deep.

Esi stands up to control herself. She goes to the bathroom, takes some tissue and blows her nose. From the door of the bathroom, she talks to Zeb.

"My kids dropped out of school. Their mates at home in Ghana were doing so well. I thought it was a curse for me to have come to America." Esi leans on the door of the bathroom.

"Come and sit down," Zeb says.

"I hoped that things would get better but when I lost my children, I almost gave up. When you can't provide the basic needs of life for your kids, it means you can't parent them. My kids began to parent themselves. I tried to control them; they resisted in a way they would never have dared to do, if things had been normal and I was the provider. If I had a good job as I have now, they would have respected me more and listened to me. I really missed my husband and wished that he was with us so that he could discipline them." Esi goes back for more tissue. Zeb is touched by her honesty in sharing her story and in being vulnerable in front of her.

Zeb goes to the bathroom door and takes Esi by the hand. She leads Esi to a chair holding her hand. Her eyes water as she thinks about her sons and she wipes her eyes.

"Don't do that," Esi says, "I don't want to upset you. Things are ok now or almost ok, but it still hurts," Esi wipes her tears.

"You didn't upset me." Zeb says. "I was already upset. I weep for myself, for you, and for all of us who left our countries. I also have sons in Nigeria. Two live with my ex-husband and my baby lives with my mother."

"It's good that they are in your country. It is a different culture over there where children respect elders whether they have money or not. Here, it's all about what you can provide and if you discipline the children, they will say you are abusing them. I was afraid of upsetting them and getting the government to take them from me." Esi twists her mouth, and wrenches her hands at the same time, with her eyes focused ahead. Finally she breathes in deeply. She exhales loudly.

"God allowed it," Esi sighs.

"So God allows qualified people to be without jobs? God allows honest people to get into abominable marriages because of a Green Card?" Zeb says.

"So they've already told you about marriage for a Green Card? Many people here advised me to do it."

"You? You were married. It wasn't his fault that he didn't return. Moreover, he too might have been suffering because of the separation."

"You're right. He was suffering, but that didn't solve my problem or the children's problems. I wasn't thinking of my emotions. Emotions couldn't pay the bills at the end of the month, and couldn't give me the Green Card that would enable me pay the bills. My Attorney told me that I could divorce him on the basis of abandonment."

"He didn't abandon you."

"Legally, he abandoned me and abandoned his responsibilities. But I didn't take that option. People in Ghana would not have understood it and it would have destroyed the little respect that remained in my family."

"This is not easy," Zeb says.

"Life was very tough for the kids and me. But God gave me a way to reclaim my kids."

"What?"

"I registered a Day Care Centre. I was allowed ten kids. I regained my sanity through the Centre, and also regained my respect as a mother. My sons loved the kids and we did the work together. I applied for Green

Card when I expanded the school. The school was such a blessing for my family."

As she speaks, Zeb begins to see Esi's face in a new light. She shifts in order to have a better view of Esi's face. She has lovely dreamy eyes that look like large ocean clamps, straight nose and moonlike mouth that gives her face a calm look. Zeb classifies her colour as the type called "yellow' in Lagos. Her skin is like a ripe *utu*. She is chubby like a ripe paw-paw. Zeb concludes that she is beautiful and probably in her late thirties."

"How old are you?"

"I'm thirty-eight. And you?"

"I want you to guess," Zeb says. Esi looks closely at her eyes. She feels there is something like burning fire inside Zeb's soul. She looks at her face and fingers. She feels that Zeb's outer face hides something going on inside. The face is very smooth and her hands have no wrinkles.

"You look very young. I would have said maybe twenty, but you have degrees and they don't do those in kindergarten. Maybe late twenties."

"I look that old?" Zeb says.

"Sorry. I can't really tell."

"I'm older than you."

"Really?"

"Yes."

"You have to tell me the cosmetics that you use. The first time I saw you I thought I was old enough to be your mother and I felt motherly towards you as you dragged your bag alone and hugged the forms."

"Where I come from, they often refer to females as mothers regardless of age."

"We do that in Ghana too. So we can both be mothers to each other."

"We're already doing so."

"Do you know that while I was going through all that suffering with my children, who were troublesome teenagers, my husband kept a woman in Ghana? He kept her for six years. I have gallons of acid in my soul. I hate my husband for abandoning me. I also hate him for having a girlfriend. I hate America for not allowing him to come back here. Why should they refuse a man visa to come and be there for his family?" Esi is worked-up again so she begins to look at the pictures on the wall again trying to control herself. She turns to Zeb.

"I hate myself for getting in the mess," Esi says.

Zeb spreads her arms. Esi allows her to hold her in her arms. Both of them help each other, shoulder-to-shoulder, and head on each other's shoulder. Esi breathes heavily.

"I'm sorry to get you fired up," Zeb says.

"You also have something."

"I do, but mine is too deep."

"It helps to talk about it. A counsellor helped me. That's why I now have a boyfriend."

"Where are your children?"

"The first one went back to Ghana and the other one is here working in a packing company."

"Let me offer you something to drink."

"No, let's go out. My boyfriend is away this weekend and I'm not working, so I have all the time. Let's go shopping. Come and visit me."

Zeb leaves a note for Anise and takes off with Esi.

28

Love-Match

Zeb wakes up with tears flowing from her eyes. She can't get off the bed. Her legs hurt. She feels very tired. She pulls the blanket and covers herself, but can't sleep. Her head aches.

"Zeb." Zeb hears Anise call her, but she's too weak to answer the call. The door opens. Anise pulls the blanket off.

"Oh, it's cold." Zeb snatches the blanket from her.

"What's wrong?" Anise feels Zeb's head and cheeks, and talks at the same time.

"You are crying?" Anise says.

"Oh-o! You are sick," Anise says.

Anise gives Zeb two tablets of Tylenol. She tells her to get out of bed and shake it off.

"Just come and have Thanksgiving dinner with us," Anise says.

"And meet our Pastor. We've told him about you and he wants to meet you," Anise says.

"I feel awful. I am not in the mood for meeting anybody," Zeb says.

"Just come. We expect a Nigerian couple. They phoned to say that they are on their way. Come down and meet them. It's Thanksgiving. You need to eat. You can go back to bed if you can't stay."

Zeb gets out of bed. Anise is gorgeous in a green wrapper and yellowish-brown blouse.

"You look great." Zeb smiles at her.

"It is Thanksgiving."

"Happy Thanksgiving," Zeb says.

"Thank you. Happy Thanksgiving."

"Thanks for caring," Zeb says.

"Don't be silly. What are friends for?"

"You are not just a friend. You are a sister to me." Zeb puts her hand on her face like she's wiping it, but she is actually covering it to prevent Anise from seeing how she juts her mouth trying to suppress what she did not say about Anise's antagonism.

"Thanks."

"When you are not in a bad mood," Zeb add mischievously,

"Your mouth is not ill! Come on and eat." Anise opens the door.

"Let us stand up and praise the Almighty God for this table that is full of His bounties." Pastor Abel says. Zeb feels her legs weaken at the thought of standing up.

"Hey Pastor!" Wendy springs up.

"Hush Sweetheart. We want to pray."

"Hey Mom!"

"God bless you, dear child. God loves children," Abel says.

Wendy sticks out all her fingers and begins to count. She wants to show the pastor that she is not a child.

"You are a big girl," Alex says.

"Hey Daddy!"

"Yes, you are a big girl, but we are all children of God. Daddy is a child of God. Mummy is a child of God. Auntie is a child of God. I am a child of God," Anise says.

"Pastor?" Wendy says.

"Yes. Pastor is also a child of God. Please Pastor, go on with the prayer," Anise says.

"Everybody stand." Pastor looks at Zeb across the table. Zeb looks back at him. Standing beside Abel, Anise smiles and winks at Zeb. Zeb ignores the gesture and remains seated. Alex holds Zeb's arm and helps her up. Zeb hesitates, but out of respect for Alex and Anise, she gets up.

"Praise God. Everybody say Alleluia!" Abel begins a long prayer in a loud voice, almost as loud as he is big, but it thins out quickly and comes alive again. His breathing is audible too, but unlike his voice, it has a steady rhythm.

Abel directs his gaze at the ceiling while he prays. Zeb has a good opportunity to observe him as he looks up. He is about six feet four and very beefy. His tummy is as if he would give birth to triplets. No wonder his shirt did not button down. The chest area is buttoned but the flabby area defies the buttons and bulges out of the shirt. His breathing is loud.

"It is a very bad flu that is going on at this time. You'll be alright." Pastor Abel sits down. Zeb does not thank him. She drinks water and watches Abel and his plate. He puts three slices of turkey on his plate. He grins and leaves a smile on his face.

"One for the Father, the Son, and the Holy Spirit." He puts three baked potatoes on his plate. Alex passes the bowl of mashed potatoes to Abel. He scoops a large portion, with a grin on his face, and puts it on top of the slices of turkey. He puts stuffing, green peas, and corn on his plate.

Zeb makes a face. It may look like she is making the face because she is feeling pain from her flu, but actually, she is disgusted. She wonders why Abel needs to pile up his plate. She would like to tell him that a second helping is allowed, but she knows that Anise would be hurt. Zeb drinks a little water. Abel takes more stuffing and pours cranberry gravy over everything on his plate. Zeb looks away.

"You like the stuffing?" Alex smiles at the pastor.

"Oh yes. It is the best dish on the table." Abel's voice is loud and hoarse as if he has lost his voice to cough.

"Do you have cough," Zeb says. Anise glares at her.

"No. The flu has not come my way and I'll not let it come. You have to come for prayers. I'll banish the spirit of flu from your body," Abel says. Everybody is silent. Even Anise does not say anything.

"I don't mean it in a bad way," Abel says. Zeb doubts that his congregation can tolerate the sound of his voice. He puts a little more stuffing on his plate. Zeb suspects that she is making him nervous.

"We have another stuffed bird, if you want more." Zeb exposes her teeth in his direction. Alex laughs.

"He likes my cooking. Right Pastor?" Anise says.

"Thank you. I miss real home cooked food," Abel says.

"But that will soon change, Pastor." Anise smiles at him first, and then looks at Zeb. Zeb rolls her eyes.

"Yaa Yaa." Abel laughs. It sounds like he has sore throat. Zeb rolls her eyes again.

"Am I missing something?" Alex looks at Abel. Anise giggles. Alex looks at her. Zeb looks at Alex. Anise pushes her chair with her buttocks.

"I'll bring the other turkey." Anise stands up.

"Don't worry honey. I'll do the favour when we are done with this one," Alex says.

Anise does not sit. She refills Abel's glass.

"There are only five of us at table. One turkey is enough," Zeb says.

"We're five at table but only four are eating. You haven't eaten anything," Alex says.

"That's why I want to pray for her. She needs deliverance from the spirit of sickness."

"Did you pray against the spirit that caused your sore throat?" Zeb says across the table.

"Zeb!" Anise says.

"What?"

"That's a good question," Abel says and goes on to explain.

"I don't have sore throat. My voice is just as God made it. It has special loud and quiet parts that reach my flock and God's ears. Ordinary people don't have it." Abel shovels food into his mouth.

Zeb drinks more water and looks at Abel and his plate. She is disgusted. She is happy that she has no appetite because she would have thrown up on seeing Abel's plate of food that looks like filth. A verse runs through her mind.

PYRAMID TRASH

You yucky pile of stuff and sauce,

Fake copy of high rise, pyramid trash,

Mountain man with wind-starved voice:

You are no pyramid, just pyramid trash!

"Do you want to go to bed?" Anise breaks into Zeb's thought about the mountain man. Zeb sees Anise's eyes shooting straight at her. She can't stand the fire in those eyes. She pushes her chair immediately.

"If you don't mind, I'll like to lie down." Zeb stands up. She has no intention of going to bed. She makes her way down the stairs to the computer room.

29

Thanksgiving Blues

Zeb sits in front of the computer, opens the drawer and brings out the forms, but she does not look at them. She is thinking. She takes stock of her experience. She is clear about where she came from and where she is going. She is a bit unsure about how to get there. She thinks about various options. She feels weak and wants to catch her breath before filling the forms. She leans on the computer desk and supports her jaw with her hands. She cannot understand why anybody who calls herself her friend will bring a man like Abel to marry her. She recalls making it clear to Anise that she was not interested in Green Card marriage and that she would not consider Pastor Abel. She is irritated that Anise went ahead with her plan. The doorbell rings. She raises her head from the desk. It rings a second time. She saves her document and goes to open the door. At the same time, Alex gets up from the dinner table. He is on his way down the steps when Zeb steps out of the computer room next to the front door.

Zeb opens the door as Alex comes down and takes Franca's coat. He introduces Zeb to the couple, Ayo and Franca.

"I've heard a lot about you." Franca hugs Zeb.

"Me too. Nice things," Ayo shakes Zeb's hands.

"We're very sorry to be late," Franca says.

"We had an encounter with the city police," Ayo says.

"They pulled us over," Franca says.

"Were you driving the new Mercedes?" Alex says.

"Yes, after all, this is a great day."

"Thanksgiving day."

"What's wrong with a new Mercedes?" Zeb says.

"It's a five hundred," Alex says.

"I don't get it," Zeb says.

"A black man driving such a car in this city?" Alex says.

"It raises suspicions," Franca says.

"It makes you look like an uppity black," Ayo says.

"Or a thief or someone doing illicit business."

Franca begins to explain how she made the money for purchasing the mercedez. "I did three jobs in three different nursing homes to save money for that car. I've watched people drive big cars all my life and I have no apologies for buying one."

"She was maid in a family that had three Mercedes Benz cars." Ayo gives his coat to Alex.

"Do you have to explain how you work hard and why you spend your money on what you like?" Zeb says.

"Yes, we have to explain it because we're not expected to have such as expensive car. As soon as the police stopped me, I knew that he wanted to check whether it was our car," Ayo says.

"Was that really why he stopped you?" Zeb says.

"He said that I did more than forty at a forty max area, but I'm very sure that I slowed down-."

"He slowed down. There was no way you could speed at that ramp," Franca says.

"Did he give you a ticket?"

"Of course. That was why Franca insisted that we go back to bring the old car."

"Yes, because I wanted to relax. I planned to enjoy myself here today. I have not seen you people for a long time and I didn't want to come here and worry about whether the police would stop us on our way back or send Ayo to jail. One ticket is enough for today," Franca says.

"So you don't relax in your dream car," Zeb says.

"Not that we don't relax. We use it to go to church on Sundays. The church is in our neighbourhood. The police there know us and know that we do honest work," Franca says.

As Zeb and Franca talk, Ayo talks with Alex. He apologises again for being late to dinner. "I phoned you, it went straight to the voice mail. I left a message."

"Then the old car had problems and this is the worst day to have car problems" Franca says to Zeb.

"Did you get it fixed?"

"Not on Thanksgiving day. It's still there to be picked up by triple A," Franca says.

As they go upstairs, the couple narrates the story of their ordeal. When one tire went down, they brought out the spare tire only to discover that it was down also. They waited for help for some time. A police officer came to their rescue.

"The police helped us," Ayo says.

"Some of them don't care about the colour of your skin," Franca says.

Zeb finds the couple entertaining so she goes back to the dining room with them. Alex motions Franca and Ayo to sit at the end of the table. Alex goes to the kitchen to bring the second turkey. Zeb's former place at table is the only empty seat. It is opposite Pastor Abel. Zeb sits. She notes that the pastor has finished the food on his plate and is eating portions of pumpkin pie.

"Enjoying your meal?" The mockery in Zeb's voice is not lost on the pastor.

"By the special grace of the Almighty." Abel does not appear to be ruffled by Zeb's sarcasm.

"Don't you know Pastor Abel?" Alex brings the second turkey and introduces the couple to Abel. Ayo tells Abel about their encounter with the police.

"Where is Anise?" Franca says.

"She's in the bathroom with Wendy. She'll soon be here." Alex puts the turkey on the table.

"What's this turkey for?" Franca says.

"You know your friend. She likes to cook as if she is feeding a crowd."

"We'll eat from this one, no need to cut that one yet," Franca points at the other turkey on the table.

Zeb puts some potatoes and turkey on her plate.

"You want to eat now?" Alex asks.

"Yes."

"Praise be to God," Abel says.

"Amen." Anise says from the steps without knowing what he is praising God for. Zeb rolls her eyes. As Anise turns from the steps, she can see Zeb through the open living room door that connects to the dining room. She is not happy about the way Zeb disrespects her visitor and pastor of her church. Anise likes to be in control of the house and she will let Zeb know that in her own way. Franca gets up from her chair to give Anise a hug. She begins to narrate their ordeal.

Zeb phones Gloria. She tells her about the day and how the police gave Ayo and Franca a ticket because of their new Mercedes 500.

"Don't believe everything people tell you. In America, you must obey the law. If you're driving sixty and all of a sudden the sign says fifty-five, you must obey. I'm not saying that racial profiling is not there but I just don't want you to think about it. Let's talk about something else."

Zeb knows that Gloria will want to talk about her usual subject of discussion which is Green Card, but she is sick and tired of hearing Gloria urge her to marry an American citizen.

"You can divorce him later if you don't like him." Gloria once told her. Zeb does not tell Gloria about Pastor Abel because she may tell her to give him a chance just because of a Green Card. Instead, she brings up the issue that is dear to her heart.

She tells Gloria that she does not like the way she judged Brian unfairly just because he is not an American.

"I didn't mean to hurt your feelings. I just want what is good for you."

"You think that you know what is good for me more than I do?"

"Peace. The guy sounds nice, but he can't help you with a Green Card. That's just my concern," Gloria says.

"The guy's name is Brian and I like him."

"You don't have that luxury yet. You need to like those who will help you."

"This is gross," Zeb says.

"The guy can't marry you anyway."

"Did I say that I'll marry him?"

"Good. Don't think of marriage with anybody who can't help you. He will find an American citizen who will give him a Green Card."

"How do you know?" Zeb says.

"I know about them. Men are sharp like razor. That's why I like Mrs. Fortney. She beat them at their game."

"I don't want to talk about her." Zeb does not want to talk about their former classmate who is living in a bigamous situation with an American.

"You don't have to talk about her, just remember her. She's happy now. She has a job and goes to Nigeria whenever she wants to see her family."

Zeb is silent. Her mind goes to her lost opportunity and she thinks that Gloria is referring to it. She feels bad.

"Are you there?"

"Yeah." Zeb's voice is weak..

"This is what we call 'though love' in America. I do this to you because I love you. You may not like it now, but with time, you'll thank me for it," Gloria says.

"I have to go."

"I'll call you next time. I love you," Gloria says.

"You are too angry to tell me to go to hell." Gloria laughs.

"Bye Gloria." Zeb's voice is still weak.

Zeb is in her room when Anise pushes open the door, "Zeb, I took you into my house as an equal or maybe you see me as someone who is inferior to you because of your degrees. Let me tell you something. You live in my house and you must respect my husband and me. Under no circumstances should you ever be rude to my visitor whether you like the person or not." She bangs the door without giving Zeb the opportunity to speak. Zeb goes after her, but on opening her door, Anise bangs their bedroom door. Zeb knocks. She knocks a second time. Anise opens the door.

"Do not disturb me and my husband." Anise shuts the door. Zeb goes back to her room.

Zeb feels that many things are against her now. She does not have anybody to tell about her revulsion for Abel. Not Gloria. Not Anise. She has no one to complain to about Gloria. She has no one to complain to about Anise. These are the only two friends that she has in America. She wonders whether something is wrong with her, since she is the one having issues with them. Things never used to be like this in the past when she was in Nigeria. She got on very well with her friends and they did not criticise her ways. The new situation is getting to her. The pursuit of green card has changed everything. Now Anise is becoming very nasty. On top of all these, Brian has not phoned her for some time now.

She believes that Brian's situation makes it difficult for him to phone her. She checks her watch. It is eleven at night. She knows that he must be at work. Poor man. She feels a connection with Brian because of their immigrant situation. She kneels down to say her night prayers before going to bed. "Thank you that I feel much better from the flu. I don't have health insurance, so you are my healer Lord. Please God, intervene in my friendship with my hostess and please get Brian to phone me." Her head flops on the bed. She feels hot and needs some fresh air. She goes to the window. She feels weak. Her legs ache. She is too weak to open the window. She parts the curtains and looks at the trees. She looks out for the birds but sees none. She goes back to bed, but her mind is not at rest. She thinks about an earlier conversation with Anise about Abel.

"Pastor Abel is an opportunity with double blessing," Anise has said. Zeb has rolled her eyes. She was not interested in knowing the blessing, but her friend volunteered the information.

"For one thing, churches can still help their workers to get work permit," Anise said.

"Why didn't you tell me all along? You kept telling me that the only way to a Green Card is through marriage," Zeb said.

"I said that it is the surest way and it is, because it is automatic. Any church can apply and you may or may not get it. Pastor Abel can apply for you if you work in his church, but there is no vacancy except one."

"Which one?" Zeb was interested.

"The only vacancy is that of being the first lady of the church. Double blessing."

Zeb agrees that marriage to Abel will open doors for her. She will become the first lady of his church but that is not what she wants to be in her life. She knows that she can just marry him, get the Green Card and divorce him. Her body shivers at the thought of such a marriage. She does not know how she can bear to be with a man she does not love, does not like, and cannot respect. She will like to marry someone for the right reason or remain unmarried. Her thoughts go to Brian. She feels frustrated that Brian does not know that she is ill. It will be nice to marry someone she has feelings for. Like Brian. She thinks of Jaja and his loneliness. She feels awful not knowing about Jaja. No job. No Brian. Abel. Zeb's mind is full of stuff as she drifts into an uncomfortable sleep and a nightmare.

In their bedroom, Anise criticises Alex for the way he indulges Zeb.

"You are the one who brought her here."

"I brought her so that we can have someone else in the house. My children are grown up and out of the house. Only Wendy."

"Your children?" Alex says.

"You know what I mean. I don't mean to exclude you. And do not divert from my concern about how you babysit Zeb. You like her because she's young. At the airport, you told her that she's thin and I'm fat."

"I thought that we settled this."

"Let me finish. You like her because she has a PhD like you. You have things in common with her. Both of you are always going to the computer room."

"Are you accusing me of doing something with someone you call your friend?"

"I'm not accusing you. I trust you."

"So you are accusing someone you call your trusted friend." Alex says.

"I like her as my friend and I'm trying to marry her off so that she can get a Green Card and make a family. That's what friends do for friends."

"Just listen to yourself. You hate Zeb's ex-husband for forcing her into marriage when she was young. Now you're trying to force her into another one."

"It's just that she has everything you admire." "But you're the one I love, the one I chose among other women." Alex tries to hold her waist but she pushes him. He falls down. It was deliberate.

"I'm sorry."

He gets up and holds her by the waist. "Don't try to pick a quarrel with me tonight." He plants his mouth on hers. It goes deep.

Zeb is asleep on her bed, but her mind struggles to resolve problems that plague her reality. She is in a long lonely road. Suddenly a figure with snake-like hairs appears on the road walking towards her. The snakes have faces. Zeb wants to run away but her legs are heavy. The figure has long strides. Zeb still struggles to run, but the figure is catching up on her. The sound of its feet becomes loud. She can make out the ghoulish faces of the snakes and one of them looks familiar. She turns to another direction. The figure is there. She looks to the left. The figure. She looks to the right. She screams for help but no sound comes from her voice.

"No!" Her hand throws the blanket off.

Anise and Alex are in her room.

"You were making such a noise. What's wrong?"

"You are so wet," Anise feels her forehead.

"She has fever," Anise says to Alex.

"We have to take her to a doctor," Alex says.

"No need. It's just the flu," Anise says.

"What if it's not the flu?" Alex says.

"What else can it be?" Anise says.

"It can be something serious like malaria."

"That's the thing with you people. You always think the worst of people from Africa. Thank God you didn't suspect her of HIV/AIDS!" Anise yells at Alex.

"Don't refer to me as you people and don't yell at me," Alex says.

"That's the least I can do now," Anise says.

"Stop quarrelling," Zeb's voice is weak.

"I'll make chicken soup for her," Alex says.

"Do that!"

Alex leaves. Anise leaves. Zeb weeps.

"Why did you shout?" Anise has come back to Zeb's room with a wet towel.

Anise cleans Zeb's face with the wet towel while Zeb tells her about the nightmare.

"If it happens again, we'll go to the Pastor for special prayers."

"You will seize any opportunity to get me to that creep," Zeb says.

"I know that you feel awful, but I warned you not to insult anybody."

"I wanted to explain that I don't like him but you shut the door on my face. Nobody has ever treated me like that."

"You need spiritual healing. People in your situation get depressed," Anise says.

"If I'm depressed, I need a shrink not a pastor."

"They do the same thing in different ways," Anise says.

"You don't give up." Zeb tries to smile, but she can't. Alex comes in with a bowl of soup.

"That's quick," Zeb says.

"It smells good too. I put *nsala* mix in it," he says.

"Honey, where is mine?" Anise smiles at Alex.

"You want to make up for yelling at me?"

Anise wakes Zeb up in the morning with a bowl of soup.

"You didn't go to work?" Zeb says.

"I'm off today." Anise sits beside Zeb with the bowl of soup.

"Thanks for the soup." Zeb sits up.

"This is from the pot that Alex made last night. Did you sleep well?"

"Very well. No nightmares."

"One of the herbs in *nsala* mix takes care of nightmares," Anise says.

"How do you know?"

"My mother used to tell me the functions of *uda, uziza, ose-oji, utazi,* and other herbs in the *nsala*," Anise says.

"Thanks for taking care of me."

"You are my sister," Anise says. She twists her mouth as she remembers her quarrel with Alex. He has convinced her that his love for her has grown stronger than it was when they first met. He really made her feel good. All the same, Anise feels that Zeb has a bit of the queen-bee syndrome. She has to make Zeb realize that there is only one queen-bee in a colony.

"The house and all in it are part of my colony," Anise thinks.

30

Queen-bee

Alex's chicken soup with *nsala mix* turns out to be good for Zeb. He touches up the soup by putting more soup mix. Zeb drinks the soup several times a day, and sleeps most of the time, without nightmares. She no longer has fever but she still stays in bed most of the time. Sometimes she watches the television. She likes to follow the news about the Maryland killer. Another suspect has been put in police custody. The latest news is that the suspect has useful information about the killer. They have generated a picture of what the killer looks like. The picture is splashed on the screen from time to time. It is a big oblong face with large blue eyes, blond hair, big nose and big mouth. He is described as a white male. Five feet ten. One hundred and sixty pounds. Tattooed a scorpion on left arm. Zeb tries to memorise the picture.

"Wendy, come and draw this man," Zeb says.

"Hei Auntie!"

"Bring paper and pencil. Let's draw."

"Computer!"

"No. We'll look at this man and draw him." Zeb points at the picture on the television.

"Right Auntie!"

"He is a bad guy," Zeb says.

"Ba-guy!"

"He kills people. You know what that means?"

"Heaven!"

"They die. They will not see their Mummy and Daddy. That man is a bad guy." Zeb points at the television.

"Run away from bad guy." Zeb points at the picture.

"Hei Ba-guy!" Wendy points at the picture.

"Don't say 'hei' to him. Run away from him and tell your mom and dad."

"Ba-guy." She goes to bring the paper for drawing.

They make two pictures.

Alex comes in. He is pleased with the pictures that Wendy and Zeb have drawn. Wendy gives one to him.

"Ba-guy. Run run run from ba-guy," Wendy says.

"Good girl. Yeah. We run away from the bad guy." Alex gives his daughter high-five.

"Hei Auntie!" Wendy reaches out for Zeb. Zeb hugs her. Alex joins in the hug.

"This is a good picture. Thanks." Alex says.

"Show Mummy when she comes." Alex gives the drawings to Wendy.

"How are you today?" Alex turns to Zeb.

"I am okay now. I'll go to the library tomorrow," Zeb says. Zeb also wants to look at some apartments that she saw on the internet. She doesn't think that this is a good time to say that she wants to move out.

"Thanks for teaching Wendy."

"I enjoy it. I love her," Zeb says.

"I show Mi Willi." Wendy goes downstairs to wait for the school bus.

"Ms. Williams is her class teacher," Alex says. Anise has opened the door and is walking down the steps.

"Honey let's go," she says.

"Wendy, show your mom the picture of the bad guy that you drew with Auntie," Alex says.

"You'll show me later. We have to go," Anise says without looking at Zeb.

After breakfast, Zeb goes to the computer room. She is busy with the forms when the phone rings.

"Hello" she says.

"Nneoma."

Zeb is so thrilled that she can't speak. She walks up the steps.

"Sweetheart. How're you?" Brian's voice sounds like music.

"Alright. Long time." Zeb is speechless.

"It's been rough. Got too busy sorting out my life. How're things with you."

"Hanging in here, as they say," Zeb says.

"Any good news?"

"I had flu but I'm okay now." Zeb is now upstairs, in front of her room. She wants to talk with him while on her bed.

"I wish that I was there to take care of you."

"My friend here did that. And her family too," Zeb says.

"Is she home?"

"No."

"What are you doing?"

"I'm filling some immigration forms that I got from Baltimore."

"Let me not disturb you. I'll call you another time."

"Why haven't you been calling?" Zeb says.

"I'll explain when I call. Bye sweetie."

"Bye." Zeb hugs herself with the phone receiver. She walks down the steps slowly. She feels that something is up with Brian. She wonders what it is. She frowns at the thought of Brian finding another woman that he prefers. Her frown disappears as she recalls that he wished to have been with her to take care of her when she was ill. It shows that he still cares, but-. But what? There is something that she cannot lay her hands on.

Zeb cannot concentrate on the forms. She is bothered about Brian. It is frustrating that she cannot phone Brian back because he uses public phones. She picks the phone and dials Tom's number

"I saw him at the weekend." Tom says.

"Where?"

"Here in Trenton," Tom says.

"Was it at a party?" Zeb says.

"Why? Isn't he allowed to go to parties?"

"You don't want to answer my question. Anyway, tell him to call me as soon as possible," Zeb says.

"It's not that I don't want to answer your question. It's just that Brian is going through a lot of stuff."

"What is it?"

"He needs to tell you about it himself," he says.

"Is he in trouble?"

"Not really. I promise you. I'll give him your message. I'll go to his work."

"You know his work," Zeb says.

"Of course. The gas station. All I need to do is go there for gas. That's how we see him."

"He's not ashamed to let you people know that he is a gas attendant."

"We all went through our own stuff in the process of settling in America. No big deal," Tom says.

As soon as Tom gets off the phone, he phones the gas station.

"Hello," Tom says.

"My home boy Tom."

"Ol boy listen. Don't mess with my sister. Phone her and talk to her."

"What'sup."

"Don't know. Just talk with her. She's very special to me. And you're my friend. Ok."

As soon as Brian gets off from the morning shift, he phones Zeb.

"What's wrong? Are you okay?"

Brian laughs gently and says, "I couldn't face you my love."

"Why?"

"I failed the board exam," he says.

"So what?"

"I've never failed an exam in my life. My whole future depended on that exam and I flunked it."

"But you can take it again. Can't you?" Zeb says.

"Not now." His voice is soft.

"What do you mean? Giving up because of one failure?" Zeb says.

"Not really. I want to put more hours into my work and make more money," he says.

"Come on! A doctor spending more time selling gas?" Zeb says.

"Not like that." He makes a little coughing sound. Zeb waits.

He sighs before he talks. "Listen. Sleeping one or two hours a day is not healthy. As a doctor, I know that, but I had to do it. I thought that it would be for a short time. But now, I can't go through it again. I have brain fatigue. I need to take it easy. I need to be alive and well."

"How?" Zeb says.

"I just have to do as much work as I can and save money. It might take some time, but it is the only way now. Then, when I prepare for the board again, I'll do it full time and use the money that I saved to pay my bills."

"It makes sense. I wish I could help," Zeb says.

"You help already. It means a lot to me to hear that you were worried about me," he says.

"You should've called me," Zeb says.

"I'm sorry. Just dealing with the bad news in my own way. I had plans for us, but I'm so disappointed in myself. I can't help you. Can't even help myself," he says.

"We're in the same boat," Zeb says.

"Mine is worse. Can't even date a woman. I'm not fit. I'm not qualified," he says.

"Meaning what?"

"Dating is a luxury that I can't afford," Brian says.

"I'm not asking you for money."

"I don't even make enough money to buy a cell phone. I don't have credit card so as to buy on credit. No bank gives a foreigner credit card. The only way I can phone is by buying these phone cards and using them on the public phones. I feel so inadequate," Brian says.

Zeb is silent. And angry.

"Are you there? Please don't be angry. I feel frustrated already," he says.

"I'm angry, but not at you," Zeb says.

"You're so kind," Brian says.

"It has nothing to do with kindness. Just situation." Anise's explanation of immigrant circumstances flashes through Zeb's mind. Anise has said that an immigrant thinks of reality and survival before any other thing. This is how Brian is thinking when he says that he cannot date a woman now.

"What about your situation? Any good lead?" Brian says.

"No. I'm still looking for more job advertisements. The problem is that they no longer advertise. Off season for the kind of job that I'm looking for," Zeb says.

"So what will you do?"

"We are talking about you," Zeb says.

"I've told you my plan," he says.

"What about marriage." Zeb wants to get him to talk about his commitment to her. She needs to know how to make her plans and move on in whatever direction, either together or alone.

"How can I think of marriage in my present circumstances?" Brian says.

"You need to think about marriage because of your circumstances? Everybody tells me that the easy way out is to marry an American." This is a very painful thing for Zeb to say, but it is the realistic thing to say. Zeb feels that Brian is in trouble, she is also in difficulty, and they both need to get out of their predicament realistically. It is painful but realistic to acknowledge that they can be together and sink together or find American helping hands and rise with them. Zeb shakes her head at the latter thought. But she recalls Gloria saying that it is easy for men. She feels that she should not be in Brian's way if he wants to take that route. If he wants her, he will resist a Green Card marriage. So she presses on.

"Brian, haven't your friends told you to marry an American and get your Green Card through her instead of torturing yourself working in a gas station?"

He is silent. Zeb is also silent. She herself will soon be looking for a gas station job. The idea of roughing it out like Brian appeals to her.

"Zeb."

Zeb notices that he calls her by her name, instead of using an endearment as he usually does.

"You? You of all people want me to do that?" He says.

"Why not? With a Green Card, you can get a job where they won't exploit you as they do at the gas station. Then you can save quickly and focus on your exam." Zeb knows that Anise will be proud of her for saying this so she adds, "We have to face reality not sentiment."

He breathes heavily. Maybe he is angry or disappointed.

"I'll understand if you do that," Zeb adds. It hurt her to say this. She desperately hopes that Brian will tell her to desist from thinking in that direction.

"Do you know how I feel about you?" he says.

"Tell me," Zeb says. She is hopeful that this conversation will bring them closer. It does not occur to her that it may pull them apart.

"I love you," Brian says. Zeb feels some relief, at last. But she still pushes her luck.

"That love will not give you a Green Card." Zeb cannot believe her own words. Tears invade her eyes. She keeps silent. He keeps silent. She feels that he probably thinks that she is callous without knowing that her heart is bleeding and that she just wants him to declare his stand.

"Are you crying?" He knows that she is weeping.

Zeb sniffs.

"I'll never do that. I am a doctor. I'll get a Green Card on my own."

"I just don't want to disturb your chances. I want you to succeed." Zeb says and sniffs.

"You don't love me?" He says.

"I do love you more than you know. I also know that releasing someone because you love him is a true expression of love. I want you to find your feet and be the man that you like to be." Zeb sniffs.

"Me too. I should not hang on you. You need a man who will help you get a Green Card," he says.

"I'll never do that." Zeb snaps and begins to sob.

"Life is not fair," he says.

Zeb sobs. She hears his heavy breathing.

"Are you crying?" Zeb says.

"I have to give all my energy to my studies." He breathes heavily.

"Did I make you fail your exam?"

"No! Thinking of you was a positive influence," he says.

"Then why say that you should not hang on me?"

"I used your words. I release you also," he says.

"I love you," he says.

"Very much," he says.

"If you want to make a call, please hang up and dial again . . ." The phone message warns Zeb to hang up, but she does not. She looks at the wireless phone receiver; white with gray buttons. She puts it on her lap. She looks at the unemotional gadget and hopes to hear Brian's voice once more. Just once more.

Zeb does not hear the Esomonus drive into the garage. She is surprised to hear their voices as they open the garage door and enter the hallway. She leaves the computer room to greet them. They all walk upstairs. Wendy dumps her backpack on the couch.

"No sweetheart. Bring it upstairs," Anise says on her way upstairs. Zeb sits on the couch and turns on the television. She waits for Anise to come down so that she can chat with her and find out what is wrong. Anise does not come down. Alex does not come down. Zeb is downstairs till late but nobody joins her in the living room.

31

Goodbye Darling

Zeb opens her eyes. A ray of sunshine seeps into her room through the window. The telephone conversation with Brian comes to her mind. She can't believe that it is over between them. The conversation plays over and over in her mind. Brian wants his space; at the same time he says that Zeb is a positive force. Zeb finds this contradictory. He said he loves her very much yet he does not want the relationship to go on. Another contradiction. One thing is clear to Zeb. He doesn't want her to hang around him, and he is honest to let her know. She pulls the blanket over her head and curls up with her hands across her chest.

It is dark inside the blanket. As she thinks about the conversation, she blames herself for bringing up the issue of a Green Card and marriage. She blames herself for releasing Brian. "He released me because I released him first." If the best way to love someone is to give that person freedom, then she did the right thing in the situation. She frowns at the thought of the word "situation." The word is like a bag that contains the load in her heart. It contains Brian, a Green Card, and joblessness. The situation stresses her out. Now Anise is adding to the stress. Zeb holds her head with her hands because she believes that it is aching. It is her heart that aches, but she feels her whole body aching. She hugs herself tight, feels the pain and enjoys the squeeze of her body. Her shoulder feels heavy. She stretches her neck, but it hurts. She feels pain in her chest. She rubs it with her palm. It still hurts. Her face feels heavy because of all the unshed tears. There are gallons of tears inside, but they do not flow out anymore. She has them bottled up, but she wants them off her chest. She wants to be free. She stretches both hands and they push the blanket. She sits up. There are tears. She wipes the tears and gets up from the bed.

In the morning, Zeb feels like leaving the house. She does not want to be alone and think of Brian. She picks an outfit that will cheer her up. She spreads the short skirt and blouse that she wore when Brian saw her off at the station in New Jersey. She feels they have too many memories that she cannot deal with now. She puts them back in the closet. She will be casual. She promises herself that she will go to the library to check for notices and read spiritual books. She needs a lot of spiritual understanding and connection. She puts her blue jeans on the bed and goes to the bathroom.

By the time she goes downstairs, everybody including Wendy has left the house. She has an uneasy feeling about it. Usually Anise would have knocked on the bathroom door or somehow let her know that they were leaving so early. She goes back to her room to dress up. She thinks that she has worn the blue jeans so many times. She really needs something special to cheer her up. The focus on bathing and picking an outfit help to divert her mind from her emotional upset. She scans through the closet. A pair of brown jeans with matching jacket catches her eyes. She picks a scarf to go with it. This attire is right for any occasion, not formal but classy. She feels like going to the American University to see Ada. She puts her address book into her handbag. She begins to dress and admire herself in the mirror.

"This is good!" she says as she glances at herself in the mirror. She turns her back to check her butt.

"Yes."

When Zeb returns from the library, she phones her sister. She talks about Brian. Kordi listens patiently and tells Zeb that Brian did her a favour by telling her to move on with her life.

"I really care for him. I had such hopes."

"Believe me; he too must also be hurting. It's not easy for both of you. But, I'm really proud of you, my sister."

"Why?"

"You did the right thing to let him go."

"I hurt."

"You'll be okay. He wants a break. And you need the break too," Kordi says.

"I'm so sad."

"It is better that it happened now than later," Kordi says.

"It would not have happened if not for this Green Card problem that both of us have."

Kordi doesn't agree with that idea but she doesn't say anything.

"Don't you agree with me?" Zeb says.

"No need to talk about what it could have been. I like your courage in letting him go. And he's clever to accept it and go. So, let's talk about what to do now."

"Why do you say that he's clever?"

"He has a lot on his table, so he needed to make a choice or have a choice made for him. You gave him the opportunity to make the choice easy for his conscience, and I really like that. You have to move on with your life. Don't worry."

"I really don't like the break now that I'm still in Anise's house. When she hears about the break, she will want to arrange marriages for me."

"Do you think that she can find a guy willing to do it for you? A guy who won't bother you?" Kordi says.

"A Green Card marriage is risky, my sister," Zeb says.

"Life is full of risks," Kordi says.

"What will Mamma say if she hears it?"

"We'll have to explain the situation, and tell her that it is not a real marriage but a legal convenience."

Zeb is surprised that her sister supports the idea, but she is revulsed by it. She thinks of another argument against such a marriage

"It might be very expensive."

"Of course. Here in London, it costs about five thousand pounds."

"Wow! That's like eight thousand dollars or something. Nobody has that kind of money to pay a man," Zeb says.

"Once you're credit worthy in London, you'll always get a loan. Don't worry about the money. I'll get a loan and pay for it. Discuss it with Anise. And who knows, you may soon find your own man, better than Brian. After all you are beautiful, intelligent and talented."

"Thanks. So are you," Zeb says.

"Has my friend, Melinda, visited you yet?"

"We spoke on the phone and she promised to visit me," Zeb says.

"I'll make sure that she keeps her promise. I really want you to meet her."

Zeb believes that one of the ways that she can move on with her life is to extend her social circles outside the Esomonus. She phones Esi and leaves a message. Aracebor sends an email message saying that he left messages on the phone for her and asks for the best time to phone her. Zeb says he should phone immediately. She waits for his call. The telephone rings. Zeb runs upstairs, picks it and says hello with her sweetest voice. She is disappointed that the call is not from Aracebor.

"Hi Gloria."

"What are you up to with that sweet voice?"

"My voice is always sweet."

"Ya-a right. You thought it was Brian."

Zeb does not say anything.

"Is this a good time to talk?" Gloria asks.

"How are you?" Gloria asks.

"Alright."

"How is Brian?"

Zeb hesitates.

"Has he proposed?" Gloria says.

"Come on! What do you care?" Zeb says.

"I don't want him to distract you," Gloria says.

"What if I want him to?"

"Well, I can just try my best as your friend to save you from future heart break," Gloria says.

Zeb tells her about the break up.

"He is a liar. He just made up an excuse to leave you," Gloria says.

"Why should he want to leave me?"

"He wants to marry an American and move on. You will not help him," Gloria says.

"He is a doctor. He can get a Green Card on his own merit."

"Ya-a right! He also knows the quick path to a Green Card. Forget the con-artist of a man!"

Zeb thinks about what Gloria said about Brian wanting to marry an American woman. Zeb genuinely believes that Brian failed the board, but Gloria has cast a doubt in her mind. Zeb's cousin has hinted that all was not well with Brian, but wanted Brian to tell her about it himself. She now wonders whether her cousin knew that Brian wanted to leave her. That might have been why he wanted Brian to talk to her. Anyway, whatever it is or was, she has to move on with her life. The telephone rings. She thinks that it is from Aracebor.

"Brian!"

"Were you on the phone," he asks.

"Not really. Just expecting a call."

"Let me not keep you," he says.

"That's okay. He hasn't called yet."

"A man?"

"Yes."

"Who?"

"This guy is somewhere in the Midwest."

"Nigerian?"

"No.Why are you asking all these questions anyway?" Zeb says.

"Nne, we are friends. I care."

Zeb doesn't say anything. So she has been pushed to Brian's pool of "just friends," she thinks and shakes her head from side to side in acknowledgement of the new idea.

"Does he want to help you with a Green Card?"

"He wants me to visit him," Zeb says. Her voice is low.

"When are you going?"

"You don't care if I go?" She yearns for Brian to assure her that she is still at the centre of his heart.

"You have to live your life. You can't keep your life on hold because of my problem. Give him the chance if you want to, but be careful."

"What do you mean?"

"I'm a doctor. And even though it hurts, I have to remind you to use condom."

Zeb is embarrassed and angry. She and Brian are not yet physical and he is thinking about her and another guy in that manner. It dawns on Zeb that Gloria is right.

"Brian, you just want to see me move on because you want to move on."

"Nne, are you offended?"

She notes that he does not refer to her with her favourite endearment, "Nneoma."

"Brian. You're just too clinical," Zeb says.

"And mechanical. Goodbye Brian." Zeb hangs up.

Zeb is very sad about Brian. Anise's attitude adds to her feeling of loneliness and sadness. Anise avoids her and when they meet, she makes it clear that she has no time to discuss with Zeb. Zeb moves from her room on the third floor to the living room and kitchen on the second floor and the computer room on the ground floor without meeting anybody. She writes a note to Anise, "I feel like a lonely ghost, please talk to me." She leaves it on the dining table. The note has been on the dining table for two days. Nobody took it. Zeb tells Esi about what is going on.

"I knew that the honeymoon would not last. Prepare for anything and let me know what happens."

"Why do you say that? This woman has been my friend for a long time."

"Just be prepared for anything. Immigrant situation is very stressful."

"Tell me about it."

"Not just for us immigrants but for friends who try to help. I learnt that from my own situation. This is why I reach out to immigrants," Esi says. Zeb is confused about Esi's idea. She will discuss this whole thing with Ada. She phones Ada.

"Hi Zeb. I've been thinking about how to make out time and meet with you before I leave."

"For where?"

"I told you that I'm going on sabbatical. I'm really busy preparing for my trip which is next week."

"What about my application?"

"The department has not made its final decision about who will replace me, but I hope that you will be the one."

"When will they decide?"

"Very soon. At least before I leave. Let's have our fingers crossed," Ada says.

"Where are you going to spend the leave?"

"In Nigeria," Ada says. Zeb's heart misses a bit. She envies Ada her freedom to go to Nigeria without fear of imprisonment.

"I'll like us to meet before I leave. I hope that the department will make its decision soon, so that I discuss the class expectations with you. Is that ok?"

"I'll love that," Zeb says. Her voice is weak.

"Are you ok? You don't sound excited."

"I'm fine." Zeb tries to sound lively.

"I'll phone you, ok.?"

32

The Colour of Chance

Zeb should be happy about the prospect of getting the position in Ada's department, but she is overwhelmed with sadness. It is because of Brian and the tension between her and Anise. Maybe she should take up Aracebor's offer to visit him in order to give Anise space to cool the tension. She wonders why he has not phoned her but decides to be proactive about it. She sends him an email accepting his invitation. But thinking of the trip makes her uneasy. It may be because of an unknown factor in Chicago or because of the tension with Anise or the sadness she feels because of Brian. She needs to tell Anise about it. She must see her even if it means staying by her door to watch out for Anise. She opens her bedroom door slightly and waits for Anise to come out of their bedroom. The strategy works. Anise has gone downstairs to the kitchen. Zeb goes to the kitchen. As soon as she greets Anise, she informs Zeb that she has no time to talk because she wants to go to bed.

"I'll leave the house very early in the morning," Anise says and makes to leave the kitchen. Zeb follows her and informs her that she wants to visit Aracebor in Chicago.

"Is he the one you'll now marry?" Anise stands.

"I don't have such feelings for him," Zeb smiles.

"It's because he's white. You quickly fell for the black doctor," Anise does not laugh.

Zeb is not sure of Aracebor's ethnicity but she believes he looks white or maybe White-Hispanic but not black.

"Anyway, I don't know whether it's because he's white or not. And what if it is? I like him. I don't love him." Zeb is tired of Anise always coming at her from unexpected angles. Her frustration shows on her face. Anise tightens her face and looks at Zeb straight in the eyes. This makes Zeb very uncomfortable, so she quickly explains so that there will not be any misunderstanding.

"Sure I know that in our culture, some people are offended when you marry outside your ethnic origin or country, but people still do it. As for me, I care about happiness and respect. And yes, someone from my background is a plus but I can't just like anybody because he's from the same background as me. There are many other qualities," Zeb rushes through the explanation. Anise is not surprised at Zeb's nervousness. Zeb likes to be the centre of attention and she has made sure that everybody in the house ignores Zeb. That should make her jumpy. Zeb is not jumpy enough for where Anise wants her to be. She thinks that Zeb is still running her mouth like the one smarter than everyone else. Zeb continues to make her point.

"As a matter of fact, I've never thought much about race or colour because it's not a big deal back home. What I want to say is that I don't really care whether someone is white or black or whatever. I know that you care about it but I don't care." Zeb smiles at Anise who appears calm and just looks at Zeb. She knows that Zeb is capable of challenging her in an argument and that Zeb is intelligent, but she does not expect Zeb to rise up to her at this time of uneasy tension between them. She now feels that Zeb is still acting like a queen-bee in her house. Someone is giving Zeb the nerve and she has to put a stop to it. First, she must find out where the influence is coming from. It is either from this new obsession of hers that she wants to visit in Chicago or from that woman who visited her. No, Anise dismisses the idea of Esi being the person because she is an African immigrant and has no influence.

"Colour is everything in America. You'll be stupid if you are in this country and you don't think about colour," Anise says. Her voice is calm.

Zeb does not like her use of the word, stupid, but she lets it pass. She says, "All I know is that I just don't have that Brian-like kind of magic with Aracebor, and it's not because he's white. It's not because of anything. It's not my fault that Brian is black and Aracebor is white. Your husband is very light skinned, so why this obsession with whiteness-."

"Shut up and listen professor! There are things that you have not read from your books," Anise yells and points her finger. Zeb knows that Anise mocks her whenever she calls her professor in an argument, but she tries to ignore it.

"Look at the black women you see on the television. What do they have in common?" Anise does not wait for a reply before she speaks.

"They are not coffee-black. They do not have kinky hair. Their skin is light; as peach as they come. Their hair is silky long like corn silk. Only very few coffee black women like Oprah get to reach up there." Anise is worked-up. She is keen on showing up Zeb's ignorance.

"At least, some coffee-black women get there. What does it matter anyway whether they are light or dark?" Zeb's voice is calm and she walks back to the kitchen wanting the conversation to end.

Anise follows her to the kitchen and stands by the dining table.

"There are more opportunities for light-skinned blacks than for the darker ones." Anise puts her hands on her waist in a challenging manner thrusting out her chest. She stands opposite Zeb across the table.

"I disagree. Look at those black footballers and basketball players," Zeb says.

"No. Look at their wives. They are either white or very light-skinned. Very few get involved with real blacks."

"Real blacks?" Zeb says.

"Yes, black women with black coffee colour. There are more opportunities for whites. So the whiter you can become the better for you. If I were you, I would consider that white man seriously, and take up the offer even if he is just doing it to help you. Make some pretty light-skinned babies who will not be at the lowest rung of the racial level." Anise does not yell. She goes to the fridge and opens the door. She does not take anything.

"This is insulting to me as a black person! It sounds to me like hating who I am and trying to have children who should not look like me! Why did you want me to marry your pastor who is darker than my black shoes?" Zeb is irritated.

"That's different." Anise bangs the door of the fridge. "Why?"

Anise does not say anything. Zeb does not insist on an answer. She thinks that she already knows the answer. She feels that what is important to Anise is that she dictates what she should do. If she likes a man, Anise will be against him and want to win. If she does not want the man, Anise will force her to go for the man and she would want her to obey. It all sounds childish to her. She twists her mouth.

Anise feels that Zeb is acting superior to her. She changes her tone. "If you don't yet know that colour is important, you'll know it when you get a job and begin to work. You'll suffer racism, and if you're the kind of woman that I know you to be, you won't want your children to suffer the same thing. You have the opportunity to have light-skinned black children now. Opportunity comes but once."

Zeb takes up the bait, "I can't do it. I don't even agree with you. All the people who rule my country are black. The newscasters are coffee-black like me, bronze-black, ebony black and different shades of black you can get. In fact, skin colour is not a huge factor."

"I'm happy you said your country. Professor, I am talking about America."

"I'm not an American."

"So all you want to do with your life is flirt from one man to the other. From the prisoner in Nigeria to the gas station doctor to this one now who doesn't have the baggage of the others? That's too fast for me. Remember that you are in the house of a married woman." Anise turns and walks away.

"Anise, you are being very disrespectful to me."

Anise stops in her tracks. Zeb has really grown wings and somebody must stop her. "Our people say that it is good for the wind to blow, so that we can see the anus of the fowl. I hope you still understand Igbo proverbs, professor." She shakes her head and drags the word, "professor." Zeb is angry at the way Anise continues to call her professor in a derogatory manner.

"More insults. You were never rude to me. The only thing that has changed is that I live in your house. Do you think that I will be jobless and helpless forever?"

"So this is what you think of me. How ungrateful of you. Queen-bee! I am only advising you as a friend and sister without knowing that you have superior and condescending attitude towards me, professor."

"Professor without job. Professor refugee. How can I be superior to you, my landlady?" Zeb tries to make light of Anise mocking her as a professor, but Anise is not amused by the joke.

"Cut that joke off. I'm serious. You know that I've never treated you like a refugee."

"I've not said that you do."

"You must leave this house and go to Chicago or wherever you've located the next man."

"Are you throwing me out?"

"You heard me. There is a man waiting for you there."

"Even if I go, I'll be there for a while. Maybe a week or two and be back before Christmas."

"Pack all your things and leave my house!" Anise says.

"What's the matter with you? What's the anger behind all these? We need an arbiter. Let's take this matter to Alex."

"Just leave my husband out of it!" Anise walks past Zeb into the kitchen. Zeb goes to her room and straight to the window.

She stands by the window and replays her quarrel with Anise in her mind. She looks at the night through the window and sees only streetlights. She wants to see the birds. "What is happening to me?" She does not see any birds, but she continues to look out. "Something is wrong with Anise." One minute, Anise is happy, the next minute, she is gloomy. Sometimes, she lashes out unnecessarily. Zeb checks her way of thinking. It suddenly occurs to her that she is the problem. Maybe she is too sensitive because of her situation. Maybe Anise is joking. Maybe she's angry about something else. Maybe she is having a problem with Alex. Zeb stands by the window speculating about the quarrel. She just cannot accept that the quarrel is about marrying a man who has not even proposed to her. This is crazy! She leaves the window and goes to meet Anise.

Anise is still in the kitchen. She is stacking the plates as she talks to herself.

"You have just thrown me out of your house," Zeb says. She hopes that Anise will contradict her. But Anise continues to mumble.

"Anise, are you throwing me out of your house for real?"

Anise stops mumbling.

"After all the assurances you gave me before I came here?" Zeb says.

Still Anise does not say anything. She keeps herself busy cleaning the plates. She throws each cleaned plate on top of another. Zeb sits on a chair by the dining table watching her clean and throw the plates.

33

Killing the Light

Zeb watches out for an opportunity to plead with Anise. She feels that since she lives in their house, and Anise is her host and mentor, she should defer to her. Another concern is that she does not know where Anise's anger is coming from. Zeb has tried to avoid this situation, but it has come upon her.

"Only God can help me now because I am so confused," Zeb says. Her voice is very low, but loud enough for Anise to hear it. Anise ignores her completely. She stores the plates in the cupboard.

"Anise, you are my friend and sister," Zeb says.

"That was in the past." The plates clatter as she stores them.

"Why?" Zeb says. She is still sitting, watching Anise, and wondering at her display of anger.

"When friends or sisters can no longer trust each other, then there is no friendship anymore." She now bangs the cupboards.

"Why do you say that? Have I done anything?"

"You lie to me." She leaves the kitchen

"Me? What lie have I told you?"

"You and your boyfriends are liars." Anise stands across from Zeb and puts her hand on her waist.

"Leave my house," she says. She puts a lot of energy in the simple sentence, and the weight of the words hits Zeb's head like boulders that cause her to break immediately. She weeps. Right there in front of Anise. Anise puts off the light in the kitchen and leaves. The callousness of her ignoring Zeb's tears and putting off the light on her is too much.

"Please put on the light." Zeb's voice shakes. Anise goes upstairs.

Zeb picks the phone, dials Ada's number and cancels it immediately. She phones Esi and tells her what has happened.

She says, "Did this thing happen as you have just said it?"

"Yes."

"There must be something else. Was there an incident with anybody in the house?"

"No."

"Any incident with her husband?"

"No."

"Did her husband make a pass at you?"

"No!"

"One thing is certain. She wants you out of the house, and you have to get out."

"I want to leave now. This night. I'll stay in a hotel and book my flight to Chicago."

"Chicago?"

"Don't ask me about it, because I don't want to discuss it now."

"I thought that there was something else," Esi says.

"I'm going to look up a hotel and call a cab to pick me."

"Don't do any foolish thing. It is too late to go anywhere. Too much violence around. Remember that they have not caught the crazy man who is killing women even though he seems to be lying low now. The person in custody is a person of interest in the case. Just pack all your things. I'll be there by five-thirty in the morning to get you. Remember to pray and thank God; it could have been worse. I'll see you in the morning."

Zeb shudders. "Anise hates me that much? She ignored me at my most vulnerable moment, and turned off the light on me. I won't spend the night in this house. I'll pack my things and call a taxi. I'll call the Yellow Taxi. They are reliable." Zeb begins to pack her things. She begins from her room. The things are just too many. She throws her clothes into suitcases and squeezes in things here and there. Her mind is not settled. She cannot get Anise's words off her mind. She believes she is reviewing the incident in her mind but she is actually speaking to herself. "She said that she can't trust me anymore. I hate being thrown out. I hate being accused of something that I don't know; something she thinks I did, which I'm sure I didn't do. I hate the unknown. I don't really know Aracebor. He doesn't even know that I'm leaving here for good. My cousin, Tom. No. He and his wife and new baby don't need my interference. But I can be useful as a nanny. No. I won't go to New Jersey. It will look like I'm coming after Brian."

She goes downstairs to pack her books. She checks her email. There is a message from Ada. "I left you a message on your phone but you haven't called back. The department met today and decided to give the sabbatical position to an Adjunct professor who is already here. No problem. Something else will come up. Hang in there. Give me a call and we'll arrange to meet before I leave. Ada."

Another blow. Zeb covers her face with her hands and breathes in and out.

Brian. Anise. Now they have not given me the job in Ada's school. She deletes Ada's message and begins to search the internet for job advertisements. She sends another email to Aracebor. "How about my coming now?" Zeb opens the drawer to pack her folders. She notices that the immigration forms are not inside the folder where she normally keeps them. They are just lying on top of the folders. She suspects that Anise must have looked at them. She puts them back in the folder and packs everything while she continues to talk to herself.

"If Aracebor says no, what will I do? Maybe I'll go back to Nigeria and see my son, but I'll go to prison. If I go to prison, I'll see Jaja. No. I won't give up because of Anise. Without Anise, what would I have done? I'll continue to navigate the web and look at adverts. Something is bound to come for me. God is there." She carries her books and papers to her room and dumps them in a suitcase. It is almost three in the morning. She cannot sleep. Just tired. She goes to the window. It looks like the birds have deserted the trees across the street. "But they always return. They'll come back," she says. She sits on the floor beside the window and tries to zip up her suitcase. She dozes off with her head on top of the suitcase.

Zebra! She springs up from the floor as she hears her name. The lights are on. Her suitcases are packed. Zebra! It is a familiar voice. She looks out of the window. Esi is already there.

"It's five-thirty. Hurry."

"I'm coming," Zeb says and runs down to open the door for Esi

Esi goes upstairs to help Zeb with her luggage. Anise gets ready for work while they take the luggage to the car. When they are ready to leave, Zeb goes to Alex who is in the dining room.

"Is there any way I offended you since I came here?"

"No."

"Have I offended Anise? Please tell me so that I will know how to apologise."

"Not to my knowledge."

"You have seen that she is throwing me out, but I can deal with it. The problem is that she has wounded my spirit by saying that I tell lies. What is the lie?"

Alex sticks out his mouth and spreads his hands to indicate that he does not know.

"Let's go!" Esi gestures with her hand.

Zeb does not move. She still has something to say to Alex.

"God bless you and your family for inviting me to your house and keeping me all this while."

"God bless you too, Zeb. Make sure you email me. We care for you in spite of the misunderstanding."

Anise is on her way out of the house towards her car parked outside. Zeb runs outside to talk to her.

"Anise, please give me a hug. We are no longer quarrelling."

Anise ignores her and continues to walk.

"Anise, this is early morning. Remember where we are from. We don't begin the day with bad blood. Talk to me," Zeb says.

She still ignores her.

Then Zeb says, "God bless you Anise." Her voice is very loud.

"God bless you too." Anise shouts without looking back.

"Thank you."

Esi revs the engine of her car.

As she drives off, she says, "I'll take you to my house."

Zeb is reluctant to go to Esi's house after her experience with a trusted friend. She must have felt Zeb's hesitation, because she says. "From my house, you can go to a hotel or to the airport or wherever you decide to go. Right now, I think that you should just rest, sleep, and think. I won't be on your way, because I'll be going to work."

There is silence for some time. Then Esi begins a story.

"I have to tell you one of my experiences while I was looking for a job, so that you will realise that I have seen this type of thing before," Esi says.

Zeb is not really in the mood for listening to a story. She now thinks that stories belittle her experiences. Ada, Anise, Gloria; all have stories of endurance and survival. But, right now Zeb hurts. She has just lost a friend. A chapter of her life is shut and nothing can bring it back. Esi goes on with the story.

"When I was looking for a job, that was before I opened the Day Care Center, an agency sent me to a place in the woods far beyond Aspen Hill. I was to go there and take care of an old couple for two dollars an hour."

"Minimum wage is more than that."

"If you find a small job now without a Green Card, won't you take it even if they pay you a pittance? You will take it if you have to pay bills. I took the job. I was grateful to be able to earn money to feed my children. I would have taken one dollar an hour."

"My God!"

"The woman had althzimers, the man was in a wheel chair, and both were in their eighties. They lived in a caravan in the woods. I arrived there on time in order to start work by seven in the night. I cooked and fed them, gave them their medicines, and put them to bed. I sat down in the living room keeping watch. I wanted to use the bathroom around two. You had to pass their bedroom to get to the bathroom. The flush of the toilet must have woken the woman up. She screamed. Her husband woke up. 'Who is this? How did you get in here?' Before I could explain, he called me a thief and I was frightened.

In panic, I phoned the agency. The manager replied, 'You have to leave if they don't want you.' 'It is too dark. There are no streetlights in this wood. Can't you talk to them and explain that you sent me here?' He just said, 'We are not responsible if anything happens to you.' That was when I realised that my life was in danger. I heard the man on wheelchair fumbling in a drawer. I thought that he was looking for his gun. I ran outside into the darkness."

"I couldn't even find my bearing. Unlike me, at that time, you have your bearing. You already have plans. If I could make it without any bearing, you can make it," she says.

"Amen," Zeb says. Zeb becomes interested in the story and wants to know details of what happened to her that night, but she is tired and sleepy and she has to plan her next move.

She has to phone Aracebor. She wishes that Brian would phone her. She just yearns to hear his voice one more time. She hopes that Aracebor won't chicken out.

Zeb opens her eyes. The window through which she watches the birds is not there. She looks around. She cannot recognise the room. It gradually dawns on her. She is not in Esomonu's residence. She is in Esi's room. She verbalises her predicament, "I'm no longer in Anise's house. She kicked me out." The next chapter of her life is about to begin. Zeb gets out of bed and tries to get used to her environment. She can hear the sound of children. She gets up from the couch. She opens a sliding door to a small deck. From the deck, she sees that it is a huge apartment complex. A couple of children are playing in the yard between two blocks. She comes back to the room. It is a one-bedroom apartment with a long closet. She slides open the closet and closes it. It is untidy. She goes to the bathroom. There is a washer but no dryer. She goes back to the couch.

Zeb wants to check her email messages to see whether Aracebor has replied. She looks at the dining table and the pantry. There is no computer. She sits on the couch and thinks of possibilities. Cousin Eddy in New York. He lives with his girlfriend. His daughter, Kim, spends half of her time in his apartment. She does not want to experience rejection from another person who is close to her. She puts off the idea of asking Eddy to take her in his apartment. She still can't believe that Anise kicked her out. Even though she was thinking of moving out, she is shocked by the idea of being kicked out and losing her friendship with Anise. She shudders. Anise's family is her new American family. She has just lost her family.

Zeb hears the sound of steps outside the door. Zeb looks through the peep hole and opens the door for Esi. She brings out two cups of soup, salad and muffins. She sits on the chair. .

"I want to check my email," Zeb says.

"I don't have a computer. Why not phone him," Esi says.

"May I use your phone," Zeb says.

"I don't have out of state. You have to use a card."

"Do you have a card?" Zeb says.

"We'll have to go to the gas station to buy one, but that'll be when I return from work. You don't need to rush anything today. You can spend a few days here to sort out things and make plans. You look awful. Just relax and sleep. Things will work out," Esi says.

"She said that I tell lies and that she can't trust me as a friend. That's the greatest insult anybody has ever given me. And to think that it is coming from a friend who knows me very well."

"Don't worry. One day, we'll know what caused all these. It might not be anything to do with you," Esi says.

"But what?"

"Maybe something else and you're the scapegoat," Esi says.

"I don't understand," Zeb says.

"Leave it alone. Just focus on your next step. I'll buy phone cards. When I come back, you'll phone. Tomorrow I'll show you Kinko's or the library where you'll use the Internet." Esi shows her where things are in the kitchen and tells her to feel free to use the kitchen to prepare whatever she wants to eat. She also says that she will bring back late dinner from her work at China Palace.

After speaking with Aracebor, Zeb begins to sort her things and pack her suitcases properly. It keeps her busy the whole of Friday while Esi is at work. She puts her journal in her carry-on bag. She removes it and puts it in her pocket book. She intends to use it at the airport and the plane. She no longer has a computer so she will use her journal more. She will write down everything that is happening to her now. Aracebor will send an electronic air ticket that Zeb will pick up at the airport. In spite of this, the heaviness in her heart is still there. She even feels heavy on her face and head. She thinks that it is because of Anise but her heart misses a beat each time she thinks about her trip to Chicago.

34

My Own Woman

They are cleaning the apartment on Saturday morning when Zeb blurts out her worry.

"Esi, I really don't know the man in Chicago very well."

"How much do you know?"

Zeb tell her what she knows.

"Will you like to hear my opinion?"

"That's why I shared this with you."

"If you decide to go, I think that you should leave most of your things here just in case you want to run back. When you get there, watch him and be very careful and prayerful. Meanwhile, let's hang out and enjoy the weekend. You deserve to pamper yourself. You've had a rough time and come out of it in one piece," Esi says. After cleaning, they have a light lunch.

"Dinner will be at China Palace."

"I've not yet met your boyfriend." Zeb sits opposite Esi at China Palace.

"He travelled to El Passo for his immigration process; that's why I had his truck that I used to get your things from Anise's house. He's alright and everything is working out. I hope that he'll be here next week. How about you? Why is it that a very beautiful and educated woman like you is not dating anybody? I don't mean for a Green Card."

"I'm not fast with men. I take my time. I fall in love. Just don't have them because they are there."

"That's probably one of the reasons why you look so young. You act young too. How many women of our age wait to fall in love before taking a guy as boyfriend? Not many."

Zeb smiles as she thinks about it. It is a kind of criticism yet it has a bit of admiration. Zeb likes it because it works for her. Esi's words break her reverie.

"I'm not sure that I believe in love. I experienced love with my husband and it's over. Now, I look at what a man can give me because he is also looking at what he can get from me." Esi laughs.

Zeb laughs also.

"I understand that very well. But I'm still who I am in a way. With my first "husband", I was cynical about love. But Jaja taught me how to love. I began a new life with Jaja. He was nine years younger but I learnt a lot from him. So physically, emotionally and psychologically strong yet so gentle, considerate and caring. He is so full of life and fun to be with. I just love him."

Esi does not want to hear about love. She finds it boring.

"Tell me about your 'first husband.' "

"I want to tell you about Jaja. I can't talk about my marriage in a public place like this. I may become emotional."

"Ok. Have you decided on what to eat?"

Zeb picks the menu. Esi knows the menu by heart.

Zeb is up early making coffee when Esi opens her bedroom door.

"Did you sleep well?"

"Very well."

"Will you help me shop for cosmetics?"

"Of course. You can begin by trying some of mine."

"Let me make breakfast. Do you know that I'm a very good chef? I've been working at China Palace for three years. I started as a waiter and trained as chef. Now I'm a supervisor."

"What's the next?"

"I'm thinking of opening my own place or going back to school."

"Both are good."

Esi brings two glasses and a bottle of what looks like Champagne.

"What do you want to celebrate with champagne?" Zeb says.

"This is not Champagne. It's apple cider. But you are right; we have to celebrate-." Esi places them on the table.

"What?"

"Life. You need a lot of cheering up." Esi goes back to the kitchen and brings two plates of vegetable omelettes and fried potatoes. She brings coffee.

"Don't spoil me-o," Zeb says.

"Why not? Get used to it because you're going to get more in Chicago." At the mention of Chicago, Zeb winces.

"What's wrong?"

"You know, I've been thinking about Chicago for the past few days and feeling very uncomfortable about it. I said maybe it's about my experience with Anise, but then, I don't feel that way towards you or this place. So I think maybe going to Chicago may not be right for me at this time or maybe it's because I don't know the guy that well. You see, I married at a very young age to a man I didn't know." Zeb pauses. She looks at the glasses and looks at Esi. Then she begins to open the apple cider. Esi watches her while eating her breakfast. She feels that Zeb is edgy, because her hand shakes a bit as she removes the foil around the cover. She squeezes the screw-top and fills the two wine glasses

"Let's drink to God's blessing on Esi and my success in America," Zeb clicks Esi's glass.

"Amen. I like the spirit. Now tell me about your marriage."

"Take it easy. You're just as impatient as I was when my story began," Zeb says.

"So you have a story."

"Of course. It began when *Nna-mu* died," Zeb says.

"Your father?"

"Yes, my Nna-a. That's what I used to call him." Zeb drinks, puts her glass on the table and adjusts her chair.

"You didn't call him Papa?"

"Papa is soft Igbo. Nna is the root Igbo." Zeb nods her head to affirm her idea of root Igbo, as if Esi will disagree with her.

"I see," is all that Esi says.

"I was the only child from my mother, but I had two brothers from my other mother who was my uncle's wife."

"Those will be your cousins then."

"Yes, but we were brought up in the same house because their father had died. I also have other sisters and brothers or what you may call cousins from other uncles living in the same compound. I hate to use the word cousin to describe them because we are close like siblings."

"You can call them brothers or cousins. I understand. Just go on."

"Nna-a used to say that I was very bright, would go to college, and be one of the leaders of Eke community. I'm from a town called Eke."

"Please go on with the story," Esi says.

"You are so impatient. I'm not running away. I have volunteered to tell you the story and I will tell it to you. Be patient."

"Ok." Esi sits back and leans her back on the chair. She has almost finished her breakfast.

"My father did not go to school in our village of Ama-Enugwu. He learnt how to read and write when he fought in the Second World War. The soldiers liked him because he was very brave."

"He was a soldier?"

"He was in the British army. That was long ago, when Nigeria was in the British Commonwealth."

"A different country?"

"Yes, before Nigeria got independence from Britain," Zeb says and continues, "After the war, he became a teacher in my town."

"Go on." Esi adjusts her chair.

"Nna-a always told me that I would become a great woman through education. I put all my effort into schoolwork and always came up on top. He was very proud of me. When they went to the farm, he would insist that I stayed at home to read my books, but my mother wanted me to learn farm work so they always argued about it."

"Was your dad a farmer also?"

"When he came back from the war, he farmed like other people in the village. But he was known as Teacher. He also traded in palm nuts and wove baskets that my mothers sold in the market. We were among the well-to-do families in our village when he was alive," Zeb smiles.

"I attended Junior Primary school in my village. I went to Senior Primary in the village of Amankwo next to our own village, because we did not have Senior in our village. After that, Nna sent me to a boarding school run by Reverend Sisters in the city of Enugu."

"I heard that your country has many Muslims and traditionalists who do not go to Christian churches," Esi says.

"That's true. My parents called followers of traditional religions 'heathens' as the Catholic priests did. They never let us visit shrines or mingle with heathens. That made me so curious about heathens," Zeb says.

"We have traditionalists too. My husband is from a Muslim family but my family is very traditional."

"Meaning?"

"We revere the earth goddess. She's the second in the pantheon of spirits," Esi says.

"Which one is the first?"

"*Nyame* is the Supreme Being with male and female essences. The female essence who created human beings also shows us the moon, while the male is shown in the sun that puts the fire of life in our veins."

"This is very interesting. In Igbo worship system, Ani is the earth goddess and the most important. Palm trees, coconut trees, forests, mountains, rivers, everything belongs to her. When Ani says that they should not farm in a particular land for years, they leave it alone and farm in another place. She says what part of the river that we should collect water for drinking, the part to swim in and the part to wash our clothes in. So even though my family is Christian, we still follow the regulation of our village and many of the rules were laid down by Ani. There are priests and priestesses who interpret what she says."

"So Ani pretty much controlled behaviour," Esi says.

"Of course. The fact is that Ani is everywhere and sees everything. You can't hide from her and you can't tell a lie in her name because she knows. We all behave ourselves in the village because we know that Ani sees everything. After all she is Earth that is everywhere. My parents never spoke about Ani but I learnt this from other people in the village."

"But when people go to the cities, they tend to forget her even though the earth is in the cities too.

I am in America and I still respect her. She is in America too."

Zeb had a Christian background but has always been interested in nature spirits, especially the female ones.

She finds the biblical stories of the Blessed Virgin Mary fascinating. The way she was very close to nature when she had her baby in a shepherd's manger, and the way the stars moved and led the Magi to her show that Mary was a woman close to nature. Zeb reveres the greatness of nature and its affinity with those who are nurturing children. She sees a lot of similarities in the stories of female goddesses everywhere. She has read about Mariamu in the Koran and has a lot of respect for her. She has read about Yemoja, the earth goddess of Yoruba people of Nigeria.

"I think that Ani is similar to the spirit that the Yoruba people call Yemoja. Hausa people have a similar goddess called Kasa," Zeb says to Esi, getting up from the chair. She takes a pillow and puts it behind her chair.

"I'll clear the table," Esi says.

"We'll clear it together."

35

Never Said 'Yes'

Zeb settles on the couch.

"Please get on with the story." Esi sits on the single seater.

"I was ten when my father sent me to Rosary High School, a boarding school run by Reverend Sisters."

"When was that?"

"1965. I loved my school and I wanted my father to continue being proud of me, so I worked very hard. The teachers loved me. I was very good in English because of all the coaching I got from my father, so they put me in the Debating society. I joined another group called Legion of Mary. On Saturdays, we went to visit the hospital, pray, and run errands for the sick. We also visited the prisons. Many times, some of us just took the time off and went to the shops and other interesting places." Zeb winks and picks a pillow.

"Did they ever find out that their good students cheated?" Esi says.

"How could they have found out? We never told on each other. It was our secret. I was so happy. Then one day, one of my uncles came to the school to take me home."

"What happened?"

"He told me that my father wanted me to come home, and I went with him, only to get home to a village that was in mourning. My father had died."

"And I did not even say goodbye." Zeb's voice quivers. She keeps silent for a while. She is trying to calm down. Esi goes back to the kitchen to bring some coffee. Zeb follows her to the kitchen.

"I still remember Nna-m as if this happened yesterday. He was very kind and loving. There was no day that he came back to our house without something for me, but I would always give some to my brothers." Zeb's voice is thin as if she talks to herself.

"Didn't he give presents to your brothers?" Esi opens the microwave to pick the cup of hot coffee.

"Sometimes he did." Zeb takes the cup from Esi. Esi picks another cup.

"He said that boys should be tough and not expect a lot of gifts. I think he just liked to give me gifts. My mother would say, 'You spoil her too much.' My brothers' mother would say, 'A girl has to be pampered. That's how she'll know the man who will be a good husband."

"How long ago was this?" Esi says picking a cup for herself.

"Over thirty years ago."

"And you still remember?"

"Why not? Nna-a's death was the end of my life. The rest has been harsh reality," Zeb goes back to the living room with the coffee. The statement jolts Esi. She is curious about how her life could have ended when she was a girl just entering middle school. She joins Zeb in the living room where she is sipping coffee. She's silent for a while; then she continues.

"After the burial, my Uncle Aghadi said that the family could not afford to pay for me in the boarding school. He said that I would live with somebody in the city of Enugu and go to school daily from that person's house. I was sad because I would miss my friends in the boarding house, but I was happy that I would still go to school. He said that the man called Igo would come and take me back to Enugu. I kind of liked the idea, because Igo was very active at my father's funeral. I felt that he must be a good man."

"Did he come as arranged?"

"Of course, he did. That day my brothers, I mean my cousins, wept so much as if they would not see me again. I still remember how Animaihe painted my small metal box. He made it look like rainbow with stripes of various colours. He got the paint from the tins discarded by workers who painted our local school. He was so talented. My metal box was so admired by my friends at school," Zeb sighs and continues.

"My mother sobbed as she advised me to clean the man's house and cook for him; a way to show gratitude for my living in his house. She also told me that I must always remember my father and work very hard because that was what he wanted of me. 'Remember that you will lead this community,' she emphasised my father's dream for me. My other mother, you know my cousins' mother, pulled me aside and whispered something."

"What did she whisper?" Esi says.

"She told me that I would no longer be in the care of the Reverend Sisters who as women knew how to take care of girls. She said that the city was full of men who wanted to deceive girls and that I must not allow them to see my laps."

Esi laughs, because her mother told her the same thing many times.

"Did anybody get through your laps?" Esi enjoys the sexual innuendo.

"Wait. I'll come to that part of the story later," Zeb says.

"So, somebody saw it. Naughty girl," Esi says.

"Do you want me to continue with this story?" Zeb is not laughing.

"Please go on."

"I consoled my weeping family, but I did not cry. I began to imagine the kind of control and strength that a leader should have, and crying was not one of them. I had a responsibility. I promised myself that I would not disappoint my father."

"Who told you that leaders don't cry?" Esi says.

"Nobody. I just knew it. Nna-a was like that. I never saw him cry, but I have seen my mothers weep. Sometimes they quarrelled and cursed each other out. They would weep and make up. Nobody ever got in-between them or took sides in their quarrel. Even my father would leave them alone.

"Why?"

"I have seen our neighbour talk to them across the bitter leaf hedging and advise them not to quarrel in front of the children. Both of them turned on the neighbour. They told her to mind her business. They told her that her children were not better than us who knew how to vent our emotions and control ourselves unlike her children who were rude and cheeky at school. Wow! They gave the woman such a rough time that she also began to weep. My two mothers then went to the fence and consoled her. They told her never to butt into their business," Zeb shakes her head smiling.

"So you see, I've seen my mothers get emotional, but not my father. So I didn't cry because I wanted to be the man as my father expected me to be. But to tell you the truth, I began to weep after I left our compound. Igo told me to stop crying, but I cried even more. I cried more than I did at the burial."

"How is Igo related to you?"

"I thought that he was my relation, because he performed tasks at the funeral ceremony. But it turned out that he was not, because of what he did to me."

"What?" Esi's mind goes to a sexual offence.

Esi thinks of how she would have reacted to a sexual assault when she was a young girl. One thing she is sure of is that her mother would have gone after the neck of the person, if her father did not get the offender before her.

"I'll kill anybody who assaults me," Esi thinks. Then she wonders what she would use to fight the person. She thinks of weapons that a little girl can use; finger nails, teeth, voice.

"Hello! Are you here with me?" Zeb says.

"Yes. Just thinking," Esi says.

"Do you want me to tell the story?"

"Please go on."

"Where was I?" Zeb says.

"The man wanted to rape you?" Esi says hoping that Zeb will contradict her, but she does not.

"He used to come to my room to make sure that I drank ovaltine and milk before going to bed. He said that I was too thin and should eat to recover the weight I lost because of my mourning. I thought that he was very nice but one particular night, he started pressing himself on me. I ran all the way to school and the Sisters kept me. They got the Matron to take me back to my home town and report the matter to my family. My mother took her kitchen knife, raised it up to the sky, touched it on the ground, and swore that she would cut Igo. My other mother wept and held me. I did not even cry. I just looked at my Uncle Aghadi. I wanted to know what would happen to my education because I would not go back to Igo's house. Uncle Aghadi talked with my mother and they decided that my uncle should take me to the school and not to Igo's house. My mother had just started retail trade in *okirika*. She would buy the used clothes from the town market and sell them in our village."

"What?"

"Used clothes. She gave my uncle the little she had made from the trade. He should give them to the Sisters when he took me back to the school. He did just that and I became a boarder again, just as when my father was alive. I was a perfect student. I did my chores and homework, read a lot, and got good grades. I won the school's scholarship of merit. I would have been very happy, but Nna-mu was not alive to enjoy my achievement with me. Then one day, my life ended. Igo came to the school to take me."

"Who died this time?"

"Nobody died, but he killed me when he said that I was his wife."

Zeb picks her empty cup of coffee, looks at it and puts it down. She picks it up again and gets up from the couch.

"What?" Esi say.

"I find this event painful, but I have to control myself somehow." Zeb keeps the cup on the table.

"I'm sorry," Esi takes her hand. Zeb sits down.

"It's not your fault. I need to tell this story. It has been there all these years like a load. I off-loaded some on Jaja but not everything. My mother knows some but not a lot because I don't want her to be mad and vengeful." Zeb says and continues with the narration.

"Igo said that he gave my uncle a lot of money at my father's funeral. The Reverend Sisters told him that he did not need to pay any school fees because of my scholarship. He threatened the Sisters. He said that they had no right over me and had no right to interfere in his personal matter. I begged him to allow me to use the scholarship to be in school. I even told him that I would marry him after high school. He refused. That was how I left school to become Igo's wife."

"Unbelievable."

"That was harsh reality. I was bitter at my uncle for taking money from him. I was bitter at my mother for allowing it to happen. I hated the man. He was huge, heartless, and ugly. He was a police officer and a very mean one. That was why my uncle and the Sisters could not stand up to him. He had power."

"What about your people? I thought that they usually come together to save their own. I heard that women can go to a man's house and deal with him," Esi says.

"I know what you are referring to. As a child, I saw women go to one man's house to sit on him. They said that they heard his wife crying at night because he hit her. They all sat in this man's house. They were inside, outside, in the shrubs, everywhere. My mother told me that if the man was not quick at accepting their demands and appeasing his wife, they would become restless and begin to destroy his things. The man said that he would never beat his wife again but he made them promise not to make songs to ridicule him and his family. It was a win win. He never beat his wife and they did not satirise him in song," Zeb says.

"That's so cool."

"That kind of thing works if you are all from the same town. Igo is not from my town. He's just a policeman who has been working in the city of Enugu for a very long time. He was so powerful that other police officers feared him. I blamed my uncle for taking the money. But he told my mother that Igo came as a friend and told him that he was in the army with Nna-a and that he wanted to help with the burial. After the burial, he began to threaten my uncle. My uncle was not strong like my father."

"So, nobody could stand up to Igo?" Esi says.

"Nobody, not the Sisters, not my uncle, or my mothers who didn't even know what happened. I really believed that my mother would come with her knife. Everyday, I would sit outside and watch the road, and expect my mother to come. When Igo realised why I was waiting, he told me that none of my people knew that I was no longer in school. He said he would take me home to see them if I agreed to marry him traditionally."

"Did you agree?"

"I refused! That was my way of getting back at him. He had taken my happiness. I knew that I would not enjoy the marriage ceremonies with a man I didn't want. I refused and I was happy that it hurt him."

"He got what he wanted, so why should he worry about a wedding ceremony?" Esi says.

"Oh no! Everybody knows that if you don't marry an Igbo girl traditionally, the children belong to her and her family. He did everything to beg me. He bought expensive wrappers, jewelry, what have you. I refused!"

"Who advised you to punish him like that?"

"Nobody. The man took away what I loved most in my life."

"Your virginity."

"And education! My girlhood! I just grew up by force. When he saw that I was pregnant, he said that he would take me to Eke and beg my mother to forgive him. He wanted my unborn child to be legally his as well. I calmed down. All I wanted was to set my foot in my hometown, and then I'd disappear from him forever."

36

Biafra War Blues

Zeb shakes her head from side to side. She is trying to control her pain. Esi wants to hug her and share the pain, but an expression on Zeb's face cautions her to keep off. Zeb folds her hands across her chest and continues with the narration.

"I didn't have the opportunity to get to Eke and disappear in a land that I knew so well. It was a bad time. That was in the latter part of 1967. The Nigeria-Biafra war had started, and people were running away from Enugu, the capital of Biafra. We ran from Enugu to Igo's village. I could not even understand their language."

"Wasn't it Igbo?" Esi says.

"One kind of Igbo dialect that I didn't understand. The people hated me anyway." Zeb flings one hand and juts her mouth as she continues.

"His mother said I was useless, that the only thing I was good at was wasting his son's money. I must be fair to him here. He told his mother and sisters that they should back off. He told them that they should not come to my side of the house."

"Did they obey him?"

"No way. His mother said that she was the head of the compound and that nobody could tell her where to go to in her compound. One of his sisters, her name was Janet; she called me *ashawo*."

"Meaning?"

"Prostitute."

"A woman called another woman a prostitute?" Esi says.

"I called her a frustrated bitch. Old unmarried bitch," Zeb says.

Esi cringes at Zeb calling another woman "old," "frustrated" and "bitch." Esi thinks it is ironical that Zeb is the one who is now unmarried, single and frustrated. She scrutinises Zeb as if she is seeing her for the first time. Zeb is just a little shorter than Esi but looks good. She is very skinny but her big butt and big breasts make her small size attractive.

"I can't believe you called another woman those ugly names," Esi says.

"What did I know then? I just wanted to hurt her. But Igo dealt with her." She slaps her hand on her laps.

"What!"

"Yes. Igo slapped his sister. 'Nobody, not even my sister can call my wife a prostitute and get away with it!' Janet fought back. She said that he did not marry me.

'You didn't marry her. She is a free woman not a wife.' The other sister joined in the fight. Their mother began to shout that he should 'remove that useless thing from my house.' She called me a useless thing. How I cried for my own mother; she would have taught Igo's mother the lesson of her life for the way she insulted me. Anyway, neighbours came."

"Who was at the centre of all this family trouble?" Esi says.

"Me!" Zeb is happy. Esi shakes her head.

"And what was your reaction to the fight?"

"I ran into our room and listened from there. The neighbours said that there had been peace in the neighbourhood until Igo returned with me. They said that he must take me away from the place. Igo did what they wanted. He took me to a place called Ede-Obala near the university town of Nsukka. He rented two rooms there, but we stayed there for only a few days. We had to run because we could hear the sound of guns in the battlefront. He said that he would take me to my hometown so that I would have the baby there with the people I loved."

"He knew that you didn't love him."

"He knew that I hated him."

"Tough."

"We went to my hometown, but it was a ghost town. People had run away. Nigerian soldiers had infiltrated the place so people knew that our town would be a battlefront soon, so they ran away. I was heartbroken. I wept so hard. I wanted to search for my people, but we did not know which part of Biafra they fled to, and the baby was kicking hard. We then went to Orlu. Igo said that Orlu was in the heart of Biafra and the safest place to live at that time. He took me straight to the hospital; Bishop Shanahan hospital. They admitted me. I had my son. He was premature so they kept him in an incubator and told me to go home. Igo rented an apartment. That was where I lived during the three years of the war. He lived and worked in the city of Owerri. He also worked in Ihiala. He moved from place to place and came home from time to time to see us. He said that bombers always targeted the cities and he didn't want his family to be in danger. I didn't even want to live with him, so it was okay by me. He used to come from time to time to see us and try to get me pregnant. I had one more child during the war and one just after the war."

Esi cut in, "You must have started to like him, for you to make the children."

"I loved my children and he cared for us. That was what mattered. During the war, I didn't have too much time to think about my hatred for him. I had other serious problems. I didn't know anything about my mother, brothers, sisters or any of my people. I used to hear terrible stories about what Nigerian soldiers did to Biafran civilians. I used to take some of our food to the refugee camp, just to be nice to them and hear their stories. I always wished that my family would come there but I never even saw anybody from my town at the camp. It was hell not knowing anything about my mother and all my loved ones. I was very angry. I wanted to join the army. Had it not been for my children, I would have joined the Biafran army to fight against Nigeria."

"Why? Just to be a soldier like your father?"

"No. Just to fight for Biafra," Zeb says.

"You liked Biafra that much as a girl?"

"Till today, I love my country."

"Are you not a Nigerian," Esi says.

"Biafran and Nigerian. I love them both. They both define me."

"It makes sense. It's like my being Ashanti, a Ghanaian and a British Commonwealth citizen. I'm now American."

"What of Igo? Would he have let you enlist in the army?"

"He would have had no say in the matter. Anyway, to tell the truth, Igo was good to us. I must grant him that. I was always happy when he came. He brought money and many things for the house. I was still interested in education. Nobody went to school, anyway. Not really. There was one or two high schools; mostly girls. The boys were in the army or hiding somewhere."

"So education pretty much stopped."

"In a way, yes, but I read any book that I could find. I read the bible in the church. I read all the books of the bible and also prayed a lot."

"At least, you didn't starve like most people in a war," Esi says.

"True, still it wasn't easy. When the war ended, Igo joined the Nigerian police. Do you know where they sent him to?"

"No."

"Abeokuta in the West. It is in the far west of the Yoruba nation," Zeb says.

"So they easily took him back after he worked for Biafra."

"Yes. When we came back to Enugu, the city was in shambles. We couldn't even locate our former house. We went to Lagos. One thing with Igo is that he knows how to use his Second World War contacts. Baba Oladimeji was good to us in Lagos. I hated Nigerians then because of the war and did not like the man. Igo begged me to accept him. He said that since we had become Nigerians again, we had to deal with them as our own people. It was easy for someone like him without emotions to say such things. You cannot switch emotions off and on as if they are electricity."

Esi is quiet.

"But we did it. We switched our emotions to accept Nigerians as ours, but it was not easy," Zeb says.

"Baba Oladimeji was well connected. He got them to take Igo back in the Nigerian Police. Then they sent him to Abeokuta. Life returned to us there, but it was a strange life. My spirit did not return to my body."

"You were broken by the war experience," Esi says.

"I was bitter. We had a big house, servants, car, chauffeur and everything. Some members of my family survived the war, but I lost my brother Animaihe and Uncle Aghadi. Both of them died as soldiers in the Biafran army. We lost so much as a people," Zeb sighs. Esi thinks about the war experience and how it affected Zeb. Zeb thinks about how the war changed people and changed the society. People were hardened by all the hardship and suffering. Many have still not been able to get back to life as it was before the war. During the war, people were killed in their homes awake or asleep. The bombers and jet fighters were the most dreaded characters of the war. People feared them more than the devil. If you wanted to frighten any one, just say, 'bomber.' Children had a song about 'bomber.'

BABOON WITH WINGS
Hunger is not seen by Bomber.
Anger is no concern of Bomber.
That you are alive incites Bomber,
That comes in metal wing of death.
When you sleep, Bomber watches.
You call God, Bomber answers,
Like lightening chased by thunder.

Uninvited Bomber comes with death,
To spray you with bomb and bullets.
I look up and cry, bomber please,
But bomber does not have ears.
Bomber has eyes that throw bombs.
Bomber has heart that loves death.

"What are you thinking about?" Esi asks.

"Just remembering the verses that we used to chant during the war."

"Let's not talk about the war; that was a long time ago," Esi says.

"For me it's still like yesterday. I was twelve years old when it started. I really don't like to talk about it because it comes with sadness, but no matter how I try, I can't tell you my story without talking about Biafra and the war. Had it not been for the war I would have left Igo or my people would have rescued me from that life. I lost my life and my spirit in that war." Zeb gets up and rushes to the bathroom. Esi hears the splash of water. Zeb returns to the living room with water dripping from her face.

"You didn't clean your face," Esi says.

"I like the coldness of the water on my face."

"Do you want to stop the story?" Esi says.

"No."

"Do you have a photo of your children,?" Esi wants to diffuse the tension by diverting Zeb to something that will make her happy. It works. Zeb goes to her suitcase and brings out a small photo album. She shows Esi her children, mother and siblings. Zeb's happy mood is cut short because Esi points at the photo of a boy whose sharp eyes focus ahead.

"That's my brother, Animaihe. He died in the war. We didn't know how he died and it hurts so much. But the family tried to bring a closure by performing funeral ceremonies for him and my uncle. When I was getting ready for their funeral ceremonies," Zeb sighs.

"What?"

"I told Igo that he should not come with me to the ceremonies. It would bring up memories of what he did at my father's funeral and he might go there to plot another crime. I just didn't trust him."

"I don't blame you," Esi says.

"But he still came. Threw his weight around. Brought in a lot of money, drinks, food and many other things. He even got some of his friends to accompany us all the way from Abeokuta to the east. My people were impressed."

"Did they take the things?"

"Of course, they had to. They had suffered a lot during the war, lost the war, lost many of our people, and lost all our property. They had nothing. And Nigeria took all the money that people had in the banks so they couldn't even get what they had in the banks before they ran from the war zone."

"How?"

"The government just made Biafran money worthless. So even if you had one million in the bank, it became zero money. The best they could do was give you twenty pounds, which might not have covered your trip to the bank. Many fathers had heart attack and died. They could not face their future without providing for their families. Of course, my people welcomed Igo's help. But they still did not regard him as an in-law because he did not marry me traditionally. He knew that also. He began to beg me again to allow him to marry me traditionally. 'After all that we have been through together' he said. I gave him a condition. I told him that I would agree on condition that I went back to school. That was the deadlock." Zeb pauses.

"I can't believe I had three children with that man!" She says as she comes from the kitchen with a glass of water. The children were the bond that held the marriage together. By the time she left Igo, she felt that children should never have been the bond. A couple should be together because they want each other. That was why she would not tell Jaja when she got pregnant and had Dozie. Angel told her to inform him immediately. She felt that if they were meant to be together, Jaja would wait for her to get the further education that she craved. She was pregnant when she heard that he was going to get married to the daughter of his parents' friends. She decided not to take her mother's advice. Jaja had chosen another woman over her and she would not use her pregnancy or baby to get back a man who had made his choice. Jaja did not know and still does not know that he is Dozie's biological father. Over the years as she got the education she craved for, her view of the matter changed and she wanted to tell Jaja her secret. Each time she wanted to tell him, the imagined consequences would overwhelm her. She will make this right. Dozie and Jaja have to know the truth.

"How did you break up with him?"

"It has a story. I'll tell you later. I want to use the bathroom."

"You used it a while ago."

"I just splashed water on my face then. I want to use it now." Zeb puts down the glass and goes to the bathroom. Esi takes the photo album.

37

Husband's New 'Wife'

Esi looks at a large photo of Zeb on the front cover of the album. Wow! What a woman! The light from the window washes over the photo and gives Zeb's face a glint. Her eyes. They look straight ahead. Esi studies the woman who lost her father when she was a child, but held on to his dream; a dream that became hers. She lost the opportunity to fulfill that dream because of early marriage, but she struggled to reclaim it. Esi views the eyes from different angles, to see whether they could look at her directly, but Zeb's head is tilted up so the eyes focus above the head of the viewer. There is a kind of smile, but the face does not glow in spite of the glint of the light. This woman might have been different if Igo had fitted into a fatherly role as a kind uncle or something. But he screwed up and became her bad guy. She became strong in the process of living with her bad guy.

Esi cannot imagine how Zeb managed to make love and have all those children. She flips through the pages to look at the children. They look alike with long limbs probably like Igo, with lovely eyes like Zeb. She goes back to the cover page. Zeb's hair is full and piled up on her head giving her face a regal look. Her neck is adorned with an expensive-looking jewelry. She looks beautiful, but something is missing. Esi tries to find the word for what is missing. Sparkle! Yes, there is no radiance on Zeb's face. On the photograph, the beauty is in her eyes and cheeks. Igo must have been happy to show her off as his trophy wife. She gave him some and stored a lot in her heart. Maybe that's why the eyes look so sad in the photo in spite of its beauty. Esi stands back from the picture, and tries to read words from the personality. Sadness. Determination. Fighter. Hidden beauty.

Esi looks at Zeb who is coming out of the bathroom. Her sexy curves are still there, but there is a difference between her real face and the photo image. The spark in her real face is absent in the photo, but there is still a mystery in both.

"When did you take this photo?"

"When I left Igo's house, I walked into a photo studio and took that photo. The photographer tried very hard to make me look at the lens but I was so focused on looking ahead at my future and wondering what it would bring that I could not look at the lens. Finally he gave up."

"It's a beautiful photo."

"Thanks."

"So how did you manage to leave Igo?"

"Let's go and shop for your cosmetics."

"We can go later. I want to hear the end of this story," Esi says.

"They sent Igo to Kaduna State in the north of Nigeria for a job that would take one year. The children were at school, so he went alone while I stayed with the children in Abeokuta. While he was away, I applied for a scholarship to go to London for a course. A husband had to endorse the form. I hoped that he would endorse it, after all the years. When he returned for a weekend I begged him to support me in getting what I've wanted all my life by filling his part of the form."

"Did he endorse it?" Esi says.

"No. But it did not end at no. He was angry and refused to eat the food that I set before him. I ate the food with my children as we used to do while he was in Kaduna. When the children went to bed, he began to lecture me. 'I give you everything a woman wants. I gave you children, a car, big house, jewelry, and I take care of you and your people.' Did I ask him to give me all those things? No. All I wanted was for him to leave me alone in my school. That was all I wanted. I was so mad at the mention of my people, but I had to hear him out.

He said that, 'Any good woman would be happy that her husband has returned safely from a very risky police job. Any good woman would want her husband to have some peace. Not so with you. You want to leave me and the children. You want to go to London to meet white men.' That was it! I was about to feel a little pity for him when he reminded me about his risky job, but when he reduced my yearning for education to desire for men, I snapped."

"What happened?"

"I wanted to tackle him with my mouth, but I saw the glint on his face and knew that he was up to something. I shut up," Zeb says.

"You didn't say anything to him?"

"No. I kept silent and just walked out to figure things out. I stood in the balcony and gazed at the night. At first, I saw nothing, just blackness. Then I began to see a little light. I could make out the figures of the trees in the compound. Then more light. There were stars in the sky, but no moon. I stood there and drank the fresh air. I opened my mouth and inhaled deeply, and then I slowly let out the air. That was what my mothers did when they were tired in the farm. But I was not tired, just angry and sad."

Esi watches as Zeb twists her mouth like she is controlling anger. It is amazing that she is still angry after all these years even with all her successes. She inhales slowly and deeply. She exhales and continues with the story.

"I later realised that he was already planning to marry another wife and was looking for an excuse to accuse me of something or have a serious quarrel with me."

"But you never really had a marriage with him," Esi says.

"True, but it was a slap on my face to sit down there, and hear that my husband had married another wife without any respect for my position as the wife."

"Appearances?"

"Call it what you like. But, that was not the way we did it at home. I mean, one of my uncles had two wives. They had their quarrels, but there was respect and friendship. And that was because the first one chose the second one and wanted her to come into their family as a second wife. When a man goes behind your back, the new wife comes in laughing at you and mocking you. She feels and acts like she is the boss of the man and you, instead of it being the other way round. The first woman should be the boss of the home."

"One way or the other, another wife is not desirable," Esi says.

"You're wrong. In my case, I didn't mind another wife, but I wanted to be the one to choose her. The man never allowed me to initiate anything. It was his house and he ran it as he ran the police department. Everybody answered him, sir sir sir. Because I didn't cower down to him, he thought that I was not a good woman."

"You also didn't make life easy for him," Esi says.

"Igo didn't make life easy for me. So there we were, making life miserable for each other."

"And making lots of babies too," Esi says.

"I love my children, and stayed with Igo for that long so as to take care of them. But that did not mean that I did not want my own life as a person."

"Did you try to prevent him from marrying another wife?"

"I could not prevent him from disgracing me. I think that he just wanted to hurt me for not being his imagined kind of wife. He married a new wife and lived with her in Kaduna. I wanted a divorce, so that I could apply for scholarship as a single person. I went to a lawyer, but he wanted a lot of money. I think that he was just afraid of Igo. Everybody was afraid of him."

"Except you," Esi says.

"Except me. I sold my jewelry and took the money to the lawyer. He took his consultation fee and then told me to bring the marriage papers. I didn't have any papers. Again he said that he could not help me."

"Where were the papers?" Esi says.

"There were none." Zeb stares above Esi's head. Her eyes look just like the eyes of her image in the photo album. The government nullified marriages enacted during the war so legally she had no marriage, but she was tied by the greatest bond; her children. She thanks God for her mother, Angel, who encouraged her to endure and wait for the right time to leave. Angel said that Igo was too powerful but God was more powerful and she would continue to "be on her knees in prayer for God's intervention in her daughter's unhappy marriage." God gave her the opportunity with Igo's new marriage. Some people saw it as a rejection, but neither she nor her children would suffer the stigma of her being a bad mother who left her kids. She seized the opportunity to get out of the marriage for good. Her mind goes to her present circumstances. She has long promised herself that she would never put herself legally under the control of another person, yet she gave a lot of control to Anise. She feels happy to be out of Anise's house even though she was kicked out.

Esi feels privileged that unlike Zeb at the time of her marriage, she was able to decide things for herself during her marriage. The problem arose from her husband's long stay in Ghana that made her resentful. When he eventually returned after six years, he thought that she was going to accept him with open arms, but instead she rejected him. She did not allow him into her bedroom because she was angry. He thought that she was acting out because she knew about his mistress in Ghana, so he begged her to forgive him saying he did not want to run around or go to prostitutes, so he kept a woman. That was how she found out. She filed for divorce. Kofi packed his things and left. Remembering this incident, Esi cannot imagine how she would have reacted if she had heard that Kofi married another woman as Zeb's husband did. Esi turns her attention to Zeb and watches her facial expressions.

Zeb's eyes are almost closed. Esi believes that she is sleeping or suppressing an emotion so she goes to the kitchen to start lunch. Zeb is just thinking about how she left Igo's house. She laughs a little. From the low window, that connects the kitchen and the living room, Esi hears her laughter.

"I thought that you were sleeping."

"No, I'm thinking about how I left Igo's house."

"Do you want to share it?"

"Of course. This story session is therapeutic for me. I'm getting to the end of it. My mother was the one who told me the best way to leave without using an attorney."

"You never married him legally, so you could have walked away."

"No. We had children and property. If I had walked away, that would have counted against me.

My mother told me what to do."

"What was it?" Esi says.

"Very simple. I should make the man to divorce me," Zeb says.

"How?"

"I asked her the same question. She said, 'As his wife, you know what he hates. Do it. You have been unhappy for too long.' That was sheer womansense. I was worried about my children but my mother said that she would keep an eye on them while I pursued my dream," Zeb says.

"Did you take her advice?"

"Right away. I got a job in a hotel."

"As what?"

"Doing the only thing that I knew how to do," Zeb says.

"Gosh, don't tell me that you began to do the thing for making babies," Esi laughs. Zeb thinks it funny and laughs.

"I thought of that. There were some good-looking guys at work with me, but my focus was on going back to school. I wanted to find a way to do it," Zeb says still laughing.

"You're crazy," Zeb says.

"So what other thing could you do apart from getting into bed?" Esi says.

"Don't be silly. I cooked for my children and my husband all those years. I was a good entertainer also. My parties were always the talk of the town. I was skilled in cooking. So they employed me as a cook in the hotel. Then he came home with his new wife."

"What?"

"He did. But she was wise."

"How?"

Zeb gets up from her seat, "I want to show you what happened." Esi runs out of the kitchen to watch Zeb.

"The so-called wife knelt down in front of me to beg me. I still remember her speech. She said 'My sister, please I have not come here to make trouble.' I almost kicked her when she called me her sister," Zeb jerks her feet and throws a punch in the air.

"Why take out your frustration on the poor woman? Your husband was the offender," Esi says.

"At that time, she was more of a poor fool than a poor woman," Zeb says.

"What else did she say?"

Zeb puts her palm on top of the other and inclines her head towards the floor in pretence of respect. Esi bursts out laughing. Zeb mimics her young co-wife's soft voice. Esi laughs at Zeb's impersonation. Zeb also laughs and flops on the seat.

"She pretended to be all innocent and full of respect, yet she managed to sneak into Igo's bed without me knowing." Zeb shuts her mouth and squeezes it into a small knot that makes her face look distorted. It looks like a mouth that will never open.

"Zeb, please tell me what she said."

Zeb relaxes her mouth and mimics the thin voice again. "I know that you are my senior and my big sister in this house. I only do what our husband tells me to do, but I really want to respect you as my mother told me to do. Please accept me. Sister, please."

"What did you tell her?" Esi says.

"I sighed, very long and loud sigh for the benefit of the husband who was watching the drama." Zeb gets up again.

"I called her 'Stupid girl!' and walked out on her. Igo shouted at me. 'Heartless woman!' I retied my top wrapper, sighed loudly again, and swaying my hips this way and that way to show my joy, I walked away without talking to him," Zeb demonstrates the actions. When she gets to the sliding door of the deck, she turns round.

"I gave him silence, which was the treatment reserved for fools," she comes back to her seat.

"Tough."

Zeb shakes her legs and continues with the story.

"The situation was tough, just as my marriage has been. I showed that I did not accept his wife. That was my way of getting back at him. The funny thing was that while we made war, my kids bonded with the girl. She was young and played with them. She washed their clothes and almost took over the house chores from my steward. I had to warn my housekeeper not to let her come close."

"Why were you punishing her?"

"Why did she come into my house without my permission?"

Esi has no answer to this question, so Zeb continues.

"In the morning, I went to work. When I returned, I purposely let out that I worked at Hilltop Hotel. That was it. Igo sprang up to hit me. That was the first time in our marriage that he tried to put his hands on me. Of course, I knew that it would make him angry but I did not expect that it could lead to physical abuse. I ran outside and made a big noise. I screamed for help. He did not like to be disgraced. He was the one who disgraced other people. But I took his role from him and began to shout outside the house. My children started crying and shouting. They had never seen me like that. They probably thought I was going crazy. The servants, drivers, and other domestic workers came out from the boys' quarters. The place was like a mad house. Everybody was shouting and crying. The new wife ran after me crying, 'Sister, please cool down, you know that our husband is hot-tempered.' I shouted at her, 'If you come near me, I'll kill you!' She ran back to the children and the house continued with its shouting madness."

"What about the neighbours?"

"When Igo saw them coming, he ran into his room. He never came out. I told them the story of my marriage; part of it. How he married another wife without my permission, how I have been a very good wife, and how he repaid me by disgracing me. I even told them that he abused his power as my father's trusted friend and tricked me into marriage. I exposed him. That was the end of it all. I moved out of the house even though he did not ask me to move out. The rest is history. I applied for Federal Government Scholarship as a single person."

"Your country was good then," Esi says.

"No. The military was still in power, but sometimes things still worked in spite of the political confusion?" Zeb says.

Esi goes back to the kitchen. Zeb follows her to the kitchen as she narrates how her mother travelled to Abeokuta to talk things over with Igo. Igo was happy to see Angel and wanted to tell his own side of the story, but Angel assured him that she did not come to fight him. She only wanted to take care of her grandchildren, but Igo assured her that the housekeeper and steward would take care of them. He went back to Kaduna without his new wife, Shatu. She stayed back to help care for the children. Angel also stayed for two months observing everything. She took to liking Shatu because of the way she took very good care of the children. Zeb went to the house often to see the children. She became friends with Shatu who eventually had two children for Igo.

Zeb helps Esi prepare *kenkey* with fish and soup. The heaviness in Zeb's heart has gone and she chats and laughs freely with Esi as if things were normal. She believes that the feeling comes from her not being beholden to Esi as a host. Since she left Igo, she never let her guard down until she entered Anise's house. She will never do it again. She will look for a place of her own and find a job. No matter how small the place is, it will be better than living in the comfort of another person's house.

"Esi? Can you help me find a place around here?"

"For what."

"To live; my own place."

"What about Chicago?"

"I'm not comfortable with that. I'll visit him later after moving into my own place."

"You can live with me for free until you get your own place."

"No, I'll like to have my own place or share the rent here."

"I understand how you feel. I pay three hundred a month. Can you pay me one hundred and sleep on the couch."

"Is that fair?"

"Yes, the lease is in my name and once in a while my boyfriend comes here."

"Does he sleep here?"

"No."

38

This Too Shall Pass

Zeb spends her first weekend with Esi telling stories, many of which she has never shared with her mother or Jaja. She wakes up early feeling much better than she has felt in a long while. She folds the blanket and bedsheets, picks the couch pillows and arranges them on the couch. Esi gives her a key and tells her how to get to Kinko's for Internet transactions. She will post a letter to her using their address so she can use it for library registration during the week. After breakfast, the two walk from their Rosecrest apartment building on 16th street to the bus stop at Lebanon Street. Esi enters her bus while Zeb waits for the bus to Langley Park.

Seated in the bus, Zeb looks out of the window to familiarise herself with the area. At a stop sign, she sees a notice at the window of a drug store by the gas station. She gets off the bus at the next stop and walks to the gas station. She goes into the drug store and reads the notice. It is a job advertisement.

"I am interested in the job opening," she says to the attendant in the store.

"It's for an attendant for the night shift."

"What time in the night?"

"From five to eleven. Are you asking for yourself?"

"Yes," Zeb says.

"You have to talk to the supervisor. Phone in the morning around eight. Here's the phone number." He gives Zeb a business card. She goes back to the bus stop.

At Langley Park shopping complex, she locates Kinko's and sends a message to Aracebor. "Due to circumstances that I'll explain later, I can't come to Chicago now. I'll call later. Sorry about the inconvenience."

Aracebor is disappointed by her message but he shrugs it off as part of what he regards as her elusive personality, which ironically appeals to him. He focuses on moving back to Baltimore and his studies, which he knows will appeal to a woman like Zeb.

Zeb goes from one store to another looking at the notices on the windows and sometimes she walks in to ask about job vacancies. She buys two Christmas cards; one for Anise and one for Esi. She sees a notice for an editorial job. She copies the information. She goes to a telephone booth and phones the number.

"Do you have a high school diploma?"

"Yes, I have more than that."

"Do you have editing experience?"

"Yes."

"Send your résumé to Our Lady of Grace at-."

I have the address," Zeb says.

Zeb goes back to Kinko's to prepare a résumé for the job. With her degrees and editorship experience, she believes that she will get the job. She closes her eyes and says a short prayer for the job. She prints her résumé, puts it in an envelope and puts it in her bag. She does not post it but goes to the bus stop. She wants to hand in the résumé personally. She wants to see the church and the work environment. She brings out her bus map and locates the area and the best means of transportation. She takes a bus to Prince George's station where she boards the metro to Glenmont station. From Glenmont, she takes a bus to Norbeck. The church is not far from the bus rank on Norbeck Street. Zeb walks leisurely on the sidewalk. She has not gone far when she sees the secluded church in a wooded background. She smiles. She likes this kind of environment. She walks into the church and kneels down on the back pew for a short prayer. She goes back to the foyer and makes her way to the office. As she walks down to the basement, and straight through an open door, someone speaks to her.

"Can I help you?" the secretary smiles. Zeb introduces herself and the secretary takes the résumé from her.

"I'll give it to Father and if he wants you for an interview, I'll contact you. Is your contact information in your résumé?"

Zeb is all smiles as she makes her return journey.

On getting back to the apartment, she phones her sister to tell her about the latest changes.

"You sound happy in spite of what happened."

"I feel like a huge burden has been removed from my shoulders."

"I didn't know it was that bad."

"I don't know what my normal self could have been without my experience with Igo."

"So it's not just Anise and Brian; you've been carrying a lot all these years."

After talking with her sister, she phones and speaks with her mother and son. She phones her cousin but he doesn't have the documents she asked for. He tells her to be patient and keep praying. She dials Gloria and quickly cuts it off. She feels like she needs a break from Gloria and all the talk about a Green Card marriage. She rethinks her strategy for survival and decides that she will change her email address, because she does not want Alex or Anise to get in touch with her. The change may affect Aracebor. No problem. If she needs to be in touch, she can phone him.

What Zeb does not know is that she won't get Aracebor on the phone if she tries, because he has a new area code in Baltimore. Moreover, she cannot trace him if she looks for Aracebor in any phone book because he now goes by his real name. He phones the Esomonus and is told that Zeb moved out of the house. Everything is confusing so he decides to wait for her to phone and explain things. Meanwhile he phones his brother to explain his new plans.

"Where are you staying?"

"In a motel and trying to straighten out my registration. I'm also loking for a job."

"You have a lot of money my brother; why bother to work, probably as a waiter or some low-class job, instead of giving all your time to education for now?" Cedric laughs before adding, "Of course you are Granma's boy. Careful with money."

"You know it."

"You are really serious this time."

"I was serious before. Just circumstances. The good thing is that I have more than the required job experience for completing my studies. So, I'm good to go."

"You have also gained a lot of maturity from your experience."

"I know; and I'm glad I did it."

"Gran Emma will be proud of you. I'm proud of you too."

Meanwhile, Zeb is still in the apartment she shares with Esi, and not thinking about Aracebor or Chicago. She is in the hallway mirror putting on her earrings when Esi is about to leave for work.

"Where are you going to?" Esi asks.

"I think that I may have an interview at the gas station."

"I like your spirit. Good luck. Remember to take an umbrella because it might rain. And don't worry if you don't see me tonight."

"Gomez?"

"Yeah."

"When will I get to meet him?"

"Weekend. See you later." Esi leaves.

Zeb is in the kitchen drinking coffee when she checks her watch. It is eight o'clock, so she phones the manager of the gas station. He informs her that the job is no longer available. Zeb is surprised.

"This early in the morning? Who could have got there before me?"

"Well ...eh."

"Well what?"

"I've made my decision." He hangs up. Zeb stands there looking at the receiver. She believes that he just does not want her. She walks back to the living room and consoles herself with the notion of the job not being suitable for her. She does not really like the idea of working in a lonely station at night just to earn a few dollars. The editorship job is more appealing so she will focus on it.

She has to go to Langley Park again to look for more job notices. This time, she decides to walk in order to familiarise herself with the area. She walks through Lebanon Street and Merrimac Road to the park from where she finds her way to the shopping complex. It begins to drizzle. Zeb uses an umbrella to shield her hair from the rain as she looks at the notices on shop windows. Not finding any notice of interest, she makes her way to the library. She walks fast because of the rain. Going through the University Boulevard, she sees a sign, The Law Offices of Rich Adams. She goes to the office and is greeted by the secretary.

"I'll like to see the Attorney."

"Mr. Adams will not be here till two. What do you want to see him for?" After listening to her issues, Liddy, the secretary, tells her to come back in the afternoon.

"How much does it cost to speak with him?"

"This is a non-profit organisation. The fees are minimal but discuss that with Mr. Adams," Liddy says.

Zeb spends time at Takoma Park Library. She creates a new email account, transfers most of her contact addresses to the new one and closes the old account. She heaves a sigh of relief. She feels good for cutting off communication link with the Esomonus. Unknown to her, Aracebor sends her an email message, but it bounces back. At one thirty, she makes her way back to the Attorney's office.

Three other people are there to check on their immigration papers. The secretary reads their papers and explains things to them in Spanish. A tall man in dark suit enters the office.

"Good afternoon Mr. Adams," Liddy says. He glances at all of them, asks Zeb what she wants and enters his office. Liddy motions Zeb to follow him. She feels lucky and smiles as she steps into his office. It is huge; bigger than the apartment she shares with Esi, but very untidy. Adams notices that she looks at the papers on top of books randomly kept on the shelf, table, and on the floor.

"I'll soon get another professional organiser to fix this office," he says removing the papers on a chair and motioning her to sit. After listening to her story, he asks her the kind of visa she came with and when it will expire. On hearing that it is a B visa due to expire in about two months, he tells her that she needs to apply for extension of the visa.

"You don't want to be classified as an illegal immigrant."

Zeb tells him about the immigration forms she got from Baltimore that will help her get a classification as an extraordinary alien. He informs her that it takes years to process it, if at all it will work. The few cases where it works are because the applicants have institutions that sponsor the application. He describes a complicated process that she can follow to get a Green Card. Zeb does not fully understand the process but she is glad that it does not involve marriage. It involves applying for admission and registering as a student so that she can get a student visa. The visa will give her a classification that will qualify her for certain jobs in the institution. Zeb cannot imagine going back to school and shakes her head to indicate her dislike of the idea.

"Come and see me after the holidays and bring all your papers."

"What date?"

"Make an appointment with my secretary."

Zebs smiles as she comes out of Adam's office, "That was a good meeting. Thanks for your help."

"I'm glad we are of help to you," Liddy says. Zeb asks to see Adams immediately after Christmas, but Liddy informs her that they will be on Christmas recess.

"You can see him on the second of January."

The rain has stopped, giving way to mild sunshine that washes over the wet ground. The smile is still on Zeb's lips as she traces her way to Langley Park. She goes to the post office and sends out greeting cards before she walks back to Rosecrest. She fixes an early dinner and relaxes on the couch in front of the television. She has a good feeling about her meeting with Adams. It's going to lead to the breakthrough she has been hoping for. She phones her cousin, Tom, to let him know the new developments. She also asks about Brian but could not get anything out of Tom.

Zeb wakes up in the morning to get ready for another day at the library. She packs her bedding and is on her way to the bathroom when the telephone rings. Thinking that Esi will pick it, she continues to the bathroom until she hears Esi's voice on the answering machine. She runs back to the living room and picks the phone.

"So you're not in your room?"

"No."

"What about work?"

"No work today."

"Why not?"

"Emergency situation. We've been ordered to stay wherever we are because of the unexpected snow."

"Snow?" Zeb runs to the sliding door and pulls the curtain.

"Oh my God." She puts her hand on her chest smiling and remembering the first time she saw the snow. It was in the winter of 1994 in New York. Her roommate laughed so hard at her running outside to make a snowman, but she called hers snow woman and used sticks to make earrings for her.

"I won't be able to return until the buses come back to the road. You too, stay indoors and keep warm."

"No way, I'm going out to enjoy the snow. I participated in snow balling in New York and enjoyed every bit of it."

"Just be careful," Esi says.

"I have good news." Zeb tells her about her visit to the attorney. Esi tells her that it is not a bad idea to go to school in order to get a student visa.

"Where will I get the money for school fees? You know it's very expensive for foreign students."

"You can do what I'm doing. I'm saving money in order to go back to school one day. You can do the same thing."

"I have to get the job first."

"You will. You are qualified and you're aggressive."

"Thank you." Zeb is happy that someone appreciates her ability. It is a far cry from Anise's attitude to her.

Esi and Zeb attend the night mass at our Lady of Sorrow's Church in Hyattsville. It is Esi's idea that they attend service at night because she will work on Christmas day. They expect a large turn out of customers and the workers will get double pay for the day. Esi invites Zeb to Christmas dinner at China Palace. Zeb meets Gomez for the first time.

"Hi Zeb," Gomez stands to shake her hands. He is about five feet seven, not tall by Zeb's estimation, but he has a groomed handsome face and charming personality.

"You must be the famous Gomez," Zeb smiles.

"I've heard a lot of good things about you and how very beautiful and smart you are," Gomez says.

"Thank you. Esi has been exaggerating?" Zeb smiles and sits.

"She's very right," Gomez sits. Esi joins them and they all go to sample the buffet. Gomez is a limousine driver at Eagle Company. He likes the job because it gives him time for his cleaning business. He has to make a certain amount every week for the company. The company doesn't care what you do with your time after that. He makes jokes about how he straddles two roles; one in a gentlemanly suit and the other in workman's jeans. He tells Zeb how he applied for green card for himself based on his cleaning business with more than ten employees. He says that she can form an organization and apply for a Green Card on that basis.

"If I have to set up something, I'll need capital," Zeb says.

"You can form a non-profit organisation. Just find a cause that you have passion for and get other people interested in it."

"It's something to think about," Esi says.

39

Stoop to Conquer

Zeb offers to organise the attorney's office for free. It's a good way of making herself useful to him and also getting American work experience. She needs to know more about a Green Card, visa and work permit options and processes. She labels folders, arranges them in alphabetical order, and begins to go through the papers to decide which paper should go into which folder. While clearing stuff in the office, she discovers a beautiful wooden figurine of mother and child lying underneath a cluster of old papers that Adams told her to trash. She cleans the dirty figurine feeling it gives her a good impression of Adams. For him to have such a piece, he must be sensitive or sentimental or something. He says he got it from a garage sale. Zeb places it at the centre of his big table. He is impressed by her work and sets her up on a small table with a computer on the corner of his office.

"At least I don't have to go to the library to line up for Internet use," she tells Esi.

Whenever Adams has the time, he chats with Zeb. They discuss politics, history, and immigration laws. She learns a lot from him about how to survive in America. He tells her his personal story; they brought him up in an orphanage and he never had parents or siblings. In High School, he fell in love with a girl who had many of the things he longed for all his life. She had wealthy parents, a sister and two brothers. He felt lucky when she returned his love and they got married and had three children. Their marriage did not work out and what hurt him most was that she and her rich family lied against him and legally prevented him from ever seeing his children. That was why he went back to school and studied law so that he would never be in such a vulnerable position again.

"So you can defend yourself and get back your children," Zeb says thinking of her hope to get back her boys from powerful Igo. Her sons are not as fast with their education as she is. Thirty years old Oli is in graduate school and his brother is an undergraduate in the same college. The third is in High School. Zeb believes that their main problem is Igo who spoils them with money and fast cars. Whenever she visited them in school, she tried to persuade them to be more serious with life.

"Are you with me? You seem to be far away," Adams says.

"I'm listening," Zeb says. She then tells him about her dreams for uniting with her sons and bringing them to America. Seeing that Zeb is competent, he begins to rely on her for researching cases on the internet and the library. She also edits what Liddy has typed before passing them to Adams. She soon begins to act as his Personal Assistant. He begins to trust her more and send her on errands, even personal ones. When Esi tries to protest and say that he is exploiting her, Zeb says that it is a good opportunity to learn American ways especially immigration matters. Working in his office stimulates her intellect. She reads newspapers in order to have some news to discuss with him. Her greatest joy is when he begins to refer to her as sister. She is happy to have him as part of her American family.

Zeb's friendship with Adams continues to grow. He teaches morning classes at the University and comes to the office in the afternoon. When he comes before lunchtime, he sends her to buy lunch for both of them and they eat together in his office. She always clears the plates and cleans the place.

"You're not good at cleaning," Zeb says laughing.

"A bad habit I picked from the orphanage. We had people who did everything for us," he says. One day he tells her about his friend, Nelly, who is having issues with him; won't return his calls or open her door to him. She returns letters and packages he sends to her. He wants Zeb to intervene by going to the woman with a parcel.

"That's kind of awkward. She doesn't know me."

"You have a way with people. Just don't tell her that I sent you before she opens the door." He gives her a package for Nelly.

Nelly not only opens the door for Zeb but chats a bit with her thinking she's missing her way.

"Where's your beautiful accent from?" Nelly says.

"I'm a Nigerian."

"That's in West Africa."

"How do you know?"

"I used to work in the children's section of the library and was in charge of geographical books."

"Mummy, who is it?" A little girl runs out from the bedroom.

"My name is Zeb Oli."

"Cool name."

"And what's your name?"

"Barb for Babara."

"That's so cool. Mine is Zeb for Zebra."

"Mummy is she coming to our house? I want her to come in."

"This is such a pretty smart girl. How old are you?" Zeb says.

"Three. Mommy is it for your birthday?" She fingers the ribbons of the parcel in Zeb's hands.

On Saturday, Zeb tells Esi and her boyfriend, Gomez, about her visit with Nelly and that Adams was pleased.

"So did he compensate you?" Gomez looks across the table at Zeb.

"He appreciated it. He gave me a bear hug and a peck. He calls me sister and we've kind of become closer."

"Just don't be too close. I don't trust police and attorneys," Gomez pours apple cider on Zeb's glass.

"You don't need to use your own personal experience to judge every situation," Esi says to Gomez.

"I have to. It's the only view I have. They know the law more than you and can set you up," Gomez says.

"I'm concerned about the way he uses her," Esi says. Zeb tells them that she has good feelings about Adams and Gomez should not worry about her.

"Adams says that my sons may be feeling resentful about my leaving them in Nigeria, so he has offered to help me bring them to America," Zeb says sipping her cider.

"You might have shown him that you feel guilty about leaving them with your ex-husband. I've told you not to feel guilty. You did the right thing by leaving them with him. He has the means to take care of them and so far he has done a good job," Esi says.

"What kind of good job? They are still in college at their age," Zeb says.

"One is in graduate school," Esi says.

"At least, they're in school," Gomez begins to eat. Zeb sips from her glass thinking about her last visit to her sons.

It was on her way back from studies in England. She had a suitcase full of presents for them. Her best friend and sorority sister, Chioma Okorji, was at the airport with a taxi that took them straight to Abeokuta to see them. Aduke Ola who lived opposite Igo informs them that he was not in the house, so she walked across to Igo's house. She was told that her son, Akinyele, was in boarding school and the other two were at the university. She had written them letters but none had ever replied any of her letters. She constantly looked out for their letters, and never got one. While in the taxi, on their way to to the university, she was excited and imagined how she would hug them but she was disappointed. Igo had lavished them with expensive cars and they seemed out of touch with reality. Oli Junior was in graduate school and obsessed with his relationship with girls. When she tried to talk about it, he looked her straight in the face, and said that he was twenty-eight and did not need her to dictate to him. That brought tears to Zeb's eyes, because she attributed it to her leaving and losing her grip on them. Her eyes water as she remembers how she named him Olima in honour of her father and brought him up with qualities of his noble grandfather.

"He would never have spoken to me like that if I had remained in the house. Shatu had no control over them and they heard all the negative things their father said about me," Zeb once complained to Esi.

"They will one day learn the truth and get wise. Don't worry. Just empower yourself," Esi said.

The second one, Igodoana, was more amenable and told her that he hardly saw his father and that his girlfriend made him feel special. It was during the conversation that she realised they never got any of her letters. She did not think that Igo was showing good parenting, but she could not complain. When she shared her worries with Angel, she told her that her sons would turn out fine. Angel used to visit them often to check on their progress.

"The children are loved. Trust me, they'll be fine."

On Sunday, Zeb and Esi go to Our Lady of Sorrows Church by Philadelphia Avenue. They are early because Zeb wants to visit the Blessed Sacrament Chapel to pray for her special intentions. She prays for her children's protection and maintenance of good behaviour and for God to make it possible for her to bring them to America. The prayers and service help to reduce her feeling of loneliness. She phones her mother to make sure that all is well at home.

"Mama."

"Zee Zee," Angel says. Dozie drops the catapult he is fixing for his playmate and runs to his grandmother as soon as he knows that his mother is on the phone. He stands there grinning and waiting for his turn to speak with her. Sure enough, Angel gives him the phone.

"Mummy, I've passed the final catechism test. I'm going to receive the Holy Communion."

"Very good boy. You're really smart." Zeb will like to be there when the boy goes through the ceremony.

"Will you like to do it when you come to live with me here in America?"

"I want to do it here. My friend Joe will receive too."

"You want to do it with your friends."

"Yes. Can I do another one when I come to America?"

"I think that it is done once only. Who is your catechism teacher?"

"We have two. Mr Ezike and Anti Dora. Grand Angel took me to the tailor. He is making white *agbada* for me. I'm very happy Mummy. I want you to come to the Holy Communion."

"I'm trying to get a job and a house so that you can come and join me."

"And Grand Angel?" Dozie says.

"Yes, she will come also," Zeb says. Zeb discusses her Immigration form document with Angel and learns that her old school is having difficulty writing a testimonial for her. Zeb phones her cousins to find out what the problem is.

"Most of the school records were destroyed during the war," Okpara says.

"Does that mean that..."

"Just wait and don't interrupt me. The principal and her staff are going through a lot of records that former students have been sending over the years. She said that there are a lot of papers, awards, stories and photos that they have to go through in order to build up the story of your stay in the school. Be patient. You know that they don't have computers and all that. Do you understand?"

"Yes."

"Ok, tell me what I've been missing. How are you getting on? Uncle Okolo brought back pictures and said you were looking very well. Is it still true?"

"I'm very healthy and happy. I moved in with a friend who lives in the area where I have a small job."

"You have a job?"

"Nothing big; more or less a volunteer kind of thing, but I'm getting good experience and the attorney is really good to me. He will help me to get extension of my visiting visa. He also advised that I register in his university as a student in order to get the kind of visa that will enable me to work legally."

"How do you feel about it?"

"I didn't like it initially, but everybody says it's a good idea."

"What about school fees?" Okpara says.

"The attorney is sponsoring me so I stand a chance of competing for scholarship under his umbrella."

"Are you..." Okpara coughs, but Zeb knows it's not a real cough. He just feels awkward about what he wants to ask her.

"Brother, he's not my boyfriend or lover or anything like that. We relate like siblings. I've told him a lot about you all and he said he will like to visit Nigeria with me when things get better."

"Just be careful. He's a citizen and an attorney who knows the ropes. These make him very powerful and he can use his power one way or the other. Be very careful."

"I'm careful."

"Don't tell him everything about yourself."

"He tells me everything," Zeb says. Okpara shakes his head. His cousin can be naïve about men. The fact that she is brilliant does not mean that she is knowledgeable in men-matters. It happened to her once with Igo, but they attribute it to her young age and the circumstances of the Nigeria-Biafra war. It happened to her again with Jaja. Okpara believes that she married too young and did not go through the normal young adult period of dating and knowing the ways of the opposite sex. She moved from childhood to motherhood and womanhood. Now that she is out, she still shows a gap in that understanding of life. When he questioned her about Jaja's marriage proposal, she said she wanted to pursue further studies and did not want marriage to stop her. It made sense then. But now, he's not sure that Jaja's marriage to another woman has ended her love for him. Now she is far away in America and getting involved without knowing it and without having family to fall back on. It sends amber signs to Okpara.

"Just be very careful. Have you met any of his relations?"

"Just his girlfriend."

"Ok. He has a girlfriend?"

"Yes."

"Still be careful."

"Don't worry about me Brother." Zeb coughs. Her brother knows she has something on her mind and guesses what it is.

He volunteers information about Jaja.

"They said Jaja started inciting the prisoners in Badagry by telling them about their right to trial before imprisonment. They mutinied, so they transferred him to the north where he doesn't know the language and won't be able to discuss with prisoners."

"Are you there?" Okpara says.

"I'm here. Just sad," Zeb says.

"I didn't want to tell you because I know it will affect you, but I guess you have a right to know. Does he know about Dozie? "

"Not yet. I've been thinking about my life and one of the things that I want to do as soon as I have the opportunity is to get Dozie to know Jaja."

"Anything can happen any time."

"I pray not soon. Jaja is too precious not just to me and Dozie but to our country."

"I know."

"But Mama hates him. Can you please find a way of getting her to be more positive about the father of her grandson?"

Zeb is awake when Esi returns after eleven in the night.

"Why are you up?"

"Waiting to break the good news. We have dealt with two sets of forms today. One is for the extension of my visiting visa. He signed as my sponsor."

"That's good. At least you won't be illegal or deported if other things don't work out fast."

"We also filled the admission forms. I filled my part and he filled his part as my sponsor. He said that I only have to pay the initial tuition as a resident. He has a strong feeling that I'll get a scholarship or at least get a resident waiver through his sponsorship."

"Looks like he can influence things."

"He kind of implies that it won't be difficult because of his sponsorship of my visa."

"A lot of things kind of hangs on the visa and his sponsorship."

"Yes. And the secretary has already posted the visa form."

"This is a big thing. You may want to ask other people about all the stuff about getting scholarship. I don't really know how it works," Esi says.

"You see, I have got more than any salary he could have paid me. My greatest happiness is that I won't be illegal and I'll get a permit to work."

"We'll celebrate it then."

"He said that he had never had our kind of closeness and intellectual match in his life. He said he feels like I'm the sister he never had."

"This is huge."

"Tomorrow we'll go to the university to give them the forms. Then we'll get scholarship forms" Zeb says.

Gloria is delighted to hear from Zeb. They have not spoken in a long while.

"You should have phoned to tell me you moved out of Anise's house and stopped me from phoning her and hearing her complaints."

"I'm sorry. I was going through a lot and wanted to get myself together."

"So who is this man you are living with?"

"I'm not living with any man."

"Anise said you have a new boyfriend you are living with. I really didn't understand because she said the man came to collect you from her house."

"I'm sharing an apartment with a girlfriend. She was the one who took me into her house when Anise kicked me out."

"Anise kicked you out?"

"Yes."

"Everything is so confusing. I'll have to come and see you," Gloria says.

"Where will you stay? Our apartment is small."

"Don't they have hotels over there?"

"Sure they do but that will be costly."

"No problem. Did Anise's husband hit on you?"

"No."

"Ok. You sound happy. Any hope for a Green Card?"

Zeb tells her about her volunteer job and her friendship with Adams. She tells her about the visa forms and his sponsorship.

"Sorry, but I have to say my mind. He sounds like a … anyway you'll hit the roof if I say it. He just doesn't sound real."

"How dare you?"

"I said I'm sorry. Things just don't add up. That's all."

"Because …" Zeb waits for Gloria to give her reasons.

"Just be careful. He's so much into your business."

"That's what siblings do for each other," Zeb says.

40

Deportation Fever

dams and Zeb go to the English Language School at College Park campus to submit the application forms. Zeb is so thankful and emotional that when she hugs him, she won't let go.

"You cannot imagine what this means to me," she says with tearful eyes. She notices how he quickly pushes her off and straightens his shirt, yet it is not ruffled. Is he embarrassed? From that episode, something changes in their friendship. He becomes distant. He enters the office and just nods his head in response to her greeting. After two days, Zeb asks him whether anything is bothering him.

"Yes." He tells her to come and sit in front of him. Then he makes his demand.

"It's impossible," Zeb says.

"Are you serious?" Zeb says.

"I just can't," she pushes her chair and walks out of his office and out of Liddys office. She feels the cold air and remembers her coat. She goes back, puts it on and leaves. The sky is dark and thick as she boards a bus to China Palace.

Zeb has a deep frown when she appears at China Palace.

"What's up my friend?" Esi notices the frown and knows that all is not well.

"He wants sex."

"What?"

"I said that he wants sex." Zeb's face changes colour. The dark chocolate complexion adds a shade and her eyes become narrow.

"Who are you talking about?"

"Mr. Richard Adams."

"Your brother and mentor?"

"Yes."

"Wait, I'm coming back." Esi goes to the senior supervisor and takes permission to go for early dinner. She comes back with two trays. Zeb does not feel like eating but Esi persuades her to eat. Zeb fills her plate with desserts and Esi goes to the salad bar. They sit in an empty booth at the corner.

"How can you have sex with someone who is your brother?" Esi says.

"Thank you. We think alike. I asked him the same question," Zeb says.

"And what did he say?"

Zeb shakes her head from side to side and a mirthless laughter escapes from her mouth.

"He said that I have no blood relationship with him."

"But you have connected with him as the sister that he doesn't have. He adopted you as his sibling," Esi says.

Zeb expresses another mirthless laughter and continues to talk, "I respect him like my brother and not just a boss. He just doesn't understand where I've placed him," Zeb says.

A waiter comes to fill their glasses.

"Is she your sister?" The waiter asks.

"Yes. Tee, how're you doing?" Esi says.

Tee fills their glasses with water and they thank her.

"She was hired yesterday," Esi says trying to divert attention from their hot topic.

"Do you know all of them by name?"

"Sure. It's my duty as their supervisor," Esi says. Zeb is not eating.

"I worked through the ranks and have been on that side of life for a long time, so I have an insider's skill for knowing them and getting along with them," Esi says. Zeb looks ahead.

"What do you want to do?" Esi touches her hand.

"I'll go back to the office and continue with my work."

"Please don't go back to him. Go to our apartment or go to the library. Let things cool off a bit," Esi says.

She does not take Esi's advice. She is at the bus stop when it begins to snow. She pulls the rope of her hood tight and waits. She begins to doubt that Adams meant what he said. Maybe he was just joking. She boards a bus back to University Boulevard to find out if Adams is serious about what he said. By the time she gets off at her stop, there is about four inches of snow on the ground and it is still snowing. Adams is there when she gets back to the office. She hangs her coat, knocks and enters his office. Before she can say anything, he asks whether she has thought about his proposition.

"There is nothing to think about. I can't do it," she says standing by the doorway.

"Close the door and tell me why," he says. Zeb hesitates, then she closes the door and stands there.

"First, you are my brother even though you want to deny it. I don't feel that way for you as my brother. Moreover, you have Nelly and shouldn't feel that way towards me," Zeb says. Adams laughs out loud at the end of which he tells her to leave Nelly out of it.

"You are very intelligent, so think of the situation like an intelligent woman."

Zeb feels conflicting emotions of sadness, anger and fear. She even feels like going to the bathroom but as she makes to open the door, Adams stops her.

"What?" she says.

"Tell me why you are angry. What have I done to you?"

Zeb is aware of Adams' habit of recording conversations with some clients. She does not want to say anything that he can record and use to get her into more trouble, sue her or use against her in some way that she doesn't know. Zeb replies that she cannot tell.

"I admire your intellect and I think that you're not likely to allow your emotion to cloud your vision. You know what to do to save yourself from a lot of problems. You are not a virgin. You are old. What are you protecting it for?"

Zeb opens her mouth in shock as she stands there. She does not leave or go to the bathroom or reply. It dawns on her that Adams is serious about his demand.

Zeb finally opens the door to Liddy's office. She is not able to stay there. She opens the outside door to go out.

"Zeb, you forgot your coat," Liddy says. Zeb walks back, picks her coat and leaves. She does not think about where she is going. She just keeps walking. The cold winter air seeps into her chest through the unzipped coat. She keeps walking. She is in front of their apartment door at Rosecrest when she realises that she has walked all the way without her purse. She begins to walk back. She now feels the cold. She tries to run but her feet are almost frozen. By the time she gets to Langley Park, she knows that she cannot go further. She goes into Casa Blanca bread factory. She sits near the fireplace and thinks about the implications of Adams' role in her applications. Adams' explanation about the implications of his sponsorship shows that he can get her deported by informing the Immigration that he is withdrawing his sponsorship of her visa extension. Zeb knows that the implication is deportation. Deportation will lead to imprisonment in Nigeria. She remembers Jaja and tears flow down her cheeks. They will not even put her in the same prison with Jaja because she will go to women's prison. She thinks of running to another State. She wonders why Aracebor did not contact her. It is true that he does not have Esi's number but he could have emailed her. She forgot that she closed the email address that he has. Men can be so unreliable, she thinks in anger looking at the blazing of the fire.

It is better to face the winter's cold than sit inside the warm bread factory and think about men. She leaves the bread shop and goes back to the office for her pocket book. Liddy calls her and invites her to sit. She does not know whether Liddy is an enemy or friend, but she sits and looks directly at her across the table. Liddy takes the flask on the small table, pours some coffee in a paper cup and gives it to her.

"You'll feel better. Its Fresnel coffee," she says. Taking the cup, Zeb sees the look of pity in Liddy's eyes. Liddy does not ask her anything and she does not volunteer any information. She drinks the coffee in silence while Liddy concentrates on her work.

On getting back to the apartment, Zeb tries to read, but cannot concentrate. She goes to the bathroom. She showers, comes out and goes back to shower. She cannot feel better or lessen the cold that she feels inside her heart. She stays in the shower for a long time. She washes her hair and her whole body. She does not feel better. She begins to clean the apartment. Esi is surprised when she returns and sees the whole place sparkling clean. They normally clean the apartment together on Saturdays.

"What's with you?"

Zeb tells her what happened. Esi wants to know what Zeb said in reply to his calling her an old woman.

"Nothing. I was too shocked to say anything."

"When you go there, remind him that he is older than you. He just wants to intimidate you."

"I don't want to confront him. I don't want to be deported."

"What if you get scholarship before the immigration denies you visa?"

"He is a professor in the same institution where I'm seeking admission and scholarship. He can ruin me there. I can't afford not to be his friend," Zeb says to Esi.

"He can be all that, but he is not God," Esi says.

"I know, but I feel like he has me in his grips and there is no way out. He knows too much about me. He knows that I face imprisonment in Nigeria. He knows about Igo. He knows."

"Let's pray," Esi says. Esi leads the prayer. She calls Adams' name so many times before concluding the prayer. "Adams, Adams, don't allow the devil to lead you astray. Adams, don't destroy the good relationship you have formed. Holy Spirit, please intervene and deal with this impossible situation, because nothing is impossible for you. You work wonders and miracles."

After the prayer, Zeb feels better and is able to sleep.

Esi leaves for work in the morning and Zeb goes to Our Lady of Sorrows to pray. She finds a convenient spot at the back corner where she will not disrupt any activity that may go on. She is on her knees for almost one hour. When she gets up, she sees a white-haired priest standing beside her.

"I am Father Augustine. My daughter, do you want us to pray together?"

"Yes father."

"Do you want to tell me a little about what we are to pray for?"

"Yes father," she says. The priest takes her to a room where they will not disturb anybody.

Zeb tells him more than a little bit and feels very good at the end of the narration.

"What is your name?"

"Zeb Oli."

"Kneel down, ask for forgiveness of sins and thank God for all the good things before what you want from Him."

Zeb's list of what she is thankful for is long, but it does not distract her from her need.

"God, please I want you to intervene in my situation with Adams."

Father Augustine tells her to be more specific. She prays that the devil should depart from Adams. The priest tells her to pray directly for herself. He directs and prays with her as she talks about her wish to get a Green Card and job through God's guidance, her wish to bring her children to America and need to trust God more.

Zeb receives a call from Our Lady of Grace in Norbec for the interview for the editorship job.

"Can I speak to Ms. Olima."

"Yes. I'm the one."

"I'm the secretary at Our Lady of Grace. Father Davey will like to speak with you about your application. Are you still interested?"

"Sure." Zeb feels that God is opening another window for her. She remembers Anise saying that churches still sponsor people for a Green Card.

"Father will like to interview you when you have time."

"When?"

"The interviews are scheduled for this week or next, so just choose any day."

"I have time in the morning."

"Can you come tomorrow at ten?"

"Sure."

Davey is a portly priest with a kindly smile. Zeb is comfortable in his presence and feels it will be nice to work with him.

"Good morning Dr. Olima." He shakes her hand.

"Good morning Father." Zeb is surprised. Not many Americans greet in this manner.

"You have an impressive résumé. I can see that you are highly educated."

"Thank you Father."

"We have a weekly journal and a committee made up of members of the church who volunteer some of their time to produce it. They collect material for publication, read them to make selection, organise and take care of all the technical aspects. We need an editor who will be in-charge and co-ordinate the production. Do you think that it looks like what you will like to do if given the chance?"

"Yes. I am a poet and I was involved in the production of a monthly magazine in our church in England. I sure like the experience."

"What did you do in the production?"

"Mostly reading, editing and selecting material. I have the ability to fill spaces with interesting bits and people used to enjoy my editorial pieces."

"You have training that helps you in those kinds of things."

"Yes."

"With your qualifications, how will you feel working in a small place like this?"

"This is not really a small place by my thinking because it is a house of God. It is conducive to creative work and appeals to me a lot as a poet. The landscape is beautiful and the kind of place that I will like to see everyday."

"I see," Davey smiles and tells her that he will get in touch when all the interviews are done.

For days, she keeps going to Our Lady of Sorrows to pray, hoping to see Father Augustine again. She never sees him. When she shares her anxiety with Esi, she tells her to go to the parish administration and ask for him.

"The secretary or somebody there in the parish office will help you find the priest. But meanwhile, let us continue to pray and hope on God."

"I'm thinking about Adams's option," Zeb says.

"What do you mean?"

"Come on Esi, is there any other option?" Zeb looks directly at Esi waiting for her reaction.

"It's just incredible." Esi moves her head from side to side.

"I don't want to live in fear of being deported. Is there something that I can use to dull my memory in order to go through it without remembering?"

"You're losing your mind," Esi says.

"A man needs to hear this and tell us what he thinks," Esi says.

"Go and find father Augustine."

Zeb does not really want to submit to Adams. The thought of what she calls "Adams' option" even makes her sick. She goes to Our Lady of Sorrows. When she asks the Parish secretary for an appointment with Father Augustine, she is told that he does not belong to the parish.

"But he prayed with me in this church."

"Did he tell you that he belongs here?"

"No."

"So he might have been a visitor like you, but we don't have record of any priest of that name visiting here."

Zeb is disappointed.

"I believe you prayed with him, but we just don't have record of him in this parish. Sorry."

Zeb is awake when Esi returns. She immediately begins to discuss the problem.

"Gomez said that it is not going to be a one-time thing. Adams wants to use you as a sex toy. He said that instead of becoming a sex toy for one man, you should think of making money through sex."

"God forbid!" Zeb says.

"That was how I rejected his suggestion. But think about it. Why should you allow Adams to gain from your body when you gain nothing?"

"It sounds like prostitution."

"Both of them sound like prostitution when you think of benefits and exploitation," Esi says.

"Doing it Adams's way will be like a Green Card marriage. In each of them, I'll be the loser once I don't submit to the man. He can make one phone call to the police or immigration and I'll be deported," Zeb says.

"Yeah."

"He would be the business man benefiting and calling the shots while I'd be the one doing the work. If I have to engage in that kind of work and be a prostitute, I'll be the boss and the worker and the beneficiary. The idea of doing it and earning money from men as Gomez said is beginning to make sense. Better be a sensible prostitute rather than one man's fool," Zeb says.

"There you go, girl!" Esi throws her bag on the couch and sits beside Zeb. She wipes Zeb's tears and weeps. Both of them hate the option.

41

Sexy Combat

It is almost eleven in the night. Esi unlocks the door. She is surprised to see Zeb sitting in a dining chair with her hands on her jaws. She stands by the door looking at Zeb. The television is not on. She is holding a book but she is not reading. Finally, Esi goes to her and hugs her. Zeb begins to weep on her shoulders. Esi takes her to the couch and pulls a chair in front of her.

"Something terrible happened."

"I know. It is written all over your face. Do you want to talk about it?"

Zeb was sitting in Liddy's office when Adams opened his office door and motioned her to come in. He wanted her to find a particular paper that she put in a folder. Zeb sensed that something was up, so she watched him with the corner of her eye as she went through the folders on his table. She knew when he moved from the shelf. She held the marble figurine on the table.

"What's that for?"

"I just held it," Zeb says.

"Why?"

"In that kind of situation, when someone pushes you to a corner, you just do what you have to do. I must have held it for defence. And it turned out to be a very good one because I had it when I turned, which coincided with when he held me from behind."

"Oh my God!"

"Don't call God yet. The struggle was between Adams and me," Zeb makes a throaty sound like guttural laughter, but there is no fun in it.

"The struggle was a physical fight between a man and a woman," Esi says.

"It was physical power versus will power. It was good that he did not take me unawares. I raised the figurine to hit him. He dodged. He pushed a chair at me and I tripped. The figurine fell from my hand. He came after me."

"You no longer had a weapon."

"Yes. He thought that he had the upper hand, but his closeness gave me the opportunity to push with my head. His glasses fell off. He lost his balance. We must have made so much noise that we did not hear Liddy come in. She stepped on his glasses. I just ran out of the office and came home."

"You poor thing."

"I was too sad and could not concentrate on thinking, reading or even sleeping."

"You should have come to China Palace."

"I don't like coming to your work every time to disturb you with my problem."

"Don't even think that way. I'll come to you if I'm distressed. So what have you been doing?"

"I took all our dirty clothes to the bath and washed them by hand."

"Why?"

"Sometimes, I don't know why I do things. So don't ask me why. Maybe I wanted to prolong the washing time. After washing them, I took them to the laundry mat and dried them in the drier. By the time I came back, it was almost eight and there was nothing else to do. I began to iron the clothes and hang them in the closet. When I was done, I had a bath and thought that I would be able to sleep from all the chores, but my mind was racing through the incidents and how to get out of the bad situation."

Esi takes her hand, "Please don't be on your own when you feel depressed. Come to my work or go to any place where there are people. You're a people's person and people can be angels."

Zeb begins to sob and blame herself, "If only I had not left Nigeria at all, I would not have found myself in this mess. Igo called me a headstrong woman. He's right. Nna-a was the one who gave me a wilful gene. My mother is also wilful. My uncles always said that I have double toughness from my parents and I used to like it.

I now hate it. Praying with Father Augustine gave me so much hope. Now he has disappeared. Now things have got worse."

"Zeb, you can't go on like this. You need to challenge him. This is sexual harassment. It is unacceptable. I'll go with you."

"No, he'll be angry."

"We'll go to the university and report him."

"No! That will make matters worse. I know a lot about sexual harassment from home, and I know that it is difficult to prove."

"You have to do something." Esi's voice is loud. She is tired from work and frustrated by Zeb's situation.

"Do something," Esi shouts.

"What can I do?" Zeb says. She is loud too.

"America cannot allow this! I'll find a sexual harassment clinic or something," Esi takes the phone book. Zeb snatches the book from her and throws it to the corner.

"What did you do that for?" Esi says.

"I don't want to involve police or anything like that. It will backfire. I don't have papers."

"We just have to do something," Esi shouts.

"Let's pray," Zeb says.

"Let's go to the school," Esi says; she does not shout.

"Let's do both." Zeb begins to laugh. Having someone who is on her side is a big relief. They neither pray nor go to the school. They just go to bed. Curled up on the couch, Zeb goes into the fetal position. She wills herself to go back into her mother's womb. She wants her children in her womb also. She curls up tighter as if holding her children, as if the blanket is her mother. She sobs. She feels a kick. Esi pulls her up.

"Stop crying. Come!"

Zeb follows her to her bed. Esi covers her with the blanket. It has been a very long time since someone did that for her. Zeb feels Esi's hand on her shoulder.

"Listen to this," Esi whispers into her ear.

"When I was a child, maybe four or five, but this is my earliest memory. I saw my mother curled up the way you were curled up on that couch. As a child, I didn't know what was happening to her. I was scared and began to cry. She pulled me into her arms and curled up around me. It was soothing, so soothing that I could feel her heart and her breath. I stopped crying. My heart began to beat with her heart. I wasn't scared anymore …"

Zeb does not hear the rest of Esi's story because she sleeps.

Esi wakes her up very early in the morning. She says that they should go to her work at Safeway, so that she will get permission to be off that morning. She wants to go to the school with Zeb. After that, she can go to her afternoon work at China Palace. Zeb is reluctant, but feels weak against Esi's firmness. It is like Zeb lost her own will, but she trusts Esi. She goes with Esi to her work, but her boss does not allow her to take time off. Esi urges her to go to Adams's department and meet him in his office.

"Confront him there. Leave his office door open and make a lot of noise just as you did with Igo. Men can't stand that kind of drama. Make sure that people gather before you say what is going on. I'm your witness. I'm a citizen. Your visa has not yet expired so you are still legal and can benefit from American justice."

"This is a desperate action," Zeb says.

"And a desperate action will solve the bad situation. This is America. Something is bound to happen. The man capitalises on your silence. Don't be silent."

Zeb is very nervous in the metro. She formulates the speech that she will make in front of Adams. She constructs it as a plea. Then she changes it to a challenge as Esi instructed. She thinks of the possible outcome. Maybe he will phone the Immigration and they will pick her from his office. Her brain is in a mess.

She is already in the English Language School at College Park when she realises that the School of Law is in Baltimore. She is disappointed, but also relieved that she is not going to confront Adams. Maybe it's God's way of preventing her from such a negative action. It's not even a good idea to go that route simply because Esi wants her to. She goes to her church to have a quiet time to think. She sits at the back of the church, the same place she sat when she saw Father Augustine.

After about twenty minutes, she leaves the church for the library. She walks along the shelves looking at the books but not seeing anything, she finally decides to check her email. Maybe something will cheer her up and something does. There is a message from the secretary of Our Lady of Grace telling her that Reverend Father Davey will like to speak with her. She immediately phones the secretary from a pay phone to find out when she should see the priest.

"If you have time, I can transfer you to him."

"The committee has completed the interviews and made their decision. All members of the committee agreed that you are highly qualified with degrees, but you are not exactly the kind of person they want for the job."

"Why?"

"They feel that because of your qualifications, you may get a better job and leave. They want someone who will not go away; someone who will make the job a career."

"Ok," Zeb cannot imagine making the production of weekly Sunday bulletin her job for life.

"You're young and hard-working. There is no doubt in my mind that you will get the job that suits your experience. I wish you good luck and God's blessing."

"Thank you," Zeb says, but she is almost in tears. This is not what she expected. She goes to the bus stop. Inside the bus, she looks out through the window, her sad mood matches the cheerless outlook of the scenery. The weather is gloomy. The former luxuriant trees of the forest now look like skeletons standing in the wood. There seems to be no life even on the floor of the naked wood. It's just white floor; no life. The bus seems to be unusually slow, making many stops even stopping where nobody wants to get out. Zeb sighs when the bus finally stops at Lebanon Street. She walks dejectedly to their apartment and flops on the couch.

"Oh yes, God, this is it. Will it get worse than this?" she says. She's loud. She thinks of what she calls "Adam's option" and immediately rushes to the bathroom. She throws up.

"Whatever will happen tomorrow should happen now. I can't live with all this anxiety." She brushes her teeth, picks her pocket book and leaves.

She knows how to get to Baltimore. She takes a bus back to the metro station and goes to Union Station where she takes Amtrak to Baltimore. Her problem starts when she gets to her destination and reads the sign, Francis King Carey School of Law. Sadness, anger and fear grip her. She stands in the hallway. She sits down. She stands up. She looks at the notice board without reading anything. She paces the hallway. People pass her. Some of them look at her suspiciously. She continues to pace, sit, stand, and stare at the notice board. A man is coming directly towards her. She recoils.

"Come," he says. He is a tall elderly man probably in his sixties. He looks fatherly. She follows him. She wonders whether she is losing her mind following a stranger. He leads her to an office. She reads the door sign: Martin Augustine, Professor of Law.

"What's wrong?" he says. Zeb begins to shiver and weep. She is not able to control her mouth as she blurts out everything. The professor opens the school's directory and looks through it.

"Richard Adams is not a professor in this school."

"He's not?"

Augustine gives the directory to her and she looks at the names starting with A. She also looks at names listed under R and does not see his name.

"Are you sure that he is in this school? There are other Law Schools and Community Colleges in this area."

"I'm not sure but he said that he is a professor."

"Do you want to press charges?"

"No no no."

"You can apply for scholarship. We need students in our International and Comparative Law unit."

"I'm not a citizen," Zeb says, her mind going to another problem. Law is not her field area, but she sees a lot of opportunity in taking courses in law like Jaja.

"There is a scholarship that you can apply for that doesn't have citizenship requirement. I have a grant for two of those scholarships. Come with me to the secretary's office." Martin tells the secretary to give

Zeb the scholarship forms. The secretary directs her to the Office of Admissions where she gets the admission forms.

"You can take it home and send it by post after filling it."

"Thank you." Zeb does not want to go home but makes her way back to Augustine's office. She pinches herself. She wants to make sure that she is not dreaming. Zeb applies for admission to the School of Law and applies for scholarship. This trip changes everything.

As soon as Esi sees Zeb, she knows that something great must have happened.

"Miracle miracle miracle," Zeb says. She is loud.

"Wait," Esi says. They are having dinner when Gomez joins them. He comes up with a plan. Zeb should tell Adams that she has changed her mind, and invite him to the apartment.

"What!"

"Do you want your buddies to harass Adams? Don't do any funny thing; the guy is an attorney," Esi says. Gomez explains his plan. He wants Esi to mix a strong drink for Adams and get him drunk so that they will find out his secrets. Gomez doesn't believe that Adams is an orphan.

"He has a past or another life that he is hiding and we must find out his secret."

"What for?"

"So that you can use it as a bargaining point? Don't think that he's done with you," Gomez says.

Zeb inhales very deeply and exhales. "I thought that this is over now," she says.

"You need to nail it and make it fast, because if he finds out that you've moved on without him, he'll make a quick move. You need to be ahead of him. I'll be outside your apartment in case he becomes violent," Gomez says.

42

Secret Evidence

Zeb is in the kitchen washing black-eye beans. She smiles as she peels off the skin of the beans for making *akara*. Akara with pap is her children's favorite breakfast. The smile is on her lips when Esi opens the door.

"Good morning Zeb."

"Good morning, I'm about to make *akara*?"

"The small cakes you make with beans?" Esi asks. Zeb nods.

"I love it. Let me help you cut the onions," Esi washes her hands to cut the onions that Zeb kept on a plate. She also begins the coffee and goes to get ready for work. Zeb blends the washed beans and begins to fry them as cake balls. They have breakfast together.

"I love the way you look so happy. The frown has completely disappeared," Esi smiles.

"I'm still concerned about inviting Adams here, but I'll do it."

"Good. Just let me know when he is coming," Esi says.

"If he will come," Zeb says.

"I bet he will. His thinking no longer comes from his brains."

"But from where?"

"Between his legs," Esi laughs.

"The place doesn't think," Zeb laughs.

Zeb relaxes in front of the television. For the first time in a long while, she watches her favourite programme *Good Morning America.* A reporter is in the neighbourhood of the Maryland prowler asking his neighbors about him. They describe him as a nice guy. Then Dr. Barkley, a psychologist, comes on and says that being nice is one of the tricks that people use to get the confidence of those they want to hurt. Zeb's mind immediately goes to Adams. Her mind also goes to Professor Augustine. Is he being nice in order to trick her like Adams? She panics. She feels he is a good guy. She is confused. She phones her sister and updates her on all that has been happening. Finally, she speaks about her latest concern.

"Do you think that Professor Martin Augustine will be like Adams?"

"Don't stress yourself. He is in his professional capacity," Kordi says.

"So was Adams."

"Not the same. The university is involved, the secretary, the admissions people."

"The same with Adams and he turned out to be a bad guy."

"You are in the same university environment with Augustine. You have rights as a student and the university will protect you. As a professor, he knows this and you must make sure you get to know all support groups in that university. I have a good feeling about Augustine. Remember the priest who prayed with you is also Augustine," Kordi says. They wonder at the coincidence in their names. Kordi says that Angel is missing Zeb.

Zeb phones her mother.

"Zee Zee, there is something."

"Is Dozie alright?"

"He is at school. Everything is fine and your brother has the documents for you. I think he posted them to you, so all is well."

"Then what is it."

"You are so impatient. It is about Jaja." Angel says and waits for Zeb's reaction. Zeb holds her breath.

"Your brother said that he is suffering too much in prison," she says. Zeb's heart misses a beat. Her mother can hear the sound of her breathing and knows that she is controlling tears. Angel nods her head at the confirmation of something she has always known but which Zeb has denied whenever she brought it up. Zeb is still in love with Jaja. Angel has tried to prevent Zeb from loving Jaja so that she can move on and have a Christian marriage with another man. For Angel, it is no longer important because Jaja is in prison and cannot hurt Zeb in America. But somebody is being hurt. Her grandson has to know his biological father even though he is not his father by Igbo tradition. And it is urgent because they can kill Jaja in prison.

"I feel very sorry for Jaja," Angel says. Zeb is surprised at her mother's feeling. She thought that her mother hates Jaja. Tears run down her eyes. She wipes them off.

"But you don't like him Mama," Zeb says.

"I don't want him to stand in your way to happiness, but the issue is now different. His survival is important. Reports in the newspapers say he is very ill, thin and weak. He doesn't deserve what they are doing to him. I'll like to do anything that can make him feel better, and I know that he loves you."

"You know?"

"Yes. That was why I didn't tell you he phoned."

"When?"

"That was the day you came home after meeting with your Vice Chancellor."

"You didn't tell me." Zeb's tears drop on her blouse. She takes a tissue and blows her nose.

"My child, forgive me," Angel says.

"I want to make it up to you right now. It's not possible for him to see you..." She does not finish the sentence. Her daughter's tears upset her. Angel remembers the first time she met her husband at a wrestling match in Onye-Achona-Okwu square of their village. How her heart swelled as she watched him in the arena. Her heart still swells whenever she remembers that first meeting, even after all these years since his death. She understands her daughter's feelings for Jaja, but never understood why she did not tell him about Dozie. Now, there is no time. She has to insist on his knowing about him.

"What I want to say is that I want to visit Jaja because of you," Angel says. Zeb cannot believe it.

"What did you say Mama?"

"I want to visit him in prison."

"Mama, please take Dozie with you."

"I will take him."

After the conversation with her mother, Zeb does not want to stay alone in the apartment and weep for Jaja or for Dozie not knowing him. She puts on her coat and goes to Adam's office to invite him for a rendezvous at Rosecrest. She greets Liddy who phones Adams immediately. He opens the door and lets her in. As soon as he closes the door, she invites him and is about to leave.

"What's the hurry? What is the address?"

"We'll talk about many things after I've paid my due," she writes the address.

"I knew you would come round."

"See you later." Zeb hurries to Langley Park shopping complex. She goes to the electronic store to look at tape recorders. She also buys phone cards and goes to meet Esi at her work place.

Adams arrives before eleven. Zeb panics because Esi is not yet home. When she opens the door for Adams, she sees Gomez and another guy sitting on the balcony of an apartment on the next building. He raises his hand. Zeb lets Adams into the apartment and offers him a drink.

"I haven't come here to drink. You know what I'm here for," he says.

"At least you can treat me like a lady."

"I'll have some juice," he smacks Zeb on the buttocks. She winces, but he doesn't see her face. They are drinking orange juice when Esi returns.

"I've heard so much about you from my friend and how you are helping her with her visa. Thank you sir," Esi says. They talk about China Palace and she offers to mix drinks for everybody. He says that he has a very important meeting in the morning and does not want to drink alcohol. Their plan does not work, so the two women stay up talking with him. He keeps winking at Zeb to send Esi away. Zeb pretends not to understand his signs. Finally, he tells Esi to go and get cigarettes for him from his car.

"Women don't go out at night in our neighbourhood," she says. He gets up immediately to leave. He is so angry. Then, Zeb braces up for her master plan. Neither

Gomez nor Esi knows about it. She learnt it from Richard Adams.

Zeb knows that Richard will phone her and he does. They have a conversation before she goes to bed. After the phone conversation, Esi comes out of her room to find out what he said. She notes that Zeb seems really happy.

"What happened?" Esi says.

Zeb presses the on-button of the tape recorder and Esi listens to a dialogue that comes on immediately.

"Zeb, why did you do that?" It is a deep voice.

"Do what?" Esi recognises this as Zeb's voice.

"You know what I mean. Why didn't you get that woman out of the way?" The deep voice says. Esi now recognises it as Adams' voice.

"Esi?"

"Yes," Adams says.

"It's her apartment. I share it with her. How can I tell her to leave her apartment? After all, you enjoyed her company," Zeb says.

"That's not what I came for."

"What do you want from me?" Zeb says the words slowly.

"Come on, you know what I want."

"Richard Adams, I do not know what you want."

"I want you Zeb."

"You had me. You came here and we talked and laughed; what else?"

"Are you suddenly naïve or you are pretending?"

"You are my brother Richard Adams. I have been a good sister to you. I don't know what else you want from me."

"You want me to say it again?" Adams says.

"Yes."

"I want pussy."

"We have no pussy cat here," Zeb says.

"I want to have sex with you. Get it?"

"You told me the same thing in your office and I said capital no," Zeb says.

"Then I'll go ahead and contact the Immigration."

"What will you tell them?" Zeb says.

"I'll withdraw my sponsorship then you'll be an illegal alien. I'll also tell them my reason for withdrawing it. You know what will happen to you."

"Will you tell them that it is because I refused to have sex with you?" Zeb says.

"Of course not."

"Then, I'll tell them that you sexually harassed and assaulted me and I refused to have sex with you."

Soft Laughter.

"They will not believe you. I am a professor, an Attorney and a citizen. You are a foreigner without status. They won't believe you." Another soft laughter.

"I have evidence." Zeb's voice is firm.

"What's your evidence?"

"I'll tell them about that day we fought in your office and your glasses got broken. Liddy is my witness."

Husky laughter.

"Liddy has seen worse things. She is an intelligent woman, and can never betray me. She has too much to lose." Another husky laughter.

"Well, then God will be my witness," Zeb says.

Deep laughter.

"God has nothing to do with this. You are smart enough to know that." Very deep laughter.

"Then you will be my witness."

Deep prolonged laughter, "Are you crazy? How can I be a witness against myself?"

"You just did. Our conversation is on tape."

No laughter. Click.

43

College Suites

September 1997 is a happy month for Zeb. She finally gets all the material for her Green Card application. She goes through the original immigration forms and goes through the list to make sure she has assembled everything. The material sent by her cousin, letters from her former universities, her book, articles, poems, magazine write-ups about her are in the large envelope. She presses the envelope on her heart and says a short prayer. She does not post it immediately, but wants to show it to her mentor, Martin Augustine, who promised to recheck the forms.

"This is perfect. An attorney could not have done a better job," Augustine says after checking the forms and attachments.

"Thank you sir. It took me a long time to get it ready."

"Good luck." He puts them back in the envelope. Zeb goes to the post office with the big envelope. On returning from the Post Office, she begins her registration as a student in the Juris Doctor programme of Francis King Carey School of Law. On Augustine's advice, she chooses courses that will make her competent in international law. Her scholarship covers tuition and boarding so she has to move out of Esi's apartment to a Hall of Residence near the school. Gomez plans a party for her and Esi in his limousine. After loading her suitcases, he opens the door and lets them in, shows them the fridge stacked with drinks and their favourite goodies in the snack box. It is Zeb's first time in a limousine. She is awed by the space, luxury and comfort.

"This must be a vehicle's version of heaven," she says.

"My friend, thank you so much. I know you put him up to this," Zeb says.

"He came up with it himself."

"I'll miss you," Zeb tears up as she hugs Esi.

"We'll visit each other."

Gomez puts on their favourite African music and takes off slowly. It takes him about one hour to drive all the way from their Rosecrest apartment in Langley Park to Baltimore while the women enjoy their party. They shake their heads to the beat of the music while they eat and drink.

Zeb elects to share a two-bedroom apartment at Fayette Square Tower. She feels a little awkward that most of the students are very young, American and white. She feels so different that she decides to adopt a typical American name in her social circles. She buys long curly-haired wig that is tinted brown. It gives her personality a new look from her usual short Afro-cut and she begins to introduce herself as Jen. She phones Ada's numbers, but her office and home mailboxes are full. Maybe she is not yet back from sabbatical. She applies for jobs at the cafeteria, library, local journals, and her department. There is a welcome party for international students at Hyppodrome Theater. She wants to go to the party but she does not want to go alone. She phones Esi to see if she and Gomez can come.

"Gomez will be at work and I really want to rest," Esi says.

Zeb goes to the party alone. She is dressed in a long skirt and blouse and walks leisurely from Fayette Square to the theatre for the party. It is at the party that she meets a bearded guy who looks familiar but his name, Robert Jefferson, throws her off completely because she has never heard it before. He is good-looking and very light-complexioned. He is soon to defend his PhD in Global and Environmental Health. Out of interest, he is taking elective international courses. Zeb is impressed that he is in a PhD programme, but feels that he is too young for her. She guesses that he may be about the age of her first son so she directs her attention to other people. Rob shows a lot of patience and politeness in the way he gives her space, but he always goes back to her whenever she is alone.

"You miss home?"

"Very much, especially after hearing disturbing news about one of my friends."

"Very bad?"

"He's not dead or anything, but they're after him." Zeb tells him about Jaja and notes how happy he is when he learns that Jaja is married.

"Any romantic attachments?"

"Not really except that we have a child together."

"Do not hesitate to let me know if you need me in any way," he takes Zeb's phone number and gives her his own.

Zeb does not have another life apart from her academic work and it pays off. She gets excellent grades in her class tests. Things work out fine with her roommate Cathy, a young woman of twenty-five. The only occasional distraction from her studies is hanging out with Rob but their time is always brief. Seeing Jen as a woman of experience, Rob does not want to rush. She appears detached and this disturbs him because he has fallen in love with her. She takes many courses and works as one of the editors in the student journal. These give her little spare time. He tries to move at her slow pace and treasures every moment he spends with her. He records their times together in his journal and enjoys reading his comments.

"Don't you think you're taking on too much?"

"The editing work doesn't take me that much time."

"Can you have at least one outing before the end of the year?"

"I'm going to spend the Christmas with my friend in Langley Park."

Rob shakes his head, "What about me. I want to spend some time with you."

"What are we doing right now?" Zeb says.

"Can we go to a movie or something or you visit me. You are always rushing to a class or library or some other pursuit."

"I can do a movie if that's what you want..."

Ada drives up to Baltimore to meet with Zeb. She is surprised to see Zeb looking confident and happy.

"I'm sorry you didn't get that position in my department."

"That's ok. I'm happy with the way things have worked out. I've applied for a Green Card as an alien of extraordinary ability. In addition, I've applied for a student visa and it's almost automatic since I have a good scholarship."

"I hope you're still applying for jobs."

"No, I want to be an attorney. I'm really working hard to finish with my courses within two and half years. I'm transferring almost forty percent of previously taken courses."

"From where?"

"Columbia, London and Benin."

"You want to change profession?"

"Yes."

"When did you make this decision?"

"I registered in order to have immigration classification as a student, but when I was selecting the courses and reading their descriptions, I began to like the programme. I've always liked Law so I won't say it's just the programme."

"Does your ex-boyfriend have anything to do with it?"

"Maybe, maybe not. The important thing is that I've realised where I belong. I enjoy the classes, but it is so time consuming that I hardly have any time for myself. In addition I'm taking many credits."

"How many?"

"Eighteen."

Ada is speechless.

The confident woman in front of her is so different from the depressed woman she met a couple of months ago.

"So what's the news from Nigeria?"

Ada does not reply immediately.

"I hear Jaja is not feeling too good," Zeb says.

"So you know."

"Yes."

"Delegates from the Association of Writers, the Nigerian Bar Association and Labour Union went to Abuja to meet with the President. Of course, he snubbed them. But their presence in Abuja received a lot of media attention. They spoke about the condition of prisoners. Many of them get sick and die because of the conditions. Jaja's prison photo was in the papers beside his normal picture. You won't believe it's the same person, but on a closer look, you'll see the resemblance."

Zeb wipes her eyes.

Zeb phones her brother and he confirms that Jaja's condition has deteriorated, but he has news that should comfort his sister.

"Mama told you that she would take Dozie to meet him?"

"Yes."

"Well, Dokki and I wanted to do it in order to save Mama from the trouble of such a long journey to the north, but she insisted on going with us. We all made the trip."

"Did you see him?"

"Yes. He's not looking good at all. Very weak but very happy to see us. And do you know what? Igo was the one who helped us. He is the Commissioner of Police in charge of the whole State. I went with Mama to see him. Dokki stayed in the hotel with Dozie. He was very happy to see us and even gave us a car, driver and police escort to assist us. It was easy to drive through checkpoints because of the car's police plate. Everything happened very smoothly."

"Tell me about Jaja."

"He was articulate. His brain is not affected by whatever is wrong with him. He was also emotional when he spoke about the struggle and the love people have been showing by visiting him. He is optimistic about the struggle and happy to be part of it. He said something that really shocked me; that his wife hadn't come to see him."

"I'm not surprised."

"Imprisonment has really taught him who really loves him for himself. He was so excited about Dozie, couldn't stop hugging him. They really look alike."

"I thought that Dozie looks like Papa."

"He looks more like Jaja now. We took photos of them. Do you know what?"

"What?"

"Jaja said that he suspected he was Dozie's father. There was a little speculation about that when Dozie briefly stayed with you in Nsukka campus. He said that it was more important to trust you and know that you would let him know at the time it suited you."

"Really. They never met. Did he blame me?"

"Not to my knowledge. Dokki and I left him with Mama and Dozie for a long time. He said that he has written lots of letters to you unposted. Their letters go through a committee and since your name is still in the Wanted-persons list, he doesn't want to post them. We also didn't want to take the letters from him because we could be searched and Igo would know about you and him."

"That will be very dangerous for him in prison."

"How did Dozie respond to him?"

"You know kids. He was very happy and full of questions."

"Like?"

" 'When are you coming back? Will you live with my mom and me?' There's one more thing you need to know before I hang up. There was a massive demonstration in the capital city of Abuja. The police rounded up many demonstrators. According to reports, up to twenty journalists and writers were jailed as ringleaders. People are now so angry that they keep challenging the military publicly. The idea is that the government will soon run out of prison space."

"Something is bound to happen. Things just can't go on like this."

"This is so so sad Bro."

Zeb likes that Dozie has met Jaja but she still feels very sad. Maybe it's because of Jaja's condition. She phones Esi and they talk about the situation. Esi says that her sadness is understandable. The two people she loves so much have met and she should have been part of it but cannot, because of her situation. Zeb tells Esi about the demonstration and the new batch of political prisoners.

"Do you still remember to pray?"

"Of course, I'm active at Christ The King. I'm a greeter at eight o'clock Mass."

"Good, just keep praying and keep busy. Don't think about what you can't control. Keep doing what you're doing. You're empowering yourself in order to be more useful in the fight later. Focus on the law programme, my friend. You're doing fine."

Zeb takes Esi's advice literally. She will not even pick the phone from Rob. Distancing herself from Rob turns out to be good for her because she discovers that she misses him. His voice on the answering machine makes her happy, but somehow she feels that she is not entitled to happiness when the lives of her colleagues in prison are uncertain. Finally, she picks Rob's call.

She tells him not to phone so often. What she is feeling is too complicated for her to understand or communicate to another person so she tells him that it is because she is too busy.

"Why don't you take it easy? You are taking on too many credits and working twenty hours at your job. That's a bit too much for the average student let alone someone taking so many credits."

"Is this supposed to be a criticism?"

"No just a concern from someone who cares for you very much." This is not what he wants to say. He just chooses words he feels will not offend her.

"Ok. Thanks. But I just want to be by myself for a while."

"I respect that." Rob does not want to put pressure on her. He thinks that he has experience of African women from the continent having previously been hooked on one of them whom he believes cut him off because he was coming too strong just because he wanted her to visit him. He will later realise that he was wrong.

During the Thanksgiving break, her roommate, Cathy, travels to her parents' place in Clinton, so Zeb is alone in the apartment. She wants to work on some assignments that will be due after the break. She cooks and stores soup and stew in the fridge, because she wants to save time and not go to restaurants for every meal. Cocooned inside her apartment, she is surprised by a phone call from Angel.

She is alarmed but Angel quickly allays her fears.

"Zee Zee, cool down. Nothing is wrong. Dozie is fine and at school. I have very good news." Angel can hear Zeb breathe out. She laughs.

"My child, I know you like I know my fingers. Your name has been removed from the wanted-persons list." Again, Angel can hear Zeb's breath of relief.

"So I can come home now."

"Not so quick. You know that things are not yet good."

"But I can visit. I miss you and Dozie and all my children and everybody."

"And who else?" Angel laughs. Zeb laughs also because she knows that her mother wants her to mention Jaja. Zeb is not sure that she feels that same fire that she used to feel for Jaja. She is sad about what he is going through … yes, and she still feels something for him … but it is now different. Since she met Rob, she has discovered another way of loving. It is calm, mature, and reasonable. It is irresistible and at the same time controlled. She has not told Rob that she feels strongly about him, loves him or is in love with him, because she is not sure of the term to use. She's probably waiting for a sign that will indicate it's right for her to let go and the real term will come naturally.

"My child, are you hearing me?"

"I'm here Mama. Where are you phoning from?"

"I cannot phone international from my house. So I'm phoning from the Telephone House here in Enugu."

"Thank you Mama for this great news."

"I've told the community to come for prayers. They wept with me when you were hunted. I'll celebrate the news with them."

Zeb brings her bank statements to find out whether she can afford a ticket to Nigeria. She will not tell her mother or siblings because they will be against it. She will just sneak in. Since her name is no longer in the list, nobody will know that she has entered and gone to Abeokuta to see her sons. From there, she will go to Enugu to see her mother and then take Dozie to Maiduguri to see Jaja. She feels happy about her decision. She is in a happy mood when Rob rings.

"Hi."

"Hi Rob, I have great news. My name has been removed from the wanted-persons list."

"Wow! This is great. We have to celebrate it."

"Sure, we have to. I'll call my friend Esi and her boyfriend. Is that alright."

"Sounds good to me." He is happy that Zeb is coming out of her mood. Zeb is also happy and hopes to tell him her real name before her friends come.

"When do you want to celebrate and where?"

"I'll talk with Esi. Will tomorrow be ok with you?"

"Yeah."

"Ok. I want it as soon as possible so that I can concentrate on going home."

"You're going home?"

"Yes."

Rob is so worried about Zeb's going to Nigeria that he decides to tell her about his feelings. He talks to his professor who supports his idea. The following day, he phones Zeb. She does not pick the phone. After two more calls, she phones him.

"Rob what is it?"

"I need to talk to you. It is urgent."

"Are you okay?"

"Not quite."

"Do you want to talk now?"

"Not on the phone, I want to see you. It won't take time, please."

Zeb waits wondering what he wants to tell her. Within fifteen minutes, he knocks on her door. She notices that he is sweating and it is not hot at all.

"Are you okay?"

"I'm scared," he says.

"Sit down." She is calm.

"I can't say it."

"Then why come here if you can't talk?"

"Don't be mad."

"What is it?"

"I love you."

"What?"

"I love you Jen. I want to marry you. I don't want you to go to Nigeria without me. Will you marry me?" He kneels down. He does not have a ring. That is because he did not plan to propose or to kneel. He feels stupid. He remembers his Grandmother Emma who taught him and his brother that they must always be respectful to women. It is disrespectful to tell a woman that you love her and not mean it. Rob believes that proposing to a woman and not having a ring can be seen as disrespectful or even a lie, but he is telling the truth. He is just nervous and awkward. Grandmother Emma will be ashamed of him. He feels like getting up and running away, but he does not run. Zeb just stands there looking at him. Finally she speaks.

"Get up."

He does not get up. She holds his hands. He allows her to pull him up.

"What did you say?" she says.

"I want you as I have never wanted a woman before in my life."

"I'm married."

Rob is confused. He steps back, turns and hurries out of the place.

Zeb leaves a message on Rob's phone telling him that Esi and Gomez will not be there, and that he should choose the time and place to meet with her. He does not call back that day or the following day. When school resumed and he still does not call her, she feels that something may be wrong with him. Maybe he is ill. If he's not ill, she still will need to explain the situation of her marriage with Igo to him. She does not even know where he lives so as to check on him there. After classes, she goes to the School of Medicine. At the information desk, they direct her to Bressler Research Building. At Bressler, it is easy to locate his office from the office map on the board of the entrance hall. He is not in his office. The secretary says he has not been in the office that day. She asks for his address but the secretary tells her to go to the Dean's office.

44

Dating Diary

 eb leaves the cold towel on Rob's forehead. She sits on the chair by his reading table and goes through the stack of books on the table. She picks a thick black album with glossy cover. She feels it with her palm. She opens it thinking she will see photos, but she sees her name. Jen. Her heart pounds. Is there another woman that he is hiding from her? She is so curious and eager to know who the woman is that she forgets her Christian dictum of respecting someone's privacy, and that a personal journal is a person's private companion. She reads.

September 4

Party organised by International Students Association.

This is a great day in my life. I met an African queen. She is the picture of the queen that Grandma Emma talked about in the folk tales she told us when we were kids. I have always wanted to meet one, maybe go to

Africa someday. Today, I met one. See how she carried herself. Like royalty. Across the hall from me, her attire caught my eyes. The fabric wound round her hips. Big bad butt. Full breasts. Wow! Like Barbie. But this was real, with the most exciting butt you can imagine. In my life, I have only once seen a butt like hers, but that is a long time ago in far away England. I wanted to meet her. But I held back just to see if she had a man. She walked slowly to the bar. Alone. I walked to the bar also.

"How're you doing?" I pushed out my shoulders.

She looked at me, trying to decide whether to respond or not.

"My name is Robert Jefferson." I did not give her the opportunity to ignore me.

"How are you?" She glanced at me and ordered a glass of wine.

I saw the most compelling eyes in the world. Piercing, alluring and yet with a strange quality I could not lay my hands on. It looked like fire that could burn you, but I could not withdraw from it. You had to deal with the fire gently.

"Your costume is beautiful," I said.

"It is not a costume." She sounded harsh.

"Oh! I'm sorry. What is it?"

"An outfit."

"It is very beautiful. From what country?"

"Nigeria."

"Great."

At this point in the reading, Zeb's heart is beating fast as she feels that she is the subject of the entry in Rob's diary. She reads on.

Wow! I danced with her. I told her she has beautiful eyes. She might have heard that many times. Who cares? She has penetrating eyes. Nobody has ever looked into me the way she did. It was as if she could see the inside of my brain. Her face was so smooth. I wanted to touch it, but I held back. I did not want to offend her or anything.

"You look like a Fulani," she said.

"I've heard that before. What do they look like?" I said.

"If you heard that before, then they must have told you what Fulanis look like."

"It was a long time ago. I want to hear it from you," I said.

"They are very tall, slim and light-skinned, just like you."

"Not as light as you, though," she added.

Dancing with Jenny was like having everything I wanted in my life. She was a real African woman and she thought that I looked like an African. As we danced, her breasts rubbed on my chest. I was aroused. I held her waist. My hands slid down her waist. She pushed me.

"Sorry, I got carried away."

"No problem."

We continued to dance. It was so hard to keep my hand from straying. But it paid off. She agreed to have lunch with me. Great!

Zeb is now smiling. In fact, her hert swells because she knows that she is reading about their meeting. She is happy to read a confirmation of her effect on him. She checks whether he is awake. He is still sleeping so she reads on.

September 12

I checked the catalogue for a course on Africa that could fit into my schedule. I added "African Migrations." I told Jen about it at lunch.

"Why did you do that?"

"Because of you."

"Me."

"Yes. I want to learn about Africa."

"I'm from Nigeria. Africa has more than fifty countries and thousands of ethnic nations and languages."

"I'm already learning a lot from you. I'll make an A in the course." "With your help," I added.

She smiled. Good sign. She liked the idea. I wanted to know a lot about her, but I held back. Let her decide the pace for now.

Great lunch. Tomorrow, I'll invite her to a movie. Wow wow!

September 14

The first class of African Migrations. White professor. Disappointment.

Will phone Jenny tonight. Great!

White professor can teach whatever. I do not care. I have a private tutor from Africa.

I checked the films. *Fire Down Below*. No. Who wants to watch Action Thriller with a woman? *The Game*. No. I want to suggest a film with love scenes. *She is so lovely* starring John Travolta. Yes, I think she'll like it.

"What movie do you want to watch?" I asked Jen.

"I don't have enough time for a movie now."

We went for a walk. It turned out to be better than a movie. She let me hold her hands. I told her about the white professor who teaches the African course. Not that I cared; just wanted to see whether she would offer to help me, but she was too smart.

"Why not? He must have learnt it, so he can teach it," she said.

"Will you teach me?"

"I did not learn about migrations."

"Just tell me about Africa."

"I can tell you about Nigeria," she said. She hardly talks about herself. I can wait.

At this point in her reading, Zeb pauses. She is very happy and confident about Rob's feeling for her. She has the same feelings for him and thinks that she also has to let him know. She is a bit guilty about reading his journal, but tries to dismiss the guilt because she did not go all out to find it. It's just a coincidence that she is in Rob's apartment and the journal presents itself. There must be a reason for the coincidence and she has to find out what it is. She flips through the pages.

September 26

Sad news.

Jenny is going back to Africa. I must act fast.

Restless. Because of Jen. I won't let her leave this country, no matter what it takes. But, what can I do? White professor should know about Africans. He's an expert on African migrations. I phone him. He says, "Come."

September 27

"Professor, it is not about the course."

"Yes."

"I'm in love with an African woman and she is going home."

"Yes."

"I don't want her to leave."

"Why?"

"I love her."

"Have you told her?"

"No."

"Don't you think that she ought to know before me?"

I felt so stupid.

September 28

Jen is a married woman and she's going home to her husband. I can't take it. Can't remember much of what happened after I left her place. I got drunk. I was happy.

I'm not a drinker but I'm going to drink again. And be happy again.

Zeb stops reading the journal. She glances at Rob lying there on the bed with the wet cloth on his forehead. So he's suffering from hang-over because he drank too much? She is relieved. She goes to check on him. She shakes her head from side to side. Men. Sometimes they act like small children. And women are always there to pick the pieces. She sits beside him on the bed and removes the wet towel.

"Jenny?"

"You are awake," she says.

"What are you doing here?"

"I looked for you everywhere. I went to your office. You've not been in school for two days. I finally went to the Dean of Students. I told her what happened. She phoned you and you told me to come."

"I answered the phone? I can't remember this."

"Yes. You gave me your address."

"Can't believe this," Rob says.

"I mopped your head with the wet towel."

"Why did you come to look for me?"

"The way you ran out of my room; it got me worried."

"Why?"

"You were upset," Zeb says.

"Did you care?"

"Why would I look for you if I didn't care? I'm a mother of four children!"

"You have four children? You told me about one."

"I just said that I have four."

"Why didn't you tell me?"

"Why should I tell you everything about myself? I don't know much about your family."

"I don't have children or wife or baby-mama," Rob says.

"The marriage is not real, has never been, but we have children; three big children, one of them is in graduate school."

Rob springs up from bed on hearing that her marriage is not genuine. There is hope for a future with her.

"We can bring them here, so you don't have to go back to them," he says.

"You see, I am not as young as I look."

"I don't care."

"You are just a little older than my first son."

"I don't care." He hugs her. He moves his mouth slowly to her own, enjoying that she is willing to let him kiss her. But she doesn't let him even though she still smiles. He gets it. He hurries to the bathroom to brush his teeth and put on cologne.

45

Dowry Fantasies

Zeb phones Gloria.

"My own dear girl, why did you cut me off like that? I phoned your number so many times. It doesn't even give the option of leaving a message."

"I moved out of Esi's house and she may have unplugged the answering machine."

"Did anything happen?"

"No, we're still friends, but I'm in Baltimore now." Zeb tells her about Martin Augustine, how she became a student.

"That's a smart and lucky move. I really like that. You're in a good place to find good American bachelors who can..."

"I have a man, for love not a Green Gard."

"Is he a citizen?"

"Yes."

"Very good. I don't care whether he's for love or for whatever. You'll get a Green Card through him."

"The professor helped me go through my Green Card application. Immigration has replied giving me a reference number."

"Have you informed them about your scholarship?'

"No."

"That's an achievement,' Gloria says.

"I'll ask the secretary for a description of the scholarship. With Immigration, you have to prove everything so I'll send the description that proves its worth," Zeb says.

"Looks like you have finally arrived in America and your life can now start. Now, tell me about this man in your life."

Robert Jefferson is originally from Alabama in the South. Grandmother-Emma brought him up with his brother, Cedric. Emma was an immigrant from St. Lucia in the Caribbean. The single most dominating concern for him as a child was the colour of his skin. He has the kind of skin colour they call *high yellow* – very light. Early in his life, he figured out that black skin colour was considered inferior. His grandmother used to clean house for a woman who allowed him but would not allow his dark-skinned brother, Cedric, to play with her kids. But things were different in Hobson community where they lived with their grandmother. There, all the kids played together but they used to regard him as a weak person just because of his skin colour. Light skin suggested that a white man raped one of your ancestors or that your ancestor was a house slave. Black people of Hobson looked down on light skin. As a child, Rob wanted to be like his dark-skinned brother and Grandma Emma. Although she treated them equally, Rob always felt different. He sensed that people thought he was not part of the family because of his colour. Grandma Emma explained that the two of them are blood brothers and children of her daughter, Thelma. Rob was a baby when Thelma died. When he grew up, he dated only dark -skinned girls.

"Where is his Grandma Emma?"

"Dead. After her funeral, he and his brother sold the house, land and property that she left to them. They invested all. Both of them were taking courses in accounting after high school."

"So he is an accountant."

"No. His brother continued with it and now he is an investment banker, but my man is an environmentalist interested in global health."

"May I talk with him?" Gloria says.

"What do you want to tell him?"

"Just to get to know him. Have you told your mother about him?"

"No, a lot is going on at home now. I want to keep it to myself and see where the relationship is going."

As they are talking, someone unlocks the door.

"Who?"

"My roommate."

"I think I have to visit you this time. I'll come before Christmas. Can you book a bed and breakfast for me near you?"

When Zeb tells Rob about the proposed visit by Gloria, he says that he can handle the hotel arrangement because of Zeb's busy schedule. She knows that it is time to reveal her real name to him. All the puzzles begin to fit in after telling Rob her story. She is the same woman he fell in love with in England when he was legally tied to Cara. She is the same woman who disappeared from his life when he was making plans for her to visit him in Chicago. Rob also unravels the puzzle of Aracebor being the same person as Rob Jefferson. She believes that these are not just coincidences. They are miracles. Everything has been designed to lead her to a good place.

Rob makes contact with Gloria and books her in Sheraton Baltimore. He also books Tom, Esi and Gomez in the same hotel. Gloria, Zeb and Rob watch *The Titanic* at The Senator before going to Sheraton for dinner. Zeb is surprised to see her friends and her Cousin Tom waiting at a dinner table. The management and everybody except Zeb know that there will be a marriage proposal. They put on one of Zeb's favorite music to create the mood. As soon as Zeb begins to sway to the beat of Toni Braxton's *Un-break My Heart*, Rob takes her to the dance floor. It is there that he proposes.

Everything is like a sweet dream to her. Later she shares her feeling with Gloria.

"That was one of the happiest moments of my life."

"If this is one of them, what are the other happiest moments?"

"There are too many. Birth of each of my children, my first degree, PhD, scholarship to Law School, uniting with my people after the war. Jaja also gave me many high moments."

"No more talk of Jaja, you now have the love of your life."

"There will always be a place for Jaja; a different place."

Before Christmas, Rob and Zeb go to the County Circuit Court Office to apply for a marriage licence. They receive their licence in the mail immediately after Christmas. Rob wants to make an appointment to have a Justice of the Peace perform the civil ceremony, but Zeb is against it. She wants her kids to be at her wedding so the wedding has to be much later. She phones her mother.

"Zee Zee. Tom has given me the good news. Why didn't you tell me yourself?"

"Mama, I have known him for some time but then everything happened very quickly. It was in a big hotel, the dining area was decorated for the purpose. He then asked me whether I would marry him. I did not have time to phone you or any other person. They stopped the music. Everybody in the place waited to hear my answer. Mama, I had to say, yes."

"Are you not my child? Why should you accept it just because people were looking at you? And what kind of man is that to ask such a private question in front of everybody?"

"That is the way they do it here Mama."

"You have to go back and tell him no."

"Mama I want him."

"Then what are you complaining about?"

"Nothing. Just that he wants us to get married in court."

"Did he ask you in front of everybody again?"

"No Ma."

"And what did you say?"

"I said I'll think about it."

"Are you sure you want this man?"

"I'm sure Mama."

"What of Jaja?" Angel is happy that someone is replacing Jaja, but she wants to make sure that it is real.

"My child, I'm waiting for you to answer my question."

"Mama I can't lie to you. I still have a soft spot for Jaja. He's my son's father. But Mama, my heart is now with Rob."

"Rob? Is that what the American is called?"

"Yes, Robert Jefferson."

"Is he a good man?"

"Yes Ma."

"Like how?"

Zeb does not expect this question.

She does not know any of Rob's friends and family members so she cannot speak about his standing in his family, but she can speak about the qualities she has observed. He is sensitive, kind and patient. He loves her. He has put in great effort and expense to arrange for her to see the people who matter to her. Angel coughs.

"Mama, I'm just thinking. He's just a good person. He takes care of me."

"Tell me what you don't like about him," Angel says.

"He's a bit reserved and sometimes it's like he doesn't like himself or his colour."

"These are not very serious. They show he's normal, not perfect. Can you put up with his flaws?"

"Yes."

"Expect more to show up when you begin to live as husband and wife. What is this colour of his that he hates? Is he green or blue?" Angel laughs. Zeb also laughs knowing that Angel is joking.

"He is supposed to be black, but his colour is almost white."

"Tell him to phone me," Angel says.

"Mama, please call Dozie for me."

"He travelled with Dokki. They went to see Jaja." Angel sighs. She doesn't want to tell her that Jaja is in hospital.

"When are they coming back?"

"Soon. When he comes back, I'm travelling to Abeokuta with him to see his brothers."

"Igo will be angry. You know how he is."

"No, things have changed for him. He's retired and no longer a Commissioner. I'm going to buy presents that I will use to welcome him back after a successful government service. At least, the children can now have a father who lives at home. That poor young wife of his is always weighed down with running the house and she's even afraid of your children. Anyway, don't let these things bother you. I'll take care of them. Just tell Robert to phone me."

"Mama, you think of everything and you go out of your way to take care of my affairs."

"They are my affairs."

"Thank you Mama. You're really my angel."

"You're my child."

After speaking with Angel, Robert no longer pushes for a court marriage. He is for a church marriage, but Zeb is still against it because her children cannot be there.

"I don't have kids and only my brother Cedric will be there for me. Why do you insist on delaying the wedding because you want your whole clan to come?"

"My situation is not normal. Thank you for being so sensitive."

"I'm sorry. I didn't mean to offend you. Look at it this way, let's get married, buy a house and bring them here," Rob says.

"I can't afford to bring them now. I'm still in school."

"But I can afford it."

"Well, I want a traditional Nigerian wedding. I never had it with Igo. I didn't have any kind with him, but I really want the traditional."

"What does it involve?"

"Your family and mine."

"I have only Cedric so that can easily be arranged when we travel. What else?"

"It involves a lot of money because your family will give my family bride price and my family will give dowry. "

"Impossible. I cannot pay your family for marrying you."

"It doesn't mean that you're paying them. Just a token of appreciation on both sides."

"I'm not going to get involved in such a ... outdated custom."

"You wanted to say barbaric custom, didn't you?"

"I said outdated."

"To me it is not outdated," Zeb removes the engagement ring from her finger.

"I don't even know why I'm wearing this expensive ring that cost more than double whatever you'll give to my family at the traditional wedding."

"It is a selfish ring for one person. I can't share it with my loved ones. But the bride price is shared and the dowry they give will be for both of us. You don't want it, yet you want me to wear this expensive selfish ring so that men will know that I have a man and keep away from me." Zeb gives him the ring. He does not take it. She drops it on the chair.

"Come on Zeb, you don't mean that you're calling off the engagement."

"You can wear the ring yourself. But don't despise my culture."

Rob tries to hold her.

"Don't touch me. You always claim to like Africa, but you look down on my culture. Please leave."

Rob phones Zeb but she does not pick the phone. He phones Tom and tells him what happened. Tom tells him that he will be having this kind of cultural misunderstanding in his marriage and he has to develop a way of resolving them in his family. He then explains the situation from his personal example.

"My family gave bride-price when I married my wife, Ije. It was our way of acknowledging the family that raised the woman who I fell in love with and chose out of all the women I've seen in the world. Her family also gave dowry that would have helped us to furnish our house if we were living in Nigeria. We gave away items of the dowry to friends and family members. Of course we brought some of the small items like special beddings and traditional plates that we use as decoration here. In this way, Ije and I, her family and my family contributed to our marriage and have souvenirs of the wedding. It was a kind of give-and-take-situation. Everybody felt included as we all ate, drank and celebrated in her family's compound where the ceremonies took place. Many of our ways in Nigeria are based on communal membership while many of our American ways are quite individualistic. It is not an outdated custom. It is misunderstood and misrepresented by those who don't understand."

"I think I'm one of those."

"Some people actually exploit the tradition and demand a lot of money from the bridegroom's family. But this is usually out of poverty or greed. It was not the case in my marriage."

"Thank you so much Tom. This explanation is so helpful. Can you suggest to me what I can do to appease Zeb?"

"Frankly I cannot. One thing I can tell you is how I resolve issues with my wife. I'm a bit like Zeb because I can walk out and not want to talk about an issue especially when we are not listening to each other. One thing that has worked is Ijeoma's ability to communicate and my willingness to listen when she is not nagging," Tom laughs. Rob shakes his head.

"It's not easy," Rob says.

"No. Marriage is not easy, but it is worth all the hard work. I mean, my wife sometimes writes to explain her point of view. I read it in the quietness of my loneliness."

"I like that. I'm so lonely. All I want is to make up with Zeb."

"Just try to understand her and her culture. I mean, I'm from the same culture area with Ije but as individuals, we come from different thinking positions. I take it as a learning experience and I hope she also learns from me."

"Thank you so much Tom. This means a lot to me."

Zeb and Rob register at Christ the King Church in Edmondson Avenue. The pastor puts them in pre-marriage class of two hours a week for six months. They buy the recommended books and attend the classes together. The classes give them insight on how to use Christian principles to engage problems in their relationship and life in general as a couple. They both like the classes and do their assignments together. They discuss the logistics of the kind of marriage that they want. They plan to have a church wedding at Christ the King and go to Nigeria later for a traditional wedding.

Zeb feels that Igo will be angry about her marriage but doesn't know how he will react to the idea of her taking the children. Rob tells her that the best thing is to write a letter to Igo and let him know that both of them should think about their children and not focus on their anger.

"Your children are adults and can decide for themselves."

"In our culture, they need to get the blessing of their parents in making such a major decision."

They phone Angel and discuss it with her. Angel tells them that the family has discussed Zeb's proposed marriage. Although Igo and Zeb lived together as couple, they were not married traditionally, so all the children belong to Zeb and her family and Igo knows that. The family has decided to be silent on that tradition for now because Igo has been good to the family in spite of his shortcomings. The family will send a delegation to inform Igo that Zeb is getting married.

"After all, he himself got married without even telling me," Zeb says.

"Leave that alone. The person who calls the police may not be the one that wins the case. He has scored those cheap points, but look at how you have used them to move to higher grounds. Do not drag my talk backwards, my child."

"You're right, Mama," Rob pinches Zeb.

"This kind of matter is not done in a hurry. Remember that he is no longer king of the police force. He is a very proud man and must be feeling bad about it. You cannot eat hot soup in a hurry. We have to handle him gently. Write a letter to him about your plans for the children. Post the letter to me. I will take the letter to him myself and talk to him. You have to rub oil to smoothen hard things so that they can move *welewele*," Angel says.

"With ease," Zeb says.

"Yes. Do you understand me, my children?"

"Yes, Ma," Rob and Zeb say.

Both of them construct a letter to Igo saying that they are willing to bring the children to America if the children want it and if he allows it.

46

From Hawaii to Lagos

Zeb and Rob sit on the floor in front of the couch facing the television. Zeb inclines on Rob's chest and he inclines on the couch. He caresses Zeb with his left hand and uses his right to use the remote control of the television channels. Zeb opens a letter from the Immigration Department. She is required to confirm her children's addresses in Nigeria. From her experience working with Adams, she knows that her application process is in the final stages. She can also apply for a Green Card through Rob when they get married. She smiles.

"What?"

"God has made sure that I must have a Green Card." She shows the letter to Rob. He kisses her and continues to flip the channels. Zeb is happy that she now has to choose whether her green card will be through marriage to the man she loves or through her recognition as a person of extraordinary ability.

There is an NFL replay of Redskins versus Cowboys on NBC. Rob keeps the remote and picks the Wedding Planner. They look at the options and prefer the picture of a small party. They decide that Tom, Kordi and Rob's brother, Cedric, will be the only family members. They plan to invite about ten people and leave for honeymoon immediately after the wedding. Choosing the honeymoon resort creates a misunderstanding. Rob likes the Mauna Lani Resort in Hawaii but Zeb thinks that it is too expensive for the persona she adopts in America.

"This is my first marriage. Can you just allow me to make it memorable?" Rob snaps.

"It is also my first."

"No, it is not."

"What do you mean, it's not?" Zeb says. She gets up from his chest where she has been lying and turns to look at him.

"Well, if it is, you will want to make it as memorable as I want it to be."

"That is the problem with you..."

"Americans!" he snaps. "Say it. I'm sick and tired of your Nigerian attitude. Everything is about your culture."

"If you resent my Nigerian ways, why do you want to go on with this wedding anyway? You put a lot of value on something because it is expensive or designer.

That's all I'm against and you're talking about culture," Zeb says. She is getting worked up.

The scene of her argument with Anise about Nigerian and American attitude to colour flashes through her mind. She is not ready to allow Rob intimidate her like Anise.

"Let me tell you something Robert Jefferson."

"No, listen. I'm proud of being American no matter what it means to you."

"America is my land of freedom where I take refuge. America means a lot to me, but that is not the issue right now. It's the way you value things. That something is expensive doesn't mean that it will be memorable," Zeb says.

"That it is cheap doesn't make it great. You have to get used to the change in your life-style. You are going to be my wife." Rob put emphasis on the word "wife."

"So?" Zeb drags the word.

"So, get used to not feeling guilty about Jaja's incarceration. I'm not gonna let him spoil my joy. If-." Rob stops talking. He sees the hurt on Zeb's face.

"I'm sorry Zeb. I don't mean it that way. I'm just a little jealous of Jaja." Rob tries to hold her. She pushes him off.

"You don't have to be jealous." She gets up and sits on the couch.

"I know. Forgive me." He also sits on the couch.

"No problem." Zeb twists her mouth. Rob tries to hold her again.

"I'm sorry," he says. He drops the magazine and wraps his hands around her.

"My concern is that you have been spending a lot of money and you will spend a lot more when we eventually go to Nigeria." Zeb still twists her mouth.

"I've told you that I have a lot of investments and you should not worry about money. I started working when I was sixteen years old and I have been investing money since then."

Zeb is thrilled by what she considers a fairy tale wedding at Christ the King Church with a gorgeous reception at *Harbor Magic*. They chose the hotel because of the proximity of the natural setting. Their guests said the accommodation is great. Kordi comments on the sea atmosphere that often tickles her nose, "in a good way," she adds. The scenery proves to be an ideal backdrop for the wedding. As the wedding party enters the hotel through the promenade, Rob smiles. He knows that Zeb is happy. She slowly inhales the mild summer air.

"I'm the princess," she smiles at Rob. She has her beau and the party of friends and family with her at her most precious moment.

Zeb is still relishing the fairy tale of her wedding as the plane lands in Hawaii for their honeymoon. She finds herself in yet another chapter of the tale in which she is still the hero. Hawaii takes her breath away with the splendid *Ahoha* welcome at the Kamuela Airport. She caresses the fresh yellow hibiscus and frangippani in her *lei* as Rob holds her other hand. She has never dreamed that her life could be like this. She no longer thinks of her extended family or her children. She savors the joy of the moment with Rob beside her. She does not even remember Jaja. Just how happy she has become. The guide takes them to a waiting loumosine that will take them to their hotel. They are at the Mauna Lani. Stepping out of the limousine, the splendid scenery of the bay and skyline greets her eyes making it water. The landscape captivates her as a work of art by an old master, but this is not just a masterpiece. It is not a painting by an artist but real life picture that you can touch and feel. Zeb stretches her hands. She breathes in slowly and exhales. Rob also likes the scenery of Mauna Lani Bay Hotel, but delights more in looking at his wife as she dramatizes her love for the place.

The luxurious ground of the bungalow where they will stay reminds her of Holywood red carpet but this is better because it is deep lushly green, which suits her mood and what her life has become. "Spring after Winter" comes to her mind as the title of a poem that should describe her joy. She squeezes Rob's hand.

"Thank you," she says looking at the beautiful landscape. Their bungalow has a swimming pool, health spa and pleasant personal staff. As they enter the suite,

Zeb experiences cold shivers on her right arm. She stops.

"What's wrong honey," Rob says. She wipes her hand. She does not know what to make of her sudden shivers on a honeymoon trip.

"Tell me, what is it?" Rob holds her face with his palms and looks at her frowning face. She tells him about her shivers that usually signal danger or that she should be careful.

"For real?"

"Believe me, it's not superstition or anything like that."

"Maybe, it's all the excitement. Let's relax." He takes her to their room. Rob picks the menu to order and they sit. The television is on at CNN. Breaking news: the president of the military regime in Nigeria has died. This changes everything. They cut their honeymoon short to plan a trip to Nigeria.

Rob is not surprised by the disorder at Murtala Muhammed Ariport in Lagos, Nigeria. Zeb has prepared him for it. What she did not prepare him for is the change in her personality. It's like she has become a different person. She laughs and jokes with Airport officials like she knows them. She speaks a different language.

"What are you saying to them?" Rob says.

"I'm speaking pigeon."

Rob has never heard her mention or speak it. He knows about her mother tongue, Igbo language, which she speaks on the phone with Angel. She sometimes explains some Igbo words to him. But this one called pigeon? He shakes his head in exasperation. Even her appearance has changed. He looks at her. She is radiant. There are many porters helping people with their luggage. Rob does not want any of them to help him. Their suitcases seem to be the only familiar things in the strange place. He pushes the cart with their luggage. All the officials are black. He likes that, but he is at a loss on how to react to them. One of them irritates him by referring to him as *oyimbo*. He is more annoyed as Zeb begins to laugh and talk to them in the strange pigeon language. How can they refer to a black man in a country of black people as 'white', and think it is funny?

Zeb's friend, Chioma, and her husband meet them as soon as they come out with their luggage. There is a lot of hugging and introductions.

"Girl, you haven't changed one bit." Chioma hugs Zeb and whirls her round.

"You're the famous Rob," she hugs Rob too. Chioma's husband, Jo, shakes hands with Rob and hugs Zeb; really close embrace. He takes the cart from Rob and hands it to a porter. As they walk to his car, Jo chats with Rob. He asks Rob whether the heat bothers him. The porter loads the suitcases. Zeb jumps into the back seat with Chioma and they continue to talk in a mixture of three languages making it difficult for Rob to follow their dialogue. Rob reluctantly enters the front passenger seat and is not happy that Zeb does not notice it. As Jo drives into the street, Rob gasps, Oh my God! The street is crowded. The only place he can compare it with is New York City. The only difference is that unlike New York, the people here are all black. He can feel a lot of vitality as people move, talk, laugh, argue and just fill the streets. You can feel the energy in the streets through the fast, slow, normal motion. Rob folds his arms as he looks through the window.

"Are you okay Hon? You're quiet," Zeb says.

"You still remember me?"

"Of course, honey. Why?" Zeb leans forward from the back seat and throws her arms on his shoulders. It is the first time she has demonstrated her love since they arrived. Rob swallows. She's been acting like she's having a lot of life and no time for him. He unfolds his arms and kisses her hand.

This is not the Africa which Rob has seen in books and films.

"Is this Africa?"

"Yes, this is Nigeria," Jo says.

"Just wondering."

"It's not as hot as I expected it to be," Rob says.

"This is not a hot period," Jo says.

He explains the seasons and their periods of the year. He tells him the names of the streets and points at places. They are in Maryland area just approaching the roundabout.

"That's the famous Saint Agnes," Jo says.

"We got married there ten years ago," Chioma adds.

"I remember the big statue of the Blessed Virgin Mary at the round-about in front of the church yard?" Zeb says.

"They have added a grotto," Chioma says.

The modern buildings and highways surprise Rob. He shudders at the number of vehicles on the road.

"What is it honey?" Zeb's hand is still on his shoulder.

"Just too many cars. Are the roads and bridges strong enough for such busy traffic?"

"Don't let your environmental safety concern get in the way, honey. A bridge has to crack before the government will notice it and begin to talk about repairing it."

"No, it is when the bridge breaks and causes a huge accident that the government will come in," Jo laughs.

"They will find a scapegoat to blame for it," Jo adds.

"Maybe the anti-government forces caused it somehow or something stupid like that," Chioma says.

"I hope that things will begin to change for the better since the dictator is gone," Zeb says.

"The military is still in power, so Abubaka is just like change of baton," Jo says.

"Is that the name of the new president?" Rob says.

"Yes."

"We have to buy some newspapers and magazines so that Rob and I can catch up on news."

"We'll do so but don't expect much in the papers. Versions of the same things; some praise the government, others condemn it and talk about everything that is wrong in the country."

They are now in Surelere area when their car slows down. All the vehicles move very slowly. Jo diverts to a side road with only two lanes.

"Why leave the six lane highway?" Zeb asks.

"Sometimes these ones are faster than the highway. Everybody knows the highway, but you have to live in this city to know which route works better at particular times."

"This is what we call 'go slow'," Zeb says, her lips grazing Rob's ear.

Jo rolls down the window. They all roll down their windows. Hawkers run to the windows trying to show their wares and convince them to buy something. Zeb buys roasted maize and *ube* and begins to eat them immediately.

"How I missed these," she says.

"Honey this is a kind of pear. It goes well with the maize," she offers some to Rob. He does not want to eat them. Something could have contaminated them out there in the open air.

"Eat it and be strong!" Chioma says.

"I am strong!"

"Oh sorry-o," Chioma says.

Zeb leans forward again and whispers in Rob's ear, "She's just trying to be nice."

Jo and Chioma have cooked and stacked the fridge with drinks. Their neighbours and friends who have heard about the visitors come to the house to welcome them. Rob and Zeb are introduced as each new neighbour comes in. Then they will hug, shake hands, thank God, eat and drink. There are just too many hugs, shaking of hands, talking and laughing. They tell anecdotes and shout like they are addressing a crowd. The hullabaloo is too much for Rob. He wants to rest. But there are just too many introductions, so he yawns. Who cares to know Jo and Chioma's connections to all "these people" who they may never see again? Rob wants everybody to get out and leave him alone with his wife. The irony is that Zeb is enjoying the rowdy attention.

Finally, Rob goes to their room. Even though he is not with Zeb, he feels some relief. Zeb stays back in the living room enjoying the company of people she has just met. He relaxes on the bed and reads the newspapers. He feels sleepy so he goes to the bathroom to take a bath and put on comfortable clothes. As he finishes, Zeb comes to the bathroom.

"You are already feeling at home," she says hugging him from behind as he is combing his hair in front of the mirror.

"I see you have better company so I have to take care of myself."

"They've all gone." Zeb takes the comb from him and combs the back of his head, gives him a kiss and they both go back to the bedroom. Rob sits on the bed with a newspaper while Zeb rummages inside the suitcases looking for presents. She tells Rob that her uncle phoned to say that he has arrived from the east in order to go with her to Abeokuta to see the children and discuss with Igo.

"I'm coming with you," Rob says.

"You know that my ex-husband will be there," she brings out a pair of shoes and handbag for Chioma.

"I don't trust that creep with you. I'm coming," Rob says.

"When I talked with him on the phone, he was nice," Zeb says.

"You already phoned him?" Rob keeps the newspaper and looks at Zeb.

"Yes. My uncle said I should phone him."

"Did you tell him that I will come?"

"No. But he knows that both of us are here."

"Well, I'm coming to protect my wife."

When Zeb leaves with the presents, Rob goes to his suitcase and takes his 38 calibre revolver, revolving cylinder. He goes back to the bathroom and locks the door to load it. Meanwhile the last visitor has left and Zeb is giving Chioma the gifts.

"These are very lovely shoes." Chioma bends down to put them on.

"Do you want to buy something from here that you want to take back to America?" Jo says.

"I remember you bought Hausa shoes when you were going to America," Chioma raises one leg for all to see her shoe.

"Very beautiful."

"Just perfect."

"I'll buy things when I go to the north," Zeb says.

"You're going to the north?"

"Yes, to see Jaja."

There is silence.

"Does your husband know about it?" Chioma says.

"Even if he knows and says 'go ahead' don't do it." Jo gets up and leaves.

"Thanks for the tie." Jo says as he opens his bedroom door.

"This man is taking all your children to America and you want to pay him by going to the north to see Jaja?"

"I love my husband, but Jaja is my comrade and father of my child. I also want to know what is going on in the YAM organization."

"The money you brought to support YAM is all we need from you. Jaja is no longer active. He's very ill."

"That's also why I want to see him. I hear he's in coma."

"Are you a doctor?"

"If I talk to him and he hears my voice..."

"Does Rob know about him?"

"Yes, I don't hide anything from Rob-o."

"Good. How does he feel about Jaja?"

"Very jealous."

"You know how white people are. He won't say anything now in Nigeria. You'll wake up one day and he's gone. You'll be lucky if he leaves a note to tell you that it's because of Jaja."

"First of all, Rob is not white. Second, don't generalise about white people."

"You're right. Black men are like that too. See how my own husband just got up and walked out. You can imagine what he will do if I want to visit an ex-boyfriend? My friend, don't do it-o."

Zeb's uncle, Okolo, comes very early in the morning with a taxi and driver. Driving through Lagos on their way to Abeokuta, Rob is shocked by the density of the population on the streets.

"New York of Africa," he says.

"Too many cars eh?" Okolo says.

"And too many people."

"About eighteen million. It wasn't like this before. People running away from the deprivation in the villages move to the cities and this leads to overpopulation," Okolo says.

"Most of them are small time farmers whose farmlands are exhausted."

"The soil can be enriched," Rob says.

"Who will enrich it? The government is busy selling crude oil and pushing people to leave their land," Zeb says.

"And stealing money they should use to repair oil devastation from which the people are running away. They run to the cities and become destitutes," Okolo says.

Rob has heard a lot about the oppression of the people by the political class from Zeb, but being in Nigeria adds a new perspective to his understanding. As they leave the city, driving becomes easy. The countryside is wide and green with flourishing vegetation. It takes them four hours to make it to Abeokuta.

47

Nigerian Wild-Wild-West

beokuta is a small city with a major advantage over Lagos. It is not crowded. There is a traffic warden at the roundabout. The driver stops and waits for the warden to give the sign to move. Rob likes the orderliness of the city. The drivers do not press the horn of their cars and make a lot of noise as they do in Lagos. The warden gives them the sign to move.

"This area is called GRA, which means Government Reserved Area."

"It is where the colonial masters used to live. Now Nigerian masters live here," Okolo says.

"Only Government Officers?" Rob says.

"Yes, very senior ones."

The houses are huge and set in acres of land. Zeb directs the driver into a large complex of one huge and two average houses. There are two other small houses near the back hedge.

"What're those houses for?" Rob points at the two small houses as they walk to the huge house.

"That's the Boys' Quarters. The domestic workers live there." Zeb points at one of them.

"What of that one?"

"The kitchen; don't you see the chimney," she says.

"Wow! The kitchen is separate from the house. That reminds me of my grandmother's house back in Hobson, Alabama"

"It's a big house. We also have another kitchen in the main house; a smaller one," Zeb says.

"We?"

"Honey, you know what I mean."

"Just teasing. What about those two near the hedge?" Rob says.

"One is where the generator is kept. The other is a spare bathroom and toilet."

As they enter the massive living room, Rob puts his hand inside his pocket. He feels his 38; cold, hard, and ready.

This is Chief Ugwogo Igodana. This is Dr. Robert Jefferson. They shake hands. Igo's handshake feels warm and firm as Rob looks straight into his big eyes. He does not see any malice in his eyes, just ruggedness. He reminds him of his brother, Cedric. Ugwogo Igo is huge, about six feet two or three. He is about two hundred pounds with balding head and grey hairs. He has bold features on his face; big nose, big mouth and eyes. Rob sizes him up. He is taller than Rob is, but Rob is certain that he can take him down with his bare hands. He puts his hand inside his pocket.

A servant brings kola nuts in a saucer. "Good morning Ma. Good morning sirs," he gives the saucer of kolanuts to Igo. Igo presents it to Okolo.

"The king's kola is in the hand of the king. Please break the kola my in-law," Okolo says as he touches the saucer in Igo's hand.

The servant comes back with a tray full of assortment of drinks.

"I want us to discuss the children's future first." Zeb does not smile.

"My daughter, wait," Okolo waves at Zeb.

"My in-law, please break the kola," Okolo says.

"Thank you. We have to break kola nuts, and have communion first as our tradition demands," Igo says.

"The kola tree comes from deep inside the earth." Igo says glancing at Rob before he continues. "We call her Ana. She bids us use her fruit for communion. They named me after Earth as Igodo-Ana and my legs are on the earth as I welcome you to my house that stands firm on the bowels of the earth. Infinite Spirit, bless this kola nut, bless the families represented here and bless our mission today. May this kola nut give us life."

"Amen," Okolo says.

"*Ise*," Rob and Zeb say.

"My in-law, take one that will go home with you." He passes the saucer to Okolo who takes one whole nut. Igo breaks the nuts. They are five pieces. The servant comes back, takes the saucer from Igo and passes it round for people to take a piece of the kola nut.

Kola nuts are bitter, but Rob eats a piece all the same. When he drinks water it tastes great.

"I have got passports for the boys. Olima Junior has finished his Masters degree in Mechanical Engineering. He wants to go to America for further studies. No problem with him. Igodoana also wants to go. No problem. The only problem is Akinyele. He's deeply involved in the YAM group fighting the government."

"What?" Zeb says. Igo glances at her and continues to speak.

"He imagines what his absent mother is like and on hearing on TV that she is in YAM, he joins up too."

"Don't pin it on me. It's your fault, you think that bringing up children is just giving them money and cars while you stay in the north with your girlfriends," Zeb says. Rob squeezes her hand.

Igo juts his mouth towards Zeb in a condescending manner.

"Look at who is talking about abandonment. You who-." Igo says.

"Stop, both of you. Leave your fight for another time. Let's talk about what we are here for," Okolo's voice is firm.

"We located where he is and brought him home. He heard me yesterday talking with my in-law on the phone about their going to America. He left before I came out this morning. We'll find him again."

"Can you make him to go to America if he doesn't want to?" Okolo says.

"I'll handle him. The first thing is to find him," Zeb says. Her voice shakes. The boy was just eight years old when she left Igo. Rob squeezes her hand.

"My in-law, Mazi Okolo, we have discussed this thing before, but I want to repeat it in front of my wife, Chizebe."

Zeb opens her mouth to contradict him and say that she is no longer his wife, but Okolo glares at her and Rob squeezes her hand so tight that she closes her mouth. Igo continues to speak.

"Initially, only Igodoana Junior wanted to go to America, but I told Olima Junior that as the most senior, he should go too and make sure they find their own place to live. I hoped that Akin would want to go if he saw that his brothers were going, but he has not changed his mind. He is stubborn like-." He stops, glances at Zeb, swallows saliva and and says, "He's passionate about politics."

He pauses, then he says, "I'll give the boys foreign exchange to help them with initial down payment for their own place. In spite of everything, Chize I thank you for taking them out at this time. The country is still not good."

Everybody is happy.

"Thank you my in-law," Okolo says.

"I'll come to Lagos to see the man in whose house my children will be staying briefly before they get their own place. I don't want my children to be with a stranger that I don't know. I have to see him and assess him to know how I'll approach the matter of placing my children in his hands, even if on temporary basis."

"This is my husband."

"What?"

"Rob is my husband." Zeb raises Rob's hand.

"This young man?"

"Yes."

"My children cannot live with a small boy like this!" Igo points at Rob.

"He is not older than my first son," he adds.

"Don't call me a small boy and don't yell at my wife," Rob stands up. Igo ignores him and addresses Zeb.

"You think that I'll let this boy take my children?" he says.

"This boy who needs his father to teach him how to treat another man cannot take care of my children." Igo still addresses Zeb. Then he turns to Rob.

"Boy, get out of my house!" he says.

Rob who grew up without his father, is annoyed by the reference to his father, but it is the word "boy" that triggers an angry chord in Rob. Growing up in Hobson Alabama, adult black men were called "boys" by white people just to put them down because of their colour. He vowed not to go back there after his grandmother's funeral. Now, a black man calls him a boy. He does not want to say, "I'm not a boy." He wants to show his superiority to Igo. With his hands akimbo and looking at Igo eyeball to eyeball, he says, "I'm not leaving here without my wife." He hardly finishes the sentence before Igo shouts, "Get out before I come back!" Igo storms out of the living room. Rob puts one hand into his pocket and positions it on the 38.

Okolo tells Rob to leave the compound.

"I'm here for my wife," Rob says.

"This daughter of mine can deal with Igo, I tell you. I'm here also to protect her. Traditionally, you don't have a right in Igo's house, so leave us."

Rob goes outside the house but does not leave the compound. He stays beside the window. Igo comes back to the living room with a 45 Gluck.

"So he has the good sense to leave my house," he says.

"If you dare touch him, America will deal with you. Foolish man! You think that you can intimidate everybody in the world as you do here," Zeb yells.

" Whom are you talking to like that?"

"You bully!" Zeb gets up from her seat. Rob sees everything from where he is standing outside the window. He pulls his gun.

"I will not shoot you. You are the mother of my children, but you will die here today if you don't get out now and follow that boy prostitute that you hired."

"You call my husband a prostitute?" Zeb moves and stands right in front of him..

"Get out of my house!"

Zeb stands her ground.

"I have more right to be in this house than you," she says.

"You! Get out of this house," she goes for his gun and succeeds in holding his hand.

"You old whore! You want to see the children that you abandoned."

Okolo pushes himself between them.

Rob's patience is stretched to the limit. He can put up with the insult of being called a boy and a prostitute, but not that of seeing his wife insulted. He has to defend her. He pushes the door open.

"Nobody calls my wife a whore and gets away with it."

Zeb immediately shifts her body to block Igo who has turned towards Rob. She loses her grip on Igo's hand.

"Igo, drop your gun!" Okolo sounds helpless.

"And you, leave this place," Okolo shouts to Rob and turns to Igo, "I'm still your in-law. Please give me that respect and drop your gun," he adds.

"Let him drop his own gun," Igo says. Zeb still blocks him.

"You drop first! Rob get out! Get out!" Okolo is desperate.

He drops the gun. Rob puts his gun in his pocket and walks out. Zeb kicks Igo's gun. Okolo goes for it and runs out through the back door with the gun.

"Sit down and let's talk about the children's future," Zeb breathes heavily as if she has run a long way.

"Why didn't you tell me that you are married to a white man?"

"He is not white. He is like Fulani," Zeb says.

"So he is a Nigerian."

"He is an African American but looks like Fulani."

"You went too far to bring him here. Never, never, never..."

"Let's talk about the children's future."

Okolo comes back without the gun.

"Where is my gun?"

"You'll never see it again. My daughter, let's go." Okolo moves to the door.

"I'm not leaving this house without my children's passports."

"My in-law, come back. Let's talk," Igo says.

They sit down. Rob relaxes, still by the window.

48

Husband of My Wife

eb and Rob look at the pile of letters. Most of them are bills, but one of them attracts attention. It is from the department of Homeland Security. Zeb's hands shake as she picks the envelope. Rob takes it from her, opens and reads. "Approval Notice for Alien of Extraordianry Ability. The above petition has been approved. The petition indicates-." Zeb screams and hugs Rob. The letter falls from Rob's hand.

"At last," Zeb says.

"Congratulations," Rob hugs her. She begins to cry and praise God. Rob picks the leter and reads the rest of it. Zeb wants to go to their church and pray but Rob wants them to check through the pile of letters.

Rob and Zeb are sitting against the headboard of their bed. They use pillows to prop their backs as they sort the envelopes, keeping aside the junk mails for the trashcan. Here is a big brown envelope with the sender's name, Ugwuogo Igodana, boldly written on the top left and back.

"You read it," Rob says.

"It is addressed to you, so read it," Zeb says.

"You know you're good at reading, my linguistic and attorney wife."

Zeb begins to read.

Dear Dr. Robert Jefferson,

This is Ugwogo Igodoana of the famous Otaebu lineage in Obea town of Nsukka North. You are acquainted with me. I am the husband of the woman whom you are now marrying. First, I must apologise for threatening to eliminate your life with my gun when you dared to come to my house without invitation. You must understand that in this land of my forefathers, taboos must be respected. Chizebe whom you call Zeb did not advise you well about Africa, but as a man who has felt her heat I understand how she can rouse the sleeping fire inside a man and make him part ways with his senses. I am sure that you understand what I mean, since you now live with her and taste what I have eaten. I write this letter to you, because you harbour my children in your house and you live with my wife. I call her my wife because I never divorced her. My marriage with her is forever and we have our children as proof of that, but I do not hold it against you for playing a role in our lives.

As man to man, husband to husband, and the one who now plays father to my sons, you are at the centre of a life for which I worked hard. I no longer swim in the ocean of good health as I used to do when I was in my hey days, so I don't want to keep this information with me in case it gets lost with me when I depart from this world that has become twisted and strange. I want you to know the father of the boys who live with you so that you will understand the root of their strength. I am a man who was castrated by fate, but I faced my fate with all my might. My sons know some parts of this story, not all. They will know all of it when the time comes, but for you, it is time, so please hear me out.

Otaebu is my great-great-grandfather's name. It means *ota-ebu-onu*, that is, "As you chew it or try to destroy it, it grows stronger and swells up in the mouth." It is a proper description of the character trait of my great ancestor, which is passed on from generation to generation.

He was bestowed with this honorable name when he was a mere boy, because of the intelligence and survival mechanism that he demonstrated when he escaped from kidnappers, and returned to our land.

Otaebu, my great-great-grandfather, belonged to the ruling class of our community, not the king's family but the king-making family considered greater than king's. He was an only child, and so his mother protected him too much. She did not allow him to go to the stream for water or go to the bush to collect firewood, because some evil animal or spirit might hurt him. But Otaebu was restless and clever. He sometimes sneaked out and joined other children on exciting ventures. One such adventure was when they went to collect *utu*, rare forest fruits with medicinal nuts. Bandits waylaid them. They fled, but they were surrounded.

Otaebu climbed a tree. A bandit climbed after him. He jumped down and injured his leg. They still took him, because they were impressed by his agility. He asked permission to ease himself. They knew that he would not be able to run away because of his wound, so they allowed him to go into the bush alone. He limped into the bush. He did not run away in the bush. Instead, he cut some *ugbugbo*, a kind of herb that purges the stomach. He wanted to develop an illness, so that his captors would abandon him. Sure enough, he developed diarrhea and had to pass feaces often. Ugbugbo shit can disband an army with its foul smell. His captors could not stand the smell and constant need to expel excrement. His condition slowed them down. They abandoned him. Otaebu cured himself with the antidote of *ugbugbo*. Everybody in my town knows the antidote.

Young men from my town went out looking for the children. They spent days searching for them. They could not trace the route of the children. It had rained and footprints had been washed away. The housekeeper of Ana, the earth goddess, went into the forest to get answers from the forest spirits. He divined that the children had gone forever and families would not have the opportunity to dance them back to the ancestral land the way they were welcomed with music to the land of the living when they were born. The town went into mourning. They were still in mourning when my great ancestor returned. He was the only one that came back. He lost his only half-brother and two cousins in that raid. He narrated how he ate the leaves of *ugbugbo*. The people began to call him Ota-ebu-onu, which refers to 'the one that eats hardship and gets stronger from the experience.' This story happened around the middle part of 1800. The story was passed down. Each generation has a story that adds more salt and pepper to the meaning of Otaebu. When someone comes with hatred, we catch it, and turn it into a survival tool that makes us stronger.

The British colonized us during that period and later wanted my people to join their army. My great-grandfather, Otaebu's son, was in the assembly that debated on whether my village should contribute men to the British army or not. He was against the contribution. The story goes that there was a debate for and against the contribution. Everybody in our community knows this story that is passed on from generation to generation. It is the history of how the British invaded our land, forced their laws on our people who were used to Obea laws and found it difficult to accept the strange ways of the British. The British then used cruelty to force their ways on the people. We still tell the history in folktales and in games. We have a game for children. It involves chanting and making hand and feet gestures. Two children play the game and act as Warrior and Kidnapper. Sometimes they add two other parts, Child and Servant, so that four children can play the game. Each performer makes gestures and sounds to support his argument. Part of the game goes like this.

At this point, Zeb stops reading the letter and gets off the bed.

"What?"

"Let me show you how to play the game. I know it very well and used to play it with the children."

"Come and lie beside me. I just need to feel you. The letter is disturbing but compelling." Rob gets up and brings Zeb back to the bed.

"Alright. Let's read the game together."

"Darling, can you do me the favour please," Rob says. Zeb slides her left hand under his neck, kisses him and continues to read.

Warrior: We do not want the people who are ruling us. Let them go away.

Kidnapper: They gave us laws of their land.

Warrior: They kill our own laws.

Kidnapper: They gave us Christianity.

Warrior: They kill Ana worship. People no longer revere the Earth. Now, they want us to join them in killing other people in their own land.

Kidnapper: They brought us white people. We now have a tribe of whites in our land

Warrior: We do not want their tribe. We want them to bring back our people that they took away. If they are dead, we want their bodies so that we can bury them in the land of our forbears. We do not know whether they sacrificed them to their gods.

Kidnapper: They did not kill them. They made them into slaves who work for them. We also have slaves here.

Warrior: We do not treat slaves like animals. Slaves become chiefs and kings here. Our gods forbid that we use people like animals.

Kidnapper: You have too much fire inside you.

Warrior: Why not? Calamity is still upon us. Now they want to take our people away to kill people of other lands. The people they took before never returned.

Kidnapper: Don't talk about it.

Warrior: Why not? We still suffer from the loss of our people. We lost our people and you know that our strength is in people. We lost more than people! We lost our morale. We lost our freedom.

Kidnapper: Past. History. Now is the present and now is a new order.

Warrior: We cannot allow our children to fight for them, and do to other people what they did to us.

Kidnapper: They can take people by force. Let us be their friends and give them what they want.

Warrior: Ana will not forgive us. I will not give up with my own hand. I will die, rather than give up. The ancestors will reject me if I give up.

Dr. Jefferson, I taught my children how to play the game, but they never play the role of kidnapper or servant, just like me. We always play the role of Warrior or Child. I have never played Servant who defends white people. And I will never play such a role in my life, even to the man who took my wife. This does not mean that I am not grateful that you ferried my sons out of this country. I know my children and I know that they will come back to Obea when it is time, but you owe it to me to know the story of my family since you took my wife and children. My story should be lodged in your brain, so that you can understand the gem of greatness and toughness in the blood of my children. My story should be told in the house where my children live. My story carries strength.

Did the British accept that my people did not want to join in their war? No. Their police arrested some elders and many men of the warrior age grade. My great-grandfather was one of them. The British sent them to the war in their colonies. That was what we were told. Our people never returned from the war to tell their story. They died in a foreign land. Each went to the spirit world alone like someone who did not have people to dance them to the spirit world.

You are a white man even though Chizebe said that you are black. I saw you; you are white and you act like them. We have a long history with your people, so we can smell them from a distance. It is a story of their taking from us. You are just continuing with a long tradition by taking my wife and children. It is in your blood, just as Otaebu is in my blood.

"This is very insulting!" Zeb says.

"Please continue reading. I want to hear him out," Rob says.

"Ok," Zeb continues to read.

There is yet another story that I want to tell you, co-husband of my woman. It happened during the Second World War. My heart was not in that war. I did not know who caused it. I did not know why I should fight. I had gone through circumcision and proved myself to be a man. I learnt what my responsibilities were as a man, and I vowed to be a good man in Obea community. I learnt that a man had to work hard for his family, and be alert so as not to miss any opportunity to take care of his community. Going to the white man's war was not my responsibility. I did not understand why I should travel all the long distance to kill people who did not harm me or my people.

One thing that my mother told me stood on my mind. She said. "No matter where you go, remember that Otaebu spirit will protect you." As for my father, he went to the great keeper of Ana shrine and got a charm for me, but that charm was seized in Lagos during inspection. I only had my mother's counsel in my brain. My father's charm was gone. I was angry. But you couldn't show anger because the punishment was brutal. The military drill was not that bad for any man who had gone through circumcision obstacles. But the punishment was something else. They will lock you up in a cell, only you. When people came out of the cell, they smelled like latrine. But that was a small part of it. They had blood shot eyes that were hollow. One day, I looked into the eyes of a recruit who they released from the punishment cell. I thought that they were holes of a skeleton. The problem was that they did not talk. They just shut their mouths. We did not know much, but their appearance told us that the cell was hell.

When we came out of the ship in Liverpool, I saw England. The sky was dull. Cold air assaulted me from every direction. I hugged myself. Before long, my nose was running like that of a sick child. I hated the place.

They transported us to a location in Swansea. During the inspection, the doctor poked my body with a short staff. He declared me unfit for combat. Me, a circumcised man, with large bones and muscles! I looked at the skinny man and his bonny fingers that were clutching the stick. His nose was red, probably from cold. I knew that it was his weak spot. I wished to knock that nose inside his head, but I remembered *ota-ebu* council, and decided to go the other way. Since I did not know enough of the language to express myself, all I said was, "I go fight." He did not acknowledge that I spoke. He wrote on the paper and handed it to the Adjutant.

"I want fight," I said. The doctor began to inspect another recruit. They motioned me to step out. That was how I lost my place beside other recruits.

"Please." I made a final effort to express myself in English, but he did not even look at me. I felt humiliated.

Zeb stops reading the letter frowning and angry that Igo has never told her about his life in the army.

"He was humiliated," Rob says.

"And he likes to humiliate people," Zeb is angry.

"I can relate to his experience," Rob says.

"Are you going soft on him?" Zeb sits up and looks at Rob before she continues to read the letter.

My initial assignment was in the kitchen of the hospital. My job was to break the coal and wood and load the furnace. I had never been near so much fire in my life. When we cleared the bush for farm purposes at home in Obea, we always piled the stuff in the middle of the field before setting it on fire. That way, we stayed away from the fire and watched it. But with the furnace, you had to stay close, and turn the coal to give them more air for better burning.

There was an accident. The side door of the furnace snapped open and huge chunks of red coal knocked me down. Hot ash topped it. That was how I lost part of the flesh on my laps. I limped for years, before I got used to walking with so little flesh on my loin. I was lucky that the fire did not touch my vital part.

They demoted me to Dr. Kent's kitchen. The work was not hard, but I hated being a "kitchen boy." That was what Mrs. Kent called me. I hated it when they called me a boy. I, a fully circumcised man, was called a boy when it was the doctor that looked like a boy with running nose! I will never forgive that humiliation. He was the one who declared me unfit for soldiering. I stayed far from him and his mountain woman who bossed him like a mother. I did all my chores and stayed very far from her so as not to hear the hated word. But she and her friends liked to talk about me. I knew it from the glances they cast at me when they talked. I wanted the war to end. I wanted to go home and be a man. Do you understand me?

At this point in her reading, Zeb's voice begins to shake because she is now feeling bad about the way he was treated. She finds the letter interesting and annoying at the same time. She stifles a tear. Rob takes the letter from her hand and keeps it. He pulls her into his arms and rubs her back.

"We can read the rest some other time." The letter agitates Rob. Zeb knows this because of the way he bites his lower lips.

Tale of the Wounded Warrior

inally, Rob takes the letter from Zeb. "Ok. Honey, let me read it. This letter is very upsetting, but I want to get to the bottom of it. It is insulting, but also compelling."

"Alright." Zeb's voice is weak. The picture of Igo that she imagines from the letter does not match the one that she knows and loves to hate. She is confused and sad. She is still lying down with her head on Rob's chest as he reads.

Dr. Jefferson, my only happiness as a soldier in the Infantry Battalion of the British army had to do with casualties. The war turned me into a man who fed on the wounded. When there were too many casualties, they would send me to work in the hospital. I swept and shined the floor. I washed beddings and made the beds. I served food. I liked talking with the patients. They helped me to learn the English language and write it. I met many Africans in this way. Sometimes I cooked

Nigerian food for them. It looked like Nigerian food. I made tomato stew with fish and mashed potatoes as fufu to go with it.

Going to the hospital to work and take care of patients was a special treat that I looked forward to. Being busy was my way of keeping my mind away from thoughts of home. I had learnt enough English to understand what Mrs. Kent and her friends said, and I did not like their references to my body parts. Women did not talk about men's body parts in the presence of men. We never did that to women either. "These are very disrespectful women," I thought, but I swallowed my thoughts with my silence. I was very happy at my next visit to the hospital. They brought shell shock patients to the hospital and they needed more hands on deck. It was at this visit that I met Ibuchi Olima, Chizebe's father.

At the mention of her father, Zeb gets up from Rob's chest and looks at the letter as Rob reads.

"I want to read," she says. She cannot wait to hear about her father, but she is also anxious about what she will learn.

"Just listen honey," Rob says.

Zeb begins to sniff.

"Ok. Here," Rob gives her the letter.

"No, go on. I don't want to read." Zeb sniffs.

Her mixed emotions confuse Rob. He pulls her back and continues to read.

They said that Olima was a good fighter with ability to stalk and hit targets. So they called him Cobra. I was proud that he was from my country and I called him King Cobra. He was a Sergeant Major and was put in a private room with three officers. All of them had shell shock, talked in thin voices, dragged their words, and were hypersensitive and prone to violence.

They assigned me to watch them. I was huge, and even though I limped, my huge size was an advantage. I did not fight them back when they struck me. I took special care of them. I made sure that I brought their food on time. They laughed at my English. Major Roger delighted in mimicking my speech and laughing at me; thin sick laughter. But he also participated in teaching me. King Cobra acted as a translator who helped me to learn the English equivalent of Igbo words. I made special dishes for them. They liked my cooking and we became more like friends.

One day, Cobra threw a plate of food at me.

"Stop it!"

He obeyed me. Then he began to weep, "*Nne, nne nne* ... She is dead."

I held him. He wept on my shoulders for his mother.

"I'll take him outside to get some air." That was what I told the other officers, but I just wanted to tell him about the secret of *ota-ebu*.

I said to him, "The only way you can go home is to eat their money."

He asked me how he would do that.

I said, "Don't get better. Your voice is okay now, but you can still act like you are still very ill with shell shock."

He asked me how he would do that. I imitated how he used to talk in very thin voice when he was very ill with combat disease.

"Like Roger?"

"Yes." I said.

He laughed and laughed. Then he imitated Roger's thin voice.

Back in Madam's house, I returned to my unhappy self. But I passed the time by being busy. Even when the yard was clean, I still cleaned it. I cleaned the house, washed the clothes, and worked in the kitchen. I looked for things to do and there was always something to do in the kitchen and the yard.

It was the first day of September 1942. Madam told me to clean the whole house. I was surprised because the house was very clean. I obeyed. She told me to bring the broom to the bedroom. In the bedroom, she told me to sweep out the dirt under the bed. I knelt down to do it. I don't know how she did it, but she pinned me on the floor, and sat on my weak lap.

I said to her, "It hurt."

She said, "I know," but she did not stop. She pushed against my crotch, pressing on my laps and using her hands to pin mine on the floor. My legs hurt. She smelled like raw meat. I felt like throwing up and pushed against her, wanting to get up. Surprise!

She swallowed me. How did this happen? I could not believe that I did it while my mind was vomiting. I cried. I shed real tears as she rode me like a cranky old bicycle, but she took my tears as a sign of enjoyment.

She said, "You love it as much as I do."

She said, "I knew that you wanted me all along."

"Animal!" She said.

"No-o," I said.

"Yes." She said.

My legs hurt so badly. I hated what was happening. But I could not understand why my waist danced a different tune from what my mind was weeping.

"Please Madam." My voice was loud and I was afraid.

She got up. I lay there, trying not to shed tears.

She said, "Get up."

I could not get up. My legs hurt. I was ashamed. I did not understand how a woman could overpower me. That my lap was weakened by the fire was not an excuse for not fighting off a woman. I covered my face.

She said, "Go and clean up!"

I crouched to push back a tear that was about to come out. I struggled to get up. That was when she realized that I was in difficulty. She helped me up. I limped out of her bedroom to my room beside the kitchen.

I dragged my feet slowly. I went about my chores in fear. I did not know whether she would come after me again. I did not know whether her husband would find out. I did not know whether he would shoot me. I did not want to tell anybody what happened. I would rather die than admit that a woman overpowered me. How could I ever admit that a woman floored a circumcised man and a soldier like me? No! It did not happen; must be my imagination.

"How's your wound boy?"

Dr. Kent strartled me with the question. He had gotten used to my limp and did not refer to it as wound.

He said, "You drag your feet too much lately."

"It hurt Sir."

He said, "Come with me to the hospital."

I wondered whether he meant it or whether he wanted to take me out of his wife's hearing, to question me, or maybe shoot me. At home, a man would not ask such questions in front of another person. Letting people know about it would be shameful. Cheating with another man's wife was an abomination. But I did not really cheat. I did. Did I? Why did my thing stand up? Did I really lust after her as she said? I was so ashamed, and confused.

I hated women; adult women. I never had a girlfriend and I never trusted women. I survived the war. I returned to Nigeria and joined the police force. My war disability was against me, but they put me on reserve. I had skills that many other people did not have. I could read and write very good English, so they eventually gave me an appointment in the personnel department. I had British experience and was trusted by the Colonial Administrators. I rose in the ranks very quickly and became an Inspector. I was in my office one day when they delivered a letter to me in a brown envelope that we used in the army.

Through his reading, Rob could hear Zeb sigh from time to time; he just placed his hands on her back patting her as he read, but now she is moaning and he feels her body shivering. He tries to pull her up.

"Please go on," she says in-between sobs.

Rob unfolds another letter in a white paper that has turned brown with age. The characters incline to the right like italics and look very beautiful. Rob puts the letter down, pulls Zeb up and holds her face between his palms. Her renewed sobs puzzle him.

"Looks like we are not going into this chapter until we get our emotions in control," he says

"I'm okay." She wipes her eyes.

"Do you want to read? Give it a try. It may help your emotions," he says.

She takes the letter and reads.

Dear Igo,

I read about you in the newspaper. I am proud to tell people that I know you. I was sad when I left England, because I did not say goodbye to you, but I was happy to come home to my town of Eke.

"What!" Zeb looks at the end of the piece for the writer of the letter.

"A man from my town was in England with Igo and he never told me," Zeb says.

"Anyway, our conversations were limited to family issues," Zeb says.

"Let me think of other Second World War veterans in my home community," Zeb says.

"Let me read and give you the answer," Rob takes the letter from Zeb and resumes reading.

Just as I suspected that day you consoled me, my mother had died and was buried the following day. I came back to many responsibilities. The colonial administration gave my father a job in the coalmine in Enugu, because his son (yours truly) was fighting for them. Unfortunately, he lost his life in a police shoot out during workers' uprising in 1948. Without a father and mother, all the family responsibilities fell on me. I have an extended family that looks up to me because I am considered privileged. I am a teacher. My beautiful wife helps me to manage my family's farm and God has finally blessed us with a child.

My daughter is the joy of my life. She is brilliant and beautiful and she will be a great man. I mean a great man not woman. I also have two sons and two daughters who are really my brothers' children. They regard me as their papa and I take care of them and their widowed mothers. I am a happy man, but I wish that my father and mother were alive to see my daughter, Chizebe, and see how well I have managed the family's fortune with the help of my wife and my brother's family. I will not end this letter without thanking you for your family's secret that you gave me. The *ota-ebu* secret worked for me. When I could not get better and even acted crazier, they shipped me home. I continued to act mad until I got to my town. If you allow me and tell me how to get to you, I will like to visit you and give my thanks.

I also will like to hear about you. So if you get this letter, please respond.

I remain.

Yours truly,

King Cobra.

By the time Rob finishes reading the letter, Zeb is a bag of emotions. She tightens her mouth, trying to control her tears.

"It is unbelievable that after so many years, the mention of your father can bring so much tears to your eyes." Rob holds her. In-between sobs, she tries to explain why she is sad.

"All these years, Igo knew my father closely and hid it from me. Telling me about my father could have made me happy," Zeb says.

"It could have brought you two closer and what would have been my fate?" Rob kisses her.

"Your father's letter is a treasure. He loved you. I don't even know who my father was or is. My mother died when we were very young and my grandmother didn't know much. It is great to know that you had a father who wrote such loving things about you. And you now have the letter in your hands for keeps." Rob wipes her tears.

Zeb's heart goes out to Rob for not knowing his father.

"You're a good man Rob," she says.

"Let's get to the end of the main letter," Rob says.

"I can't go on right now. Let's take a break. There are too many issues."

"So Igo was raped; and by a woman. Nobody will believe it, but I believe him," she says.

"Such strange circumstances. Poor man," she says.

"Are you going soft on him?" Rob says.

"You don't know how it feels to have someone force himself on you." Tears flow from her eyes again.

"Igo did that to you many times."

Zeb slumps on Rob's shoulders. Many things that puzzled her about Igo are beginning to make sense. Igo was a victim when he was vulnerable; without family and in a foreign land. She became Igo's victim when she was vulnerable without her father and cut off from family in a distant place. In spite of her former feelings towards Igo, she feels pity for him. She is disturbed by the compassion she feels for Igo; a man who took her girlhood and deprived her of sexual womanhood. She must make peace with him before he dies. At the thought of Igo dying, she remembers Jaja's situation. "If my little boy's father dies without my seeing him-." She shakes her head to banish the thought of Jaja passing away.

"Are you going soft on Igo?"

"He is the father of my children. He might have been a better father to them if not..."

"Do you mean to say 'a better husband to you?" Rob snaps.

"Rob, you can't be jealous of him. I hate what he did to me. I'm just beginning to realize why he has a monster inside him."

"Or maybe why he put a monster in you," Rob's voice is harsh.

"You think that I have a monster in me?" Zeb is alarmed. She does not want to continue with the conversation. Her monster is her secret.

"Do you want to get to the rest of the letter?" Rob says.

"Yes."

Rob reads.

Mr. Jefferson, I send this letter to you so that you can see the beginning of the friendship that I had with Chizebe's father. Note also how effective my *ota-ebu* counsel was to his survival in England. When he died, I was heartbroken. I helped his family as much as I could. In fact, I gave a lot of money to his brother. When he told me that he needed someone to take care of Chizebe, I obliged because I knew how much my friend loved her. Chizebe was the first woman who excited me. How could I let her go? She was the only key to my survival as a man. How could I let her go? I took her as I was taken. I regret it and know that it was wrong. Two wrongs do not make one right. But how else could I have cured myself of the spell put on me by Mrs. Kent; a spell that made my thing to shrink whenever it saw a woman?

I have been a good husband to Chizebe, a good father to our children, and a good in-law to her people. I have always provided for my family and her family. I even lost the respect of my mother and sisters because I married a "foreigner." As a white man, you may not understand the concept of "foreignness" in my community. Anybody who is not from my community is regarded as a "stranger," which means "foreigner." They did not accept my wife, but I forgave them, because they did not know the burden that I bore. They did not know that Chize cured me and made me a man.

I know that it was hard for her all those years that she lived with me but I tried to love her as much as I knew. I learnt how to fight but did not learn how to love a woman and this is my penance. I have paid for it and paid more by now losing my kids. Chize never really gave me a chance. She never understood me. She always plotted to leave me. I fought hard to keep her, but at a point, I had to let her go. I married another wife, Shatu.

This is all that I want to tell you. I am very ill, not physically, but in my mind. I've lost my work, my wife, and children. I drink to keep my mind dowsed so that I don't remember the good life that I would have lived if

your people had not come to the land of my forefathers.
Now, my wife Shatu runs my show. Women have always
run my show.

Even though a white man, you are a man like me,
and must have some understanding of my plight. I have
narrated the secret part of my life for the first time, to
you, husband of my wife and father of my children. We
have a lot in common.

I have told you a lot, so that you will understand the
background of my two sons who live with you. Do not
use them as slaves, because they have *ota-ebu* blood.
The blood is still potent and has been strengthened by
travails. My children with you will have experiences in
America and their *ota-ebu* will grow stronger. They will
triumph and still come back to me because the Earth
Mother that holds the umbilical cord always calls back
a child to the land of his birth. My children will make
Obea town, Nigeria and America proud. Thanks you for
hearing my story.

Yours truly,

Igodo-Ana

Zeb gets out of the bed. She is in a hurry. She runs to
the bathroom and bangs the door. Before she gets to the
toilet bowl, she throws up. She kneels beside the bowl
crying, retching, and thinking.

50

The Home in Her Heart

Zeb does not tell her mother about her trip to Nigeria. She does not tell any of her friends. It was her sole decision and she knows that it has put her relationship with Rob to risk. Her heart feels heavy. She rubs it with her left hand and drags her small carry-on bag with her left hand. She walks close to the wall of the aisle to allow other passengers bypass her. One of the two airhostesses standing near the entrance of the plane go forward to help her.

"Are you okay Maam?" she takes Zeb's carry-on bag.

"Thank you. Just a little tired," Zeb says, not knowing how to name the heaviness in her heart and the throbbing on her head. The host tucks her bag in the passenger loft so Zeb has only a small pocket book as she takes her seat. She rubs her head with her hand not minding strange looks from the woman beside her. She knocks it lightly a few times. The knocks did not give her relief. She closes her eyes to shut off reality, but her mind recreates the scene with Rob.

Rob was against her proposed trip to Nigeria because he did not understand the need for it. He said that if she convinced him of the necessity for the trip, he not only would let her go but would also travel with her. Zeb cooked Rob's favorite dinner of stake and vegetables with potato pie. They had just finished eating when Rob brought up the issue of the proposed travel.

"My grandmother Emma taught me good values and how to be the man for my family. She was a widow but she did not forget the greatness of my grandfather who toiled in the Smith plantation to keep the family together. I promised Gran-Emma and myself that I would grow up to be the good man that she raised me to be. To know that you have gone soft on Igo just because he was raped..."

"No just that..."

"Ok. Because he knew your father, give me a break! Your father died long ago and if you still grieve for him, you need a therapist not your rapist ex!"

"Don't raise your voice on me and do not belittle my experience." Zeb was desperate to break Rob's focus on his emotion.

"I can yell. My family's future is at stake for God's sake!" Rob banged his hand on the table. His cutlery rattled and the fork fell on the floor but he did not pick it up. Zeb went round the table and picked it in order to do something and cool her own temper. She hugged Rob from behind, but he shook her off.

"Just sit down and let's talk about this issue dispassionately." Rob said. His reaction really confused Zeb. It was the first time that he reacted in that manner towards her. She fell on the floor, deliberately wanting him to pay attention to her.

"Zeb, just sit down and let's talk as adults. Put yourself in my position."

Zeb had tried this kind of trick before when she rebuffed Jaja's marriage proposal, wishing and expecting Jaja to wait for her. Not wanting to hang in the loop, Jaja acceded to his parent's pressure. Zeb remembered this and promptly got up from the floor and went back to her chair with tears in her eyes.

"Don't tell me that you broke a bone; if you did I'll call 911," Rob was harsh.

"Rob, I'm not going home because of Igo. I'm not even sure of why I want to go there. The only good reason that I am compelled to go..."

"Who is compelling you?"

"I don't know. I just feel this great need or force drawing me to Nigeria. I don't know whether it has to do with my son Akin who has joined the movement in the bush. I don't know whether it has to do with my child Dozie or my mother, but then if anything is wrong with any of them, my brother would have phoned me. I don't know whether it has to do with my brothers. I don't know what it is. Rob, you are my closest relative, you are my love, please understand me and support me. I do not and can never love any man as I love you. Please Rob, understand that something is happening to me in the spirit. I just feel that something terrible will happen."

Zeb believes that her plea had effect on Rob because he kept silent. Finally, Rob broke the silence with a question. "Zeb. Do you want me to be honest with you?"

"Yes, my love."

"Zeb, I know that you have suffered great abuse that has distorted your life, but you have also been spoilt."

"By whom?"

"All of us who love you; your family, friends and me especially."

"That's so self-serving. You barely know me."

"Sure, I barely know you and that's why I do not understand or support you in this. If some unknown spirit is pulling you, why can't you allow me to accompany you?"

"If you come, who will be there for the boys? You promised to take them as your own..."

"They're adults."

"But also new in the United States. Please understand. This is a journey that I have to make alone. Let this be a test of my love and devotion to you, my darling."

"I know that people use Americans for Green Card and after using them and getting everything they want, they just dump them like that." Rob snaps his fingers.

"I didn't even get a Green Card through marriage." Zeb's voice was calm.

"But you would have..."

"So this is what you think of me eh?" She wiped her tears.

"I also want to see Jaja. I won't forgive myself if he dies without my seeing him. I want closure."

"And that closure does not include your husband?" Rob got up from his chair and went to the room. Zeb began to clear the table, thinking. Then she went to the closet where they kept their empty suitcases.

Seated in the plane to Nigeria, Zeb does not realize that she is knocking her head again with her hands until the host asks whether she needs a doctor.

"There is a medical team on board that can help," he says.

"No thanks, just a kind of headache that won't go away."

"You need tylenol or something?"

"Yes thanks."

Two tablets of Tylenol do not help Zeb. Instead of abating the heaviness, she begins to sweat profusely. She removes her jersey and uses tissue to wipe the sweat. After cleaning the sweat, she begins to feel cold and puts on her jersey again. Then calmness overwhelms her and she doses off to a disturbed sleep. She wakes up at the smell of beef dish being passed to the woman sitting next to her. She drinks two small bottles of red wine with her dinner. Over-indulging herself with wine is deliberate and quickly achieves its purpose and she goes into a deep sleep.

The plane touches down by five in the morning. Zeb looks at her watch and smiles. For the first time, she arrives at Murtala Mohammed airport in Lagos without looking out for anybody who has come to pick her from the airport. This is part of her plan to achieve her aim of going to see Jaja secretly. She is surprised at the way her heart lightens at the thought of Jaja. She has not felt this way for him in a long while. Does it mean that Rob is right to feel some jealousy towards Jaja? She is confused about her feelings. Her thought goes to Igo. She no longer feels any bitterness towards him. This is not altogether surprising because she has been feeling a lot of empathy for him since she read his letter. She has read it a couple of times, and her compassion grew with each reading. She no longer drags her carry-on-bag. She straps it on her back as she walks through the customs. She goes through "Nothing to Declare" but an officer calls her back.

"I do not have anything to declare," she says still angry about the fight with Rob.

"Everybody has to undergo searching," the officer says.

"Why do you have the sign of "nothing to declare," if you have to search everybody?"

"Madam, please just come and be searched like everybody."

She moves to the line of people to be searched. She is amazed that the few people on the line have so much luggage. Most of the people are still trying to get their bags from the baggage-claim. Then she smiles as she remembers that she also used to carry a lot because of all the presents that she usually bought. But for this trip, she has no presents. When it is her turn to be searched, she unstraps her bag.

"What do you have in your bag?"

"Books and clothes."

"Can we see them?"

"Sure," she is about to unzip the bag when the officer asks her whether she has anything for them.

"What do you mean, sir?" Zeb says even though she knows what he wants.

"What do you mean, are you not a Nigerian?"

"I am a Nigerian but I don't understand what you are referring to."

"We are hungry."

"I don't really have any food, but you should be the one welcoming me with food instead of asking a visitor for food."

"This woman, you're tough-o. You can go, but next time, try to bring something back for your brothers in Nigeria. We have not been paid for three months."

"Then you should not work."

"If we don't work, you won't be able to enter this country and we still need our country to function even though we are hungry."

"That's sad."

"And we need the support of people like you."

"Next time."

"Ok. Next time Ma."

As Zeb walks out, she can hear two attendants joking about her in pigeon, probably thinking that she does not understand.

"Dat kaind-a woman, I sorry for di man wey de marry am."

"You tink say dat kind of woman go fit get husband?"

"Im go get, she beautiful. But im no go fit keep man. She too tight with money and her mouth sharp."

"Na di same ting we dey talk. She can't have a man because she can't keep a man."

Zeb hesitates in her track, wanting to go back and challenge them about their corrupt thinking. She feels like asking them why she must give them her money or her husband's money when they are paid for their job. But she does not go back. She just shakes her head in disgust for such ideas that come out of a corrupt mind. She sighs as she makes her way to the bank.

Zeb goes to Bureau de Change and changes two thousand dollars to naira, the local currency. She already has her ticket to Maiduguri, so she knows that the money will be enough for her other travel expenses. She takes a taxi to the local airport, but she is disappointed at the airport when she is told that Dana Airline flights to Maiduguri have been cancelled due to bad weather.

"What are we supposed to do?" She looks at the officer through a miniature window.

"Madam, you can check tomorrow." The young woman replies.

"Where am I supposed to stay?"

"Don't you have relatives or friends in Lagos? You can stay with them or if you like you can stay in a hotel."

"Who will pay?"

"Ah, Madam, all these questions are too much-o. The plane is not going. Come tomorrow. That's all," she says and closes the window. Her attitude annoys Zeb. She wants to find her supervisior and not only complain but also find out the real status of her flight.

She goes through the crowded foyer to the Information booth. Many people are standing by the counter but none seems to be waiting for information, so Zeb asks her question.

"Please I want to see the Dana Airlines manager," she says.

"They don't stay here-o."

"Where do they stay?"

"I think somewhere in Allen Avenue," the officer says. Zeb shakes her head in annoyance.

"Is there no manager in this airport?"

"Go to that window and ask them." He points at the same window that an officer closed earlier.

"The woman at the window is not the manager and she doesn't seem to know much," Zeb says.

"She can tell you where their office is."

"But the window is shut."

"There is nothing I can do, Madam. It's not even my job to work for Dana Airlines."

"But you are the Information officer."

"I work for Nigerian Airways not Dana Airlines. This woman your trouble is too much."

"Madam, are you coming from America?" This question was from one of the young men standing by the Information counter.

"Yes."

"Where do you want to travel to?"

As soon as Zeb says that she is traveling to Maiduguri, some people gasp and others laugh.

"Madam, you don't live in this country," one man says.

"Maiduguri airport is not functioning-o," another says.

"Since when? I got my ticket just last week."

"Ah! I don't know –o." He turns away indicating that he is no longer interested in the matter.

"Madam, the best thing for you to do is to travel by bus." Another man steps in to help.

"They have air-conditioned buses and the journey takes only two days." The man tells her the names of a number of buses that travel from Lagos to Maiduguri.

"Which one will you take? I can help you." This offer is from the man who previously turned away from her. Zeb suspects that something is fishy.

"I know my way. Thank you." She leaves the information Booth.

"Madam, I'm hungry–o. Give me small thing for food. I have not had any food since yesterday. "

"I still have to change my money." Zeb is loud.

"I can take dollars – o," the man shouts running after her.

"Let me go and change your dollars for you." He catches up with her.

"Make I help you," he says trying to take her luggage but Zeb refuses. Another man catches up with them saying, "Madam, don't give him your money-o. Na thief-o. Make I take you to the place where you go change ya money by yaself."

Zeb walks away from the "hoodlums." She just wants to find out the true status of her flight. She knows that if she phones her friend, Chioma, she will find out the true situation of things. She shakes her head indicating her reluctance to make that contact at this time. She is on a journey that she needs to make alone. She sees a uniformed officer go through a door and she walks to the same door and opens it. It is an office.

"Yes, can I help you?" the officer says. He explains that they are carrying out some repairs at Maiduguri airport so no plane can land at that airport at this time. She has the option of flying to Kano and making the rest of the trip by bus or taking a bus from Lagos straight to Maiduguri. Zeb decides to take a bus from Lagos.

It is almost nine in the morning in a mild August weather that Zeb tells a taxi driver to take her to Yaba. Instinctively she takes the passenger seat beside the driver. She wants to be next to him in case he is up to any tricks. She tells him to shut all the doors and put on the air-conditioner.

"Yes madam." The driver does not argue. He is used to the ways of these Americanized women; one of them attacked his friend because he wanted to take a route that was not in the map held by the woman. Another one once shot a gas gun that blinded his mate for days. He will not take any chances; after all, he is handsomely paid. That is one thing about these people; they have a lot of money and they are generous.

51

The Abuja Expressway

aba Station is not a single lot but a collection of different vehicle parks that stretches for miles. The taxi stops her at Obey-God lot. The lot is a collection of orange-coloured mini buses. Two touts rush to take her luggage, but Zeb stops them because she has heard many stories about passengers who lose their luggage to thieves pretending to be touts. She drags her luggage, but one of the touts does not give up. He follows her closely asking her where she is going to.

"Don't you have big buses?" Zeb says. The tout does not answer her question, but goes ahead to tell her how good the bus is.

"It is air-conditioned."

"It has good music that makes your body go je-lee, like jelly fish inside cool water," he says.

"I need more than music and air-condition. I want comfort too." Zeb walks along but she can hear the tout still trying to convince her.

"They get comfort Madam; plenty comfort. The cushion soft like pillow-o and ..."

"Ice water-r!" Zeb goes to a boy hawking bottled water. She does not really want water but just wants to get information from the boy. It is after mid-day that she boards a bus called God-is-Good.

Zeb sits by the window and puts her bag under the seat. She was told that the trunk of the bus will remain locked until they get to their destination so she has taken towels, soaps and other items for freshening up from her luggage before they put it in the trunk. She enters the bus and sits comfortably by the window. She watches other passengers enter and take their seats. She also looks outside at people lining up to get into other buses. A couple cuddling beside the bus attracts her attention. She feels that they may be foreigners because Nigerians don't usually demonstrate affection in that manner in public. She glances at the line-up of people wanting to enter different buses. There are many lines and many people hustling to break the lines. Typical of our people – some try to be considerate and lawful, some continue to disrupt, and cut corners, Zeb shakes her head from side to side. A young woman grabs a young man by his shirt and pulls him back.

"Sir, there is a line here!" She says and the man behind her supports her.

"We are not stupid!" The man says.

"I'm in a hurry," the young man tries to maintain his ground.

"We are all in a hurry."

"And even if we're not in a hurry, you must go to your spot," the young woman insists.

Zeb laughs thinking that this is part of what adds vitality to street culture – argument, vibrancy, public opinion and judgment.

"Good morning everyone. Peace be unto this bus."

Zeb shifts her gaze from the line outside to the front of her bus to look at the woman who is greeting everybody. Zeb smiles – she also likes the way people are always sharing greetings. The greeter is the same woman who was just making out with her partner. She is a smallish woman about Zeb's height. The tall man with a smiling face follows her.

"How are you?" He greets the man sitting behind the driver's seat.

"Good day ma." He greets the next person.

"Hey pretty girl, making a trip with Grandma?"

"She's my mom." The little girl does not seem to like the man.

"Oh. Sorry. Your mom is so cute," he says.

"Yes." The girl does not smile.

"Say 'thank you,'" her mother says. She is on the window seat beside her daughter.

"I don't like him," the girl whispers to her mother who quickly reprimands her.

"*Mechie gi onu!* Angela Ifedi. Your mouth will put you in trouble one day." Mama Angela says. Angela not only shuts her mouth as her mother instructed, but stretches her right hand and covers her mouth with her palms.

The man puts his bags in the rack above Zeb and beams a charming smile.

"Hello," he says.

"Hi," Zeb says.

"Looks like I'll have the pleasure of sitting next to two beautiful women," he says as he lets the young woman in to sit next to Zeb while he takes the aisle seat.

As they exchange greetings with her, she tries to guess their nationality from their accent but is unable to detect any foreign accent.

"My name is Miriani and that's my husband Pastor Gosdon," she points to the man beside her.

"I'm Zeb."

"Where are you travelling to?" Miriani begins a conversation.

"Maiduguri. What about you?"

"We are going to a convention in Abuja." She gives Zeb a pamphlet titled, "The Only Way."

As they chat, the bus fills out and the driver enters the bus. He is bulky with a pouch. He immediately turns on the ignition and revs the engine.

The driver's mate jumps in as well, grinning. It looks like the bus is about to move.

"Ladies and gentlemen. I am Peter Rock, the Officer piloting this God-is-Good bus number 4040 from Lagos to Maiduguri. This is direct drive through, no lingering, no shaking, and no stopping for anything until we get to Ibadan where we stretch our legs before proceeding to our first pick-and-drop in Abuja. The lavatories are at the back of the bus. Please throw the toilet tissue that you have used into the blue bucket there. I repeat. Please do not throw it inside the toilet bowl. If you do, it will block the passage and we will all die of foul odour here." A few people giggle.

"Please turn off your cell phones, black berries, blue berries, talk berries and other kinds of berries that give or get information from people outside this bus. It is the law. Obey and don't complain. Thank you ladies and gentlemen." He salutes like a soldier laughing and happy with himself. People laugh at his antics and funny way of talking.

"We shall serve jollof rice with *dodo* and chicken. Later, we will stop over in Ibadan where there are different restaurants and *bukas* for everybody to eat what they want before we take off for our first destination. Please do not throw your dirt anyhow and dirty this clean bus. Throw your trash into the small buckets on the aisle. If you have blankets or wrappers or coats or sweaters or any kind of cover, use it because we are now transforming this Bus-Craft Unlimited to winter in Nigeria with our powerful air-conditioner! We shall provide good music and fun movies for your relaxation. If you have any questions, ask me and do not disturb the driver. Please relax and enjoy the ride. Thank you." He bows. Angela claps. The passengers also clap and laugh. "Thank you, my brother," Miriani claps. He bows to the people in front of him, turns round and bows to those behind him. As he goes to take his seat, Miriani's husband gets up.

"Praise God!" he says. A few people respond "Alleluia."

"Let me hear you shout greetings to the Big God. Praise God!" He stretches the word 'God' for effect. His voice booms with enthusiasm and more people respond this time. Zeb does not like the way he is trying to convert the bus into a church and forcing everyone to join his congregation. She brings out a book and begins to read, but she cannot concentrate because the man's words disrupt her attention.

"I am Pastor Gosdon of the Free Church of the Living God. And this is my loving wife, Mrs. Miriani Gosdon. She is the mother of my two lovely children. God is good. Alleluia! You all know the condition of this country that we live in. It is tough. It is rough and the devil works full time right now as I am talking to you. But God is on the throne."

"Yes!" Miriani shouts.

"That's right," someone shouts from the rear of the bus. A few other people echo their words.

The driver presses the horn. Zeb looks out and sees that he is overtaking a long line of cars. She wonders why they allow him to intimidate them with the size of the bus and of course, the sound of the horn that roars like a lion.

"I want to pray for our trip, so cover your eyes," Gosdon says. Zeb opens her eyes and looks at him. The pastor has closed his eyes and Miriani chants a simple verse. Most people join her. Zeb does not open her mouth but she follows the lyric of the song.

Hail Almighty
Hail Divinity
We bow down before you.
We kneel on the ground.
We roll on the floor.

"We pray for our God's protection on this trip. Let no evil people come our way. Let them go their own way and we on our own way. Cover this bus with your protection and lead us to our prosperity, our destiny and destination. Amen and alleluia."

"Alleluia!"

"Praise God!"

"Alleluia!"

"My prayer is brief. My wife, Miriani, and I are going to the grand convention of Church of the Big God in Abuja. I am going to hand out fliers with information about what we do and where we have the convention. If you can attend our gathering, we will happily welcome you and you will gain abundance from the Lord. We do not solicit for donations, but if it pleases you to support our programme for the poor by donating alms and tithes, we will thank you. What I am soliciting for are your souls. Do not focus on money but on saving your souls. Money is the root of all evil and money is the devil that is killing this country."

Some people agree with interjections.

"Yes!"

"That's right!"

"It's true."

The manager hands out packaged food and bottled water. Zeb likes the chicken in the package.

"This is really good," she says as she eats the chicken.

"I like it too, it is garden-grown chicken; not the type that was fed with artificial feed," someone says. She is the mother of Angela, the little girl who did not like Pastor Gosdon.

"I think that you're right," Miriani says.

"Our people leave the chickens to feed on whatever they find in the shrub around; mostly vegetables," Mama Angela says.

"What vegetables?" Zeb wants to know.

"Like soft greens and water leaf." Mama Angela says.

"Are you from America?" Miriani says.

"Yes." Zeb is used to people asking her the same question.

"You have to be very careful," Miriani says.

"What do you mean?"

"Like keeping your dollars safe."

"I don't have much to keep safe. I'm here on a mission and money is not part of it."

"Anyway, just be careful. This is just how I warned some of my foreign friends from England when I was studying at the university but they didn't listen until they lost their passports and all their money," Miriani says. Zeb does not ask her where she studied and when this happened. She just does not want to continue the conversation with her.

Zeb rubs her arms.

"You are feeling cold. How can somebody from America feel cold here in our warm Nigeria?"

Zeb rubs her arms some more. She is wiping off goose pimples. For her, it is not a good sign. She relaxes when she remembers that she put her passport and money in her luggage before they loaded it in the trunk. Even if anyone steals what she has in her pocket book, it will not hurt her that much. She relaxes and soon sleeps.

When she opens her eyes, she notices that the road is boarded by thick forests and it is getting dark. She likes to know where she is so she turns to her neighbour.

"Do you know where we are?"

"We are near Ibadan and will soon be getting off the bus to eat."

The bus pulls into a resting area with different kinds of eating places. There is a huge building painted orange colour with a sign, "God Dey Kamkpe." It looks like most businesses attach God to their name, Zeb smiles. There is a line of sheds that function as mini-restaurants. They seem to be popular as many people line up in front of the sheds. Zeb walks from one shed to the other inhaling the aroma of different dishes. She makes to line up at the bitter leaf soup shed because it smells delicious, but she sees a toddler with runny nose playing on the floor near the cashier of the shed. She imagines the woman wiping the toddler's nose and not washing her hands properly. She proceeds to the big building. It houses two restaurants that specialise in Nigerian dishes and American fast food. She orders pounded yam with bitter-leaf soup and goes to the restroom.

Back in the bus, she feels heavy and sleepy, but she struggles to keep awake in order to know the route that the bus it taking. The large expanse of wooded area is fascinating as she recalls tales of spirits and wild animals of the forest that she heard as a child. Of course those tales are not true but somehow they give the forests an eerie feel. The wood evokes magic in her imagination. She loves and reveres it, but also fears it. She wants to experience life in the forest and at the same time abhors such a life. She shudders at the thought of her son Akin choosing that life. She shakes her head. The road winds round the contours of the hills and Zeb imagines the workers that dug out roads from the hills and valleys without much technology. She is still musing on the green landscape when she fell asleep again with her head beside the window. It is a deep sleep.

She springs up to the sound of loud voices. Before she can find out what is happening, someone shoots a gun. There is a loud scream.

"Shut up! I won't hurt you if you co-operate. Just get out of that seat!" Pastor Gosdon is ordering the driver.

"What is going on?" Zeb is loud.

"Sh-h-h! Armed robbers."

The pastor is now in control of the bus. He drives it through a narrow road that is barely big enough for the bus. There are three beeps from a car behind the bus. Zeb hopes that it is a police car. Gosdon stops the bus.

"Go and unlock the trunk of the car! Quick!" Gosdon shouts his orders.

"What is going on?" Zeb says again. She notices that Miriani is not beside her.

"Hey boys, there is enough meat for you in the bus." The voice sounds familiar to Zeb.

Some young men rush into the bus.

"Everybody, come out and surrender your purses as you go!"

"Turn left as you come out!" A robber with a shotgun collects personal effects from the passengers.

"And don't look right as you leave the bus!" A robber shouts as he collects bags from the racks.

"And flat on your stomach!" One of them shouts outside the bus.

There are screaming and wailing.

"Better co-operate before I handle you!" A robber snatches a bag from a woman who is screaming.

"Olodumare-e!" A woman calls on God in Yoruba language and begins to pray.

"Shut up!"

Instead of shutting up, she becomes louder and adds the name of God in other languages, "Chineke God-o! Oseloblua! Jehovah! God of Abraham!"

A man keeps shouting, "Oghene! God! Oghene! God! Oghene."

"Stop crying like a woman and lie flat on your face.

"Yekp-a! Yekp-a! Yekpa-a!" The man changes his words of exclamation.

A robber pulls Zeb's hand. Something cold touches her forehead.

"Madam America, surrender ya-a bag." The man scratches his crotch and makes a kissing sound.

"What the ..." Zeb does not finish the sentence because the man stops her with a slap on her cheek.

"Take your hands off-" Her sentence is cut as the man slaps her on the face again. This one blinds her momentarily and makes her dizzy.

As they push Zeb and other women into the bush, she can hear orders from the same familiar voice.

"I'm off boys. Enjoy your loot." the familiar voice says.

"Hey Don, you can't take off like that with all the juicy stuff."

"Come and get me." The same familiar voice is drowned by the sound of a car driving off. Zeb now knows that it belongs to Pastor Gosdon.

"I'll surely get you." There is a volley of gunshots. Screams. A car drives off. Another volley!

"Make una move fas-fas!" A robber yells at Zeb and Mama Angela.

"I no like di way Captain Don take dat small gal and leave us with deez ol pigs."

In spite of her pain, Zeb winces at being referred to as an old pig. She drags her feet.

"Move or I move you!"

"You can't get me to move to anywhere. I'll rather die," Zeb hears a woman shout and resist being dragged into the bush.

"You go move. You go open ya fat legs. You go kneel down or lie down and do whatever I tell ya to do. Fat Mama!"

Zeb can hear a big slap, probably the woman's face or buttocks. There is a loud blast of a shot. Loud screaming!

"Sexy mama, move or you go down too!"

Zeb is now barely aware of what is happening. She staggers. Her leg is caught in the web of thorns and shrubs. She is vaguely aware of being pulled from the mesh, of her jeans being cut off her body, of her legs being pulled apart.

52

Ojoni-Mi

Zeb is now conscious but disoriented. She does not know where she is. Maybe she is dead. She tries to raise her hand to touch her body but her hand cannot move. She hopes that she is recovering from a nightmare. Powerful firelight beams on her face. She cannot see the source of the light but she tries to hold her breath. She knows that someone puts his ear near her nose. She hears him talking to another but she cannot understand their language.

"A human, Papa, not an animal," Idris tells his father.

"She is still alive," Idris tells his father after listening to Zeb's breath.

"Who is she?"

"Not a spirit."

"But what?"

"Let's find out."

Ojoni has just come out of the hut and is about to go and milk the cows when she sees something on the horizon. She peers into the distance to determine what it is. She lets out a shout of jubilation when she realises that her husband and son are carrying something. From a distance, she thought that Zeb was a forest animal. Neighbours run out from their huts to see the prize of the hunt. They run across the small yard towards the veldt to meet the hunters, only to discover that they won't be sharing meat from the hunt. The women take over immediately. They take Zeb to the bathing hut.

Zeb is aware that the women are removing the remaining part of her jeans, her big shirt and remnants of her brassiere. She is grateful that they are washing off the dirt from her body. She tries to speak her thanks but her mouth is too heavy to open. She cannot see through the swollen eyes. She is not aware of where she is but she feels the kindness of the people. On seeing the condition of the wounds on her head and laps, the herbalist knows exactly the seeds and roots to use in healing her. She instructs the women to shave her hairs so that she can treat the wound. Ojoni grinds the medicine and begins to apply it to Zeb's bald head as instructed. It hurts but Ojoni continues to put more of the paste until it masks her head and face. She is left on a mat beside the fire even though there is heat from the sun. This is to be her bed for a very long time.

It is one week since Zeb left for Nigeria and Rob has not heard from her. He knows that her plane landed in Lagos and he feels that her friends would have picked her from the airport. What he does not understand is why she will not phone him. He begins to work long hours at the School of Medicine. Dean Cringage is happy when he presents a proposal to design a Global Health project on Africa. If Rob does a good job as he hopes to, the school will have better funding opportunity with the Federal Government and private funders like Rockefeller and Bill Gates. Rob's office at Bressler Research Building of the medical school is busy with graduate students whom he has enlisted to help in making phone calls, getting statistics and designing the time-line and other logistics of the project. He spends very little time in the house, but the few times he spends there are restless because he thinks about his wife.

Rob is not the only one wondering about Zeb's silence. Her two sons, Olima Junior and Igodana are in the family room watching the game between the New York Giants and Dallas Cowboys. It is during commercial break that Oli Jr. declares his intention to move out of the house.

"Why not wait for our mother to return," Igodana says.

"Your mother cannot change in her old age. This is not the first time that she has abandoned us. Amber has invited me to live with her and I'm moving tomorrow."

"How can you move into your girlfriend's house? Are you not a circumcised man brought up by our father with all the stories of Otaebu?"

"It is because of Otaebu that I want to make it quickly in this country and go back to Nigeria."

"What will happen to me when you go?"

"I'll have my own place soon, you will come and live with me. Meanwhile, stick with Rob. He's a kind man and will take care of you even if our mother has abandoned him as I believe she has."

"Mom really loves Rob and loves us too."

"I love her but I'm moving on."

Rob sits on the sofa where he usually sits with Zeb watching the football game and sipping a glass of dry wine. He enjoys the burning sensation of the wine as it goes down his throat. He looks around the living room and his eyes rest on their wedding photograph on a stand above the fireplace. It looks like Zeb is smiling down at him as he sits on the couch. His wine-red eyes see a tinge of mockery in the smile. He immediately directs his eyes to the wine cellar and thinks of another bottle. He gets a bottle of brandy and goes back to the couch, but his mind goes back to Zeb. Did this woman just use me to get a Green Card? He tries to shake off the thought as he drinks the brandy. It burns his throat. He gets up again and goes for another bottle. He studies them and finally decides that Bourgogne Chardonnay will soothe his lonely heart. He cannot think of anything that will prevent his wife and her siblings from getting in touch with him except their embarrassment at Zeb's behaviour. His common sense tells him that she has gone back to Igo whom she pities but his heart tells him that it must be Jaja. Two times she has called Jaja's name in her sleep. It shows that he still has a major place in her heart, but when he questioned her about it, she not only denied it but was angry at him for being supersticious. He decides that he will not call anybody in Nigeria and get the bad news. He should move on with his life.

He blames himself for spoiling his wife and enabling her to go out of control. It is high time he showed that he too has ego and dignity. The phone makes a beeping noise. He rushes to pick it up. It's just false beeping. He holds it, wanting to make the call just to hear her voice. Against his resolve, he dials Zeb's number. It is silent. He waits. Then it begins to ring.

"Hello."

"Zeb?" Rob says at the same time a deep voice says "hello." There is a click sound. The person has switched off the phone. Rob is sure that it was not Zeb's voice. It was a male voice. He dials many times but never gets through to anybody.

Meanwhile Zeb is still recovering from the battering. Her recovery is very slow because the damage is physical and psychological. The swelling has gone down but as she heals from the physical wounds, scenes of her assault and rape come to her mind and she weeps. Thinking that she is in pain because of the wounds, Ojoni complains to the herbalist who prescribes some herbs for sleeping. This brings some relief to Zeb and they no longer hear her crying in the night. She still weeps during the day and wipes off imaginary dirt from her arms. She does not understand Kebba language but the rhythm and music of Ojoni's soothing words calm her nerves. They put the open tail of an old calabash in her slightly open mouth and pour goat milk into it. As soon as she is able to open her mouth, she eats whatever they put into it – bananas, yams, mangoes, avocados, and a lot of fish and seafood. They usually roast the fish in open fire. Lying on a mat beside the fire, she watches stages of the fishmeal. Umaru cuts the fish to pieces and Ojoni seasons them with salt, pepper and herbs. Their son, Idris, usually strings and puts them beside the fire. Zeb soon learns how to roast the fish and plantains. She is able to know the names of her benefactors because she has listened to details.

Like a child learning how to speak, she utters her first word to the delight of onlookers.

"Ojonimi," she calls the long version of her caregiver's name as she has heard her husband call her, without knowing that he adds the 'mi' as an endearment.

"Thank you," she says in English attempting a smile. Everybody applauds. This was when Idris steps up as her interpreter. Idris is a pupil in a community school a couple of miles away in Adonkol. He informs Zeb that he and his father walked about a mile to another hamlet to report her presence to the chief. It is now the chief's duty to report the matter to the government.

Zeb has spent three weeks lying down and healing from the wounds inflicted on her thighs. She is now able to explore her surroundings. It is a small fishing and hunting hamlet near the banks of the River Niger. It consists of about seven huts made of mud walls and raffia roofs. A baobab tree marks the center of the hamlet where the children congregate for story telling in the evening. While many adults are away in their canoes fishing and taking their fish to markets, and some of the bigger children walk the miles to school, Zeb joins the women doing domestic work. Without shoes, she does not find it easy to walk in the stony landscape that is heated by the sun, but she does not care. She accompanies the women to the stream to get water that they pour into huge water pots in the barn behind one of the hamlet huts. She learns about the stream and its different areas for washing clothes, bathing, fishing and getting water for drinking. She has developed a habit of wiping her arms as if she is wiping off dirt. Ojoni thinks that it is because of the heat and tells her to go to the stream as often as she likes to bathe and swim, but Zeb is frightened of the idea. When they understand that she is afraid of men in the village, they get Idris to explain the village taboos to her in English in order to assure her that nobody will harm her.

Dr. Jefferson's team has almost completed writing the project proposal and he already plans to write another one, something outside his normal routine that will be more challenging for him. In spite of the project challenge, he is still lonely, restless and constantly thinking about Zeb. Even if she has decided to ditch him and go back to Igo or Jaja, she should have informed him after all these weeks. He decides to phone her friend Chioma in Lagos but discovers that he does not have her phone number. He phones Gloria and Esi but none of them has heard from Zeb.

"Don't even think that Zeb will ever leave you for another man. I just think that something is wrong and we have to find out what it is," Gloria says.

"You can speak up for her. She's your friend. But you don't know how she has softened towards Igo. We quarrelled about him and I wanted to travel with her, but she refused. Anyway, you know your friend, she's always right. I don't want to fight about love."

"You'll be proved wrong. Let's just wait and see," Gloria says.

"I can't wait anymore," Rob says.

Zeb soon finds a following in the young children who are too young to walk the miles to the nearest school. She becomes a kind of babysitter and teacher. Taking care of children is just the therapy that keeps her mind out of many concerns. Going to Maiduguri to see Jaja has receded from her mind as worries about the anxiety she must have caused Rob take over. She tries to keep busy in order to relieve her mind of worries.

She teaches the children the alphabets in song, takes them to the children's area of the stream to play and bathe, and tells them stories even though they do not understand her language, but she uses a lot of gestures and songs. The children are eager learners and always follow her. She is concerned that the people of this village do not benefit from the oil and mineral wealth of the country. She now thinks that providing all Nigerian children with educational opportunity from their early childhood should be of primary concern.

Everybody in the hamlet knows Zeb and she has learnt how to greet in the local language. She performs duties happily because she is grateful to be alive and is happiest when Idris returns from school so that he can communicate with her. From him, she hears that the chief has reported her presence to the authorities in Adonkol. She is therefore not surprised when the chief turns up with two government officials.

53

Heart Throb

he paper work at the Maximum Security Prison takes almost two hours. The officer at her last stop is very friendly and explains that it normally takes days or even weeks to do the paper work.

"Your paper work is easy because you are connected to very powerful people."

"What people?" Zeb is surprised because she only knows the Welfare Officer in Adonkol who arranged for her travel, and Bisi who took her to the station. Sitting in a large room with other visitors, she figures out that this is the last stop. The visitors put the contents of their bag in one of the baskets on a long table for inspection by the guard. They have presents like clothing, food and money. After the search, they are taken to the window to speak with the inmates. Tears well up Zeb's eyes as it dawns on her that she has nothing for Jaja. She really has nothing.

She remembers how she got the clothes she is wearing from the Welfare Office in Adonkol. The Welfare Officer had called the woman who was cleaning his office.

"Bisi, take that woman to the store and make her look more decent," he said pointing at her attire.

"Yes sir."

Zeb's mind darts off to her host, Ojoni, who nursed her to health. She remembers how grateful she was when Ojoni opened a big metal box at the foot of her bed and gave her the black and white *iro* and *buba* that the Welfare officer looked down on. She remembers feeling humiliated and casting down her eyes in shame when the Welfare Officer said that her outfit was not good enough. She also knew that the shame was nothing when compared to the big shame buried in her heart. That was why she humbly followed Bisi to the store-room where they kept used clothes. The room had a damp dusty smell but Zeb did not notice it because of her erased dignity.

"Let's find something more decent for you," Bisi said.

"What's wrong with my clothes," Zeb asked.

"Nothing really. Just too washed out."

"I like it." Zeb could not imagine what would be better for her psychology than the feel of Ojoni's clothes. She rubbed her hands on her chest feeling the comfort of Ojoni.

"Ok. You can take some clothes that you will use later," Bisi said untying one of the two bundles in the store.

"Sure?"

"Yes. Take as many as you want. They are remnants from what we give to the poor."

Zeb found a pair of blue jeans that looked like her size and a big shirt.

"Take a scarf too," Bisi said, "your hair is not good."

Zeb's reminiscence is interrupted when she hears her name called by a Prison Guard.

"Yes sir."

The guard says, "Follow me."

Zeb is surprised that she is not directed to the window like other visitors. They walk through a long hallway.

"Where are you taking me to?"

The guard feels the alarm in Zeb's voice. He laughs and explains, "The inmate you want to see is a special inmate and cannot come to the window."

"Is he crippled?" Zeb is still alarmed. In reply, the guard opens a large door and Zeb smells strong disinfectant. He opens another door and Zeb stops walking. She has always imagined how she will rush into Jaja's arms, but this is not her reaction as she sees Jaja propped up on the bed looking like an invalid.

"Come on," the guard says.

Zeb and Jaja just look at each other without saying anything, without hugging or kissing, without greeting, weeping or laughing. Zeb is not surprised that Jaja has lost a lot of weight but she feels some comfort that his vitality is still there. Jaja looks at Zeb's disheveled low cut white hairs and wonders how her hair could have turned all white within a few years. He is surprised that a woman like Zeb has given up on grooming. What he finds most shocking is her timid demeanor.

"Something is wrong with you my love; there is a deep shadow inside you. Tell me. Tell me everything. What happened to you?" Jaja uses a lot of power in his feeble body to hold her face with his hands looking closely at her; eye ball to eyeball, his nose breathing into her nose. Zeb feels so happy; this is where she has always belonged, she thinks as tears run down her cheeks. She does not wipe them. Jaja does not wipe them. He just feels them on his own cheeks as they run down her cheeks to soak her blouse.

"They raped me."

"Who raped you?"

"Robbers waylaid our bus. They took everything and after that, they took the women to the bush. They were so ruthless on me, Oh Jaja," she weeps.

His hands slide down her cheeks to her shoulders. She holds him tight, enveloping his thin frame with both her hands, their chests heaving in unison.

"My poor baby, I'm so sorry. You have suffered a lot because of me." He holds her tight. She wraps her hands around his thin body. They just hang on their closeness as they breathe in and out, smelling each other and loving it.

"Forgive them my love. I do not know these men who did this horrible thing to you but I think that they must be victims of rape too. For them to do such awful things to you or to anybody, they too must have been raped in one form or another. I was raped too. You were raped even before you were raped." He inhales deeply, having used so much energy. She does not say anything, but the tears keep flowing down. They still hold tight, their bodies merging like one body. There is silence, except for the beat of their hearts.

"Where is my poet?" Jaja has used so much emotional strength so he gasps for breath. Zeb holds him tighter. He just rests in her arms.

"I'm no longer a poet? I have not written much of anything since I left this country. Too busy struggling for survival."

"The creativity is still there and will come out of you at the right time. This surviving country needs all her survivors and resources including poetry."

"I have lost the will Jaja."

"No. The will is there. Just work on forgiveness and with time, the will and its poetry will come out. Promise."

"I'll try." Zeb says. There is silence as they both enjoy the touch of each other. Zeb wants Jaja to focus on getting well instead of worrying about her so she tries to show understanding of the rape.

"I understand all these Jaja. They were probably raped by the corrupt system and they are violently assaulting others and expressing some little power in the process. I understand all that, but I still hurt."

"We must keep looking ahead at the bright future. Look at me. I wished, yearned and dreamed that my eyes would once more see my only love before I die. Look at me now; I not only see you but I am holding you and I am assured that our hearts still beat together, so even if I die..."

"You're not going to die. I'll arrange to take you out of this country..."

"And leave YAM? I'm an inspiration to the people and when I die, they will know that it is because of our cause. My funeral will be used to strengthen the movement."

Jaja tells Zeb how the military government subjected him to severe torture aimed at forcing him to reject the movement, and be rewarded for it or continue with his journey to certain death.

"I have a fifty-fifty chance of death, but also chance of survival through well-wishers like guards who cleverly counteract my journey to death. Seeing you has given me more life. And you want to take me to America?"

"Yes," Zeb says without thinking about Rob. Her main concern now is for the dying man.

"What will your husband say?" Jaja looks at her, amused and even enjoying the reflection of shock and confusion on her face. He knows that Zeb will open her mouth and leave it open for some time because she is confused about what to say. She does just that, and then she becomes silent.

"Angel told me about him. He is a good man," Jaja says.

"My mom? And she didn't tell me." Zeb is relieved to have something to say.

"Not long ago. Angel was worried when she heard about my wife; that she left our kids with her old parents in the village in order to move on with her life. It was easy to open up to Angel. I told her that I was worried about the kids especially Zebra Junior who will be getting into a difficult age without the guiding hand of her mother. Mama was very sympathetic and even offered to take the kids so that they can go to a better school in the city with Dozie."

Zeb opens her mouth. "I don't know what to say," she says.

"You don't have to say anything. Just hear me out. I have initiated divorce proceedings against Aney on grounds of abandonment. She has never visited me in any of the prisons all these years. Some of my friends have at different times offered to bring her with the kids to see me but she always refused. In fact, I was a bit relieved because my heart was never there, but I would have loved to see my kids. I don't blame Aney for leaving but I'm worried about the kids. If Mama Angel really is able to take them, their maintenance money will not be a problem for me but it will be a huge task for Mama at her age. Oh, if my kids can grow up with our son Dozie ..." Jaja does not conclude his sentence, he closes his eyes to take a breath. He breathes heavily like he has come from a long journey.

While he rests, Zeb thinks about Jaja's kids. She wonders how Rob will feel about adopting them. She knows that Rob likes a house full of kids, but he may not want Jaja's kids. She will try to make him realise that it will make her happy to have Dozie grow up with his half-sisters. "Rob is a caring man. He loves me and will support anything that will make me the best that I can be for him."

It is almost two o'clock at night. Rob is still working in his office when a member of his project team knocks on his door. Janice is an elegant medical intern who is interested in global health.

"Just want to let you know that I've input the statistics." She yawns and stretches her hands. Rob feels that she is tired.

"Thanks. You can go home now. We'll wrap it up tomorrow," he says.

"You look so tensed up. Are you ok?" she says.

It's a long time someone has paid attention to him. He swallows saliva before he replies. "I think you're right. I have to leave." However, he is reluctant to go to his house.

Rob has got used to having a family but members of the family seem to have deserted the house since their mother travelled to Nigeria. He no longer sees Oli Junior and his younger brother, Igodana. On their own part, the young men feel vulnerable because they are not sure of what is going on between Rob and their mother. Zeb has not phoned them as she promised. They have made phone calls to their father and he does not know anything. Angel asked them about Zeb when they phoned so she also knows nothing. Only Rob appears normal in their eyes because they are not aware that he misses Zeb. They only know that he hardly stays in the house. It's like he avoids them and they suspect that he may be spending time with a woman. Oli Junior has also got a girl friend who takes a lot of his time. Only the younger one, Igodana Junior, stays in the house watching the television and surfing the Internet. He was happy when his brother suggested that they move out of the house.

"We have to get out before Rob kicks us out," Oli said.

"I think that he has someone he is hiding from us. He leaves early and comes back late unlike when Mom was here," Igodana said. "We have to tell Dad what is going on."

"Let's leave him out of it. When we move out, we can phone and tell him," Oli said.

It is almost twelve noon. Zeb has been with Jaja for over an hour and the prison guard comes to inform her that she has overstayed. Teary eyed, she tries to get up from the bed but Jaja nudges her.

"What?" she says.

"You're not going to leave with that gloomy face. You have brought a lot of joy to me, so let's not spoil it."

"I just hate to say goodbye to you in your condition." Her mind goes to the last time she saw him when he came to her place in Nsukka. She smiles at the memory and cheers up.

"Ze-Ze," Jaja smiles. "I'm a happy man. My legacy is preserved in the struggle and in you. To see you again and also know that the children will be in your loving care ... our son Dozie, Zebra Junior and little Ebere. What else can I wish for? You have always been my wife, you stubborn goat." He laughs. Zeb laughs also. The empty cell echoes their laughter. The echo is so loud that the guard opens the door to find out what is going on. He smiles and shuts the door. They stop laughing when Jaja begins to cough.

"You said that the robbers took everything."

"Yes, my luggage, all my money and even my passport. This dress that I'm wearing was given to me in Adonkol before they put me on the bus to Kano."

"Don't worry Zee. Money is not a problem. Our friends will give you all the money you need. You also have to report the incident at the American Embassy. Please remember to see a doctor."

"Who are these friends who will give me money?"

"Don't you know that you are a hero in the movement? Friends of YAM will do anything for you. You have inspired many."

Zeb bites her lips as she remembers how her children's father, Igo, blamed her for their son's membership of YAM.

"What is it?" Jaja says.

"Nothing," she says, but seeing the doubt in Jaja's face, she makes up a lie because she does not want him to worry about her son. She tells him that her mind momentarily went to her ordeal. He pulls her to the bed and she lies beside him.

On the bed, Jaja puts his head on her shoulders as he speaks. "I am ill Zee, but the power of our people gives me strength. My imprisonment has helped to galvanize a new wing of the movement. The guard that brought you in will give you money. Friends will help you along the way even as you travel to Mama Angel in Enugu and to my village to get the kids. They will assist you along the way. The good thing is that you are no longer a wanted person, so everything will be done without undue attention to you." He gasps for breath. She adjusts the pillows so that he sits up with his back on the pillows.

She is about to get up. He uses one hand to pull her back. Zeb is amazed at the strength that comes from his frail body. He draws her to him on the bed and whispers in her ears. "My love, one final promise."

"Hei. Too many promises," Zeb laughs.

"Just one more. I know that it will be hard, but work on it one step at a time."

"What is it?"

"Stop drinking liquor. You deserve a better life."

"How do you know?"

"Your breath, my love, smells like a beer parlor."

Zeb feels mortified and tries to explain how it helps her to forget. "To forget the rape, I use..."

"Sh-h. I understand you more than you can ever know and I love you unconditionally, so don't explain anything, my love."

Rob is at a meeting with his research team. It is not a formal meeting but just a thank you dinner at Fuji on Maple Street. They drink and get to know each other better, which is good because Rob intends to use some of them for his next research project. Janice has a lot of background information about the project. She grew up in the southside of Chicago where poverty and crime made it almost impossible for kids to get quality education in the poorly equipped schools. She is one of the few examples of success from such backgrounds and she is very proud of her achievement, and passionate about improving the environment. She dominates the conversation at dinner pushing her agenda for the inclusion of American inner cities in global health programmes. She dares to ask Rob about his personal life.

"Dr. Jefferson, we pretty much know the background of many of us here and it is important for our team work, but we hardly know anything about you except that you have an African wife. When do we get to meet her?"

This question surprises Rob especially as everyone looks at him expectantly. He sips from his glass of wine before telling them that Zeb travelled to Nigeria. The sadness in his eyes does not escape Janice who as they are leaving the restaurant asks Rob another question.

"When is your wife coming back from Africa?"

"She is actually from Nigeria."

"Oh. That country that is riddled with malaria and corruption," she laughs.

"That's why our project is important for that region."

Janice hopes that her statement will not undermine her campaign for including American poor communities in the project. She wants to know if he is available for dating.

"When is your wife coming back from her country?"

Rob wants to tell her to mind her own business but he does not say it.

54

New Beginnings

The weather is almost one hundred degrees fahreinheit in Lagos as Zeb steps out of the taxi that brought her from Maiduguri. The prison guard had arranged for a taxi to take her all the way from Maiduguri to her destination in Lagos. She slept most of the two days' journey. She steps out of the taxi and wipes her arms as if wiping out dirt, but she is not dirty because the taxi is fully air-conditioned. She looks to her left and to her right like a child learning how to cross the road. She hesitates before walking to the door. She presses the doorbell once. She waits timidly at the door with her face cast down.

Jo opens the door to find a woman he does not immediately recognise.

"Hi, Jo!" Zeb is relieved to see the familiar face of her friend's husband.

"Can I help you?" Jo says stepping back.

"Jo, don't you recognise me?" Her new circumstances have altered Zeb's appearance.

"That's Zeb," Chioma rushes out and hugs her.

"Why didn't you tell us that you were coming?" Chioma says.

Zeb is silent. She is filled with mixed emotions of regret, love, anger, self-pity and relief.

Jo tells them to enter the house.

"What's wrong?" Jo says as they enter the living room.

"What happened?" Chioma says. It is obvious to her that something tragic happened to Zeb. Her dress is not flattering. Her hair is very short and dirty grey. Her outdoor life in the fishing village has given her skin a hue darker than her normal one. In addition, she has lost her confident personality.

"What will you drink?" Jo says.

"Do you have liquor?" Zeb says. Jo raises his eyebrows. Chioma goes and sits beside Zeb. Tears flow from her eyes. Chioma also begins to weep for her friend because she feels that whatever has dumbfounded her friend must be a very serious matter. Jo takes a pack of tissues from the dining table, puts it on his wife's laps and goes to the cupboard in the dining room where they keep hard drinks.

Chioma is surprised at the way Zeb gulps down the beer brought by her husband. In-between drinks, she narrates bits and pieces of her story. Chioma pulls the chest of drawers where they keep old newspapers and brings out three different papers that reported the robbery of God-is-Good bus travelling on 128 Highway. They diverted the bus to a bush-path between Kabba and Lokoja. Four people including a woman died in the shoot-out purported to be between the driver and his mate on one hand and the robbers on the other hand. The husband has claimed the woman's body, but the three other bodies are yet to be claimed. They discovered a little girl in a get-away car that crashed on the 128 highway. She is the key witness. She said that the driver of the car, whom she calls a pastor, bled to death from gunshot wounds. She said that some men led her mother and other women to the bush while the pastor whisked her away. The police rescured some of the passengers. Others presumably took rides from other vehicles. Some of the male passengers said that the robbers raped the women, but none of the women confirmed the allegations.

"I would have blamed you for not letting me know of your trip to see Jaja, but you have gone through so much hell that I can only be happy that you are alive," Chioma says.

"Thank you." Zeb's voice is weak.

"What do you want to do?"

"I need to see my mother and my son."

"True. You really need to curl up under your mother's embrace and also give your son some love."

"I also need Rob. I want my life back. Oh how I hate this body." Zeb wipes her arms.

"What can I do to help you, my friend?"

"Nothing, except to get my husband on the phone and then go to the American Embassy. I just hope that my Rob is okay and my kids over there are okay."

Chioma dials Rob's number and hands the phone to Zeb. It does not go through. Chioma reminds Zeb that, "That's how our Nigerian phone works; by not connecting people." She laughs and assures Zeb. "We will continue to phone his number until it goes through. I have a good feeling that he will help you to recover."

"It's not just about me."

"But about what? Don't tell me that you want to take Jaja to America."

Zeb laughs. It is the first time Chioma has heard a real sound of laughter from her. Chioma laughs also, but stops when she sees that Zeb's mirth has turned to tears.

"I just want to beg Rob to forgive me. I don't want to take Jaja to America. I do not want to go back to America."

"What?"

"I want to live in this country, that is, if Rob agrees. I want to fight for children's education in this country. I'll begin by getting Rob on my side. I don't know whether he will agree that we adopt Jaja's children."

"You are really crazy."

"It is a promise I made to a dying man." Her face is stern.

Rob is about to drive to work when he sees a note under the wiper like a police ticket. He takes it and reads.

"Dr. Jefferson. This is just to let you know that I have moved out of your house. Thank you for everything. I will keep in touch. Olima Junior."

Rob is angry. He goes back to the house to speak with Olima's brother. He has not done anything wrong. Instead, he has made sure that the young men are comfortable because he does not want his issue with their mother to affect them. He makes sure that he stocks the kitchen and fridge with food. In addition, he makes sure that their biweekly allowance is remitted from his account to their accounts.

"Where did your brother move to?"

"He stays with his girlfriend," Igo says.

"What's the address?"

"I don't know," Igo grumbles. He feels that everybody has let him down. His brother said his stay with Amber would be temporary while he looks for an apartment where the brothers could live together, but Igo still feels alone and abandoned.

Zeb's first night in her friend's house was smooth because beer knocked her out. She wakes up in the morning with a premonition that all is not well with Rob. She has tried his number several times and now believes that something might have happened to him. She knows that the American Embassy can help with information. She goes to the Embassy to get another Green Card and ask them to help her contact Rob. When she walks out of the taxi at Raymond Njoku Close, one young man runs to her asking whether she wants to take a passport photograph.

"I am the photographer for the Embassy. I know the exact dimensions," the man says.

"Good morning Madam," another man runs across the road with a camera hanging on his neck.

A young woman sitting on a chair under a red canopy shouts at the men. "Do not harass her. She knows what she wants," she says getting up from her chair. She walks up to Zeb saying, "Good morning Ma."

"My name is Abbey. I sell phone cards. I can show you where you can take good photos if that's what you want."

"Who are you?" Her politeness surprises Zeb.

"Abbey Okeke. I graduated from Lagos State University two years ago."

"And you sell cards? How much profit do you make from selling cards?" Zeb says.

"Not much Ma, but it's better than joining gangs of robbers or prostituting."

"Don't mind her Madam. She is a prostitute at night." One of the touts behind them laughs as he runs away.

Abbey shouts a curse word at him, "Ewu!"

"You are calling me a goat?" The tout shouts from a distance, "I'll punish you at night."

"Hooligan!" Abbey shouts back. The allusion to punishing Abbey at night evokes sinister images in Zeb's mind. She begins to sweat profusely.

'Maam. Where do you want to phone?" Abbey says. Instead of giving her Rob's number, Zeb asks for gin.

Inside the embassy, Zeb picks a tag and waits for her number to be called. She has no identity of any sort to prove who she is and hopes that the Immigration Officer will somehow be able to trace her Green Card number. As usual, her mind goes back to images of rape. She shakes her head. She begins to sweat profusely from the heat generated by her suppression of her nightmare and the large dose of *ogogoro* that Abbey bought for her because it is cheaper and stronger than foreign gin. It is at this time that they call her number. In-between wiping sweat and struggling with choice of words to recount how she lost her things, the officer stops her.

"Maam, do you have a police report to collaborate your story?"

"No."

"You have to get a police report."

"That's no problem. Can you please help me contact my husband? He is an American and I have not been able to get him on the phone since I returned. I'm afraid that..."

"What's his name? And what's your SS number?"

Zeb is no longer sweating but sitting quietly and reading the newspaper articles about the robbery incident. She is upset that none of the women on the bus could own up to being raped. They know that people usually blame and scorn rape victims. Each of them prefers to carry the demon of rape alone rather than compound it with the shame of slander and exclusion. On her own part, she has only told her closest friend, Chioma, and of course Jaja. She recalls that Jaja was compassionate and did not blame her as people normally do to rape victims, but he offered an intellectual assessment of the incident and pleaded that she should understand and forgive the rapists. She understands too, but she still hurts deeply. How can she begin to forgive and forget something that has rocked her being and has settled at the center of her heart? This is something that is redefining and directing her personality. It is easy to intellectualize the incident but to live with it is painful, life wrecking and forever-hell.

She has always advised her students to fight oppression and lift the society up. Her students understood the fight against the oppressive government, but are they educated on the issue of fighting other oppressions? Thinking about it, Zeb realises that none of her students ever complained about sexual harassment personally even though it was talked about generally. None has ever reported a case of rape. Zeb remembers when she was a student in Benin. They never ever went anywhere alone at night. They usually hung out together or you went with a trusted male friend. Everybody understood that it was not safe for women. She now feels that she could go to the police and talk about the rape instead of hiding the matter like other women. It is the right thing to do. How can the police do something if nobody acknowledges rape? Her face sags as she thinks of these things. Zeb springs up as soon as she hears her number.

She moves fast as the window opens. The Immigration Officer looks at her, and hesitates for a second before speaking. "Ms. Jefferson, your husband filed for divorce five days ago," he says. Zeb hears the words but does not retain their meaning.

"What did you say?" Zeb is woozy from shock and alcohol.

"Robert Jefferson filed for divorce on grounds of abandonment. I can give you his attorney's phone number."

Zeb opens her mouth to talk but no words come out. Her mouth hangs open as the Immigration Officer calls her name, "Ms. Zebra Jefferson."

"I did not abandon Rob. I was going through hell." Her voice is low. She is recovering from the shock. She barely hears the Officer says, "I understand but he is not aware. What do you want to do?"

Zeb does not reply. She is recollecting herself.

The officer continues, "You are still entitled to a new green card, but you have to bring a police report."

Zeb stares at him with her mouth closed.

"Did you go to a clinic for medical evaluation of the rape?"

"No."

"Just bring the police report and the newspaper report of the incident. Doctor's report will help too. This is your file number. When you come back, pin the number and your papers together. I wish you good luck Ms. Zebra Jefferson."

"Thank you." Zeb's voice is firm. Her legs are steady as she walks out.

Stepping out of the Embassy building, the mid-morning sun hits Zeb hard on the face. She squints and refocuses her eyes on the road. She stretches her shoulders as if bracing for a fight. It is not a fight against Rob but a fight for her love.

I SHALL FIGHT

I shall fight for my love.

Fight for my children.

Fight for all women raped and unraped.

I shall fight for fairness and justice.

I shall fight and fight and fight until I die.

Zeb is busy reviewing her poem when Chioma comes back from work anxious to know the outcome of her visit to the Embassy. She does not believe the bit about Rob divorcing her because Zeb is so calm.

"You're making this up."

"No."

"Are you ok?" Chioma is confused by Zeb's reaction. It is as if she does not care, but Chioma knows that Rob is the love of her life.

"I'm fine. I just have a new dream."

"I know. Children's Education."

"I've modified it. Right now, I need your help. Can you help me to call a press conference. I want to talk about my rape and all that happened on that fateful trip. I want it on camera and in all the newspapers. We have to change this mentality of silence about the abuse of women."

"I thought you want to get Rob back and fight for children's education."

"All of them go together because they come together in my body. It will not be difficult for a doctor who examines me to testify that I am physically and emotionally wrecked." She coughs and continues to review her poem as she sips from the glass of *ogogoro*, which Abbey bought for her.

Chioma throws her hand around Zeb's neck "I am worried about your constant coughing and itching. I hope that they are not symptoms of something more serious."

"Like what? What can be more serious than what I have gone through?" Zeb says coughing.

"You are thinking about AIDS. I don't have AIDS," Zeb says.

"You were raped by unknown men."

Zeb mocks, "According to the government's study, there is no AIDS in this country."

"Do you trust this government?"

"You know that I do not. What do you want me to say? Do you want me to worry about HIV/ AIDS? I have enough worries already."

"You're right, my friend. Let's not talk about it."

"Let's focus on the work ahead!" Zeb begins to cough. It is a prolonged cough. Chioma rubs her shoulders and reads Zeb's poem.

TREASURE IN THE WELL
Beyond the heat lies the promise,
Like labour before baby's entrance.
Beyond the spikes lies abundance
Of rosiest oil and fruity superstars.
Hei! I have drunk of the cup of bile,
What is the hurdle of divorce to me?
Yank it with a finger and claim my love,
Education unlimited is my goal for all.

55

Breaking the Ice

ob is having late dinner with Janice when Igodana Jr. comes home from work. Rob notices his gloomy countenance.

"Good evening, Rob," he says in a flat voice devoid of his usual warmth. Rob notes that he did not greet Janice before quickly galloping down the stairs to his room in the basement. Rob declines Janice's invitation to come to bed because he wants to review the new project proposal that is due the next day. It is one thirty in the morning and he is still seated by his computer editing the report. He is cross-checking the reference for lassa, a rare fever prevalent in the northern part of West Africa, when he sees a Nigerian Guardian newspaper article captioned, "Female University Professor in a Rape Scandal." He reads:

History was made at the Headquarters of the Young African Movement (YAM) in Lagos when Dr. Zebra Olima, a mother of four young men in their twenties decided to break the silence about rape of women in Nigeria. She narrates how she was in a bus travelling on Route 128 to Abuja when it was diverted to a lonely patch where the passengers were robbed at gunpoint and the women were ordered to enter the bush where they were gang-raped by gun-wielding young men. She has vivid memory of the incident. Wide-eyed and smelling of *ogogoro*, which she claims is very helpful in dulling the pain in her heart, she describes the three men who verbally abused her and other women as they were marched to the bush where the rapists abused and slapped them around. She could not recall how the ordeal ended for the women because she passed out. In an incredible twist to her story, she claims that two hunters discovered her body in a ditch in the forest and took her to a fishing village where some women nursed her for weeks. We cannot easily dismiss her claims because she gave real names of villagers, local government officials and Welfare Officers who helped her along the way because she was penniless. She wore a washed-out blue and white wrapper, which she said is symbolic. It was given to her by her host, Ojonimi, whose husband and son rescued her on their hunting trip. She urged other women who were raped to come out of the closet and "end the tradition of silence that is killing our people."

Rob stops reading the long article because of the tears that have covered his eyes. He goes to the basement to look for Igodana. The television is on in the family room and Igodana is sitting in front of it, but he is asleep.

"Igo, wake up!" Rob kicks his legs.

"What?" Igo Junior opens his eyes.

"Come."

"What is it, man?" He sees that Rob is crying.

"Come and read this," Rob says.

"Is it about my Mom?"

"So you know. Why didn't you tell me?"

"You had a visitor. I came here and cried myself to sleep."

"I'm going to Nigeria. I'll phone my travel agent and take the next flight."

"I want to go with you. I want to go home and see Mom. She's in Enugu with Grand Angel and the rest of the family."

"No need for you to disrupt your classes. I'll bring her back to the US where she will get the best care."

"No point. Its better she dies at home in Nigeria."

"What are you talking about? My wife is not going to die."

"She has AIDS."

"No." Rob's voice is flat.

"I read it on the Internet."

"No."

Clear faced and impatient, Rob and Igodana surf the Internet together. Rob pushes his papers to the side and adjusts the computer monitor so that both he and Igo Jr. can see as they search for articles about Zeb.

"I've been phoning Nigeria but can't get through. I just want to talk with my Mom," Igo Jr. is emotional. Rob places his hand on Igo's shoulders, patting him and consoling himself as they search the Internet. They soon see the article that Igodana is referring to.

The effort to deal with Human Immunodeficiency Virus (HIV) in Nigeria has been thwarted by concerted attempts to cover evidence of it and deny its existence in the country. An unprecedented event has forced the issue to receive serious attention after a landmark press conference at the University of Nigeria, Nsukka where a former lecturer, Dr. Zeb Olima announced that she is HIV positive. She is purported to have contracted the disease through a gang rape incident three months ago. The viral transmission of HIV virus is purported to have occurred during the gang rape of the popular professor the day she returned from the United States of America.

In a bold attempt to draw attention to the disease Dr. Olima says, "There is a great need to acknowledge the existence of HIV and AIDS in this country. Sweeping them under the rug will not eliminate the disease. The pattern of distribution, including rape of women and girls should be stopped. I call on the Federal Government of Nigeria to use its powers to deal with these issues and liberate our people from the silence on HIV and rape. Let us all join hands and break the silence of our jail!"

"I'm so proud of my wife." Rob says. He goes to the telephone to phone Angel's number and tell Zeb that he will be with her soon.

"I told you that the lines are out of order," Igo Jr. says.

Rob leaves a message for his travel agent and begins to get ready for the trip.

Glossary Of Unfamiliar Terms

Ada	First born female. In its wider use, the term stands for any daughter, not just first.
Agu nwa	Nickname that alludes to the exceptional and strong person. It is derived from agu (leopard) and nwa (child) that make up the compound name.
Akara	A kind of bean-cake.
Akwa-a akwuru	Literarily push-and-it-stands firm means unshakable or immovable.
Ashawo	Prostitute.
Baule	An ethnic group in West Africa, particularly Ivory Coast.
Boubou	Grand free-flowing gown for women.
Buba	Yoruba (Nigeria) word for loose blouse worn with iro (wrapper).
Bukas	Cafes or Eateries usually affordable by average-income earners.
Dodo	Fried ripe plantains.
Dogon-yaro	Very tall and leafy tree in the family of neem whose botanical name is *azadirachta indica*. It has medicinal benefits for numerous illnesses including malaria.
Edi ka-ikon	Thick soup prepared with a variety of vegetables, palm oil and assorted ingredients that include fish and meat.
Egusi	Soup made with ground melon seeds as the main ingredient in addition to dry fish, meat, vegetables and seasonings.
Fufu	A kind of glutinous dough usually eaten with soup. It is made by mashing or pounding the food item such as yam, cocoyam, plantain, and cassava.

Garri	Dry granular flour made from processed cassava. It can also be used to prepare fufu also called garri or eba.
Gele	Large head wrapper usually tied in flamboyant shapes.
Hausa	An ethnic group in the northern part of West Africa with concentration in the northern part of Nigeria.
Ibe	Community of people related to an individual through the father.
Icheku	Small dry fruit with velvety black cover, usually in clusters in its tree.
Ikwu	Community of people related to an individual through the mother.
Iro	Yoruba (Nigeria) word for wrapper.
K'ewe-e sikwa	Translates as "So that people will say" and refers to the habit or style of showing off what the individual perceives as superior in order to impress people.
Kia-kia	Mini-bus.
Mechie gi onu	Shut your mouth (Igbo, Nigeria).
Moyin-moyin	A kind of pudding made from beans.
Na atabi anya	Opening and closing her eyes. Blinking.
Nna-mu	My father.
Nne	Mother.
Nne-oma	Igbo endearment for women. It derives from *nne* (mother) and *oma* (good) that make up the compound name.
Nsala	It is also called naked soup because of the absence of red palm oil and a lot of vegetables. Their absence makes it easy to see through the soup and notice the fish and other items in it.

Nweje	Obscure, but connotes pretense of excessive goodness or holiness.
Ogbolo or Ogbono	Soup thickened with ground Irvingia or Wild Mango seeds in addition to vegetables, fish, meat and condiments.
Oghene	God in Urhobo (Nigeria) language.
Ogogoro	Alcoholic drink, usually distilled from palm products. It was illegal during the British direct government of Nigeria, in order to ensure the monopoly of imported British alcoholic drinks.
Okada	Motorcycle used for local transportation. It is not to be confused with Okada town in Edo State, Nigeria.
Okirika	Used clothes also called second-hand clothes. It is different from Okrika, which is a community in River State, Nigeria.
Okwa	A kind of dish for serving *ose-oji* (the peppered nut paste for eating kola nuts).
Omumu	Igbo (Nigeria) word for the ideology of female potential that promotes the prominence of women in all spheres of the soceity.
Ose-oji	A kind of paste made from peanut, pepper and other ingredients. It is usually served with Kola nuts.
Oseloblua or Osanobua	God in Edo(Nigeria) language.
Ube	Small black fruit with star-shaped hard seed used for marble-like flooring. This is different from the bigger oval *ube* that is usually blue or dark-blue in colour – usually eaten with maize. It is also different from the pear-shaped *ube-oyibo* called avocado in English.
Uda	A kind of medicinal root and seed obtained from a rare forest tree.

Ugba	Salad prepared from oil bean strings and other ingredients.
Utazi	Medicinal herb noted for its sharp bitterness.
Utu	Succulent forest fruit with a hard outer shell usually yellowish in colour.
Uugbugbo	Medicinal root.
Uziza	A highly spiced seed and vegetable.
Wallahi	Hausa language affirmation of truth in the name of Allah. Also used as exclamation.
WalahiTalahi!	Hausa language emphatic affirmation of truth in Allah's name.
Yekpa	Exact meaning is obscure, but it connotes the cry of extreme pain or wonder.

Printed in the United States
by Baker & Taylor Publisher Services